Praise for *Six Wicked Reasons*

'Jo Spain interweaves the lives of her multiply flawed
characters with great skill. The clever twists and
cracking dialogue make it hard to put down'
*The Times*

'Enthralling – Spain dissects her characters'
secrets with razor-sharp precision'
JP Delaney, author of *The Girl Before*

'A intriguing Rubik's Cube of a book that kept me
urning the pages to get to the truth. So well
plotted and beautifully written'
Liz Nugent, author of *Unravelling Oliver*

'Won fully drawn characters and more secrets and motives
n you can shake a stick at. Loved, loved, loved'
Caz Frear, author of *Sweet Little Lies*

'A clever and unusual premise . . . a
brilliant hook and rapid-fire ride'
*Irish Independent*

'This is her best yet. *Six Wicked Reasons* will cement Spain's
position as st names'

'Jo Spain is at the vanguard of Ireland's
flourishing crime writing scene'
*The Irish Examiner*

'A cleverly constructed and thoroughly immersive
thriller that seamlessly links past with present'
*Irish Independent*

'Fresh, witty writing style . . . an eye for details
which make the characters instantly believable'
*Daily Mail*

'With its eclectic cast of characters, isolated setting
and knockout twists, this gives a certain
Ms Christie a run for her money'
*Heat*

'A contender for the most arresting opening paragraph
of the year . . . This is crime fiction for grown-ups, taking
its time to explore the ins and outs of human psychology'
*Sunday Express*

'Clever, pacey, compulsive'
*Sunday Mirror*

**Jo Spain** is a full-time writer and screenwriter. Her first novel, *With Our Blessing*, was one of seven books shortlisted in the Richard and Judy Search for a Bestseller competition, and her first psychological thriller, *The Confession*, was a number one bestseller in Ireland. Jo co-wrote the ground-breaking television series *Taken Down*, which first broadcast in Ireland in 2018. She's now working on multiple European television projects. Jo lives in Dublin with her husband and their four young children.

Also by Jo Spain

*The Confession*
*Dirty Little Secrets*
*With Our Blessing: An Inspector Tom Reynolds Mystery*
*Beneath the Surface: An Inspector Tom Reynolds Mystery*
*Sleeping Beauties: An Inspector Tom Reynolds Mystery*
*The Darkest Place: An Inspector Tom Reynolds Mystery*
*The Boy Who Fell: An Inspector Tom Reynolds Mystery*
*After the Fire: An Inspector Tom Reynolds Mystery*

# SIX

# WICKED

# REASONS

## JO SPAIN

Quercus

First published in Great Britain in 2020 by Quercus
This paperback edition published in 2020 by

Quercus Editions Ltd
Carmelite House
50 Victoria Embankment
London EC4Y 0DZ

An Hachette UK company

A CIP catalogue record for this book is available
from the British Library

PB ISBN 978 1 52940 028 1
EB ISBN 978 1 52940 025 0

10 9 8 7 6 5 4 3 2 1

Typeset by CC Book Production

Printed and bound in Great Britain by Clays Ltd, Elcograf S.p.A.

MIX
Paper from
responsible sources
FSC® C104740

Papers used by Quercus Editions Ltd are from well-managed forests
and other responsible sources.

For Jim and Julie, always remembered

# JUNE 4TH, 2018

You didn't swim in the bay.

The locals knew that.

The sailors who had lost their lives in the South County Wexford inlet over the years had all been from other parts of the world. They hadn't known about the treacherous rocks and tricky rip currents of Spanish Cove, so named for its first recorded casualties – members of an Armada vessel that had blown off course and found itself dashed on the jagged ridge.

Within sight of shore, the sailors, to a man, had drowned.

The tide lifted and pummelled their bodies against the very rocks that had caused their demise, painting the stone crimson.

Some claimed they'd been lured to their deaths by otherworldly creatures.

Other cultures called them mermaids. Sirens. In Gaelic, *moruadh*. Dangerously beautiful beings with icy skeletal fingers and a grip like tangled seaweed.

Superstition. Folklore. The stories that endure in places like these, away from the bright lights and modern cynicism of the city.

The family who'd hired the yacht for the party on the night it happened were all locals.

It would *never* have occurred to them to strip off and go swimming.

Now that family was gathered in the harbour master's office, blankets and crinkled silver foil wrapped around their shoulders. Bedraggled, cold and in shock.

Nine had boarded, only eight returned alive.

There'd been fireworks, earlier in the evening. The strains of music could be heard from shore. Crates of champagne had gone on board, delicious canapés, everything to make it the perfect luxury night at sea.

It was a much-anticipated reunion.

A brother, who had vanished from their lives ten years ago, leaving untold grief in his wake, had come home.

The party to mark his return ended when a body was pulled from the water, already deceased.

The victim's head bore the marks of a heavy blow. The water had washed away most of the blood, revealing an ugly gash, so deep the white bone of the skull was visible.

It was entirely plausible that a boom or some other piece of sailing equipment had swung at the victim, making him lose his balance – except the deck from which he'd fallen seemed free of any such dangers.

He'd been drinking; he could have slipped and banged his head, then somehow managed to topple over the side rail – although it was quite high and designed for safety.

The detective sergeant in charge wanted to know if the victim had displayed any symptoms of ill health, dizziness or confusion? Had he been depressed?

What, exactly, had happened prior to the alarm being raised?

There was a lot of broken glass on deck. Two of the brothers had fought, if their bruises and bloodied noses were anything to go by.

The detective, now living in Wexford town, had once been a local himself. He knew the family, way back. He could have asked to have been excluded from the investigation. But in a small, remote village like this, where everybody ate and drank each other's business, being seen as one of their own was often to the advantage of the police.

Anyhow, this was a busy night for the county police force, with two serious incidents elsewhere in their jurisdiction. There *was* nobody else, his boss cheerfully informed him.

But it would be resolved quickly. An accident, wasn't it?

Wasn't it?

The family comforted each other, as they waited to give their statements.

The unity, however, was forced.

Their brother had returned and now their father was gone.

Frazer Lattimer, sixty-one years of age, native of Scotland, resident in Ireland most of his adult life, was dead.

His children looked at one another, and wondered.

Which of them had murdered him?

# PART I

# ONE WEEK EARLIER

# CLIO

*Adam's home.*

The words still rang in her ears.

Said so casually. Like he'd just popped down to Four Star Pizza and returned with a sixteen-inch deep pan, extra pepperoni.

Or had just arrived back after a long day at work, the headlights of his car illuminating the driveway.

Adam's home.

The sentence hadn't been uttered with the weight it deserved, the gravity that captured the fact their brother had been missing for ten years – at worst, presumed dead, at best, presumed dead.

Clio was still reeling from Ellen's phone call, the imparting of the news.

Adam's home.

*Does he know about Mam?* Clio had asked. *Does he know what he did?*

Once upon a time there was a family.

A father, a mother and six children. They lived in the most scenic part of Ireland, in a beautiful house on a hill, and were wealthier than everybody they knew. Rich in every sense, but mostly in the way that mattered. They had class. They had status. They had each other.

And then it all went to hell in a handbasket.

Clio picked up the photograph that had captured the Lattimers at a happier time – her whole family at the beach.

Her parents sat on scratchy, striped towels. Kathleen's smile came easily; Frazer's was less enthusiastic but even he looked to be enjoying the day out. Clio's sisters, Kate and Ellen, shielded their eyes from the sun as they looked up from placing pretty shells on a giant sand monument that Adam had built. Adam grinned happily, his uncomplicated nature apparent in his features. James was self-absorbed as usual, licking an ice cream he'd made last far longer than any of his siblings'. Ryan had pulled a last-minute cheeky face, tongue out, eyes crossed, fingers in his ears.

And there was Clio herself, a chubby little thing sitting at the front, the baby of the family, adored by one and all.

Who'd taken that photo? She was too young to remember. Probably Uncle Danny.

She placed the framed picture in her holdall.

Then she started to move around the room.

It was years since Clio had done this. Said goodbye to inanimate objects.

Goodbye, bed. Goodbye, alcove. Bye, wardrobe. Bye, stairs.

A little OCD in an otherwise chaotic life.

Her eyes scanned the small apartment for the last time. The tiny, functional kitchenette with the pan on the two-ring hob, still burnt on the base from the time she'd got drunk and decided to make popcorn with barely a dribble of oil. The single bed, half the slats broken. She'd propped it up with boxes but it still creaked like hell whenever she had somebody in it with her. The cracked window, through which the sounds of Bleecker Street seeped night and day, reminding her that, no matter how lonely she felt, she was always surrounded by other people.

This was her world. These days, you couldn't get next nor near Greenwich Village for the rent she was paying for this place. But when Clio had arrived, four years ago, at the tender age of twenty-one, her then-boyfriend had already secured the rent-controlled studio from a departing expat and Clio had clung onto it ever since.

At the time, the boyfriend had told her she'd never grow accustomed to New York. Clio was used to sleeping in the blackest of nights, a blanket of stars overhead, to a soundtrack of lapping waves and gulls.

Bleecker Street was sirens and pneumatic drills and nightclub revellers and car horns.

In the end, it was the boyfriend who ran home. Clio stayed, working in various bars or restaurants, taking cleaning work and other jobs – any position that would pay her cash in hand.

She'd told herself she didn't need much money once the essentials were covered.

Walking along the Hudson was free. The city's art galleries and libraries regularly ran open-house nights. Shows could be seen for half price if you were happy to queue or knew somebody on the concession stand. Drinks flowed liberally if you found the right barman to screw.

It said a lot about her personality that she could see the positives. Most people who'd been done out of fifty-plus grand on their twenty-first birthday and endured what she had would have been bitter about their circumstances.

Clio zipped up her holdall and looked around the room one last time.

There was a definite nostalgic lump in her throat.

Here, in a small apartment in a big city, she'd found independence. She'd found peace. The space to be just Clio, and not *Clíodhna Lattimer, youngest of the brood, daughter of Frazer and Kathleen, sister to . . . you know the ones.*

But it hadn't all been easy.

In fact, at a certain point, it had been spectacularly shit.

But even prisoners find it hard to leave their cells and face the outside world.

People ran out of empathy, somebody had once told her. They could listen to your pain for a while, but then their worlds moved on. Nobody stayed long in the company of a victim.

So, she would never let anybody know the full truth of what she'd endured.

Clio picked up the white rectangular envelope she'd left on the bed.

She'd taken the letter out of its original envelope. This one was plain, no name or address inscribed on its front.

The letter had started it all. It explained everything.

She'd promised herself she'd get rid of it. If anybody knew she had it, if they read it, they'd learn what she'd learned. But she couldn't destroy it. She needed to keep reading the words, to remind herself why she was returning to Spanish Cove.

She tucked it into her handbag and grabbed her holdall and wheelie suitcase containing the sum of her worldly possessions.

'Goodbye, home,' she said, her voice caught on a sob, and left.

★

The screech of aeroplanes braking on the runway at JFK airport.

A long line of yellow cabs; a wide expanse of stone-grey buildings; glass-fronted terminals; a mass of travellers, the experienced and the wide-eyed.

Inside, in a tiny office, a twenty-five-year-old woman pretending not to give a damn but, truthfully, trembling like a little child.

'It's Clio. Clio, like the car, you know? Renault Clio? Not Cleo like the queen. But you pronounce it like that.'

'It says here on your passport Cleed-na . . . Clee-odd-ha-na, ma'am.'

'It's Clíodhna. Clee-oh-na. This is exactly why I use Clio. For the love of Christ, is this going to take much longer? Can't you hear the announcements? That's my fucking plane they're talking about.'

'Ma'am, please refrain from using expletives.'

The large black security official's eyes bored into Clio's. She felt the heat burning red hot in her cheeks. She blinked first, lowered her gaze. This small interrogation office she'd been brought to, after being plucked out of the passport control line post-security, already felt like a prison cell. She wanted out.

'You will be accompanied through the terminal to your flight. You will stay in the boarding lounge. You will be . . .'

Clio switched off at that point. She had no rights, no argument to make.

She'd overstayed her welcome in the greatest country in the world and now she was being chaperoned out of it. Make America great again. Deport Clio Lattimer.

It wasn't her fault the plane was running late. Some minor technical fault Aer Lingus was dealing with last minute. Clio tried to tell that to Betty, the female security official she'd been assigned, hoping it would put an end to the dirty looks Betty kept flashing her. Built like a brick shithouse and humanity-weary, Betty's whole demeanour further diluted the *'You have a nice day, ma'am'* the previous security official had sarcastically bid as Clio was carted off to the boarding gate.

Now, sitting at the sushi bar in terminal two – because Betty recognised Clio was entitled to eat as long as she didn't plan to eat anywhere off airport property – Clio relayed the whole sorry experience to a County Galway man perched on the next stool.

'And their drugs dog ripped a ladder in my tights going past with that stupid thing on his back,' she said. She turned to her guard. 'Didn't he, Betty? Does he need to walk that close? I mean, if he has to get that close to smell the drugs, is he any fucking use, Betty?'

The Galway man, whose name Clio couldn't be arsed to remember, blushed at the security official's obvious irritation. He ordered another two vodka tonics from their server. They arrived in seconds, served up on square napkins. Clio knocked hers back, shot-style. Betty pursed her lips. Betty probably had three kids at home and no doubt just wanted to get through her shift so she could fuck off to Stop and Shop and pick up some groceries. Clio almost felt sorry for Betty.

'So, why are you going back?' Galwegian asked. 'If you knew you'd get stung going through JFK? Did somebody die or something?'

'Why don't you get another round in while I pee?' Clio said. She swivelled on her stool. 'Betty, how about we gals go powder our noses?'

The security official's features were so scrunched they were starting to disappear into themselves. Clio reckoned if the Aer Lingus flight took much longer, Betty might consider sticking Clio on any plane, going anywhere, just to get rid.

And maybe that wouldn't be a bad thing.

'More vodka for the lady on a mysterious trip home.' Galwegian smiled.

'Oh,' Clio said. 'There's no mystery, really. The prodigal son has returned. My brother. Disappeared ten years ago and now he's back.'

She hopped off her stool.

'Jesus,' her companion said, taken aback at the turn in the conversation. 'He vanished, like? Where was he?'

'God knows.'

'And he just came back? That's incredible. So that's why you're going back. Makes sense. I'd say you're dying to see him.'

Clio felt her breath shorten, her chest constrict.

'Actually,' she said, 'it would have been better if he was fucking dead.'

# AFTER

'How drunk would you say you were this evening, Clio?'

'Do I sound drunk?'

The detective sighed.

'Earlier,' he said. 'During the party.'

'Does it matter?' Clio shrugged. 'I wasn't driving the boat.'

'Everybody was drinking, weren't they?'

'More or less. What's your point?'

'I'm trying to get a sense of the atmosphere. Were people merry drunk or tense drunk?'

'Ah. Because you think there was a big fight and Dad got caught up in it. Well, there wasn't. James and Adam argued, Dad wasn't even there. Nobody saw him go in the water.'

'If you were drunk, how do you know?'

Clio blinked.

'When can we go home?' she asked.

'When I get all these statements straight. I'm not going to lie, Clio, it's a bit like pulling teeth at the moment. Which I'm putting down to shock and, perhaps, the after-effects of alcohol. Not deliberate obstruction of justice. Which I know you know is serious.

Whatever the reason, I need to know what happened on that boat.'

'You can't keep us here all night.'

'I can, actually.'

Clio frowned.

'So, James and Adam evidently had a physical altercation,' the detective said. 'But did your father argue with anybody?'

Clio felt her body slump. Might as well just get it over with.

'We all – except Ryan – had a few drinks. We were tense. Over a week, we'd gone from being a family that had learned to live with Adam's disappearance, to one that had to deal with the knowledge that he was alive and well for ten years. We had to get to grips with the knowledge that he had left us, deliberately. We weren't exactly happy, to begin with, having that party. As for Dad, he didn't – um – he didn't *fight* with anyone in particular. But . . .'

'What?'

'Nothing.'

The detective studied her.

'Okay. Let's go back to the start. Why you all came back to Spanish Cove.'

'Aren't you listening? Adam . . .'

'I'm aware your brother returned. It's a big deal, I know. But I can hear how angry you are with him. And, yet, you went to a lot of effort for him, very quickly. Ryan had to come home from Italy. James and Kate both have full-time jobs and busy lives in Dublin. You returned from the States, getting yourself into plenty of bother in the process. He could have visited you. You could have Skyped while you planned how to manage the reunion. Instead, you all dropped everything.'

Clio bit her lip. There was nothing for it. She'd have to tell the truth.

'We . . . we had no choice,' she said. 'And – I wanted to leave New York.'

'Why?'

'I wasn't . . . I wasn't happy there any more.'

'No, why did you have no choice?'

'Oh. Dad did his usual.'

'And what was that?'

A pause. Then a smile.

'He threatened to cut us off.'

'And that's something your father did frequently?'

'I'm sorry?'

'You said, he did *his usual*. Was it a recurring theme?'

'Dad holding money over our heads? Pretty much.'

'I see.'

The detective looked down at his notes.

'Did it upset you, your dad's – what will we call it – controlling nature?'

'I was used to it.' Clio shrugged.

'Then why emigrate?'

Clio stayed silent.

There was only so much truth she was willing to reveal.

# JAMES

This was utterly humiliating. Mortifying. Standing here, people ignoring him, like he was a nobody and mattered to no one.

James wanted to die inside but he was working desperately not to let it show.

Time was, people had recognised him wherever he went. His face had been in all the society pages. He'd guested on chat shows and appeared at red-carpet opening nights. Ireland's celebrity pool was shallow and James, for a short time, had been its whale.

But that had been a few years ago, when he was hot stuff, the twenty-something producer who had his finger on the button. The man who was going places.

He'd peaked too soon.

It was six years since he'd had a show.

To be washed up at thirty-five — James wouldn't let it happen. It was ludicrous. Everybody else's career was just starting. James' couldn't be finished.

He glanced at his watch while neatly stepping over cables that were being dragged out of view of the scene shot. He'd been told when he rang ahead that this production was going to picture lock and yet, here they were, still shooting. James had heard the director was a perfectionist but had James been the executive producer, he'd have pulled the plug days ago. It was so easy being one of the *creatives*. Never having to worry about the little things, like who was going to pay your wages or finance every last detail of every goddamn thing.

His phone rang in his pocket, buzzing silently against his leg. James ignored it, like the professional he was. They were filming the same lines for the fourteenth time and if anybody so much as breathed heavily, they risked being massacred by the rest of the cast and crew. James had heard the urban myth about the crew member hanging himself in the background of a shot that had remained in the final reel of *The Wizard of Oz*. He'd also heard the cynical reactions of people who didn't believe anything like that would ever be left in a movie.

None of those people knew how many times a single scene needed to be filmed to get the various angles, let alone everything else, correct. Movie bloopers weren't so much mistakes as footage editors and directors saying, collectively, *ah, fuck it*.

He didn't want to answer his phone, anyway.

Everything was building up to a head of steam. James felt it in his gut. But he couldn't deal with it. Not right now.

Adam's return – that's what he had to focus on.

'Cut!'

James looked up as the director called time.

'And we're done. Break for thirty, then back to the unit base, guys and dolls.'

There was a collective sigh of relief, some half-hearted clapping.

James hurried over to the actor he was seeking before somebody else could grab him.

Darius Lefoy was a star in the making: early twenties, face of an angel, the gaunt-haunted look that women wanted to fuss over and men weren't threatened by. It came across beautifully on camera.

The young actor now worked mainly in London and there was talk of an LA move.

James' supposed trajectory, some years previous.

If James could secure Darius for the part in his new production, it would seal the deal. He'd only need him for an eight-week shoot. It wouldn't interfere in the slightest with the actor's route to stardom and it would do everything to put James back on the same track.

'Darius, hi, James Lattimer.' James tried to sound more confident than he felt as he approached with his hand out, weaving through the crew. The young actor was surrounded by costume assistants who were helping to remove the bulletproof vest and gun-belt he wore for his part.

Darius shook James' hand limply.

'Eh, hi,' he said, uncertainly.

'From Red Productions?' James said. 'Your agent, Naomi, she told you I was dropping by to see you in action, didn't she?'

'Eh, yeah. I think so.'

James bristled. He'd come here specially; it had taken weeks to set up.

Behind him, he heard a whisper:

*'Who the fuck is your man?'*

The voice was young. One of the costume assistants, probably. James swallowed.

Be careful who you kick on the way up, he wanted to say.

The actor lifted his arms into the air and let himself be unshackled from his detective gear. It was a ridiculous role for him. He looked good on screen but in real life he stood about five foot in socks and weighed in at nine stone. The director of photography would have his work cut out angling those action-man shots.

'Listen, I'm starving, man,' Darius said. 'I gotta grab a bite on the bus. Were you looking to chat or something?'

James glanced over at the canteen bus, then at his watch. He rubbed the back of his neck, anxiously.

'I was,' he said. It was time to play his ace. 'But, maybe we can reschedule. I've got a meeting at two with these Netflix guys and, you know yourself, nobody is too big to be late for them. Especially when they've flown over for you.'

Darius was a good actor but not that good. James watched as the wheels turned.

'Oh, shit; yeah, of course,' Darius said. 'James *Lattimer*. Here, why don't you grab a salad with me and we can talk?'

James hesitated, then he threw his hands out in submission.

'I guess if they think it's a good enough idea to come over from LA for, they'll wait five minutes for me,' James said. 'Go on, then.'

It was all a big game.

But, this was important. When he returned home, he had to arrive as a success.

He needed this weekend to go smoothly. He couldn't risk anything else.

# KATE

Kate wasn't sure what to pack. It was warm in Dublin but Spanish Cove had its own mini climate. It was a combination of being so far south and also surrounded by hills on all sides, including right over the bay where County Waterford acted as a buffer. This time of year, it should be swelteringly hot, but if a cold breeze came in from the Atlantic, the Cove would act as a wind tunnel, bringing the temperature right down.

She placed two neatly folded sweaters on top of the strappy vests and linen trousers she'd already packed. Kate liked to dress strategically; looking good took a lot more than just going to the gym frequently.

Her mam had been a pear-shaped woman. Not a good shape if you're after conventional good looks, if you believe the magazines. She had always carried a little bit of weight but it had never mattered. She was beautiful. Her face and smile were all people really saw. The kindness within her. Ask anybody, they'd have described Kathleen as the most attractive woman they knew.

Kate wasn't a great beauty. At least, she didn't consider herself so. And she had the same body shape as her mam. She didn't carry weight well.

In her teens, Kate had carried a lot of weight.

An awful lot.

'How long did you say you were going for, again?' Cheng was searching the walk-in wardrobe for his golf shoes. He hated golf, forced himself to play it, he said. Kate reckoned the anarchist in him really enjoyed turning up in the clubhouse populated by utterly Irish, entirely white, overweight and overpaid men. Cheng was wealthier than all of them, but would never be one of them, even though those very same men frequented Cheng's hotel – a hotel that was, in fact, thriving, with full occupancy, a restaurant going for its first Michelin star and a basement cocktail and jazz club that was jam-packed every weekend.

And at the helm, Cheng was fond of saying, a poor Chinese man from Beijing.

It was a total exaggeration. Cheng's mother might have been from a lower-class rung by Chinese standards, but his Irish father was very well-to-do. The son of a well-known industrialist, Kate's father-in-law had travelled to Beijing on one of the first foreign student exchange programmes in the late seventies. He'd gone to learn about a culture that was just opening itself up to the rest of the world; he'd come home three years later with a wife and child.

Now he looked into her bag, swollen already.

'Just the weekend,' Kate said. 'But you never know.'

She turned back to the rails, cheeks burning.

'Hey,' Cheng said. 'Are you sure you don't want me to come down with you?' Then, gentler: 'I know this must be tough for you.'

Kate froze.

'Why do you say that?'

'Eh, you haven't spent a single night in your father's home since I've known you. I've only met your father and James once, and none of the rest. And I know why.'

'Do you?' she said, her heart beating that bit faster.

'Come on,' he said, and laughed thinly. 'It's hardly rocket science.'

He wrapped his arms around her from behind and accented his voice.

'You young white girl. Me big bad China man. East met West and stole its woman.'

She pushed him away, laughing.

'Wear your Black Lives Matter tee shirt down and see what happens,' he said. 'Test how racist they really are.'

'You're not black and you've lived here since you were two,' Kate said.

'Don't you dare rob me of my agency. I'm a shade on the scale, white girl. Anyhow, the only time I did meet your brother, he asked me if I knew any Asian actors because his colleague needed baddies in his show. I'm not even going to repeat what Frazer said. Suffice to say, it's obvious why you're practically estranged. The rest probably wear white pointed hoods to dinner.'

Kate paused and looked inside her bag.

What the hell was she doing? Why was she travelling down at all?

She'd been to Beijing more often than Spanish Cove in the last few years. They travelled to China at least once a year, usually staying near where her mother-in-law Yin had grown up. The village had once been full of clothing manufacturers and cheap restaurants, but it had been gentrified in the nineties as it was swallowed up by the expanding city. Kate loved it there. Visiting LaiTai flower market, eating in Cai Yi Xuan in the Four Seasons (where Kate and Cheng dreamed about the five-star hotel they'd open to rival it one day), strolling through the Forbidden City.

Perhaps they should move to China, when all this was over and she'd made it through this hellish weekend.

'You poor love. You're all over the place, aren't you?' Cheng put his arms around his wife.

Kate looked up into his serious, dark eyes.

When she first met him, this gorgeous man, five years older, more experienced – more everything – she'd melted. She wasn't worthy of him. May he never find out.

'You sure you don't want me to drive you? Or wait until you get your car back from the garage? At least then you won't feel stranded down there.'

'No, it's fine. I was due a trip down with James, anyway. And he won't want to hang around, either.'

'Okay, but it doesn't matter how sick your father is, *qīn*,' Cheng said. 'If it gets too much, just call and I'll be down to pick you up in a heartbeat. Where is my phone, anyway? Have you seen it? I heard it ringing earlier; I've no idea where the thing is.'

Kate only half-listened as her husband continued to talk, now from out in the bedroom.

From the moment she'd got the phone call about Adam's return, she'd found herself reverting to all her bad habits.

Snacking unconsciously.

Lying awake at night.

Lying.

For years she'd had everything under control. Cheng often joked that if Kate was sliced open, the word willpower would run through her like she was a stick of rock, that if she'd been born in China, she'd have been an Olympic gold medallist by the time she was five.

She should have said no, refused to go to Spanish Cove for the long weekend. She was a grown woman, after all.

Yet, when her father had picked up the phone, she had become a child again. No longer Kate Grant but Kate Lattimer. Daughter, not wife. Sister, not friend.

It killed her, lying to Cheng, but she'd had to come up with a reason for why she was going down in such a rush. What was the point in telling him the truth?

All families had their secrets. The Lattimers might be a bit more . . . abnormal than most, but wasn't that, in itself, normal?

So what, if none of them talked to each other?

And, anyway. Adam was back for now, but who knew?

Tomorrow he could take flight again.

And she could go back to having nothing to do with her relatives.

# AFTER

Kate kept her hand clutched to her stomach. She felt ill, properly ill. Had felt that way all weekend, in fact.

Now, at least, she knew there was a reason for it.

Detective Downes handed her a cup of hot something, but she didn't even look at it, just appreciated the warmth in her hands. He was being nice, she reckoned, because they'd met each other earlier that day. Briefly, in better circumstances, in the village, before they'd had the party, before Kate had got on the yacht, before her father had . . .

Less than twelve hours ago, everything had been normal.

'So, James attacked Adam,' he said, scribbling something into a notepad that looked like it had been pulled from his school bag. He was an odd-featured man, one of those people who looked older than he was but still seemed too young to be doing a proper adult job.

'Yes,' she answered. 'But Adam had a go at him—'

'Still,' he cut her off. 'It was James who threw the first punch, you said.'

'Yes. I'm sorry – but what does this have to do with my dad?'

The detective looked up at her, then back down at his notepad.

26

He probably wasn't writing anything, Kate thought. He'd be playing hangman, trying to look important until his boss came along. Or maybe he was making juvenile observations about them all. How they looked. Kate had known plenty of people like that. She'd seen the nasty things they'd scrawled about her, inside lockers and on the corners of desks.

'Before the fight,' the detective said, 'you told me the group split up for a little while. Why? Had there been an argument, even before James attacked Adam?'

'I . . . Not an argument, as such. Dad had just, he mentioned something about the house.'

'What?'

'Nothing important. But we all sort of drifted away to our own corners, for a while.'

'And this was around 8 to 8.30 p.m.?'

'Yes. I was trying to phone my husband, that's why I know what time it was. From the call log.'

'How would you describe your relationship with your father?' Detective Downes interrupted.

'How would I describe . . . ?' Kate looked at him blankly. 'Fine. It was fine. He was my dad.'

'You didn't see him much – before this weekend, I mean. You don't come home often.'

'Yes. Well.'

Kate felt herself colouring.

'I work,' she said. 'I run a very busy hotel in Dublin. I can't come down here every other weekend. I have my life and . . . it was just, with Adam home, I had to come back to see him, obviously. It was . . . great news.'

'Was it?'

'Of course it was. What does that mean?'

'So, you rushed home to see your brother, who vanished for ten years, but you never had time for your father. You mustn't have been that close to him.'

'We weren't *not* close. We just . . .' She floundered again.

Detective Downes looked up and met Kate's eye.

'Did your dad ever hurt you? Did you have cause to wish him harm?'

Kate blinked rapidly.

'Absolutely not!' she said, appalled. 'I loved my father and he loved me.'

# AFTER

Detective Downes stepped out of the harbour master's building and walked the few hundred yards to where the yacht was anchored, surrounded by emergency vehicles, their blue and red lights pulsating against the darkness.

Over in Albertstown village, the bars and restaurants had suddenly become busier. Every passing car slowed for its occupants to stare across at the unusual activity by the water.

Frazer Lattimer's body still lay in a body bag on a stretcher in one of the ambulances that had been summoned. It would be moved shortly, transferred to the pathologist's office.

When the detective had seen the corpse, it had looked relatively unscathed, bar the wound to the rear of the skull.

The family had nothing so peaceful to look forward to. Frazer's head would need to be shaved, for a start. Then his torso would be cut open and all his organs taken out, before being replaced and his body sewn back up.

The man they buried would not look like the man they'd lost.

One of them, at least, wouldn't be too bothered by that.

From the start, Detective Downes had had his doubts about this being an accident.

That was being borne out by the statements of those on board the yacht.

It was absolutely apparent they were holding back.

And there was no reason for that unless there was something to hide.

Well, in the absence of testimony, he still had facts.

Forensics had done their job on board the vessel; the detective was welcome to look around.

He walked the entire circumference of the yacht. It was long – twenty metres by his reckoning, with enough deck at the sides for two people to comfortably stand together or pass each other; a large party area to the rear; and a sailing cabin at the front, with windows on all sides. A small set of stairs led to a smaller, upper party area, and he'd already noted a sizeable below-deck space, which also contained the toilet.

When he was happy he'd the specs properly memorised, the detective moved to the right, or starboard, side of the vessel, where he'd already established Frazer Lattimer had last been seen.

He nodded at the besuited forensics officer taking samples from the deck using small cotton buds.

If Detective Downes turned his head left and right he could see the sailing cabin at the front, and the far rail at the rear of the vessel.

The detective examined the steel safety barrier. It came up to just under his chest and he was a man of average height.

It would take a lot to accidentally fall over that rail.

He looked behind him at the perfectly smooth white surface that ran around the side of the yacht. No windows looking into the cabin below. And, more importantly, nothing that could swing at a person if the yacht suddenly jerked.

He looked back down at the forensics officer and the small pile of plastic bags the man had already collected. Each contained samples from the blood spray on the side of the yacht and the deck beneath their feet.

Frazer's head wound had been deep. And those sorts of injuries caused a lot of bleeding. But, after the initial splatter, blood generally reverted to gushing in the direction of gravity. Down the neck, onto the clothing.

There were enough drops on board to indicate that that's where the blow to Frazer's head had been sustained.

And, then, before more blood came, before it began to pool under his feet – Frazer Lattimer had been pushed into the sea.

That was Detective Downes' theory, anyway.

# ELLEN

Saturday, that's when they were all arriving. Ellen polished the bannister harder. The pine spray made her nose tingle and she was pretty sure she'd inhaled too much of it. It felt pleasant, in an entirely unhealthy way.

Maybe that's what was giving her palpitations.

It was only Thursday. She had enough time to get everything ready. There was no need to stress. But she had to show them how well she'd been looking after the place.

It might not mean much to them but it meant everything to her.

Her father was in his study. He hadn't come out all morning. She could hear him on the telephone, a soft, familiar mumble. Coughing. The smell of cigars seeped from under the door. Ellen had opened every window in the house, but you could still catch the sharp tang of Villigers in the downstairs rooms. The poor dog was in there with him, no doubt well on his way to secondary-smoke lung cancer.

She'd made up the beds with crisp white linens and comfortable feather duvets, and left new toiletries in all the en suites and the family bathroom. The cushions in the sitting rooms were freshly plumped. Every surface in the kitchen gleamed. The fridge was stocked – Frazer had planned a big dinner on the first night. A case of Laurent Perrier had already arrived and catering staff had been ordered in.

Ellen couldn't put her finger on it but something was niggling at her. Some missing piece. She paused and glanced through the fan window atop the front door overlooking the sea.

'It's clean. Would you not go have a cuppa or something?'

Ellen jumped. Adam was standing at the top of the stairs, his expression one of concern. Adam, the ghost. Who'd returned so unexpectedly, without a call or letter or warning, four days earlier.

'It's been a long time since we were all together,' she said. 'I just want it to look nice.'

'When *was* the last time they were all here?' Adam asked.

Ellen looked down at the cloth and the Mr Muscle bottle in her hand.

'That often, huh?' Adam walked down the few steps towards her. He was still recognisably Adam. The dark evening shadow that had started in his late teens and couldn't be vanquished, even with a close shave. The furrowed eyebrows, so thick they looked like caterpillars had taken up residence. The blue-green eyes, startling, like he'd been gifted gemstones from the sea they lived beside. Ellen hadn't doubted it was him for a second when she'd opened the door and saw him standing there on the step. A single bag on his back – a bag she'd already been through but discovered nothing of note in. No clue as to where he'd been or who he'd been with or what had happened all those years ago.

'Are you hungry?' she asked. 'I can make you something.'

'I'm not hungry.' Adam hesitated a couple steps above her. 'What do you do for money? You haven't left the house since I arrived.'

'It doesn't seem fair, you asking me about my life when I'm not allowed to ask about yours.'

'Of course you're allowed,' Adam said.

Ellen cast a glance over at the study door.

When he first saw Adam, Frazer had started to cry. Not blub, exactly, but there had definitely been tears. Ellen had been as shocked as Adam. It was not something their father did regularly.

Then Frazer had taken Adam into his study.

They'd spent hours in there, speaking too softly for her to eavesdrop. There was no screaming match, no remonstrating. Not that she could tell.

It was so very peculiar. She'd expected her father to be furious, with Adam turning up like that. Raging.

But when they'd both emerged from his study, Frazer had seemed . . . *happy*. He'd then announced to Ellen and also Danny, who'd shown up by that point, that rather than Adam going over and over what had happened, they should get everybody home the following weekend and Adam could tell them all together. It would be fairer that way.

Fairer to whom, Ellen wondered? Didn't she have as much right as Frazer to know where Adam had been?

But Danny, the family's oldest friend, had agreed.

Ellen didn't want to be the one causing upset. Especially as Adam had looked so stunned and grateful to be on the receiving end of such a warm and considerate welcome.

Still, Ellen was sick with suspense.

Why had he gone and, more importantly, why was he back?

'Hello?' Adam said. 'Your job?'

Ellen was shaken from her reverie. She'd been doing that more and more this last week, drifting off. Remembering.

Of course, the most important date in her life was approaching. There was that, too.

Thirteen years.

'I tutor online,' she said.

Adam raised an eyebrow.

'Tutor what?'

'Accountancy.'

'Fascinating.' Adam smiled.

'It's a good job,' she said, defensively.

'I'm only winding you up.'

He continued on down the stairs towards her.

'Lucky Spanish Cove has decent broadband, hey?' he said. 'Otherwise you might have had to move out.'

Ellen wouldn't dignify that with a response.

Instead, she asked the question that had been burning inside her since his return.

'Are you coming back here to live? To Spanish Cove, I mean?'

'Why do you ask?'

'I just – I'm just wondering.'

'No. If I settled back in Ireland, it wouldn't be here.'

'I could help you,' Ellen said. 'With a deposit. On a different place, I mean.'

'I don't need your money, Ellen.'

Ellen bit into her bottom lip.

Was he lying to her?

Was he after the house?

She forced herself to smile.

'Where are you going, now?' she asked.

'The shore. Want to come?'

'No. I'll see you later. For dinner.'

He touched her arm as he passed. She resisted flinching.

Human touch. She was unused to it, but she really shouldn't show it.

Still, there was more at play here. It unnerved her, having him back like this.

And it wasn't just Adam's reappearance that had her on edge.

Just what was her father up to?

That's what was playing on her mind.

He was in the middle of something. Had been for a while, she was sure of it. There was no other reason for him to hole up in his study like this, for days at a time, talking on the phone, click-clacking away on the computer keyboard. Why make such a big thing of this weekend, to the point where he'd told Kate and James to hold off coming down any earlier?

And all the mysterious outings he'd been making lately, returning in the wee hours.

Had he . . . had he known Adam was coming?

Was that why he seemed so relaxed and happy about it all?

Or was there something else going on?

# AFTER

The room was tiny. A table, two chairs so close the occupants were almost knee to knee. A computer, phone, some box files stacked on a shelf. A bright light overhead, unshaded. A mini Burco water boiler and a tray of tea and coffee necessities. Ellen took it all in. It was her first time to speak to Detective Downes but she had an awful feeling it was going to be a long night. He had that look about him. A terrier, who wouldn't rest until he'd dragged every painful secret from the surviving Lattimers.

He claimed that he and Ellen knew each other. That his family were local. There were a few Downes in Albertstown, sure. And he looked vaguely familiar. But she couldn't place him. It might have been because she never went anywhere these days, never saw anybody.

Or maybe Ellen didn't know Detective Downes at all and he was trying to trick her. Build a rapport, that's what the cops did in the shows Ellen watched. She mightn't leave the house much physically, but TV and books were a great window into other worlds.

'You say your father was happy to have Adam home?' the detective said.

Silence.

'Ellen?'

'He, um, yes. He was glad.'

'So, they didn't argue? I gotta tell you – I think if I disappeared for a decade and then rocked up at my house, my mother would flay me alive.'

She shook her head.

'Over the week, then – did anything change? What I mean is – maybe Frazer was shocked to begin with and grateful to have his son home. But as the days went on, he might have had time to think about what Adam had done. Maybe he got angry. Perhaps lashed out a little?'

'No. No, my dad was happy Adam was back. He said nothing to the contrary all week. Not that I heard.'

The detective looked at her, then scribbled something down.

'So, what about Ryan?' he said. 'Was Frazer happy to have him home? There was some trouble, before, wasn't there? Between Frazer and Ryan? I thought I heard something, way back.'

Ellen's thoughts were racing.

But she tried to keep her face as placid as possible.

'Ryan and my dad?' she said. 'No. They got on fine.'

# RYAN

It was only midday and Ryan was already on his second shirt and his third glass of wine. The sweat formed puddles between his shoulder blades as he swatted at fruit flies trying to take up residence in his Amarone.

'Fuck off and get your own drink,' he said, into the silence.

He was the wine bar's only local patron. Limone's residents were at one of their all-too-frequent religious events, the populace gathering en masse in the church at the top of the steps while tourists wandered cluelessly around the Marie Celeste-like town.

It was still early season at Lake Garda in northern Italy. It might be late May, but July and August were the most popular months. For now, visitors still numbered small groups, not the hordes they could expect later in the year. Ryan liked it either way.

After many years as an awkward child, then a gangly teenager, followed by a skinny, gaunt adult, Ryan had emerged from his cocoon as a striking-looking man. The Lattimer gene had only been latent, it transpired. The skeletal look, once he'd filled out a little, had lingered in his cheekbones, and his eye sockets still looked a bit deep, the lids lazy. He'd been mistaken, on several occasions, for the actor Cillian Murphy and it didn't displease him in the slightest. The drugs had left something positive, at least.

Now, at twenty-eight, he was clean – relatively speaking; what were a few glasses of wine among people you barely knew? – healthy (he walked everywhere, could afford little else), tanned, well-fed and relaxed.

I am a happy man, he repeated to himself every day in the old, speckled mirror that hung in the dimly-lit bathroom of his lodging house. Then, he did whatever odd jobs Signora Romano had for him. Ryan didn't have the willpower or inclination to be a starving artist, and for just a couple of hours' work, Signora Romano made it her business to keep him fed, clothed and housed. On her heaped plates of pasta primavera and rosemary focaccia bread, Ryan could walk and think for hours on end, even write when the mood struck him.

Italy was his home now, or at least this little part of it was.

Nowhere made him feel quite as at home as Limone, with its terracotta roofs and colourful small houses, the quiet, narrow lanes and the vista of the lake at every turn. Maybe, just maybe, it reminded him a little of home. Spanish Cove wasn't as pretty but it was . . . alluring.

Home. Ryan looked down at his mobile. It had been flashing all morning and he'd been ignoring it all morning. Of course, if he really didn't want to hear from anybody, he'd have switched it off, wouldn't he?

There they were. Missed calls from Dad. Ellen. James. Kate.

Abracadabra, it rang again. Clio.

He answered.

'Are you fucking joking me?' she said. 'Is that a foreign dial tone?'

'Hi, hello, it's lovely to hear from you, too, Clio. You sound well. How's life? I'm just tickety-boo.'

Silence filled the line.

'You're drunk,' she said.

'I've had a few, I won't lie, but they're small glasses. The Italians drink it like water, you know.'

'You're bloody drunk. They didn't let you on the plane because you're drunk.'

'*Au contraire*. They didn't let me on the plane because I'm sitting in a bar in Limone and Milan Bergamo airport is over one hundred kilometres away. Apparently, you can't fly if you're not at the gate. And they call that customer service.'

'Ryan.' With one word, Clio sounded utterly despondent. All his big brother-ness wanted to make her feel better. But what could he do? He was here, she was there. And here he planned to stay. He couldn't go through with it. He just couldn't.

'What can I say, my darling sister? It's not meant to be.'

'I'm going to book you a new ticket for tonight. Ryan, you have to be on this one. Promise me. I know you have your bag packed. Just do it. Please.'

Ryan shook his head, silently. No way in hell was he getting on a plane back to Ireland. They'd have to drag him kicking and screaming; they'd have to wrestle his passport from his cold dead hands; they'd have to—

'Ryan. Don't make me go home alone. I'm still in Dublin. I'm with James. We're driving down to Spanish Cove tomorrow. Even Kate's coming with us. He's back, Ryan. He's really back.'

'Don't care. Is James with you now?'

'Yes.'

Ryan sighed.

'Christ, I'll be on the late flight,' he said. 'And if James, or anybody, so much as sniffs my breath—'

Rustling: Clio walking away from James, Ryan imagined.

'I won't say anything,' Clio cut him off. 'Why are you in a bar?'

'They're good thinking spots,' Ryan said. 'I have it under control. I *had* it under control.'

Silence again.

'You're mental, Ryan.'

'Ha!' He looked out at the placid lake and the set of stone steps leading down to it. 'We all know who made me that way, don't we, Clio?'

He held the phone to his ear and listened to her short, anxious breaths, the two of them thinking about the past and the hole that had been torn through their lives.

# CLIO

Clio couldn't wait to get out of James' house and on the road to Spanish Cove.

James was welcoming in his own way and his teenage daughter, Bella, appeared to like Clio, the little Clio saw of her. But Clio still felt uncomfortable. James' wife Sandra had styled their Dublin suburban home clinically white, and the clean, minimalist lines had sanitised anything resembling personality. Clio had felt scruffy the entire time she'd been there. No wonder sixteen-year-old Bella preferred to hide in her turret. Clio had caught a glimpse inside Bella's room and it appeared to be a haven of pink, cluttered fluffiness.

Sandra herself left Clio on edge. She'd been a model, once. And she had the blond hair and big blue eyes that held a certain appeal. But she also had big teeth and bone structure that reminded Clio of a horse. Clio just couldn't warm to her.

James also seemed eager to get going; once Kate arrived, they got out the door at speed.

'I'll see you soon.' Sandra beamed at Clio, hugging her before she could get into the back of James' car.

Fucking hope not, Clio replied in her head.

And now she had to survive being in a car with three of her siblings. God knew why Kate had condescended to travel down with them. *Guilt,* Ryan had suggested. Because she owned a five-star hotel and still hadn't offered to put Ryan or Clio up.

As with all dreaded events, the reality was nowhere near as stressful. As the four of them piled in and took to the road, a strange peace descended.

The brand new Audi's air conditioning was top notch, so they could enjoy the summer sun beating down on the windows without baking under it. The radio was tuned to Sunshine FM and mellow music filled their ears. They'd missed most of the June bank holiday weekend traffic by leaving on Saturday morning instead of Friday evening. And as soon as they left Dublin, country smells started to filter in through the car's vents, trumping the exhaust fumes of the other vehicles.

James and Kate, the grown-ups, sat in the front; Clio and Ryan in the back.

'How do you feel, Clio, darling?' Kate asked her, somewhere just outside County Wicklow. 'About leaving New York?'

Clio shrugged.

'I had a good innings,' she said. 'It's hard, you know. Living like that.' She fell quiet. She knew they were all waiting for her to articulate exactly what 'like that' was.

'Looking over your shoulder all the time?' James suggested.

Clio glanced at him in the rearview mirror, surprised. She'd never considered James to be the most insightful.

'Yeah,' she said. 'Exactly. Waiting. Wondering. I know people who have families there now. Their whole lives are built in the boroughs. They have Google alerts on their phones, waiting to see if Trump will say anything about an amnesty for the Irish. Like he's going to give the Irish an amnesty when he's building his wall. Unless he wants us to build the fucking thing—'

'And how is the writing going, Ryan?' Kate interrupted. Her tone said the questions were tick-box exercises. Clio wanted to tick off her own list, which started with asking why Kate insisted on speaking in that ridiculous accent these days.

'I sent an MS out to a rake of agents a couple of months ago,' Ryan said. 'And now I'm waiting for the fuck-you slips to start popping into the letterbox. Like my story is any more fascinating than any other poor sap's.'

Clio shook her head and reached over to squeeze Ryan's hand.

'Maybe you should try getting a real job,' James said.

'Piss off, movie man,' Ryan shot back. 'Who's going to hire me?'

'My industry is full of recovering addicts,' James said. 'It's practically a requirement.'

Clio snorted. There was a cheap irony there, that it had been Ryan and not James who'd ended up with the drugs problem.

James turned up the radio. The strains of Prince's 'Purple Rain' filled the car.

Clio watched him. She could almost see the stress in her oldest brother's shoulders.

What was going on that had him so wound up?

Then the music was abruptly cut off by the Bluetooth and James' phone ringing.

The name of the caller flashed up on the dashboard screen.

*Lena.*

James knocked it off.

'Who's Lena?' Clio said. 'The other woman?'

'Work,' James said, his voice almost choking on the word.

Albertstown, the village nearest to Spanish Cove, was quiet, despite
the heat and all the chairs and tables set up outside the gastropubs
that nowadays dotted the pretty seafront.

The Audi glided down the single main street and turned onto
the coast road.

To the left, boats bobbed in the harbour, fishing nets strung
across their decks; men in tee shirts and waterproofs bringing in
the day's haul, and it not yet twelve o'clock.

And then they were driving the two short kilometres up to
Spanish Cove, so close and yet a world away.

While at a remove, perhaps because of it, the Cove had always
attracted artists and writers and those wanting to shut themselves
off from the world amid breathtaking surrounds.

Clio's great-grandparents, the O'Hares on their mother's side,
had moved there long before it became popular and built the house,
which was still the largest in the small hamlet. Their great-grand-
father had been a successful publisher who'd socialised with Yeats,
among others. His son hadn't been as artistic, but he'd managed to
make a successful living from academic publishing. By the time
Clio's mother Kathleen came along, the O'Hares had built up solid
wealth. Kathleen, the only child, would inherit it all.

'Is that . . . ?' Kate squinted at the man walking the coast road
towards them. Clio followed her gaze as James slowed the car.

Danny McHugh. Uncle Danny.

Danny held his hand up to shield his eyes from the sun and peered
in the now open car windows.

Danny's face had been tanned and aged for all the years the Lattimer children had known him, his days sailing in all weathers carved into his skin. His hair was thinner now and he seemed less strong, less fit. But he was in his early sixties, Clio told herself. You couldn't expect everybody to stay the same.

'There you all are,' he said.

'Missed you, Danny.' Clio smiled.

'Aye, right enough,' Danny said, as emotional as he ever got. 'You're all headed up above?'

'Is everybody talking about it down in the village?' Clio asked.

'Course they are,' Danny said. 'Should be minding their own business. No family 'round here that hasn't got skeletons leppin' around their closets.'

'Christ, Danny,' Ryan drawled. 'Don't dilute our only talent. Surely it's the Lattimers' job to keep this place in salacious gossip?'

'Ryan, really,' Kate said.

'Have you been up there?' Clio asked, cutting across her sister. 'How is he?'

'He's back,' Danny said, simply.

'Well, look, we'll go on ahead,' James said. 'Nice to see you, Danny.'

'I'll see you later.' Danny started to walk away, towards the village.

'Will you?' James called after him, but Danny just raised his arm in a goodbye gesture.

'Why will he be back up at the house?' James asked. 'It's a family dinner tonight, isn't it?'

'Danny is family,' Clio said.

James didn't answer her. He put the car back in gear and sped up the road.

Seconds later, they rounded the bend. The first houses of Spanish Cove began to appear, bright-coloured roofs and blossom-filled terraces built into the slopes on which the homes were stacked, white fences adorned with decorative handmade ornaments and wind chimes that twirled and tinkled in the breeze as the light flashed on their spirals and tubes.

And then they were climbing the hill towards their home, two storeys of taupe grandeur, white curved-bay windows facing the bay and the Passage East ferry, palm trees swaying in the gardens.

Clio shivered, just as Ryan leaned over and took her hand.

*'There is nothing either good or bad but thinking makes it so,'* he said.

'You're Shakespeare now, are you?' James said. 'Can't understand why that publishing deal hasn't landed for you yet.'

Clio reached forward and flicked James on the back of his ear.

'Don't be so bloody mean,' she said. Then, after a moment: 'That's my job.'

He smiled and flapped her away, too thrilled with his cleverness to be apologetic. Then he raised a key fob and pointed it at the control box erected at the side of the entrance to the gardens.

The black wrought-iron gates began to open.

Their home was part of the community. But it was apart, too.

It was important everybody remembered that.

# AFTER

'You're quite an old friend of the family, Danny, am I right?'

Danny studied the young pup interrogating him. Detective Downes, that's how he'd suggested Danny address him, when he'd started asking all the questions. Before Danny gave him the eye and the pup baulked and whimpered, *or whatever.*

The notions. He might live in the city now, but Danny had known *Detective Downes* when he was the kid being egged on by his older brothers to steal sweets from the old newsagents in Albertstown. He wondered if any of the Lattimers remembered him. Probably not. They'd cut themselves off from the world after . . . after Kathleen.

'I am, yes,' Danny answered.

'You know them all well.'

'As well as any outsider can know a family – which is, not well at all,' Danny said.

'I'm sorry?'

Danny shifted uncomfortably on the small plastic chair, feeling pain shoot up his back and around into his abdomen.

'Behind closed doors and all that,' he said.

The young fella looked none the wiser. And he was in charge?
Christ.

'Right. And, eh, can you tell me again what were you doing when Frazer went into the water?'

Danny stroked his jaw and stared down Detective Downes.

'Do you know what a captain does on a boat, son?' he said.

Detective Downes blushed.

'He sails the bloody thing,' Danny said.

The detective baulked a little. But then his lips set in a thin smile.

'I ask because you were the first to notice that Frazer was in the sea. But, you didn't see him go in?'

'Nope.'

'How did you spot him, then?'

Danny sighed.

'I'd had some engine trouble. Got the vessel going, she jerked a bit. I steadied her, went back to check everybody was okay. Saw the blood on the starboard. Don't know what made me look out. Instinct, mebbe? There he was.'

'You don't sound too upset.'

Danny stared at Detective Downes. Then he shook his head, slowly. What did this *child* know of feelings?

Just because Danny wasn't wailing and gnashing teeth.

Frazer was dead. A man who'd been his best friend for nigh on forty years.

Danny would feel what he wanted and express it in whatever way he saw fit.

'There was a lot of fighting on board tonight?' the detective continued.

'I wouldn't say a lot,' Danny answered, cautiously.

The young fella waited. And waited. Danny let the silence grow. The pup broke.

'There was broken glass everywhere and Adam and James did a fair bit of damage to each other.'

'Aye,' Danny said.

'Eh . . . how did it start?'

'How does any family fight start?'

Silence.

'Drink?'

Ten points for the little detective.

'Was there anything else?' he asked. 'Did Frazer argue with anybody?'

'Mebbe.'

'Who?'

Danny pursed his lips.

'What you have to remember,' he said, 'is that Frazer was my friend. This weekend was hard going for him. That's all I'll say. Even if I am fond of those kids.'

'You think one of Frazer's children may have attacked him tonight? Is that what you're getting at?'

'I'm getting at I'll bet they're not all being entirely truthful about their motives for coming back home. That's all I'm saying.'

# ADAM

Adam kicked at the pebbles that lay along the shoreline, pulling his foot back as the wash from the waves curled at his toes and dampened the fabric of his trainers.

He'd seen the car coming around the coast road, had known it was his siblings, felt it, a change in atmosphere.

He sucked on the cigarette, so short now he was almost at the butt. The skin around his nails was red raw. He'd been picking at it for days, an old, childish habit that resurfaced in times of acute stress.

Ellen had been relatively easy.

His sister was the same as ever – her brown hair in an old-fashioned plait that hung lankly around the front, face devoid of make-up, her plainness worn like a badge of honour.

She was, of course, convinced everybody would be focused on her this weekend: judging her, gossiping about her, discussing her past. She'd never gotten over her personal tragedy; she never would, not if she stayed here.

Adam's disappearance and reappearance was a mere distraction from her own sad history.

Frazer's reaction . . . now that had left Adam puzzled.

For one thing, he'd cried. Then he'd listened, carefully, as Adam gave his father a version of what had happened all those years ago. The version he knew the old man would want to hear. The one where Adam was the instigator and Frazer the victim.

Apologies were uttered, redress made.

Adam had still expected to see anger from Frazer. More, even. Hatred. Adam would have understood that.

Instead, his father seemed unnaturally calm. Happy, even, to see Adam home.

*'I'm glad you realised it was time to come back, son,'* Frazer had said. *'I'm old, but not too old. We'll all be the better for this.'*

*What?* Adam had heard himself screaming in his head. It didn't make sense.

His father always had an angle.

Adam had returned on his own terms. Successful. Wealthy. His father admired that, even while he begrudged it. It was important to Frazer Lattimer to be needed. He fostered it. At the same time, he resented neediness. The man was nothing if not a mass of hypocritical contradictions.

If his dad was happy to have Adam home, it had to be because it was useful to him.

Ellen said the others rarely came back. Maybe Frazer was lonely and Adam's return was an excuse to get everybody home again. To fill the house with Lattimers once more.

Whatever was going on, Adam would watch his father carefully.

His dad and Ellen were one proposition.

Adam knew his other siblings would be more difficult to deal with.

Kate might be a bit oblivious. She wasn't Ellen, but she, too, was unhealthily obsessed with herself.

James was sharper. He'd be desperately trying to establish Adam's reason for returning.

As for Ryan and Clio . . .

They knew him, through and through.

They were the only ones who could really spot if he was lying or not.

When he'd discovered their mother had died, Adam had known there would be no forgiveness. It had been the ninth anniversary of her death, that's what the newspaper had said.

He wasn't the sort to scan Deaths and Anniversaries notices. Too young. But something had led him there, he told his father.

Lattimer. The name had jumped off the page.

*'How did you feel?'* Frazer had asked.

*'Like shit,'* Adam told him, truthfully. Not only had he missed his mother's last months alive, he'd missed her funeral and the years afterwards, when he should have been grieving.

How could anybody forgive him when he couldn't forgive himself?

That was a side point, though. He could learn to live with that.

It was everybody finding out the truth about why he'd left.

And why he was back.

That's what he had to avoid.

Adam flicked the butt into the lapping water. He glanced up at the house, then down at the ground. Shoulders hunched, he began the long walk back up the hill to face the music.

# CLIO

Frazer greeted them when they arrived, obviously happy to see them. So happy that the knot in Clio's stomach temporarily unwound. She had expected to feel guilty once she was in his presence, at being away for so long and for making no effort. But, right now, that didn't seem to matter.

Teddy, their old collie, padded into the large hallway behind her dad and slumped onto the floor at his feet, staring up at them all with milk-glazed eyes and no recognition.

'Ach, there's the baby of the family,' Frazer said joyfully, in the Scottish accent he'd never lost, even though he'd lived in Ireland twice as long as his home country. He wrapped his arms around Clio and her senses were assaulted by his scent – books and the sea and Molton Brown.

'Aye, I've missed you,' he said. 'Have they Americanised you? Let's have a look.' Frazer peered over the top of his reading glasses and stroked the bristles on his chin for effect. Once red, they were now full-white, uncontainable by any razor, just like Adam's had always been. His hair had gone the same colour, though there were still flecks of red and auburn here and there. He was as tall as ever, but age had hunched him over a little.

Clio blushed under his scrutiny, knowing she looked perfectly normal but suddenly conscious of all that her father couldn't see beyond her long-sleeved blouse and skinny jeans. The tattoos on her lower back and ankle. The streaks of colour on the underside of her thick brown hair. The piercings in her navel.

Clio escaped her father's gaze by dropping to her hunkers, where she tried to pat Teddy, noticing the more prominent rib-cage and the patches on his skin where the hair was less thick. What age must he be in dog years anyway, she wondered? They'd homed him as a pup, at least thirteen years ago now. He was getting on.

'Is he okay, Dad?' Clio asked. 'He's lost weight.'

'Old age,' Frazer replied. 'Bugger won't eat anything but treats. I'm the same. Don't know if he's got like me or I've got like him.'

The dog shrugged away from her hand and rested his chin on his paw.

Clio stood, reluctantly, hurt.

Teddy had slept in her bed practically every night when she was growing up. Four years away, and now he wouldn't even look at her?

Frazer's attention was back on his other children.

'Kate and James, you look terrific, the pair of you!' A pause. Long, painful. 'Ryan.'

Frazer stood back and looked at Ryan, who was hovering at the rear of the group.

'Dad.' Ryan stepped forward slowly, reluctantly, his head bowed. When he was in front of his father, he looked up. Frazer placed his hand on his youngest son's shoulder and examined him. Only Clio saw the flinch.

'How are you, son? Healthy?'

'I am.'

Frazer nodded curtly, satisfied.

'Well, now, is this not terrific, having you all together again? I've such a hooley planned. It's been a long time coming. Too long. But what better reason than Adam coming back!'

'Where is he?' Clio said. With the mere mention of Adam, her mood darkened.

All wasn't well. The past had happened. This wasn't a joyous reunion. 'What has he told you?'

'He's round and about,' Frazer answered her. 'But look, you've only arrived. Go on, drop your bags in your rooms. Freshen up.'

'I'd rather just—' Clio started. 'Where the hell was he, Dad? Did you tell him what happened to Mam?'

'He knows,' Frazer said. 'Later, Clio. Settle in, go on.'

'Good idea,' James interrupted before Clio could protest any more. 'I need a shower. We can hang on another half an hour, eh?'

'Ach, you'll have plenty to talk about.' Frazer smiled, his eyes on his eldest son.

Clio didn't imagine it. A shadow crossed James' face. It disappeared as abruptly as it had arrived, and he smiled broadly.

Her room looked almost the same.

The personal effects were more or less gone. Posters and make-up, junk she'd strewn across her dressing table. But the duvet set on the single bed looked familiar, and she recognised the jewellery box that sat by the mirror, black, engraved with oriental flowers. In the window, the large terracotta vase her mother had bought in a market in Granada sat on the sill, filled with fresh flowers. Gardenias.

Clio walked to the window and pulled the sparkling white net curtains aside. She looked out at the sea and breathed. The window was open; the smell of seaweed and molluscs and brine filled her nostrils. She'd gone to the waterside often in New York, but it hadn't smelled like this. New York, no matter where you stood, filled the nose with the scent of industry and food and hot air vents and other people. Like the heroine in *Brooklyn*, Clio had forgotten. Nowhere held her heart like Ireland.

Clio walked to the bed and sat down, felt the give that had always been there, ever since herself and Ryan had broken the middle slats when they'd decided to use the mattress as a trampoline. Clio, it seemed, was destined to always have a bed that didn't work properly.

Their mother had threatened to break the pair of them when she saw the damage.

Only Ryan had been punished.

Clio crossed to her bag and took the envelope out of its pocket.

In the corner of the room, she knelt and pulled back the carpet that she'd torn from its tacks decades earlier.

She placed the envelope on the floorboards underneath and patted the carpet back into place.

It would be safe there.

# AFTER

Back in the station, Dave Murphy was working a late one and he was, he patiently and not so politely explained to Detective Downes, *up to his fucking eyeballs.*

'I appreciate that,' the detective said, holding the phone slightly away from his ear in an effort to negate the worst excesses of the sergeant's volume and cursing. 'I'm up against it myself down here, Murphy.'

'Thought all these call-outs tonight were accidents, for Jaysus' sake. They're saying the pile-up on the N11 involved a fucking Yank driving the wrong way up the motorway, half-pissed. The boating incident up in Curracloe included two teenagers who'd stolen a speed-boat. And now you're saying there's a murder. For the love of f—'

Detective Downes placed the phone on the table. Even without it being on loudspeaker, he could still hear his colleague. He just hoped the family in the small room down the way couldn't hear him, too.

'So, I reckon I take priority, then,' the detective said, when the tirade had drawn to a conclusion.

'What? Why do you sound so tinny? Are you losing signal?'

Detective Downes hastily picked the phone back up before Murphy seized the opportunity to hang up.

'You speak French, don't you?' he said.

'Where did you hear that?' Murphy answered, full of suspicion.

'You tried to seduce Bernadette in the canteen by singing every word of *"Je t'aime, moi non plus"*.'

'Well, I didn't know she was married, did I? Anyway, I can sing *"Joe le taxi"*, too. Doesn't make me a Francophile.'

'Didn't you live there for a year when you were in college?'

'Ah, for fuck's . . . what is this about?'

Detective Downes smiled.

'I need you to get on to whatever pals you have in the Sûreté and find out if Adam Lattimer has any record over there. I'll send you his details. If we do it through English, they'll make us wait for being ignorant Anglo twats, you know they will.'

'Sure, sure, I'm doing nothing else here, it's not like—'

Detective Downes hung up.

He'd cite loss of signal.

Murphy would stew for a few minutes, then he'd get on it. He was good like that.

# ADAM

It was weird. Like they didn't know each other and were meeting for the first time. Yet, they all knew each other too well for the politeness of strangers. So, nobody knew quite what to do.

Adam stood in the hall watching as first James, then Ryan, Kate and Clio all came down the stairs, agog, mouths hanging open at the sight of him. Ellen hung back, standing in the shadows of the hallway, letting him have his moment.

'Hi,' he said, lightly.

They stopped at the foot of the steps, gathered in a little group, staring at Adam like he was behind a glass wall and they couldn't touch him. He glanced at each of them, nervously, his eyes returning more than once to Clio and Ryan.

'Adam,' Kate choked, then she was on top of him, squeezing the life out of him. 'I thought you were dead.'

Adam let her hold him, surprised at the outpouring of affection. He kissed the side of her head. She felt familiar, but smelled different. Expensive.

'It's okay,' he said. 'Kate, it's okay. I'm okay.'

She let her arms fall, then, and just looked at him, embarrassed. It was James' turn next. He shook his head, incredulous, then pulled Adam into a bear hug.

'Man,' he said. 'You gave us some bloody scare.'

'I know,' Adam muttered.

'I thought the whole life and death shit was my job,' Ryan said, dryly.

Adam smiled thinly as he embraced his younger brother.

Clio stood on the bottom step. She remained motionless.

Adam swallowed the lump in his throat. If Muhammad . . .

She kept her eyes to the side, refusing to meet his gaze, though the step meant they were just about face to face.

'Hey,' he said, gently.

Clio said nothing.

'Clio, I know I screwed up,' Adam continued. 'And I know I've a lot of explaining to do. But, for now, can we just say hello?'

Clio's green, cat-like eyes slowly angled until they met his.

He didn't even see her hand move, just felt the sting of the slap as it landed on his cheek, the noise rebounding around the high-ceilinged hall, followed by gasps of shock from the others.

'Your disappearing act killed our mother,' she said, coldly.

Adam raised his hand to his cheek, felt the heat that had nothing to do with the slap.

'Clio,' he choked. But before he could add anything else, Frazer arrived.

'All right, lass,' he said, his voice firm.

'It needs to be said,' Clio snapped, tilting her head at Adam. 'Mam thought he was dead and it killed her. And he strolls in here like nothing has happened, like we can play happy families—'

'I know, pet. Come with me for a few minutes.'

Frazer took Clio's arm and began to walk her towards his study; she resisted at first but then her body slumped and she reluctantly followed, without even a glance cast back at Adam.

'Why don't the rest of you sit out on the verandah,' Frazer called. 'It's a lovely evening. Enjoy the last of the day's heat. Have a chat, eh? Try not to go too Jeremy Paxman on your brother. We've the whole weekend ahead.'

Adam made a move in his father's direction, almost reaching out to Clio. But he halted, nodded obediently.

He watched the back of her head disappearing down the hall.

'Verandah,' Ryan muttered. 'Still a fucking snob.'

Had they been there for any other reason, sitting in the garden that sunny, summer's afternoon, sipping cool drinks, it would have been an entirely pleasurable experience.

But Adam had barely raised his G&T to his lips when the first question landed.

'Well,' Ryan said, his eyes on Adam. 'Are you going to tell us, or do we have to drag it out of you? You're the main event, bro. Spit it out. Where were you?'

'Shouldn't I keep it for the grand dinner?' Adam said, half-heartedly. 'The da has ordered in lobster.'

'When you've followed dinner with a line of cocaine off a hooker's arse, all other eating experiences are tame in comparison,' Ryan retorted.

'Jesus, Ryan,' Kate exclaimed, while Ellen wrinkled her nose in disgust. 'Must you always be so vulgar?'

'Moi, vulgar? By the way, why do you keep talking like that, Kate?'

'Like what?'

'Like you're from a quaint village in Suffolk.'

'There is nothing wrong with how I speak.' Kate sniffed.

'Adam, come on,' James said. 'Before this descends into shit none of us are here for. Ryan's right. We're dying to know.' He stood and walked to the drinks table, where he uncapped the gin and refilled his glass with more than one measure, more than a double.

'Woah,' Ryan said. 'Easy, tiger. My sobering up doesn't mean there's a vacancy.'

'This is a celebration,' James said. 'Big difference.'

But Adam was watching James carefully. He didn't look like he was celebrating.

And now James was staring at Adam. They all were.

Adam took a deep breath.

'It's no mystery,' he said. 'It's probably how you imagined it.'

'How do *you* think we imagined it, Adam?' Kate said. Her voice sounded thick with distress and confusion.

His siblings' shocked surprise at having him back was quickly being replaced by their memories of losing him in the first place.

'The night it happened,' Kate continued, 'we didn't even realise. It was only as the days went by – we knew something wasn't right. You would have said goodbye; you'd have told us if you were just going back up to Dublin. All the stuff you'd brought down was still in Spanish Cove and we couldn't get hold of you in your college digs. Your phone was dead. Then we thought you might be with James. Mam rang him, asking had he seen you.'

James shook his head, answering a ten-year-old phone call.

'We tried all your friends here. You remember, Ellen, don't you? We drove the length and breadth of the county. Nobody had heard from you. Mam and Dad went to the guards. They rang all the hospitals. Danny got the coastguard out; they started to search the bay. We were devastated, convinced you'd drowned and we'd gone and left it two days before we started to look for you.'

Kate's voice broke.

Adam felt shame churning in his stomach, burning through him like white heat.

'Clio was inconsolable,' Kate said. 'The only one who had faith was Mam. She was *convinced* you would come back. You were facing your final year in college and she figured you'd panicked, that maybe you'd failed your exams. And when that turned out to be true, and we found out you'd given up your lease in Dublin, we knew then that something had been up for months. But Mam still believed in you. When we discovered your bank account was empty, she thought, he's gone into hiding, he can't face Dad. She waited a year for you, until . . .' Kate trailed off.

Adam hung his head.

'I was depressed. When I left, I mean. I was suffering with depression. Badly.'

Adam looked up. His siblings were silent. Kate's mouth hung open. James looked confused.

'You weren't depressed,' he said, blankly. 'We know what depression is. Mam and . . .'

James flashed a quick glance at Kate, then cast his eyes sideways. Adam caught it, though.

'You were at a party a week before,' James continued. 'You rang me from a party. You asked . . .'

James stopped abruptly. Adam stared, unblinking, at his brother, waiting to see if he'd fill in the blanks.

But James didn't want to say any more. He didn't want to admit his own culpability.

'Wait,' Kate said. 'Did somebody diagnose you with depression or did you decide this yourself?'

'There was no diagnosis. Not then, I mean. I only realised later. Years later. I didn't know what was going on at the time. Only that I couldn't cope and I needed it all to end.'

'Why didn't you talk to any of us?' Kate said.

Adam shrugged, blushing.

Kate shook her head, incredulous.

'Oh, Adam,' she said. 'And what? You just walked out of the house? Decided to leave?'

'Something like that,' he answered.

Kate struggled to form the next sentence. Ellen got there before her.

'Were you planning to kill yourself?' she asked.

'Yes.'

They all fell silent for a moment.

'That's what we thought had happened,' Ellen said, glancing sideways at Kate.

'It's what I intended,' Adam said. 'I . . . I couldn't stand the thought of any of you finding me. I didn't know where to go or what to do, at first. Then it came to me. I got on the ferry.'

His voice was clipped. Robotic. Adam was conscious of it, but he couldn't make it sound anything other. Even though he'd practised this story, over and over. Maybe he'd practised it too much. And yet, this was all true. In a manner. And he had felt suicidal. On plenty of occasions.

James shook his head adamantly. He was studying Adam, his face disbelieving.

'You didn't get on the ferry. We spoke to the guys who run Passage East. They knew you; Ryan had worked there, for God's sake. They would have remembered you, easily. And your passport was here. We found it.'

'I didn't get on the ferry to Waterford,' Adam corrected him. 'I hitched to Rosslare. I got on the ferry to Cherbourg. I knew if I killed myself in Ireland, you would find out. In Cherbourg, I was nobody. I could just vanish. If I even made it that far. And I didn't take my passport because I didn't want you to know I'd gone abroad. To come looking for me.'

'Then how did you travel?' James asked. 'How did you . . .'

'It doesn't matter,' Adam said. 'I went. That's all you need to know.'

'But you didn't kill yourself,' Ryan said.

'Obviously.'

'So, why didn't you come back, then? Why didn't you let us know you were okay?'

'I couldn't,' Adam said. His voice had adopted a pleading tone. 'At first it was embarrassment. Then it was worry. Then fear. It was like, every time I thought of picking up the phone or sending a note, I'd end up down this cul-de-sac. You would all hate me and it was probably just better to . . . to not say anything. I can't explain it.'

Adam swallowed.

'What changed?' Kate asked. 'You're here now, so what happened to make you change your mind? Why did you come back?'

'I found out about Mam,' Adam said. 'It was just there, in the memorial notices. First time I'd ever looked. I didn't even get Irish papers until recently and even then, it was just a fluke I saw it. Or maybe I was looking for something. I don't know.'

His siblings looked at each other, shock mixed with discomfort.

'The memorial didn't go in every year,' Ryan said, finally. 'Dad put it in the first year and didn't bother again. I noticed last year and sent one in for her ninth anniversary.' He paused. 'Just to piss the old man off.'

'Wait,' Kate said. 'Are you saying if you hadn't seen that, you wouldn't have come back? But, *it nearly didn't go in*. And, she's dead. She's gone. Wouldn't you have come back for us?'

'I did come back for you,' Adam protested. 'I missed the chance to say goodbye to Mam. I couldn't bear the thought of that happening again.'

Adam looked around them all. His eyes lingered on James, who was still studying him intensely.

James looked away first. He peered into his empty glass, then back over at the diminished bottle of gin on the drinks table. Adam knew he was planning to get himself another one.

James was sweating, beads visible on his brow and over his lip.

*James,* Adam thought, *looks like he's hiding as much as I am.*

# CLIO

Clio felt cold, even though her father's study, heaving with expensive mahogany furniture and dusty, groaning bookshelves, was warm. Airless, in fact.

Frazer had just relayed what Adam had told him when he returned. Clio was still mulling it over. She studied her father's face, keen to figure out if he believed her brother.

Depression.

If Adam had been depressed, he wouldn't have been alone in their family.

He was, however, the first to admit to it.

Teddy was on the floor near her foot. He'd looked up once or twice and she thought she'd seen him sniff the air around her.

She'd leave him be until he familiarised himself. Let him come to her.

'I don't care if he was depressed,' Clio said. 'He still walked off the face of the planet. And, yet, you seem okay with him coming back. Aren't you . . . ?'

She held out her hands, unable to find the words.

'Angry?' Frazer said. 'Of course I am, lass. I'm furious. But what should I do? We've lost a decade. He's my son, Clio. He was always my . . . well, *you* understand. You and him were easier to love, I guess, even if I shouldn't say it. Should I lose another ten years raging at him? What would that achieve? My parents rarely spoke to me when I moved over here. I'm sure it didn't make them any happier.'

Clio blinked.

'You don't understand, lass. But you were younger, when your brother left. More of your life has been affected by it. Maybe old age has given me some perspective, eh? I've learned to take the good where I can. And there's a lot of positives to be had from Adam's return. You're here, for a start.'

Clio didn't know what to say.

Frazer stood and walked to the bookshelf by the window. He ran his hand along the spines of the books. It rested on one; he pulled the book towards him, blowing dust from its hardback cover.

Those books.

She used to love those shelves.

The sun was in her eyes. She brought her hand to her brow to shade them. Her forehead felt clammy.

'Do you remember this?' he said, showing her the cover.

Clio looked at him blankly for a moment, then her face filled with recognition.

'*The Witches,*' she said.

'Your favourite read at bedtime.'

It had been. Every night, the time her father devoted to her and only her. In a large family, you took what you got.

'I wish I could have done more to protect you,' he said eventually, placing the book back in its place. 'From everything that happened back then.'

Clio's shoulders tensed. Any tighter and her neck was going to spasm.

'Dad, I don't want to talk about me,' she said.

Frazer sighed and sat heavily in his chair.

'Do you think Adam is telling the truth?' Clio asked.

'Why would he lie?'

'I don't know. To make us feel sorry for him? It's hard to lash out at somebody when they're telling you they had no control over what they did. When they're using it as an excuse.'

'But why would he need us to feel sorry for him?' Frazer said. 'Why come back at all, if he doesn't want to be here?'

Clio shrugged.

'It does make sense,' Frazer said. 'So many young men, too many, from around here, have suffered with depression. Adam wasn't a big concern for your mother and me. There was Ryan, and each of you had your own – stuff. It pains me to say we could have missed it, but then, if he'd been hiding it well . . . There has to be some reason he did something so stupid. Why would anybody in their right mind want to cause so much hurt? To others or . . . to themselves?'

Clio tugged on her bottom lip. She knew what her father was getting at. She knew *who* he was getting at.

'Anyhow,' Frazer said. 'We all have our reasons for doing things. Even you, Clio. You might not want to talk about why *you* felt the need to run away for four years, but perhaps you might want to have *this* conversation.'

'What conversation?' she said, startled.

Frazer sat back, let the pause grow. Clio's senses prickled.

'I'm thinking of lifting the stay on your trust. Yours and Ryan's. Though, I'm not sure about Ryan's. I want to watch him over the next few days. Make sure he's not . . . ach, you know why I froze it in the first place.'

'Yeah,' she snapped. 'Because none of us could be trusted. Because Ellen and Kate and James had screwed up with their inheritances and then Adam disappeared and left an empty bank account.'

'And Ryan was in rehab when he was due to receive it,' her father added. 'How could I let him? With everything that had happened?'

'I'd done nothing, Dad,' Clio said. 'Mam . . .'

'I know what your mother wanted,' Frazer said. 'And I can see how you would have preferred her way of doing things. But how well did it end up for the others, eh? It was my job to take care of you, Clio, when she'd gone. And she wasn't always the best at making the right decisions.'

'Our grandparents left us that money for a reason,' Clio said, trying to swallow her anger. Her mother's parents had been good people. Fair. Their grandchildren would eventually inherit the family portfolio of investments but they'd also set trust funds aside for each of them. In case they needed money earlier. Fifty thousand, with interest, upon turning twenty-one. They'd made Frazer and Kathleen trustees. If one of the children became ill or incapacitated, the trustees could retain their money in the fund, earning interest, until a more suitable time for its release.

Her father, in Clio's opinion, had used the conditions and his power far too liberally.

'Ryan's trust amounted to over sixty grand with the interest it had accumulated, Clio. Think of the damage that could have done to him when he turned twenty-one. How would you have coped with his death, I wonder? You barely survived your mother's.'

Clio couldn't take any more. Her eyes kept finding the bookshelf and the sight of it made her want to vomit.

She knew, now, where all the family secrets were kept.

She stood and walked to the door but before opening it, Clio paused and turned.

'You never considered the damage that might be done without that money,' she said. 'Did you think of us at all, Dad?'

Her father looked terribly sad for a moment.

'I think of you all, all the time,' he said. 'But I'm allowed to think of myself, too. You know it was hard on me, Clio, when all of you upped and left. After your mother died, Kate couldn't get away quick enough and as soon as you had the means, you were gone.'

Clio blinked back tears.

At the desk, Teddy attempted to get to his feet.

The dog was trying to follow her.

A couple of steps.

Come on, boy.

But he couldn't make it. He lay back down.

Poor fucker.

'Clio, don't keep running from the hard stuff,' Frazer said.

'I'm not,' she said, lightly.

Her father held his arms out in surrender, in apparent apology at having upset her.

She smiled, tried to make it warm.

Then she walked outside and closed the door behind her.

And that was when she realised that she'd barely been breathing.

# AFTER

Ryan kept taking nervous sips of coffee, between jiggling his legs up and down and generally being unable to keep still.

It was familiar to him, this nervous anxiety, though it was a long time since he'd experienced it this bad.

It made him crave.

If he could lay his hands on something right now, he knew he'd take it.

The danger zone. Those moments in the shade, when the sun could come out or you could tip into total darkness.

He started to rock back and forth.

'Are you okay?' the detective asked.

'No, I don't think I am, actually,' Ryan said.

The detective looked puzzled for a moment. Ryan watched him and felt himself relax, just a smidgeon, now a witness to somebody else's discomfort.

No doubt all his siblings had answered that question with 'I'm fine'.

'I'm just shocked, I guess,' Ryan said.

'Of course. Sure. You, eh, you're okay, though? In general, I mean?'

Ryan couldn't really remember Detective Downes, but when he'd arrived earlier the man had introduced himself to Ryan as a former local of Albertstown. And everybody around this way was aware of his sordid past. The addiction. The trouble and pain he'd inflicted on his family.

Well, they knew some of it.

'Yeah,' Ryan answered. 'I'm good. Have to remember to not slip when, you know . . . stress.'

'Absolutely.' The detective nodded sagely. 'Was this weekend particularly stressful, would you say?'

'It got fairly fucking intense in the last few hours.'

A pause.

'How did you feel, about your father summoning you home?' the detective asked.

'I only came home because Adam did. I wouldn't have been here otherwise, put it like that.'

'Were you angry with Adam, then?'

Ryan shrugged.

'He's my brother.'

Detective Downes cocked his head, examined Ryan.

'So, you were annoyed by your father, but not by Adam, the very reason you came home. Given the choice, would you have met Adam somewhere else, on your own terms?'

Ryan clamped his lips shut.

'I see,' the detective said. 'Did you tell Frazer that? Did you and him argue?'

Ryan hesitated.

'You never really fought with Frazer,' he said. 'Not in the sense you mean.'

The detective waited for him to clarify.

'I mean,' Ryan said, 'it wasn't as simple as a stand-up row, with yelling on both sides.'

'No?'

'No.'

'What was it like?'

Ryan looked down at the floor.

'The thing with Frazer was that you never really knew what he would do or say next,' he mumbled. 'You might think you had a handle on the situation and then it would flip. The only thing you could expect from him is that he would always be the centre of attention and he was always the victim. Right to the fucking end.'

Ryan breathed heavily into the silence. He knew it oozed out of him. Just how much he hated his father.

'You ever want to harm your father, Ryan?'

'Me?' Ryan said. He tugged on the inside of his lip so hard, he felt the skin give. 'Mainly, I just tried to avoid getting harmed by him.'

# CLIO

She'd spent the afternoon lying in her old bed, remembering.

If she closed her eyes, she could almost hear her mother's voice echoing through the years. The house even *smelled* the way it used to.

But when she opened her eyes, she knew instantly that everything had changed. Her world was still on its axis. The door to her mother's old room was still closed, and Clio was still skirting around it as though it, and the person who'd died in there, had never existed.

Clio's mother had been the sort of woman to bring warmth into a room with her. When she talked to you, it was only you she was focused on. She oozed kindness. Clio, growing up with her, had thought that was normal. She only realised, when Kathleen was gone, that her mother's personality was rare, that she'd been a gem. It ruined you, a person like that loving you. Once you'd had that, it was devastating to realise nobody else would ever care for you in the same way. You would never be that important to anybody else.

Fucking Adam.

In the corner of the room, the letter lay hidden beneath the carpet, every word of it seared into her mind's eye. The truth that revealed how unnecessary it had all been. All the loss and grief that had marred Clio's life.

At one point, her door opened. Clio half-turned her head to see who it was, but there was nobody there.

She frowned, puzzled, until she heard the laboured breathing of another presence and then Teddy was pulling himself up, with huge effort, onto the end of her bed.

'Now you want to know me, huh?' Clio said, sitting up.

He fell in a heap at her feet. Clio reached down and tickled the back of his ears. The dog sighed, contentedly.

Two parts, joined again. Clio still remembered him as a little bundle, a hot, wriggly mess of panting and fur and wet tongue and big brown eyes, nuzzling under her chin.

Adam had given Clio the puppy. Kathleen had nearly had a heart attack, until Teddy turned his eyes on her and she'd melted, then instructed Frazer to do the same.

'He's part of the family now,' Kathleen had said. 'A smelly, hairy, loveable part.'

Teddy sighed again.

'I missed you, too, boy,' Clio said, her voice thick.

She lay back down, resting her feet against his back, and felt his heart beat, long and slow.

And they stayed like that until she heard her sisters' voices on the landing outside and Clio forced herself to sit up. She had to continue to act like she was normal. Normal-ish.

'Do you have tonic?' Kate asked, when Clio arrived in her sister's bedroom, brandishing a bottle of vodka.

Kate was sitting on the edge of her bed, the Empress Sisi, Ellen behind her running a comb through Kate's immaculate bob.

Kate had suggested the sisters spend some time together before dinner. It felt odd. Ellen had never done girly and sisterly. Not in Clio's memory. And even now she looked out of place. Still, she was trying, Clio thought, charitably. Quickly followed by the less kind thought that Ellen was probably afraid she'd miss something.

'You've mistaken me for fucking room service,' Clio answered. 'Slug it from the bottle.'

'Like savages,' Kate said.

Clio sat on the rug on the floor, her legs tucked under her, and watched her sisters to the tune of Billy Joel's 'The Longest Time'. Kate had obviously found her old CDs.

'Your hair is like silk,' Ellen said, bringing the comb back to the crown of her sister's head. 'How do you keep it like this?'

'Cut and condition, once a fortnight,' Kate said. 'There's a salon in the hotel.'

'I'm surprised you've time for it.' Ellen sniffed. 'What with how busy you are. I didn't think you were a lady of leisure.'

'Looking good is part of my work,' Kate said. 'You know, Ellen, we've all got the same hair. If you put just a little effort in . . .'

'Catty,' Clio said. Then, to Ellen, 'She can afford to be pampered.'

'It's not like any of us were born without silver spoons,' Kate retorted.

'Some of us did better than others, remember?' Clio said. 'Though fuck knows what Ellen did with her money. Unless you have it squirrelled away, Ellen, I'm assuming you lost it. I can't think of any other reason you'd still be here.'

Kate and Ellen exchanged a loaded look.

Clio noticed, wondered what the secret was.

'What did Dad say to you?' Ellen asked, preventing Clio from probing. 'Earlier?'

'He said he's so happy to see me home that he's been on to his solicitors and changed his will. Turns out, I'm getting the family homestead.'

Ellen's face paled.

'Jesus, relax,' Clio said.

'It's no joke,' Ellen said. 'You all left. This is my home. I stayed, I cared for him . . .'

'Cared for him?' Clio snorted. 'You make him sound like an elderly invalid.'

'Whatever,' Ellen said. 'I stayed.'

'The spinster sister who wouldn't leave in case the house was gifted to somebody else from under her, right?' Kate said.

Ellen flushed bright red and lowered the comb.

'Except that's not true, is it?'

Clio stretched back and observed them, entirely fascinated now.

'Just shut up,' Ellen hissed. 'Clio, sit up here. I'll do *your* hair, instead.'

Clio didn't think she could say no.

She handed Kate the bottle of vodka, and took her place.

As Ellen brushed her hair, Clio realised this was the closest anybody had been to her in a long time. Anybody who hadn't been about to have sex with her. Clio did her own hairstyling, always had, even when it didn't go well. She didn't like the small talk that went with hairdressers. She'd nothing to contribute.

'What on earth?' Ellen paused, and Clio felt cold air on the nape of her neck as her hair was lifted.

'What have you done to your head?' Kate gasped, appalled.

'It's in fashion,' Clio said.

'So were white jeans, once,' Kate said. 'Not all abominations should be slavishly adhered to.'

'Leave it down,' Clio said, raising her hand and batting her sisters away.

'God, what would Mam say?' Kate said, laughing lightly.

'Mam's not here,' Clio snapped.

The casual introduction of their mother into the room, the missing piece, shook Clio more than she wanted them to know. She reached over and took the bottle off Kate, ignoring now the look that Kate and Ellen gave each other.

'You might have been a bit hard on Adam, earlier,' Kate said, quietly. 'I mean, whatever he did, he can't be blamed for Mam dying.'

'Are you shitting me? You were *here*.'

'She died from a heart attack, Clio.'

'She died because her heart was broken,' Clio retorted. 'And we all know that wasn't what killed her, really. We all know what happened.'

Kate fell silent.

Clio took another drink of vodka and blinked rapidly.

'Why are you defending him, anyway?' Clio said. 'You've refused to speak about him for years.'

Kate opened and closed her mouth. She got up and walked away from the bed. Clio watched as her sister opened her wardrobe and began to rummage through old clothes that still hung there. Elasticated tracksuit bottoms and long woollen jumpers. Clothes for hiding in. Some of them were three times the size of Kate now. Nothing like the delicate, designer-label clothes she'd brought from Dublin.

'Why is all this still in here?' Kate grumbled.

'You want to know what Dad wanted?' Clio said, speaking to her sister's back. 'He wanted to tell me he was thinking about lifting the stay on my trust.'

'Well, that's good news, isn't it?' Ellen said, brightly, slowing the strokes of the comb 'That could help you set yourself up, find a home. In Dublin, I mean.'

'Yeah, you can stop running away,' Kate said.

'For fuck's sake, I'm not Adam. I told you all I was going. You don't give Ryan a hard time.'

'We never heard from you,' Kate countered. 'Ryan stayed in touch. You only gave us your new number last year. If Adam had come back before that, we'd have struggled to track you down. You'd have been the one who'd disappeared, then.'

'I was living in the States illegally! I had to keep a low profile. I sent cards, didn't I? Anyway, you're one to talk, Kate.'

Clio watched as her sister's whole body tensed.

'How's Cheng, your husband of seven years?' she continued. 'Any chance we might meet him one of these days?'

Kate said nothing.

# AFTER

'Talk to me about that Saturday night, James,' the detective said. 'The first night you were all together.'

'Saturday?' James said.

The detective nodded.

James gritted his teeth. He was cold, he was wet and he was pissed off.

His father's death had been an accident. Couldn't they just leave it at that?

'You want to talk about Saturday,' he said. 'It's bloody Monday. My father just died. What does Saturday night have to do with anything?'

'Maybe somebody did something on Saturday that caused your father's death on Monday.' The detective shrugged.

'Nobody caused anything. You know what, I want to go home, get dry and ring my wife and daughter. This is starting to feel like you think something heinous happened, like we're suspects.' James frowned. 'I think I want a solicitor in with me if we're going down this route.'

'Are you saying you need a solicitor?'

James half-laughed, a surprised sound.

'Don't pull that smart-ass shit with me,' he said. Then he swallowed.

'Anyway,' he said. 'I've nothing of note to say about Saturday. If you want to know what happened on Saturday, you should talk to Kate.'

'Why? What will Kate say?'

James opened his mouth, then raised his hand to his chin.

Maybe he should wait for the solicitor.

Then again, if the detective was looking for people who might have wanted harm to come to Frazer . . .

Well, better that he was looking elsewhere.

# KATE

'Cocktails in the lounge before dinner,' James said, as they walked around the landing towards the stairs. 'Sounds like a plan to either put us all into a good-natured drink coma or have us sufficiently steaming to tear each other's heads off. With us, it could go either way.'

Kate said nothing. She didn't mind the thought of numbing herself with another drink. The tension in her stomach was growing, and she couldn't put her finger on why.

Her reaction to Adam had taken her, as much as everybody else, by surprise. She'd had no idea she would be so overwhelmed and so happy to see him. They hadn't even been that close as kids. Adam had that way of looking at you, looking through you, from a very early age; Kate had always felt he could read thoughts that even she wasn't comfortable with. She didn't like feeling that exposed. And yet, him standing there, in the flesh, had brought back all the sadness she'd felt when he'd gone. That fear that he was dead and her guilt that she had never really liked him that much anyway.

The universe had given her a second chance. She *would* love him this time.

Maybe she could start making more of an effort with all of her family.

She just had to deal with a few fairly substantial issues first.

They heard them before they saw them. Whatever James had planned to say next died on his lips. He stopped and listened. The strains of new voices carried up from the lounge.

'Is that . . . ?'

James dropped Ellen's arm and took the rest of the steps at a trot.

Time slowed for Kate.

She noticed the tiny balding spot on the top of James' head.

She realised how alike Clio and Ellen were from behind, the same height and body frames.

Then James opened the lounge door and Kate found herself standing in the hall. She followed her siblings reluctantly.

Sandra and Bella were there, talking to Frazer, a huge smile plastered on Sandra's perfectly made-up face, a bored scowl on Bella's.

'What . . . ?' James' face was how Kate imagined hers looked.

'Surprise!' Sandra squealed. 'You really had no idea!'

Frazer put his arm around her and beamed at everybody.

'Well, it's hardly a family gathering if we don't have the whole family, eh?' Frazer said. 'Sandra and Bella are as much Lattimers as the rest of us!'

Was Kate imagining things? Was her father watching her, in particular?

'Well, this is terrific,' James said, sounding both surprised and a little horrified. 'You devil, Sandra. You didn't breathe a word.'

'It was all your dad's idea, but I can keep a secret when I have to,' Sandra said, and winked coquettishly at Frazer.

Kate continued to see and hear everything in what felt like slow motion.

Sandra's wearing fake eyelashes, she realised. Who the hell wore fake eyelashes to a family dinner party? And she was clearly revelling in being the centre of attention and completely oblivious to the strain in James' voice. How could a wife be so out of tune with her husband's moods, Kate wondered?

Bella continued to hang back, seemingly more aware than her mother of the change in atmosphere.

'Sandra was just telling me about her fortieth,' Frazer said. 'You should have invited us all, James.'

'Oh, it really wasn't a big thing,' Sandra said. 'I'm too old to celebrate my birthday now.'

She giggled, apparently not too old for that. Frazer smiled indulgently.

'Ach, you don't look like you've five years on my son, lass,' he said. 'And look at your beautiful daughter.'

They all looked at Bella and Kate was momentarily distracted from the panic building in her own chest – her heart went out to the girl, who was blushing furiously, her face the same colour as her hair.

'She's the image of you, Sandra,' Frazer said. 'A total beauty. You must have looked just as stunning when you were young.'

Kate winced. Typical Dad, two feet first.

Sandra's face froze, but then she smiled so hard at Bella it looked like she had lockjaw.

'Oh, she's much better looking than I ever was,' she said.

Bella rolled her eyes. She made a show of tossing her vivid red curls over her shoulder and rearranged her face into a bored expression.

'I can't believe you managed to lure Bella down here,' James said. 'I'm sure you'd rather have a free house in Dublin, sweetheart.'

Kate tuned out as they uttered more small-talk inanities. She felt like she was going to vomit. She knew, she just knew where this was going.

'Kate, are you keeping an eye on the dinner from the door, or are you planning on joining us?' Frazer said.

Kate looked at her father, examining his face.

She couldn't see any trace of what she was most worried about.

Her father couldn't think it appropriate for them to meet Cheng like this.

Not in these circumstances.

He could be an idiot, but not this. Surely.

'Hi, *qīn*.'

Kate felt every muscle in her body seize up.

She turned, and there he was. Cheng. Stiff, confused, doing his best to act normally.

'Your dad rang a few hours ago and invited me,' Cheng said. 'He said it would be a great surprise for you. I . . . I didn't realise it was a big family party you were coming down for.'

'I—' Kate started.

'Ach, your husband must think we're right strange folk,' Frazer said. 'But this weekend is all about putting the past behind us and new beginnings, eh?'

'You should have phoned me,' Kate said weakly, still looking at her husband.

'Well, I was curious,' Cheng said coldly. 'And, as your dad said, maybe it was time for me to meet the rest of my in-laws.'

He was staring at her. Kate knew what was going on in his head.

He was angry, wondering why she'd lied about her father being ill, but no doubt he already suspected that she thought she'd been protecting him. Because she wouldn't have had any bad intentions, surely? Not his Kate.

Kate wanted to die.

'I need to talk to you—'

'Kate, let the man come into the room,' Frazer boomed. 'What'll you have, Cheng? Jack on the rocks? You look like a whiskey man.'

'I won't drink, thank you, Frazer,' Cheng said. 'I might be driving.'

'Ach, you've come all this way, you have to spend the night. And one won't hurt before dinner. Kate, I can't believe you haven't told him the news. Don't worry, I didn't spoil it on the phone. I suppose you wanted to see him for yourself. Well, go on then, you break it!'

Little dots started to dance in front of Kate's eyes.

'Cheng, lovely to meet you.' Clio stepped forward and pulled him into an embrace.

Kate watched as Clio whispered something, barely audible, in Cheng's ear. It might have been *take her outside*.

'Well, Adam,' Frazer said. 'I think you're going to have to introduce yourself.'

Kate watched Cheng's head whip around at the name.

Adam put down his glass reluctantly, and walked towards them.

'Kate?' Cheng said, looking at his wife. Kate started to shake her head. She swallowed. She couldn't bring herself to say it.

'Adam,' Cheng repeated. He stared at him, then looked around at the rest of the Lattimer siblings, all refusing to meet his eye. Frazer appeared confused, Sandra ill at ease and Bella openly fascinated. Cheng looked down at Adam's hand, then back at his brother-in-law.

'Kate said you were dead.'

# ADAM

Cheng didn't hang around long after the big reveal. He headed straight out the front door, followed at a pace by Kate.

An embarrassed hush had descended momentarily, followed by forced small talk as everybody tried to gloss over and move on from what had just happened.

It wasn't the done thing in their family to overanalyse.

Or analyse at all.

They were too middle-class for that.

Nobody noticed Adam slip out.

He made his way to the front porch and stood in its arch. He needed air. He needed out.

He took a cigarette from the box in his pocket and lit it, sucking the smoke in until his lungs felt their usual abnormal selves. Then he listened to Kate and her husband as they fought beside Cheng's car.

Cheng wanted to go back to Dublin. He looked furious – not just with Kate but with all of them. Adam had met his sort of man before. Proud men. Good, honourable men, unwilling to be taken for fools. And boy, his sister had taken Cheng for one.

He wasn't the first whose eyes she'd tried to pull the wool over. He wouldn't even be the last, Adam acknowledged, reluctantly.

They were standing on the road now where Cheng had parked – Adam could see them if he stood just to the left of the doorway. Cheng had his hand on the driver's door but Kate wasn't budging out of his way.

As the cigarette smoke dispersed, Adam inhaled the night air. Lavender-scented, diluted and mingling with the briny smell from the low tide and the seaweed it had washed up. The bay, serene.

'Why did you come?' Kate's voice travelled across the garden. 'You know I want to keep our life separate!'

Adam could barely hear Cheng's response but he could detect the tone. Furious.

'It was easier to say Dad was sick than tell you the truth,' Kate cried, in response.

Ah. She'd been caught in another lie. Adam shook his head. Kate was screwed.

'You let me think your brother was dead for seven years,' Cheng said, louder.

'I thought he was!'

Kate clamped her hand over her mouth. She glanced back up the drive. The windows of the house were all open, soft light spilling out into the dusk, moths beginning to gather and flutter against the glass. She couldn't see Adam, standing in the shadows. But in the deafening silence of the surrounding countryside, Kate must have known that her fight with her husband would be heard far and wide. The cottage home of their nearest neighbours, an artist couple who'd moved over from Leicester, sat a mere fifty metres down the road.

Cheng shook his head.

'You didn't say you thought it. You said he was. You cried, when you told me.'

Adam watched Cheng's body language. He was facing away from Kate, still determined to get in the car and escape the madness.

'When I met you,' Kate said, 'I had no idea that we were going to end up married. And once I'd lied, I couldn't think of a way to tell you that I'd lied. Can't you understand that? I just didn't want to talk about Adam any more. Or any of them. I'd one brother in rehab. Another who'd disappeared. A sister who's determined to be a bloody spinster. Our family was all anybody talked about down here for, God, I don't know how long. I just wanted you to think I was normal.'

'You wanted to impress me or something, is that what you're saying?'

'No, look, it's not like that. At one point, we did think Adam was dead.' Kate's voice was firm, assertive. 'Dad had found something . . . Oh, look, it doesn't matter. As time went on, I just chose to believe that he was. I had to.'

Adam tensed, listening harder now.

Cheng said something, low again, half speaking into the car.

'I know I should have told you everything when he came back,' Kate said. 'But I had to see Adam in the flesh to believe it.'

Cheng seemed to hesitate. She was winning, Adam realised. It was convincing. But then Cheng looked up at the house and Adam could practically see his hackles rise.

His brother-in-law turned and looked at his wife, her face tilted up to his, beseeching.

'I respected your decision to stay away from your family,' Cheng said. 'I thought . . . Well, you know what I thought. That they were a bunch of prejudiced arseholes. And you let me think that because you had to protect yourself from the lie you'd told. All those years, I felt guilty that I was the reason for the distance between you and your relatives.'

Cheng's voice broke.

'It's unforgivable,' he said.

Kate visibly recoiled.

Cheng got into the car and slammed the door before driving away, even his engine sounding angry.

It was only then that Adam realised he wasn't the only one inadvertently spying. Perched on the sill of the dining room window, half-hidden by a mauve-blooming hydrangea, Bella was swinging her legs and also sucking from a cigarette, a black hoodie zipped up to her neck, the laces on her pink Adidas trainers open and dangling towards the ground.

She tossed the butt and jumped down from the sill as Kate walked up the drive, dejected, slowly. Adam watched Bella approach his sister, her arms folded in a way that mirrored Kate's.

'That went epic pretty quick, Aunty Kate,' she said.

Kate looked Bella up and down, slowly.

'I'm not your aunty,' she said, coolly. 'So don't call me that.'

Bella almost tripped, she backed off so quickly. Adam felt sorry for her.

He stayed still as his sister approached.

Kate bit her lip and went to go past him without saying anything. But at the last moment, she stopped.

'Do you know how much trouble you've caused?'

Adam tugged at his bottom lip, but said nothing.

'It was one bloody fib!' Kate cried, distressed. She was speaking to herself.

'Was it?' Adam said. 'Your husband knows everything about you, does he?'

Kate stared at him, shocked and angry at once.

But then he saw the mask come down on her face and he knew he was right.

Kate hadn't changed a bit. She was still a liar.

# AFTER

'Were you alone with your father at any point this evening, Kate?'

'Is that why you asked me to come back in here? Can we not do this another time? I want to go home.'

'I appreciate that. But I want to make sure I have everybody's statement correct, first. Were you alone with your father?'

Kate tensed.

'No.'

The detective was still scribbling in his little pad.

'But, you were alone?' he asked.

'I . . . yes. I was trying to phone my husband and I wanted some quiet in which to do it.'

'But you didn't go below deck?'

Kate's mouth suddenly felt very dry.

'I couldn't get a signal outside, there was no way I'd get one below deck. I went up the side.'

'The port side. Not the same side as your father.'

'No.'

'I see,' Detective Downes said. 'Could you see anybody, from where you were?'

'Danny. He was at the front. In the steering cabin. But it's got windows on all sides. He could see me, I'm sure of it. I could see him, anyway.'

'Right.' The detective paused. 'Things were tense between you and Frazer, weren't they? After he invited your husband Cheng down without your knowledge.'

'How do you even . . . ?' Kate started. 'Actually, it doesn't matter. You know everything, right?'

She laughed. It sounded hollow. But, if she was honest, she didn't feel hollow. She actually felt quite . . . content. It wasn't right, that she could feel so happy when her father lay dead somewhere.

'Do you think your father invited Cheng down to deliberately upset you?' the detective asked.

Kate shrugged.

'I don't know. Yes? Maybe. Detective, I really want to ring my husband. I've been trying to get through, but his phone is off. If I can just ring his mother . . . she'll talk to him. This is important.'

'*This* is important.'

Kate looked up from the phone in her hand. The detective's tone had turned distinctly snippy.

Wasn't he supposed to be gentle with her? She was a relative of the deceased. And yet, here he was, pulling her back in for a second interview in the space of half an hour. Was he going to bring everybody back in, she wondered? Because if that's where things were headed – if they were going to start talking about each other's secrets . . .

Kate had to take care of herself now. It was imperative.

'Fine,' she said, putting down her phone. 'You want to talk about Saturday. I was irritated with my father, yes. But I was more annoyed at myself. What happened was my own fault. And anyway, it wasn't the biggest bloody shock of the night.'

'No?'

'God, no. That was my dad's announcement.'

The detective's pen was poised over the notepad.

'I'm surprised Ellen didn't mention it,' Kate said.

# CLIO

Clio didn't immediately follow the others into the dining room for dinner. Instead, she waited in the hall for Kate, tracing the grooves of the stair bannister with the nail of her forefinger, feeling the familiar carvings.

She'd stood at the foot of these stairs, in this same spot, when they'd brought her mother's body down the morning after her heart attack.

Clio's parents hadn't shared a room in years so Kathleen had been alone in bed when it happened. That was something that had really bothered Clio. That her mother might have called out, in pain, in a house full of people, but nobody heard her. Nobody helped. She'd died on her own.

When she was thirteen, Clio had suffered from a particularly violent vomiting bug for several days. Kathleen had slept on a mattress on the floor of Clio's room, waking up every time she did, getting the bowl to her in time, cleaning Clio's face, mopping her brow, and not resting until Clio fell back asleep.

She'd bend over backwards for all of her children.

*It's just what mammies do,* she used to say, cheerfully.

She'd died alone.

It was why Clio couldn't go into the room. Why none of them did.

She would have hidden the letter in there, if she'd found the courage.

Kate appeared on the top step.

'You okay?' Clio asked, as her sister descended.

'I'm fine,' Kate said.

Clio hesitated. Kate had fixed her make-up and combed her hair. She looked perfect, as usual. She would carry on for the evening like nothing had happened. It was what she always did, even if everybody else around her was dying with embarrassment on her behalf.

Kate was a machine.

Still, it had been years. Clio wanted to at least try for a normal sisterly exchange.

'I'm sorry that happened,' Clio said. 'Did Dad know, do you think? That you'd told Cheng that Adam was dead?'

'No.'

Clipped. Certain.

'Did anybody?'

Kate sucked in her cheeks.

'James.'

'James?' Clio repeated. She was stung. It wasn't like she and Kate had any sort of relationship but, Clio supposed, the notion that Kate didn't have a relationship with any of them had made that easier to come to terms with. Now, the knowledge that her older sister might in fact be close to James, well . . . it hurt.

'I told James because he lives in Dublin and I worried that he and

Cheng might bump into each other when I wasn't there to steer the conversation,' Kate said.

Oh. That was different then.

A sudden thought struck Clio.

'Would James have told Dad?' Clio asked.

Kate glared at her.

'Why would you even say that?'

Clio blinked.

'Forget it,' Kate said. 'We just have to get through the next couple of days.'

She walked towards the dining room. Clio followed, confused.

Why on earth was Kate staying in Spanish Cove?

The old Kate would have run back to Dublin the very same night to get away from her family.

Unless she had something planned.

The dining room's centrepiece was a large oval-shaped mahogany table their mother had received as a wedding present from her own parents. It was covered now with a pristine white tablecloth, candles and flowers running along its centre. The bay window at the end of the room ran the length of the curved wall, and the fading evening light, mixed with the soft orange glow from the candle wicks, cast everybody in gentle warm shadows.

Danny had kept the seat beside him free for Clio. She could have kissed him. Kate was sitting to her other side, and Clio knew there wouldn't be much conversation out of her tonight. Nobody would be mentioning Cheng, that was for sure.

She picked up her champagne glass just as Frazer prepared to make the first toast.

'It's been a long ten years, son,' he said, nodding to Adam. 'A lot has happened. In your life and ours. I know we're all feeling rough at the moment and there's bound to be a few tense exchanges.' A brief look at Kate, who barely blushed. 'But what we should all feel more than anything else is gratitude. You're home now. You're alive. That's all that matters. Everything else, we can talk through.'

Clio stared at her father. The words sounded sincere and heart-felt. She looked at Adam. He swallowed, then lifted his own glass and tipped the air with it.

'Thank you,' he mumbled.

'To Adam,' Frazer said.

Clio sat with her hands placed firmly in her lap until Ryan kicked her under the table. And then, even if it was only for form's sake, Clio toasted her brother.

'And to your poor, dead mother,' Frazer said, before taking a sip. Clio had the glass to her lips when he spoke. It chinked against her teeth, and that was followed by a spill of liquid into her mouth, and an involuntary swallow that nearly made her choke. When the tears cleared from her eyes, she saw the look of abject shock on Adam's face.

Before any of them could say anything in response, the door opened and the first of the catering waiters came in carrying starters. Saved by the staff.

Clio was about to start eating when she felt something soft and hot land in her lap. She lifted the tablecloth and looked under. Teddy had taken advantage of the open door and sneaked in. Now he rested his head in between her knees, waiting to be fed.

Clio smiled and slipped him some cured ham. She started to eat; the food was tasty, wholesome, and she needed it, along with the alcohol. She and Danny made small, enjoyable talk. She might have been drunk. She must have been drunk. Because, for perhaps the first time since she'd arrived, she felt herself start to relax.

Their plates were cleared and the lobster was brought out dressed in the brandy sauce. It looked and smelled delicious.

When she'd gone into the kitchen earlier to get the vodka, she'd heard them squealing as they were boiled alive. It had almost made her laugh, the delicious irony of it.

'Ach, you never let us down, Danny,' Frazer said. 'Caught fresh this morning! You remember, man, when we used to take the boat out and lay the crab cages? Honest work for your supper, eh?'

'Frazer, boy, you never caught so much as an old welly boot.' Danny smiled.

'Minor details.' Frazer puffed his chest out. He caught Clio's eye and winked.

The lump in her throat felt like a rock when she swallowed.

Minutes earlier, he'd toasted his dead wife and Clio suspected it had been done to see Adam's reaction.

She'd never begin to understand how he could do that – slip so easily from provocateur to avuncular.

She shook her head and passed a small boiled potato down to Teddy, and felt his tongue, wet and hot against her fingers.

'I know what you're up to, Clio,' her father called over.

Clio looked at him, alarmed.

'No tidbits from the table. I broke that dog of that habit as soon as you left.'

Clio smiled.

'At least he's eating,' she said.

'Aye, all right then,' her father said. 'Adam, now you've given this lot the highlights, tell them the details. He's done well for himself, the lad. We should be proud of him.'

Clio caught herself before she swallowed her own tongue.

'Is that right?' James said. 'Do you have a family? Whereabouts are you over there, anyway?'

Adam lowered his knife and fork.

'I live in Paris.'

'Live?' Ellen said. 'You're going back there?'

'I have a business there. No family. I'm . . . wealthy. Probably not as well-off as you, Kate, but I do okay.'

'I'm not wealthy. My husband is wealthy. Thankfully, there's no prenup.'

Clio flinched. Sounded like Kate was on her way to drunk, too. It was the only time they ever saw the true Kate, when she'd had a few too many glasses of truth serum.

'What's your business?' James asked.

Clio watched him. It was just like James to zone in on the money aspect of Adam's life. James counted happiness units in dollar signs.

'I run a construction company.'

'Construction?' Ellen said. 'Really?'

'Is there something wrong with that?' Adam said, mildly amused.

'It's just, you were two-thirds through a degree in computers before you . . . you know. Did what you did.'

'My options were limited when I arrived,' Adam said. 'I didn't speak French. I worked my way up the ranks, got to gaffer and then I set up my own firm.'

'How come you could do all that but not ring home?' Kate said.

Clio winced. Her sister had that tone, the one that said everything was just fine, if fine meant absolutely not fucking fine but we're all smiling anyway.

'It's not like that,' Adam said. 'I thought about ringing. Every. Single. Day.'

It was so bloody obvious he was hiding something. To Clio, anyway. Couldn't the rest of her family see it?

'All right,' Frazer said. 'The lad's being honest. Let's remember, this is a happy occasion. We're having a nice family dinner.'

'And it's bloody delectable,' Ryan said. 'I've just realised I've a pain in my hole with pasta. Why aren't we Irish renowned for our cuisine?'

'Thermidor is French, idiot,' Clio said, dryly.

Ryan shrugged dismissively. Bella, beside him, started to laugh.

The tension was dissipating again. Up and down, like an old-fash-ioned kettle struggling to boil.

'Aye, we're back to the good old days, all right.' Frazer smiled. 'You lot bickering. Well, I have something to tell you all that I hope will make this weekend the celebration it should be.'

Clio shared a look with her brothers and sisters. She felt Teddy, who'd settled on her feet, tense.

'Ach, I'll just come out with it,' Frazer said. 'I've met somebody.'

Nobody said anything. Nobody was sure where this had come from or where it was going.

'I've spent a long number of years grieving for your mam. But, you know, I'm still a relatively young man. And . . . I've found happiness again.'

Clio frowned. What the hell was this?

Frazer shifted uncomfortably in the silence.

'Aye, well, I didn't think it would be right to introduce her early

on, not when we were having our first family dinner in I don't
know how long. But I figured it might be an age before I have you
all together like this again. So, I was hoping none of you would
mind if she joined us for coffee. The next bit is for the two of us
to announce. Ana!'

Clio realised what was happening just as the door opened. A woman
came in – she was small, dark, pretty. Her hair was greying at the roots,
the rest of it a dark auburn. And she'd styled it in those Danish plait
buns that Clio thought only characters in fairy tales wore.

How long had she been standing out there, Clio wondered,
waiting for her cue? Where the hell had she come from?

The woman's face was friendly, heart-shaped, but right now
she wasn't smiling. Instead she was looking at them all with barely
concealed panic.

'Come in, come in,' Frazer said, standing. 'Ana, this is my family.
Family, this is Ana. You know Danny, but everybody else is new
to you.'

'Hello,' she said, blushing.

Accented. Clio couldn't decide where. Eastern European?

Nobody moved for a moment. Clio heard Kate mutter something under her breath that sounded like *fucking idiot*.

Frazer, so wrapped up in his own excitement and happiness, was
oblivious.

'Ana and I have been seeing each other for a few months now,'
he said. 'Her husband passed away a few years ago, too.'

Ana, evidently more tuned into the silence in the room, was
growing increasingly unsettled. She let Frazer take her hand but
didn't come any closer to the table. Instead, one of her feet remained
planted facing the door, indicating she might run at any moment.

'And we have decided to marry.'

Clio actually felt her jaw drop.

Frazer dragged his eyes from his fiancée and looked around at his children, then back to Ana. His expression switched from pleasure to momentary concern when he saw his fiancée's uncertain face.

'Well, congratulations, you old bugger,' Danny said, raising his glass.

Clio, out of habit, started to reach for hers, too.

But then Ellen pushed her chair out abruptly, causing her fork to fall off the table. At Clio's feet, Teddy stood up as fast as his ageing limbs would allow, banging his head off the underside of the table.

'You're joking,' Ellen said, staring at their father like she could kill him. 'You're fucking joking.'

# AFTER

Detective Downes turned up the dial on the electric heater. Then he picked up his mobile phone. Adam could see him open Safari and type something into Google. His eyes narrowed as he scanned the search results.

Adam busied himself examining his hands.

His knuckles were cut from where he'd landed successful punches on James.

Worth it, he thought.

'So, what I'm gathering is that before tonight, you'd already had quite a fractious weekend,' the detective said. 'Did you know what you were letting yourself in for, when you came home?'

Adam took a deep breath.

'I'm not going to lie to you, Detective. Our family has always been hard work.'

'So, why come back?'

'Right now, I can't tell you why. Before tonight, I guess I just felt like I had to. If I'd known what was going to happen . . .'

'Why did you leave in the first place?'

'I had a . . . I think you'd call it a breakdown.'

'It wasn't that you'd fallen out with anybody?' Detective Downes asked. 'Like your father?'

'I never fell out with Frazer. That's the truth. The others . . .'

'What about them?'

'I – nothing. It's not my place to say.'

The detective sighed.

'What was life like in France?'

'Good,' Adam said. 'I mean . . . not good. I had to live with what I'd done. But, if I hadn't had that . . . I made good for myself, is what I'm trying to say.'

'I see. And then you came back to all this.'

Adam shrugged.

'Tell me, Adam, how did you feel when your father announced he'd be getting married again? You only recently learned that your mother had died. You must have been feeling pretty raw about that. What did you think when Frazer revealed his news?'

'Nothing,' Adam said. 'I didn't think anything. I hadn't been in any of their lives for ten years. He could have said he'd been taking hormone injections to become a woman and I wouldn't have had a right to an opinion. I might have been late to the news of my mam passing, but that was my fault. Not his.'

The detective smiled.

'Your sister, Ellen, she was surprised, right? She hadn't known he had a girlfriend, let alone was planning to get married. I'm thinking that might have had ramifications for her? Like possibly losing her home, if that's where she'd decided she was spending her life? That sort of thing could make a person very resentful.'

Adam stretched out his hand, felt the pain shoot up his wrist. He might have sprained it, when he'd thumped his brother.

'Ellen was with us the whole time on board that yacht,' he said, answering the detective. He could hear the note of caution that had crept into his voice. 'She didn't leave the rear deck when we were all together and then she, Ryan and I went downstairs. With Ana. Ellen went into the toilet. She was . . . a little upset.'

'Upset? I see. And you're sure you didn't lose sight of her before that? Or when she came out?'

'Positive. She wasn't upset because she'd just killed our dad, if that's what you're getting at.'

'Why was she, then?'

'I don't know.'

'I see.' The detective sighed and scribbled something down. He studied his notes, pursed his lips, then looked back over at Adam.

'Talk to me about James,' he said.

'What about him?'

'Was he in good form over the weekend? Did he mention anything about the show he's producing at the moment?'

'He said something, yeah.'

'What's it called, by the way? The thing he's working on?'

Adam frowned.

'I've no idea. Why do you ask?'

'Because I can't find anything online,' the detective said. 'Isn't that interesting? He's this hugely successful guy, but there's nothing online about his work.'

'I don't know what you're getting at.'

The detective inclined his head.

'Don't you?' he said.

# ADAM

They'd gone down to the shore after dinner. Adam, Ryan and Clio.

Ryan lay on the sand, his head in Clio's lap. She was sitting upright, her hands planted on either side of her. Both of them were angled away from Adam.

Clio was still treating him like he was carrying the plague.

It was a bit over the top, in Adam's opinion. He didn't know what else to say. He'd been apologetic – humble, even. She'd have to give him a break at some stage. Wouldn't she?

She hadn't objected to him joining her and Ryan on their walk, though. That was progress.

'I knew Dad would do something like that this weekend,' Ryan said. Then, before either Adam or Clio could say anything, 'Jesus, Clio, you're terribly skinny. Your thighs feel like chicken legs. It must kill Kate being around you, seeing how little effort you have to make.'

'A diet of stress,' Clio said. 'Works wonders.'

'Fuck, who's this, now?' Ryan said, his voice low.

Adam watched his brother's face closely. He could tell Ryan was struggling being in their father's company.

They all heard it, the crunch of footsteps on the pebbles that led down to the sandy part of the beach.

It was James.

'Wondered where you lot had got to,' he said, as he plonked himself down and held his hand out for Adam's cigarette. 'Give us a drag on that. I didn't know you smoked?'

'You knew me a long time ago,' Adam answered. 'You've probably forgotten a lot.'

He passed it over, bemused at the momentary panic on James' face.

'Where's your lovely wife?' Ryan asked, winning their brother's attention.

'In my room. She and Bella are heading back tomorrow.' A pause, as he inhaled the smoke. 'I prefer my dramas on the screen.'

'She's interesting, that one,' Ryan said. 'One to watch.'

'Sandra?' James said, surprised.

'Bella, fuckwit.'

'She's sixteen, Ryan,' James hissed.

'I mean, she's a nice kid,' Ryan said. 'She seems smart.'

'Isn't it weird that none of us have children yet?' Clio mused. 'I mean, I guess Ryan and I are sort of young, but the rest of you should have made the leap by now.'

'Bella *is* my kid,' James said.

'God, I know you helped raise Bella, James. But she's not *yours*. She was, what, already four or five when you and Sandra met? Why didn't you want to have a brother or sister for her? She seems like somebody who'd have benefitted from a sibling.'

'Like we all benefitted?' James snorted.

'Is that why, do you think?' Clio pondered 'Our family is such a hot mess we think we can't be good parents? James, don't look at me like I just shit on you. I know you're a good dad.'

'Ellen can't have children,' Adam said, staring out to sea.

Out of the corner of his eye, he could see Clio scrunch up her face, puzzled.

So, there were still things she didn't know about their family.

But then there were still things she didn't want her family to know about her, either.

He'd lay his life on it.

Slowly, slowly.

'Can't she?' Clio asked.

Adam shook his head.

'No,' he said, softly. 'She can't.'

'How come you know that and I don't?' Clio asked, defensive and offensive at once. 'Does Kate know?'

'We all know,' Adam said.

'*I* didn't know,' Clio said. 'And I don't see why you, of all of us, are entitled to that information and I'm not.'

'I probably have kids all over the place,' Ryan said. His tone was light but he caught Adam's eye and sent him a warning look. They didn't talk about Ellen. Adam knew that, even if it had been ten years. Some things hadn't changed.

'You're a dog,' Adam said, taking his cue.

'Wuff.'

Ryan bared his teeth and started to pant.

'Is that why Ellen's so set on having the house?' Clio asked.

Fuck. She wouldn't let it go.

'Is that why she won't leave? She can't have her own family?'

'She won't leave because she's smart,' James answered. 'If she moves out, then that house will end up going to all of us. As it stands, she's in residence and I bet she reckons that gives her a right to stay there. It's not on.'

'You think we should all get a share,' Adam said, a statement, not a question. 'Even me? After what I did?'

'Damn right I do. I'm not saying she shouldn't get hers but, Christ, what are house prices like now? That house has to be worth a million. She's not entitled to it. And whatever you did, Adam, you're still family. We're family.'

'You're quick to suggest it be sold off,' Clio said. 'It was our mother's home.'

'She's not in it any more, is she?' James responded.

'She is for me,' Clio said.

'It's a redundant conversation,' Ryan cut in. 'Frazer is not exactly decrepit. And shagging Mother Russia will give him a new lease of life. He'll probably leave her everything in his beloved will, anyway.'

'Is she Russian?' Adam pondered aloud.

'I wouldn't be so sure he has much time left,' James said. 'Let's be honest, Ellen looked like she was going to kill him.'

'You all looked like that.' Clio snorted. 'What was he thinking, springing that on us in the middle of everything?'

'It's his way,' James said. 'He never thinks what he says or does will affect anybody outside himself.'

'Is that what you really think?' Adam asked, curious. 'You reckon he invited Kate's husband down here without knowing what would happen?'

It was too dark to see the colour rising in James' cheeks but Adam knew it was there. James looked away, shrugging.

'Will somebody just fucking tell me why Ellen can't have kids?' Clio asked, returning to the question.

Her brothers said nothing.

Ryan kicked off his shoes and stood up. He started to unzip his jeans.

'It's been an age since I was in the sea,' he said. 'Lakes are nice and all but they're not . . .'

'Freezing?' Adam suggested.

'I was going to say the real thing,' Ryan replied. 'Adam, come on, then.'

'I'm not getting in there.'

'Yeah, you are, you little pussy. You haven't really come home until you've swam. You're going in the sea if I have to drag you in.'

Ryan unbuttoned the top of his shirt and pulled it over his head.

Adam got up reluctantly and started to undress. James shook his head, stood and began to walk away, wanting no part of the madness.

Ryan was in his boxers now and, once sure Adam was following suit, he took off at a run towards the waves.

Adam watched his brother's body tense as he hit the water.

'Holy fuck! Shit! Jesus Christ!'

'Stay close to shore, fuckwits!' Clio shouted after them.

Adam waded in behind his brother, more cautious.

Ryan turned and began to splash Adam with large armfuls of water.

'Pack it in, arsehole,' Adam hissed.

'Get in properly and I'll stop throwing it at you.'

Adam went further in until Ryan could reach him. In one quick movement he was on top of Adam, pushing him under the water.

Adam went under, the salt water rushing up his nostrils, stinging his eyes. He emerged for a moment, saw Clio, standing now. Then he was under again. When he came up this time, he saw James hesitating at the top of the beach, watching his brothers. He was deliberating whether to come back; whether it was play-acting or more serious.

Adam found his feet and blew forcefully through his nose, spitting out seawater at the same time. He swayed for a moment, then gave Ryan a shove, toppling him in.

'We're even!' Adam shouted when Ryan surfaced. 'Stop.'

'Push me again!' Ryan said.

He made to have another go, but then he followed Adam's eye-line, and looked back to Clio, and at James in the distance. James had pulled his phone from his pocket, its blue screen lit up. He started to walk away, towards the house, the phone to his ear. Within moments the tall reeds on the dunes obscured his body and only the back of his head was visible. Clio had her hands on her hips, annoyed at both of them.

Ryan shrugged, threw himself on his back and began to backstroke.

Adam did the same, kicking away from his brother, swimming in the opposite direction.

He had to keep it together, stay on top of his temper and all the rage he was carrying. Not rise to anything, or anybody.

Calm, he told himself. Calm.

# JAMES

Sandra was still awake, applying one of her many expensive creams and examining her face for new signs of ageing, any extra crow's feet or puckered lines at the mouth.

James knew the five years she had on him played on her mind a lot these days.

His job didn't help. James, even without a green-lit project, seemed to spend a lot of time around young, pretty actresses and Sandra had a vivid imagination. Sandra could write for screen, if she were so inclined. *Dynasty*, perhaps. Every female with a beating heart was a lurking vixen. Sandra's suspicions were draining his bank account, between the clothes and make-up and pampering.

If only she knew. The truth was so much worse than an affair.

'Where's Bella sleeping?' he asked, as he threw his shoes under the bed. His old room bore no familiar furniture or markings. He'd been one of the first to move out and his mother had gently asked if he minded her turning his space into a guest room. He'd had no objection.

James was destined for LA. Spanish Cove would be but a distant memory.

'Your sister put her in the attic,' Sandra said. 'I don't think your father told Ellen that we were coming. She seemed put out. Started going on about bed linen. You'd swear it was her house. And anyway, I don't see why a house this size doesn't have more than seven bedrooms.'

'It has eight,' James said.

'Well, why isn't she in the eighth?'

'It was my mother's,' James said, his voice turning a little hoarse. 'Nobody sleeps there.'

'Oh,' Sandra said. 'I forgot. You never brought me down here much, baby. I think I'm starting to see why.'

James lay back on the bed and sighed. He missed his mother, too. He hadn't actually realised how important she was in his life until she was gone.

'What were you doing, anyway?' Sandra asked. 'After dinner? You missed coffee. That Ana is very nice, by the way. Quiet. Good manners, though. Unlike that sister of yours. She should be ashamed of herself, reacting like that to your father's good news. It's not all about her, you know—'

'I went for some fresh air.' James cut Sandra off.

'I saw you down in the garden. On the phone.'

James sighed.

He loosened the belt on his jeans and began to unbutton his shirt. His stomach hurt a little from the size of the meal they'd had on top of the alcohol throughout the day. James wasn't used to eating or drinking so much. He liked to stay in shape. It was half about talent, half appearance. Station bosses wanted you to look the part when you strolled in to pitch a drama. It might only be Ireland but it was still *the industry*.

'James,' Sandra said. 'Is everything okay?'

*Do you care?* he wanted to say.

'Why wouldn't it be?' is what he actually said.

'It's just, you seem so stressed lately and . . .'

James filtered her out. Instead, he thought about the phone call he'd taken on the way back from the beach.

It was going to hell in a handbasket.

His French co-producers had pulled a fast one on their financing deal.

The broadcaster they'd secured would only be putting up thirty percent of the required funds and James' company would have to find the rest.

It had been a devastating blow; one he was still trying desperately to keep under wraps.

It was all about appearances. And James had done a spectacular job of convincing people he knew what he was doing.

He'd had one hit, a cop show that ran for three series. Since then, he'd had too many non-starters. But he'd successfully painted the picture that his absence had all been through choice; that he'd decided to not work on any other projects until he found the one that was good enough.

That he could afford to wait.

And then *the one* had come along. A sentimental drama set in post-WWII Ireland. Arty, but soapy enough to draw the crowds. The Yanks, in particular, would love it.

From the off, though, he'd struggled to bring other backers on board. In this business, you were only as lucrative as your last big project and that had to have been on TV yesterday. Not years ago.

The clock was ticking.

'Everything's fine,' he heard himself tell his wife, his voice floating above his body, not really connected to him. 'The French are still playing hardball but I'll get them over the line. It's too good a show not to make. It'll be payday soon.'

He closed his eyes so he didn't see Sandra move, barely felt the depression on the bed.

But he did feel her wet kisses on his stomach, her hand trace the line down below his belt, and then her mouth travel in the same direction.

This again.

She'd sprung it on him a couple of months ago.

*'I want to have a baby. I want us to have a baby, together.'*

He didn't know if she couldn't see he was stressed or if she could and thought a pregnancy would help. Maybe she didn't care, one way or the other.

It was the last thing James wanted – somebody else reliant on him, somebody new to take care of.

Still, if it kept her distracted from the extent of his money woes.

He kept his eyes closed and let his head fill with thoughts of Lena.

And the promises he'd made her.

Beautiful, twenty-two-year-old, desperate for a big part, Lena.

# ELLEN

Ellen was up before the rest of them that Sunday morning.

The others, she knew, would be reeling from the last twenty-four hours. Their reunion with Adam and the news their father had dropped into all their laps. Not to mention the forced proximity.

She'd bet none of them were thinking about her. Or what today was.

Every year had been hard. This year should have been no harder. But there'd been so much disruption in the last week. All the little routines and habits Ellen had put into place had been pulled to pieces.

Suddenly this anniversary felt important. Really important.

Thirteen years ago, her life had ground to a halt.

She didn't get out of bed immediately. Instead, she lay looking out at the bay, thinking how peaceful it all was. The early mists were rising from the sea, indicating today would be warm. Birds chirped in the sycamores in the garden. The County Waterford fields across the bay in the distance, lush green, were dotted with grazing sheep.

There was nothing to say that today was any different or there was any turmoil in the world, or anything bad at all to worry about.

Every morning, this was her view.

Ellen was thirty-nine and she had only lived in two other places in her entire life. And that had all been over the course of one year.

A year that had started so gloriously and ended so horrifically.

Thirty-eight years in Spanish Cove. In this house.

It was *her* house.

Ellen shuddered as she remembered the previous night.

Who was this Ana woman? How had Frazer kept her a secret for so long?

They shared a home, for God's sake.

She'd thought there was something up. Not this, though.

Frazer had been out a lot more recently. And they didn't live in each other's pockets. The house was big and Ellen tended to keep to her part of it, Frazer to his.

But, still.

Shouldn't she have noticed he was seeing somebody? Wouldn't she have noticed?

Unless he had been deliberately keeping it from her, going out of his way to make sure she didn't know.

Ellen flung the duvet back and sat up.

She didn't know what this meant for her. But she wasn't going to find out, either, hiding in bed all day.

Best to keep going like everything was normal.

But it would mean so much if one of them, just *one* of them, remembered what today was.

# CLIO

By the time the others had started to emerge, several of them the worse for wear, Ellen had laid out breakfast in the kitchen: sausages and bacon, scrambled eggs, fried tomatoes, mushrooms and soft, floury Waterford Blaas.

'You could run a B&B, Ellen, you little gem,' Ryan said, heaping his plate. 'Did you do all this on your own?'

Ellen shrugged. On her own plate, she'd placed a slice of toast and a spoonful of marmalade.

Clio watched her as she spread the preserve across the bread.

'Jesus, mortification of the flesh, is it?' she said.

Ellen looked up.

'What?'

'Are you depriving yourself of a proper breakfast for some reason?' Clio said. 'Have you joined Opus Dei?'

Bella was sitting beside Clio, eating forkfuls of baked beans and watching them all. She laughed, a little too loudly, at the joke. And she kept smiling at Clio.

It was making Clio uncomfortable.

'I'm not hungry,' Ellen replied. 'I ate while I was cooking.'

'I doubt that,' Clio said. 'You look like you weigh four stone.'

'You're one to talk,' Ellen snapped. 'There aren't a lot of calories in vodka and Pop-Tarts. You should try red wine. Iron, at least.'

Clio snorted. She wasn't used to Ellen being so witty.

'Where're Adam and Kate?' Frazer asked, without turning around.

Clio's father was standing by the kettle. He had his back to them but she knew he was taking in every word.

'The question is, where's the gorgeous Ana?' Ryan said. 'What age is she, anyway, you old goat? Late forties?'

'A lady never tells,' Frazer replied. 'But, aye, she's closer to fifty than sixty.'

The door opened and Kate appeared, looking like hell.

'Have you seen Adam?' Frazer asked.

Kate shook her head, gingerly.

'Maybe he's done another runner,' Ryan said.

Nobody laughed.

'I think he's gone for a walk,' Ellen said.

'I wanted to talk to you all together,' Frazer said. 'Ach, anyway. I know Adam is staying on for a while. I'd like to ask the rest of you to stay until Tuesday also. I plan to have a little engagement party tomorrow evening. Danny has organised a yacht and it's all arranged.'

A chorus of voices rose in protest.

'I'm going back to Italy,' Ryan said.

'I need to get back to Dublin,' Kate added.

'A party!' Ellen choked.

Christ, she looked miserable, Clio thought. Poor Ellen. Now expected to attend a celebration of an event that would in all likelihood see her home pulled from under her.

Their father raised both his hands and made a shushing motion.

'I know, I know,' he said. 'You all have very busy lives. But how often have we all been together like this?'

'Did you plan this?' Ellen asked.

'Of course I planned it.' Frazer laughed. 'You can't organise a party with no preparation.'

'Before you told any of us you were expecting us to stay three days,' Ryan interrupted. 'I thought long weekend meant going home tomorrow morning. It's already the interminable fucking death march, two whole days.'

'Not everything has to be a big drama, Ryan,' Frazer said. 'And you might try thinking about your siblings, for once. Not yourself.'

Ryan opened and closed his mouth.

'Well, I think it's a good idea,' James said.

'But James . . .' Sandra piped up.

'I know you need to go back later,' he said. 'But I had planned to stay on longer, anyway.'

Clio noticed the quick glance James gave Frazer.

And she knew her father saw it, too.

'I don't think I can stay,' Kate said.

'Please, lass,' Frazer said. He turned and handed her the plate of food he'd been building. 'It would mean the world to me.'

Kate looked around her siblings.

'Fine,' she said, decided but unhappy.

Frazer nodded, content.

'Excellent,' he said. 'So, about today.'

'When do the pubs open?' Clio asked.

'We can go to the pub tonight.' Frazer smiled. 'This morning, though, I've something else planned.'

'What?' Clio said.

Frazer, by her chair now, leaned over and kissed her head.

'Just come with me,' he said. 'I think I've some making up to do.'

Clio was in the back of her father's car, squashed in between Kate and Bella – who was now glued to Clio's hip – like an agreement had been reached to keep her from the door handles and any last-gasp effort to leap out of the moving vehicle.

Clio was sorely tempted.

She'd been so reluctant to go with them. So much so that Teddy, poor Teddy, who could barely summon the energy to pad from room to room, had nuzzled into her legs and started whining. Clio had rubbed his head and tried to avoid whimpering herself as she was chaperoned towards the car. The dog knew her better than her own family.

'I miss Kathleen fierce,' Frazer said. 'I hope you all know that. Marrying Ana is not about moving on. It's just, your mother wouldn't want me on my own any more. And I've been on my own for so long now . . .'

Sandra, sitting beside Frazer, made what sounded like a mewing noise.

Clio ignored them both.

She didn't want to hear the catch in Frazer's throat. Or the sadness in his voice.

She refused to hear it.

If he wanted to atone for deciding to remarry, he could do it on his own time. She didn't see why they all had to be dragged into it with him.

When they arrived at the small cemetery on top of the hillside, she found herself herded along before she could come up with a reason as to why she should stay behind.

After her mother died, Clio had cycled up here a lot, dumping her bike by the old oak outside the warped railing, tracing the uneven, broken path towards her mam's final resting place.

She followed those same steps now, knowing the names on the headstones to either side of her – dates stretching back as far as the 1800s, inscriptions fading on stone, grass and weeds overtaking any memory of human touch.

This place had been the hardest thing to leave behind when she'd boarded the plane for New York, not knowing if she'd return. Clio didn't believe in God. She didn't believe in spirits or an afterlife, so for her, that cemetery was where her mother was. In the pale blue dress they'd buried her in, the cross and chain that said her mam at least believed something better awaited, her hair coiffed in an unfamiliar style and her lipstick perfect, all ready to meet her maker.

If her maker would forgive her.

Clio looked around and saw Adam get out of James' car and catch up with their father.

He had no right to be there.

'You look like *you* belong in a coffin,' Bella said, tucking her hand under Clio's arm. 'You're white as a ghost.'

Clio said nothing.

She didn't know why Bella was latching on to her. Maybe because Clio was young and not the archetypal aunty. Maybe because she quite clearly didn't give a fuck about Bella.

Something spoke to her niece, anyway.

Clio pulled away and walked faster, suddenly determined to be the first to the grave. She turned in between two headstones and cut across the grass.

And there it was, her mother's final resting place.

Kathleen Ann Lattimer. Fifty-one years of age. Beloved wife and mother.

Clio dropped to her knees on the grass verge.

The grave was in good shape. Somebody had been maintaining it.

A mound of rocks from the beach was heaped at the base of the headstone. Over the years, the children had all taken turns bringing up stones and heavier rocks that they'd found on the shore; pretty, ornamental types, their edges and colours shaped by the sea. Their mother had loved to walk on the beach; she'd loved collecting shells and stones and driftwood.

Fifty-one was no age, really.

Adam, arriving just behind Clio, leaned over and ran his fingers along their mother's name. Everybody else hung back.

He looked up, straight at Clio.

She blinked and turned away.

'Your mother would have been so happy to have us all here like this,' Frazer said. 'Especially you, Adam. I hope this brings you some peace, lad, eh? Best to get it out the way, I think. Coming up here, like this. We can all start to move on. Together.'

Adam nodded, grimly.

Clio stood and wiped the dirt from her knees.

'The O'Hares are buried just over there,' Frazer said, as though they were tourists and he was their guide.

'We know, Dad,' James said. 'But Mam always said she wanted to be in the sun.'

Clio couldn't help but smile. James had said their father's next line for him.

Frazer nodded, distracted.

'Cost a fortune,' he said. 'Opening a new plot and two perfectly good ones already in the family.'

'We'll put you in over there,' Clio said. 'Save money.'

Frazer glanced at her sharply.

Clio smiled.

'I'm not sure how my fiancée would feel about that,' he said. 'She might want us to rest together.'

Clio flinched. Game, set and match to her father.

'Remember the Pattern?' Ryan said. 'Fucking days long.'

'You're in a cemetery,' Kate said. 'Would it kill you to construct a sentence without resorting to cursing?'

'Stone fucking dead,' Ryan quipped.

Clio smiled, genuinely this time. At her brother and his memories.

The Pattern was a Mass said annually in the cemetery, always in summer, when the families of the parish would gather at the graves of their loved ones. Their mother had brought them every year; the day was a calendar event for her. She'd get up at the crack of dawn to fill baskets with sandwiches and pork pies and sausage rolls. Then they'd all troop up to the graveyard, hats on their heads to protect them from the worst excesses of the sun. Their father never joined them. He considered himself an intellectual atheist. It meant their mother had to pray twice as hard to ensure both of their ascents into heaven.

Kathleen knew everybody at the Mass and she'd do a social turn of the cemetery before tending to her parents' plot. Then, because her mother and father were buried in the shade, she'd settle her own family around a grave in the middle, the resting place of some man called John Doyle, who'd lived locally but had no family left to visit him.

Clio recalled that, at the time, she'd found the whole thing mind-numbingly boring. Sitting on the hard stone grave-surround, she'd entertain herself by killing ants and blood-red mites, while listening to decades of the rosary being intoned as though the walking dead were performing it.

There'd be a break in the programme for lunch, which was always a relief, then it would resume again, dull and duller, as the priest criss-crossed the cemetery to bless each grave individually. The whole thing went on for about four hours.

Yet, now, Clio looked back on it fondly.

'One of those priests felt me up,' Ryan said. 'Father O'Toole. He taught in our school.'

'He didn't feel you up.' Kate sighed. 'He was like that with everybody. Tactile.'

'He was tactile with my arse cheek,' Ryan replied.

'He probably thought you were a pansy,' Frazer said. 'Maybe if you'd played sports, like your brothers.'

'Oh, of course,' Ryan said. 'We all know that the homosexuals don't engage in any physical activity outside of riding each other.'

Frazer ignored his youngest son, instead busying himself with deadheading a small dahlia at the foot of the grave.

Clio placed her hand on Ryan's arm and shook her head gently.

Ryan never learned. With the rest of them, Frazer's little digs were hit and miss. With Ryan, he always pressed the right buttons and Ryan reacted every single time.

And came off worse.

She felt her brother's arm tense, then relax.

Not today. Not at their mother's grave.

Clio started to walk away, trailing her fingers over the other headstones. A Holly Blue butterfly fluttered past and Clio felt its wing brush her cheek.

No afterlife, but perhaps small symbols that the universe had some meaning.

At the gate, she saw Danny, parked a little down the hill. He hadn't been at the house when they'd left, but he must have guessed where they were when he arrived and found it empty.

She'd gone only a few metres along the road when she heard footsteps behind her. Bella was at her side again.

'Bella, I want to be on my own.' Clio sighed.

She kept walking. Bella kept pace with her. When Clio realised, she stopped short.

'What?' she said.

Bella shrugged.

'Tell me about New York.'

'What? What about New York?'

'I want to move there,' Bella said.

'To do what?'

'To work.'

Clio sighed, again, loudly.

'As what?' she asked. 'A waitress? Bar girl? Selling concessions? Or do you think you'll get a job in *Vogue*?'

'I want to vlog.'

Clio had started to walk again but now she did a double-take.

'What?'

'Vlog. Like, video-log.'

'I know what it is,' Clio said. 'What do you plan to vlog about?'

Bella hesitated.

'Lifestyle stuff,' she said. 'I know it takes a while to build up a following. But if I work at it . . .'

'Don't go to New York,' Clio said.

'But . . .'

'Just, don't. Don't be so fucking stupid. If you want to talk shite into a camera, you can do it from your nice, cosy bedroom in Dublin.'

Clio started to walk away.

'Just because it didn't work out for you,' she heard Bella call out, petulance seeping through the hurt.

Clio ignored her. She made her way over to Danny, who'd got out of the car and was resting against its bonnet.

'Teenagers are thick,' she said.

Danny smiled.

'You look like you want a lift,' he said.

Clio nodded gratefully.

'And she's no worse than you were at that age,' Danny added.

'I didn't go to New York to *make it*, trust me.'

'I seem to recall you wanting to be famous at some point.'

'When I was about ten,' Clio said, but she blushed anyway.

It hadn't taken long before she'd been disabused of any notion of life in New York being glamorous.

'Here's Ellen as well,' Danny said. 'Glad I came now.'

They watched as Ellen made her way towards the gate.

'Why did you come up, anyway?' Clio asked, as they waited. 'Were you looking for us?'

'I do the grave every Sunday,' he said, shrugging.

Ellen arrived beside them.

'Thanks for waiting. I have to get out of here.'

She got in the front, as though Clio had been holding the door open for her, and slammed the door. She was in foul humour and Clio had no idea why.

Once Clio was in the back, Danny began to drive.

'I don't know what Dad's doing, bringing Adam up to visit the grave like that,' Ellen said, her voice filled with anger. 'Why did Adam even come back? It's caused nothing but trouble!'

Clio caught Danny's eye in the rearview mirror.

'What's got into you?' Clio said.

'Don't defend him,' Ellen said. 'You're the one who accused him of killing Mam.'

'And you and Kate told me to rein it in. Whatever he did, it's not his fault Dad has a new squeeze, Ellen.'

'Stop,' Ellen said. 'I don't care. I don't want to talk about any of them. Adam, Dad, they're both to blame. For all of it. Dad . . .' She caught Clio's eye in the rearview mirror. 'Sorry, Clio, I know you were always his favourite, but you know as well as I do, Dad didn't help things with Mam. We don't talk about that, but it's true. They're both responsible.'

Clio felt tears prick in her eyes and looked up, an old trick she'd learned.

An uncomfortable silence filled the car.

Danny shifted in his seat and changed gears. He grimaced, as though in pain.

Clio noticed and watched him with concern. Ellen saw it too and met Clio's eye again, her expression puzzled, curious.

'I'm sorry, Danny,' Ellen said. 'I know Dad is your best friend.'

Danny said nothing. But Clio could see his jaw was set. In anger or acceptance, it was hard to tell.

'Dad is to blame for a lot of things,' Ellen said, her voice filled with vitriol.

Clio sat back, surprised. She had her own issues with Frazer. But, apparently, so did Ellen.

# AFTER

The clock on the wall said it was just after half eleven. Danny stared at the second hand, watching it go round and round.

Detective Downes said he was waiting for his superior to join him. He needed his boss to go over their statements and check that they were thorough before he could let them go home. This way, he didn't need to bring them down to the station, where they might have to sit all night. Or call them back in again tomorrow. It was for their benefit, he said. But something was wrong, Danny figured. The pup's questions had become more . . . probing. More targeted. He had the bit between his teeth, that was for sure.

'So, earlier this evening, the party broke up into smaller groups,' the detective said. 'There was a period, roughly between 8.00 and 8.30, after the initial drinks and the fireworks, when the family wasn't all together on the rear deck of the yacht. Did you speak to any of them?'

Danny sighed.

'James came up to me,' he said.

'What did he want?'

'He wanted me to talk to his father. There had been a few words. They were all wound up about him marrying Ana.'

'What did you tell him?'

'I told him it was none of my business,' Danny said. 'Christ, all these bloody questions and the body of my best friend is still lying out there, cold and getting colder, while you try to figure out which of his children killed him. I have to tell you, it's making me sick to my stomach.'

'Maybe I'm wondering if you killed him.'

Danny placed his hands on the table, out flat. He didn't know why – perhaps he thought if they were both keeping an eye on them, he wouldn't be tempted to punch the detective.

'Arrest me, then,' he said. 'Frazer wasn't perfect. We go back a long way. I, more than anybody, maybe even more than his kids, knew his flaws. We fell out, from time to time. Frazer was a stubborn old boot. Selfish, very selfish at times. He'd get in his head he was right about something and that was that, no matter what you said or how much you proved he was wrong. There were points when we'd argue about something and I would know, I would *know* I was right and he'd tell me black was white, night was day. I'd be sore pressed not to grab him and strangle him.'

Danny sat back.

'Now, you tell me this, you cheeky wee fuck. You tell me what happened tonight that would make me kill a man in a sneaky way like that. Because I'm telling you, if I ever wanted to murder somebody, I'd just do it. I'd do it on a crowded street, I'd do it in front of you. If anybody ever enraged me so much that I was driven to take their life, God forgive me but I wouldn't be worrying about getting away with it, do you get my drift? I'd just fucking do it.'

Danny caught himself.

It needed to be said but Danny hadn't wanted to show how angry he was.

The detective nodded, slowly.

'I understand you're upset,' he said, gentler now. 'Listen, Danny, just bear with me. Before everybody spread out on the yacht tonight, Frazer made some sort of announcement, am I right? What did he say?'

Danny stared at the detective and then turned his head, raised a handkerchief to his mouth and coughed up some unhealthy-looking phlegm. He hadn't dived into the water to fish Frazer out – the younger lads had got there before him. If he were honest, he'd been too shocked to move.

'I'm saying nothing more,' Danny said.

The detective put his head in his hands.

'Well, what about this,' he said.

Danny pursed his lips and waited for the question.

'Is it possible none of them wanted to murder Frazer? Is it possible his death was an accident? That maybe, just maybe, somebody had been angling to hurt somebody else, instead? Like Adam?'

'Why would anybody want to kill Adam?' Danny said, leaning forward.

'Because his coming home kicked all this off, didn't it?' the detective said.

Danny opened and closed his mouth.

Detective Downes was right.

# CLIO

Clio had Danny drop her down in the village. Home barely a day and she had to get away.

The village had expanded a little from the place she remembered. There were at least three extra pubs, one of them almost exclusively targeted at tourists with prices on its menu that no local would ever pay. The newsagents had expanded into a mini-supermarket, stocking every essential your heart could desire. Bread, milk, buckets and spades, nappies, shellac nail varnish, gate paint.

Toilet brushes, even.

There'd also been an explosion of restaurants in the last couple of years. A shellfish farm had opened along the coast and Kate had told Clio when they'd arrived yesterday that one of the eateries was even garnering international attention.

Clio struggled to get to grips with the notion of the village as a gourmet culinary destination when the only food she'd ever enjoyed there had been over-battered fish and chips that needed a vat of vinegar to taste of anything.

She walked along the wall by the shoreline for a few hundred metres, looking out over the harbour. Nestled in among the docked fishing vessels was a larger vessel, a white yacht.

The party boat, presumably.

Clio shivered and turned her gaze inland.

She was hungry. Her appetite had returned with a vengeance since the return home.

The sea air and familiar flavours.

A restaurant's outside seating area was starting to empty out and it was there that Clio headed.

She ordered crab claws in garlic butter on sourdough toast and a glass of sparkling water from a waiter she didn't recognise and who, she realised, didn't recognise her. This was also new. The village used to be so small that everybody knew everybody and somebody was always someone else's mother or father, son or daughter, sibling or cousin.

She'd just begun to enjoy her anonymity when the boy who'd taken her virginity sat down at her table.

'As I live and breathe. Clíodhna Lattimer.'

Rob had barely changed. In the face, anyway. His grin was still drop-your-knickers charming and his eyes had retained their twinkle. His body, however, had taken a beating from life. Clio remembered his naked, sinewy twenty-year-old form. Three years older at the time, he'd still been skinnier than her. With such a slim frame, the added weight didn't suit him. His blond hair, too, had lost much of its shine. Not even thirty, and the grey was starting to take hold.

He was morphing into an overweight Daniel Craig.

Still, she smiled. An involuntary response, the natural reaction to Rob.

'Sorry,' she said. 'Who are you?'

She picked up her water and drank it, amused eyes watching him over the glass rim.

He clasped his hand to his chest.

'I'm wounded, girl. How could you have forgotten me and that night, eight years ago, the passion, the orgasms, the . . .'

Clio snorted the water, spraying her hand, the table and possibly him.

She looked around at the handful of other diners, who cast curious glances before returning to their meals.

'Tell me you remember every minute or I'll have to give you a run-through,' Rob said. 'Loudly. Like the moans you made in the throes of our lovemaking.'

'I swear to Christ, Rob, shut the fuck up or I'll pour this water over your head.'

He laughed and sat back.

'Plus,' Clio said, placing the water back on the table, 'from my recollection, it was only a few minutes' worth. Not a lot to remember and certainly not enough time to raise the roof.'

'Ooh,' he said, laughing. 'Burn, as my Johnny would say.'

He stood up and leaned across to hug her. She let him, enjoying the feel of his arms around her, the scent of his sweat. They hadn't parted on acrimonious terms. It had just fizzled out. Clio had no more interest in relationships back then than, well, she'd ever had, really. Sex was a release, not a contract.

'Who's your Johnny?' she said, when he sat back down and signalled to the waiter he was staying. 'Come out of the closet, have you? And have you joined me for lunch, now? Just invited yourself, like?'

'Slimline tonic and whatever the lady is having.' Rob ignored her as he spoke to the waiter. 'Will you not have a glass of wine, Clio?' She shook her head.

'Me drink wine while you're on a slimline tonic?' she said, when they were alone again. 'You used to be a pints man.'

'Johnny is my son,' he said. 'Two years old and getting bigger and more of a handful by the day. I don't want to miss his graduation because I've had a heart attack at fifty, which was exactly where the pints were taking me. Plus, I'm working.'

Clio tried to take it all in. Rob had always been a talker, something that had drawn her to him. He talked so much, it didn't matter that she was quiet. And here he was, spilling his life story, filling her in on the gap of the last few years, like they were still the best of friends.

'What local filly did you manage to trap?' she said, as he accepted his drink from the waiter. 'Or did you wander outwards because you'd run out of girls to shag in Albertstown?'

'You always thought the worst of me. I only slept with all those women to get over you, Clio, after you refused to become Mrs Rob.'

'You never proposed to me.'

'I didn't have to. You owned my heart from the moment you let me pop your cherry.'

Clio laughed.

'You don't know Johnny's mam,' he said, his face growing more serious. 'She's from Wexford town. Still lives there. I met her not long after I moved up there. After you dumped me.'

'You're not together?' Clio asked.

'Nah. Tried, for a while, for the sake of the baby. But we gave the kid a better chance by living apart. No child should hear his parents bickering day in, day out. A lovely-looking girl but not a lot going on between the ears, if you know what I mean. He got my smarts, thankfully. Sharp as a tack.'

'I'm sorry,' Clio said. But she wasn't sure she felt it. She could imagine Rob with a child – a little mini-version of him. But not with a wife. Rob had never seemed the sort to settle down and twenty-eight would have been indecently young for somebody like him to be married – even if it was practically elderly for most of the people they had grown up with.

'Clearly, fate wanted me single for your return,' Rob said, smirking. 'What has you back, anyway?'

'Haven't you heard?'

He shook his head, blank-faced.

'Been down south buying equipment for the farm.'

'You're not still working on your parents' farm?'

That explained why he was back in Spanish Cove, anyway.

'We're not all jet-setters,' Rob said, with a smile, though there was a hint of defensiveness.

'I didn't mean . . . You were smart,' Clio said, backtracking.

'Still am. But I give the parents a dig out when I can. I've another job on top. Full-time, as it happens.'

'Two jobs?' Clio said. 'You can get lunch, so.'

'Ha! Buying lunch for a Lattimer, that's a new one. Ripped through the inheritance already, have you?'

Clio wasn't going there. Rob might be happy to reveal all but Clio didn't want to give away her secrets.

'Adam is back,' she said, deflecting.

Rob's eyes widened.

'You're shitting me.'

'Turned up at the homestead just over a week ago.'

'Where was he?'

Clio shrugged.

'He says he was in France.'

'He says? Don't you believe him?'

Clio shrugged again. Rob studied her and she started to feel uncomfortable under his gaze. She'd forgotten how soul-searching his eyes could be. Like you were the only person in the room, or on the planet, for that matter. A bit like Adam.

'So he was there, all this time?' Rob shook his head, incredulous.

They both fell silent. Clio knew that Rob, too, remembered the huge search parties ten years ago, the ones the younger teenagers had been refused admission to, as though, if sent off searching, they might also disappear. His parents would have helped. Gangs of locals, beating through tall grass in the fields, trawling woods and barns, combing the cliffs, scanning the shore.

Being forced to help with flasks of tea and mounds of sandwiches and scones, that's what Clio remembered most. Her mother in the kitchen, barely standing, but keeping the worry at bay so she could run a military-style operation and ensure all the volunteers were fed and watered.

And all that time . . .

'Did he tell you why?' Rob asked. He had a right to know. Everybody did.

'He just had . . . a breakdown or something,' Clio said. 'Do you mind, Rob, if we don't talk about it? I'm still struggling to get my head around it.'

'Jesus. Not at all. None of my business.'

He reached over and took her hand in both of his. His skin was warm, rough, his palms and fingers calloused by the farm work he was allegedly not doing too much of. And she remembered him taking her hand before, when he had found her almost passed out drunk on the beach, a few weeks after her mother's funeral. Then, the next year, when he took her hand and led her into his room, while his parents were up shopping in Dublin and his brothers were in the pub.

She'd cried when they'd had clumsy, awkward sex, not because it hurt or she regretted losing her virginity, but because it didn't make her feel anything.

And if somebody as kind as Rob, a person she was utterly at home with and even fancied, couldn't provoke some kind of emotion in her, what did that mean?

It meant she was lost.

It meant she was dead inside.

'Tell me you're staying for a while,' he said, gently, hopefully.

Clio let the little glimmer spark in her stomach for a moment before she doused it.

'Not long,' she said, and pulled her hand back. 'You know I can't stand this place, Rob.'

'Well, you sure I can't take you out for a drink? Or back to my apartment? You're aged a few years, but I'm a modern man, I can look beyond the wrinkles and saggy boobs and do cerebral . . .'

'Tosspot.' She laughed. 'You wouldn't stand a chance with me now. But, I guess somebody's hand is getting lucky tonight.'

Then she stood up, kissed his cheek lightly and started to walk away, trying not to give in to the abject disappointment on his face.

She stopped and turned just before she hit the pavement outside the enclosed seating area.

'What's your full-time job?' she asked.

'I joined the police.'

Clio frowned.

'What?' Rob said.

'You? You joined the police? What do you do?'

'Catch baddies.'

'But you're . . .' Clio looked Rob up and down. If she had to choose a policeman to pursue her, she'd be happy with Rob. She could stop and think about the world for a while and he still wouldn't catch up; he looked that unfit. 'Not being funny, Rob, but you're carrying a few pounds.'

He tapped his head with his finger.

'I do my policing up here. Detective Sergeant Rob Downes, nice to meet you, ma'am. Unprecedented for somebody my age but I was always a grafter. My traffic duties are well behind me. I'm the thinking sort, now.'

'Well, um, congratulations.'

'Bet you wish you'd married me now.'

Rob grinned at her and she forced herself to smile back.

Then, his features became serious.

'In a weird way, I think it was your brother disappearing that made me want to go into it.'

'I'll tell him,' Clio said. 'Say hello to your parents for me.'

Then she really did leave.

As she walked away, she wondered if Rob was the sort of cop who could smell badness in somebody.

She'd met a few of them over the years.

They'd spotted the badness in her straight away.

# RYAN

Ryan had chosen to walk back to the house from the cemetery. Being stuck indoors and in cars, being confined with other people for any length of time, didn't suit him at the best of times, but today, he really needed to be away from his father.

When he'd been hospitalised, it was the one thing that had got to him.

Never mind the shakes, constant vomiting, cold sweats and the general desire to kill himself.

Being in company, all the time, really bothered him.

But while Ryan had wanted to escape for a bit of solitude, his niece had other plans.

Bella had been sitting on a tree root outside the graveyard, puffing furiously on a cigarette; her mascara was smudged, making her look like an angry, chain-smoking panda.

She fell into step with him as he started down the hill, roaring back at Sandra that she was walking.

'It's a long way,' Ryan said, looking down at the sandals on her feet; diamanté-studded things, not suitable for anything beyond showing off.

'Clio is a bit of a bitch, isn't she?'

Ryan nearly choked.

'You what?'

'She like, pissed all over my parade just there? More or less told me to give up on life and go on the social.'

She tossed her hair, irritated, and he caught the intense scent she was wearing. Overbearingly fruity.

Ryan narrowed his eyes, but kept facing the road ahead.

'I doubt she meant any harm, whatever you're talking about,' he said.

'I told her I wanted to go to New York. Like she had. I thought she'd have some tips, you know? That she could help me.'

'Ah.' Ryan reached into his pocket and took out his own cigarettes. 'I don't think things worked out that well for Clio in the States. Don't take it to heart.'

Bella said nothing. She held her hand out – it took a few moments before Ryan realised what she wanted. Then he handed her a cigarette.

They continued in silence, keeping to the edge beside the low ditch and gnarled tree roots, even though they would hear a car coming from miles away.

Ryan inhaled. Up here, the smell of the sea didn't dominate. Instead, the aroma of gorse bushes and mown grass filled the air, joined by ancient tree bark and distant agricultural smells carried on the warm breeze.

'What can you smell?' Ryan asked Bella.

'Manure.'

Ryan smiled.

'And cheap smoke,' she said. 'What are these cigarettes, anyway? I usually smoke Benson & Hedges.'

'Usually!' Ryan snorted. 'How the hell are you smoking at all? Aren't you millennials the ones who look after yourselves?'

'Aren't you a millennial?' she retorted. 'You and Adam smoke like troopers.'

'We started it to annoy Frazer, but, turns out, it's quite addictive.' Bella held the cigarette up pointedly, quizzically.

'821 Biancas,' he said. 'Aside from cheap smoke and shit, what can you smell?'

She inhaled theatrically.

'Nothing,' she said.

'That's the unsophisticated nostril at work,' he said. 'Try harder. Distinguish. In Limone, I could tell the time of day from the smell. Croissants, freshly baked, was morning. Frying garlic, lemon tang, exhaust fumes – that was afternoon. Mosquito spray, candles, bitter grapes, jasmine meant the evening.'

Bella stared at him, her mouth hanging open slightly, the wheels turning behind her eyes as she calculated how insane he must be.

She shut her mouth, tilted up her head and sniffed. He could see she was about to utter a sarcastic line but something had interested her. She smelled again.

'Coconut?' she said.

'It's the gorse,' Ryan told her. 'Not everybody can smell it. You're special.'

She laughed dismissively but he could tell she was pleased. Teenagers always were, when you told them they were unique.

It was what the dealers had spotted in Ryan when he'd been one. That desperation to be told he was important, that he stood out.

'Train your nostrils, you might start picking better perfumes,' he said.

'Wanker,' she spat back.

He smiled.

'I just want to go somewhere,' she said, sighing. 'I want to start again.'

'You haven't started at all,' Ryan said. 'You're only a kid.'

'And what are you?'

'Older than my years.'

She snorted.

'What were you doing when you were my age?' she asked.

Ryan kicked a stone on the road into the ditch.

'You don't want to know what I was doing at your age.'

'That good, huh?' She laughed.

'What's gone so wrong with your life?' Ryan asked. 'How hard can it be, living in a nice house with wealthy parents and no worries except what colour you want to dye your hair this week?'

'We're not rich,' she said, quietly.

Ryan pursed his lips.

'Money problems?' he asked, his voice light.

Bella didn't answer.

Ryan watched her for a moment. Since yesterday, she'd worn this bemused, bored, mischievous look on her face, seemingly thrilled to be in among the Lattimer madness. But now she looked upset, younger, more vulnerable than you would imagine her to be.

She reminded him a little of Clio. No wonder Bella had sought her out. A kindred spirit.

'It's not as fun as you think it might be, moving abroad,' he said, gently.

'You . . .'

'Whatever you do, do not use Clio and me as role models. We

have our strengths. And our flaws. Clio is better than me. But it's one thing to emigrate for work or, I don't know, a different climate or something. Don't go because you're running away. You'll be bringing yourself with you.'

'I'm not running away from myself,' she said, and even if she'd added *duh,* she couldn't have sounded more dismissive. 'I'm happy with myself, thank you very much. I want to get away from other people.'

'Who? Your parents?'

Bella glanced sideways.

'I . . . it doesn't matter.'

'Is James still an arsehole to live with?' Ryan prompted.

'I don't know . . . He's the big success story. But when he's at home . . .'

She trailed off.

'See,' Ryan said, tightly. 'Arsehole.'

Bella laughed, but then she looked so small that Ryan put his arm around her shoulder.

'I think there's something bad going on,' Bella said. Ryan felt her body slump a bit. 'He might be . . . he might be cheating on Sandra. She's a bit of a pain, but she's still my mum. I don't know what to do.'

'Why should you do anything?' Ryan said. 'They're the grown-ups. Let them sort it. It's not down to you.'

'But she'll be so unhappy if he leaves. She's so bloody . . . grateful to him. She used to say that to me – he took us in. She'd never tell him that. But that's how she feels. Like, he's five years younger than her? It's embarrassing. I never want to feel like I need somebody to take care of me. But Mum does. It will crush her if they split.'

Ryan stiffened. Under no circumstances was he going to feel sorry for James. And in Sandra's case – he'd searched and searched for something of substance and been left wanting. This kid was the only good thing either of them had ever done.

'People always think they know how they'll feel in certain situations but it's rarely what they expect,' Ryan said.

Bella shrugged. She seemed comfortable with Ryan's arm on her shoulder. There wasn't anything sexual to it. She was just a niece being comforted by her uncle and Ryan, oddly, was quite enjoying it.

Whoever thought he'd be at home in a nurturing role?

They hadn't, contrary to what Ryan had expected, heard the car roll around the bend behind them. The hybrid engine on James' Audi was too quiet.

The vehicle slowed to a halt and James rolled down the window.

'Bella, why aren't you with your mother in your grandfather's car?' he snapped.

Ryan hastily removed his arm from the girl's shoulder. He didn't like the way James was looking at him.

'She's all right walking,' Ryan said.

James ignored him.

'Get in the car. Sandra has decided to leave for Dublin early. You're going with her. Now.'

Bella frowned.

'I want to stay with you.'

James looked back at the wheel. Kate was in the passenger seat beside him and looked uncomfortable. Adam sat in the back, interested, but not intervening.

Ryan glared at James. Did he really think . . .?

150

Bella walked around the car and got into the back, beside Adam.

Ryan leaned down to the driver's window, his hands placed on the car door. He looked down the road, then back at James.

'Don't judge me by your own warped standards,' Ryan said, quietly.

Then he looked in the back at Adam.

'Thanks,' Ryan said. 'I can see why you came back, now.'

Adam raised his eyebrows in a *what do you want me to say?* expression.

Ryan pulled his hands back as James pressed the button to roll up the window.

He watched the car drive away.

# ELLEN

After they dropped Clio to the village, Danny had offered to drive Ellen anywhere she wanted to go.

She *was* thinking about going somewhere and genuinely considered Danny's offer.

She could go into town. Ask around. According to Sandra, who'd talked non-stop at breakfast before the others came down, Ana had told her she was Polish and that she worked in a shop in the city. Worked in or owned, Sandra couldn't recall.

Ellen could investigate a bit. It was a Sunday, but everywhere opened on Sundays now, didn't they?

Ellen, though, knew she wouldn't be going into Wexford town. And if she did, it would be in her own car, so she could scarper the hell out of there if she needed to.

Even after all these years, she was scared of running into people. Running into one person in particular. Him.

She was terrified of what he might say.

So, she had Danny drive her back up to the house and instead she went on her computer, her link with the outside world, to do her research.

She wondered if she'd need Ana's surname but decided to start by looking up Polish-owned stores.

She hadn't expected there to be so many.

Wexford town, it seemed, had come on in leaps and bounds since Ellen had been there last. The directory for Polish-owned stores was longer than she could have imagined.

Ellen scanned the names, her eyes wide. She'd need more information. She'd need Ana's surname, after all.

She typed in Ana + Polish + Wexford. She had begun to click out of the windows she already had open when a news item at the top of the search page caught her eye. It mentioned a Polish store in Wexford town.

One was just about to go into receivership.

Ellen's finger was hovering over the link when the sitting room door opened.

Ana stood in its frame.

'Oh,' she said. 'I am sorry. I did not know anybody was here. Frazer . . .'

She trailed off.

Ellen tried to say something. She wanted to ask this woman questions. Get to the bottom of everything.

But the presence of her, the fact Ana had been able to let herself into the house in their supposed absence, shocked Ellen to the core.

She shut her laptop and rushed from the room, almost banging into Ana as she did.

The woman barely moved to let her past.

# AFTER

The detective took a gulp of night air into his lungs and let himself stand still for a moment and process.

It was approaching midnight. He had an hour or two left with this lot before he had to allow them to go home. Or to the hospital morgue to be with their father, though he doubted any of them planned on doing that.

A couple of hours.

And nobody willing to tell him anything significant, yet. It was like dredging a murky lake – the net finding plenty, while he, the man in charge, was still unsure what he was looking for.

Was Frazer the intended victim? He'd sure got on the last nerve of several of his children.

But, then, their relations with one another didn't seem the best, either.

Still – Frazer was taller than any of his sons. His hair was grey, whereas all his sons were still dark. It was a calm night and the moon was bright.

A person would have to have been very drunk indeed to make that mistake.

In any case, a picture was already starting to form in Rob's head, between what the Lattimers were saying and not saying.

He'd already done some cursory research on his phone. God bless Google.

At least two of them hadn't been entirely honest.

But who was lying the most?

He walked over to the remaining ambulance still parked at the harbour.

Ana Wójcik had been given a mild sedative for shock but she was resisting being brought to the hospital. A friend was apparently en route and would take her home to Wexford town.

Rob stood at the ambulance door and watched as a young paramedic sat stroking the woman's hand.

There was no doubt Ana was in shock. She sat very still, her eyes fixed forward, blank and somewhat glazed. Occasionally she blinked, and raised her hand to the sides of her hair and patted the plaited buns. A habit. Checking her hair was still in place, even in the midst of trauma.

'I'm sorry, I don't think she's in a fit state—'

Rob held up his hand. The paramedic wasn't much younger than him, maybe early twenties, but she had the air of somebody trying very hard to look like she could do her job very well.

Rob didn't even bother pulling out the old tropes.

He just looked at her.

She moved to the side of the ambulance, making room for Rob.

The detective climbed in and sat facing the dead man's fiancée.

'I'm very sorry for your loss,' he said.

'That is kind of you.'

There was no tone in her voice. She was robotic. In shock. Proper shock, unlike the family he was interviewing.

'Can you tell me what happened on board this evening?'

Ana shook her head.

'Did you see anybody with your fiancé before he died?'

She shook it again.

Rob pursed his lips. He looked down at his notepad, flicked back to Danny McHugh's statement.

'Frazer went up the side deck on his own to smoke a cigar at approximately 8 p.m., after the fireworks,' he said. 'There'd been some sort of incident prior – with his children, I believe? And you? A fight, of sorts.'

'I did not fight with Frazer.'

'No.' Rob consulted his notes. 'But you weren't happy with him?'

Ana said nothing.

'You didn't go with him. You went below deck, with several of the others. You sat alone. You were, according to what I've heard, unhappy.'

Rob looked up. She caught him by surprise. Ana was staring at him, her eyes fully focused now, not drifting, not traumatised.

'Frazer did a very bad thing,' she said. 'I ask him not to make any more big announcements, not to do the things that would upset his children. This was important to me.'

Rob ran his fingers over his chin.

'What did he do tonight that upset them?'

'You must ask them this question.'

Ana's eyes glazed over as she spoke but her voice was strong, furious. It took Rob by surprise.

'Ana,' he said. 'Do you think your fiancé deserved to die?'

'No,' she said. 'Of course not. Nobody *deserves* to die, unless they are very bad. Very evil.'

Rob paused, thought about how to frame the next question. Fuck it, best to just ask it.

'How did your first husband die?' he asked.

# CLIO

Clio walked slowly back up to the house from the village. She was in no rush to return, but even she couldn't drag out a couple of kilometres for more than a half hour.

She was so deep in concentration when she finally arrived that she barely noticed Bella in the garden. Her niece was sitting on the grass, plucking daisies with a face so miserable even Clio couldn't pass her by.

Bella only looked up when Clio's shadow obscured the sun.

'Hi,' Clio said.

Bella raised an eyebrow, then returned to her task.

'Where's your mum?' Clio asked, undeterred.

'Packing. We came for one night. She brought down enough clothes for a world tour.'

Clio lowered herself onto the grass, crossing her legs in a position that mirrored Bella's.

'What?' Bella said.

'What, what?'

'You going to tell me I'm a fucking idiot again?'

'I didn't say you were a fucking idiot. I just said, don't go to New York.'

'You said I was fucking stupid.'

'I'm sorry about that.'

'Whatever.' Bella shrugged.

Clio tugged at her bottom lip with her teeth. She didn't find this any easier than the girl sitting in front of her, but she also knew she couldn't leave Bella sitting there, looking so unhappy.

It was too familiar a sight.

'Don't mind me, anyway,' Clio said. 'I'm a moody bitch. Everybody says. It's just . . . New York is hard, you know? It isn't how you think it will be.'

'You don't know how I think it will be.'

'True. But I know how I thought it would be and we're not that far apart in age. I don't know. Maybe you'd be fine. You have your mum, she'll look out for you. If you need money or that. It's a difficult place to get by in, that's all I'm saying.'

'She doesn't,' Bella whispered.

'What?'

'Mum. She won't look out for me if I go. She says eighteen is old enough to take care of yourself. She did.'

Clio sucked in the inside of her cheeks.

'Is that what she's told you?'

Bella nodded.

Clio hesitated.

'If she was doing such a good job of looking after herself, why did she go looking for James?'

'Mum thinks that *was* looking after herself.'

'I see,' Clio said. She reached over and started to lace the little pile of daisies in front of Bella's legs.

'Something tells me you're not somebody who will need a man to take care of you,' she said.

Bella shook her head, vigorously.

Clio nodded.

She continued to work on the flowers. When she'd made a bracelet, she reached out and took Bella's hand. She slipped it on, over her wrist.

Bella looked down at it, surprised.

'That's because you're smart, Bella,' Clio said. She took a deep breath. 'You're pretty and funny and you're smart. Don't ever forget that. And forget what I said earlier. Fuck the begrudgers, okay? Fuck 'em.'

It came out stiffer than she'd intended, but Clio was still glad she'd said it.

Bella nodded, her eyes wide, red spots in her cheeks.

'Eh, yeah,' she said, almost flippantly, but Clio could see what she'd said had meant something.

'I'm going to make coffee. Want some?'

'Coffee ruins the complexion, Sandra always says.'

'So does Botox. Eventually.'

The two smiled at each other.

'I'm okay,' Bella said.

'Yes, you are.'

She stood up and, after a moment's consideration, leaned down and kissed her niece's head. Having made as much effort as she could, she walked away.

In the kitchen, Clio found Ana at the table, writing in a small notepad.

'I will leave if you wish it,' Ana said. 'I do not want to be in the way.'

'You're not in my way,' Clio said.

She poured water into the back of the coffee machine and turned it on. Then she rested against the counter and looked across at Ana. The woman's face said she was still trying to make up her mind whether to stay or go.

'How long have you and Frazer been an item?' Clio asked.

'I . . . Not long,' Ana said. 'I am sorry, I mean, long enough. For him to ask the question and for me to accept the proposal.'

'Have you lived in Ireland a while?'

'Fifteen years,' Ana said.

'You're . . . Polish?' Clio hazarded a guess.

'Yes.'

'Whereabouts?'

'You not know it,' Ana said, doubtfully. 'Wieliczka.'

Clio shook her head. She'd never been to Poland; she only knew its major cities.

'It is famous for salt mines,' Ana added, a note of pride in her voice.

'What made you come over here?' Clio asked. There was no judgement in her voice, no hostility. She, too, had been an emigrant.

'My husband got job here. Then, he die. But I was settled.'

'How did he die?'

Ana hesitated.

'I do not like to talk about it,' she said.

Clio studied her.

Behind her, the coffee machine hissed its readiness. Clio turned and poured herself a cup.

'How did you meet my father?' she asked.

'He like my buns.'

Clio whipped her head around.

'What?'

'I have a Polish bakery in town.'

Ana's face was inscrutable but Clio thought she detected a hint of amusement at the corner of her lips.

Of course Ana owned her own business. Frazer could always spot a good thing.

So much for the gold-digger theory.

'Do you want one?' Clio said, nodding at her coffee cup.

'No, thank you. I should go.'

'Go where? How come you don't live here, in the house? I presume you will be moving in, at some stage?'

Ana hesitated.

'Perhaps.'

Clio stared at Ana. She was difficult to figure out. She was pretty and ageing far better than Clio's father. Quiet, but happy to talk if you asked her questions. Clio suspected she was smart, perhaps smart enough to not make it too obvious. Frazer would never be able to live with somebody stupid but he also had to believe he was the most intelligent person in the room.

The door opened and Frazer came in, a book in his hand, reading glasses perched on his nose. Teddy came in behind him, close to her father's feet, but as soon as he saw Clio, he moved towards her. She felt him, warm and comforting, against her legs.

Whatever happened after this weekend, she was taking her dog with her when she left.

'Do you have the final order worked out, Ana . . . ?'

He spotted Clio.

'Ah, Clio. Are you lassies getting to know each other?'

Clio and Ana shared a look, then both nodded.

'Excellent,' Frazer said. 'You won't mind if I steal her, Clio? Ana's business is catering for our party tomorrow. I just have to negotiate down her extortionate prices, eh?'

Ana blushed furiously.

'Are you sure it's a good idea?' Clio said, watching the pair of them. 'The party, I mean.'

Ana gathered her things and started to move towards the door.

'I will wait for you in the study,' she said to Frazer. She barely glanced at Clio.

'I'll be right behind you.' Her father smiled.

When the door closed, Frazer turned to face Clio.

'Do you like her?'

Clio shrugged.

'It only matters if *you* do,' she said.

'You always were the thoughtful one.'

Clio raised an eyebrow.

'You didn't answer my question,' she said. 'This weekend was meant to be about Adam, not you getting engaged.'

'Can't it be both?'

'Dad.'

Frazer sighed.

'Haven't the last ten years been about Adam?' He said it lightly, but Clio could hear the simmering emotion beneath. 'Adam or

Ryan or Ellen or all of you. It's hardly unreasonable, is it, to ask my children to do something for me? For once?'

Clio bit her lip and swallowed her retort.

In the silence, Frazer leaned down and stroked the dog's head.

'He's abandoning me for you, isn't he? Aren't you, boy? And me the one who fed and walked you all these years. I'll try not to take it to heart, you bad doggy.'

The dog panted and licked Frazer's hand, then nestled against Clio again.

Frazer stood up.

'You look desperately like you want to say something but you're keeping it all in and that's not exactly the fresh start I was hoping for,' Frazer said, scrutinising her over his reading glasses.

Clio could feel beads of sweat start to form on her lower back, a cold tingle run through her body.

Ellen had sown the seed and Clio couldn't stop thinking about it. It had to be said.

Now or never.

'You know what, Dad? Fine. Let's talk about it. Let's talk about what you said to Mam all those years ago.'

Clio could see her father brace himself. He must have known this was coming. The minute Adam returned, and he'd asked them all to come back, he must have realised one of them would be brave enough to confront him.

Maybe he hadn't expected it from Clio. She hadn't expected it from herself.

But Frazer probably didn't realise how much she knew. She'd been young at the time. Kept out of the loop.

Well, that was then.

'You told Mam to accept Adam was dead,' Clio said. 'Over and over. Even though she was at her wits' end. But you were wrong. He was alive.'

'I didn't know that, though,' Frazer said, his voice a mixture of anger and regret. 'You have no idea how bad your mother got that year, Clio. She was at breaking point. She refused to give up.'

'You say it like that was a bad thing.'

'Your mother needed closure,' Frazer said. 'We all did. We couldn't search for Adam indefinitely. We had all of you to worry about. And we had to start living our own lives again. I don't feel guilt for that.'

'But you *lied*.'

There. It was out. There was no going back.

'You said you had proof,' Clio continued. 'The private investigator you hired had found evidence that Adam had been in London, and that he was dead. But now we know he wasn't even in England!'

'That's what my man told me, and I believed him. Why wouldn't I? Christ, lass, I've never been so glad to be wrong.'

'But it was too late for Mam. And you knew how delicate she was.'

Clio and Frazer stared at each other.

He blinked first. He knew she was right.

The vial of tablets, empty, by her mother's bedside.

But it had been the heart attack that did it. The coroner had confirmed it.

*He confirmed it*, Clio repeated to herself.

But there was no doubting how fragile her mother had become.

Kathleen had put all her hope in the private investigator finding Adam. And when Frazer told her what he'd discovered – the investigator's belief that Adam's was one of several bodies pulled out of a burned-down building in a part of London notorious for housing cheap immigrant workers – Kathleen refused to believe it.

Frazer believed it, though. He believed it immediately.

The investigator had done his research. The building had been deemed a fire hazard months previous and its residents were all Irish, Polish and other Eastern European labourers. Somebody resembling Adam had been known to be living there and a local building-site manager claimed he had an Irish lad on his books called Adam, who hadn't been back on site since the fire.

The blaze had spread so quickly and so efficiently, the Met police were still trying to identify the victims for months after. Even dental identifications were proving difficult.

Frazer told Kathleen over and over to accept the inevitable.

He made her believe it.

That's what Clio felt.

By the time they discovered the investigator, and Frazer, had jumped the gun, that Adam wasn't among the fire victims, Kathleen was dead.

'I'm sorry, lass.'

'For what?' Clio muttered.

'I thought you understood. I only did what I thought was right. I hoped your mother would grieve for Adam and just . . . move on. That's what you do, isn't it? When you've other children to think of. I'm ashamed to say it, but I wanted him to be one of the victims. Just to put an end to the torture of not knowing. To put an end to the misery your mother was in. I should have explained myself to you, I should have told you why I didn't wait until Adam was categorically confirmed dead before I told your mam. Why I gave up hope. I can see now how much it's been on your mind. I can see now why you went away.'

Clio scrunched her eyes closed.

She so badly wanted to believe that he'd had all their best interests at heart.

She so badly wanted to get through the rest of this conversation without vomiting all over him.

'Lass, it's all in the past. We can't go over and over it. It's not healthy. But I know we can't pretend it didn't happen, either. I'm not having a party to block out all the bad things. I'm having it to celebrate the good. Wait and you see, now. Ach, you'll be delighted when you see what I've put together.'

Clio nodded back, dumbly. Her father was already moving on, thinking about his own happy plans, blinkered to everyone and everything around him.

He left the kitchen then, and she was alone.

'*These violent delights have violent ends,*' she whispered to herself.

# AFTER

'Who smashed all the glasses on board tonight?'

Detective Downes was staring at her, waiting for an answer.

Clio shifted uncomfortably.

'Clio, did somebody smash those glasses on purpose or did James and Adam knock against the table?'

'I don't know.'

'You do know.'

'Kate. It was Kate.'

'Why?'

'I don't know. It was when the boys were fighting. She just lost it. Maybe she thought it would stop them or something. I'm tired, *Detective*. I don't know why anybody did anything tonight.'

'So, she's prone to losing it, is she? Fits of rage?'

'What? Jesus, don't be fucking stupid.'

'There's blood, Clio,' he said. 'Somebody hit Frazer. Somebody was angry. Maybe it was Kate. Didn't your father used to have some name for Kate? Some mean moniker. What was it?'

Clio closed her eyes.

Remembered.

*And the biggest slice of the cake is for our lovely Kate. Go on, Kate, lass, eat it up. Ach, it's nice to see a girl comfortable in her skin. Have another piece.*

Clio shuddered.

'We all have our moments. Kate wouldn't hurt anybody. Not physically.'

'Well, Clio, if you keep ruling everyone out, who will we rule in?'

'How about accepting it was a fucking accident?' Clio snapped.

Rob sighed.

'James attacked Adam. Hadn't he also fallen out with Ryan, earlier? What about Ryan and your father? They had quite a difficult relationship, didn't they?'

Clio stared at Rob.

He knew fucking well they did.

'I thought you wanted to know about James, not Ryan,' she said.

Rob smiled again.

She was falling into his trap. He was cornering her.

'Go on,' he said. 'Tell me about James.'

'There isn't anything to tell. You're all over the place. This is ridiculous, Rob. Kate, Ryan, James, all of us. We didn't do this. None of us would have. Are you trying to make a name for yourself or something? Is that it?'

'King Kong Kate,' Rob said.

Clio's eyes widened.

'What?'

'That's what your dad used to call your sister. You told me once. Not to her face. But you thought she'd overheard him, didn't you? You said, *Kate got skinny because of Frazer*. What an awful thing for a father to call his daughter.'

'I don't . . . I can't remember.'

'Is James broke?' Rob said. 'Did your father cause an argument about money tonight?'

And Clio felt a wave of nausea rise up inside her.

Rob wouldn't let this drop.

She'd known, hadn't she, when she ran into him in the village yesterday?

He was police.

What else had she expected?

# JAMES

James could have left with Sandra and Bella.

It might have been easier. Taken him away from his family and the feeling that the bomb could be dropped at any moment.

But it would have only liberated him in the short term.

He'd had another call from his chief financial officer that morning. She'd reiterated that the well had run dry. They'd contacted all their go-to funds, the ones who had come through in the past. Then they'd gone outside the normal channels and tried the people who'd refused them before, in the hope of, what? Nothing. It was still worth a try. They moved on to cold-calling venture funds, angel networks – James had to hand it to his CFO. She was innovative and persistent.

But she'd still come back empty-handed.

She'd spoken to a solicitor after their conversation the previous evening. James' house had been remortgaged at the start of the year so he could provide for his initial end of the deal. There was no more money to be generated there. James had inquired as to whether he could take a second mortgage out on Sandra's apartment, a vanity project she'd embarked on when she'd decided turning properties around for market could be her thing.

It wasn't her thing.

The solicitor had explained that, because the apartment was still technically in negative equity (Sandra had bought it at the height of the boom; the accountants were doubtful it would ever recoup what she'd spent), the bank wouldn't look at it. Plus, James' request that only his name be used on the papers if the bank came through, like they had on his house, had been laughed out of the room. Even if it had been his money Sandra had used to secure the loan for the apartment, it was in her name.

He was running out of options.

Which meant he had only one left, unless he wanted this project, and everything he'd sunk into it, to collapse. The writer alone had been paid almost twenty thousand for the show's treatment and drafts of the first two episodes, and the crew James had been slowly assembling had required sweeteners to bring them on board. James had let down this particular director before, on another show that had collapsed, thankfully off the radar. He'd had to pay him twenty thousand up front just to get him onside. And James had only done that because the French had demanded that particular director.

He was finished if this didn't come through. He'd owe money left, right and centre, with no way of earning any, and this time, he could end up losing his house as well.

Frazer was in his bedroom, holding up ties against his white shirt while he tried to decide which one to wear that evening.

'Dad, sorry,' James said, knocking on the open door lightly. 'Could I catch five minutes with you?'

Frazer glanced at James' reflection in the mirror, then nodded, before returning to the hanging ties and selecting a dark blue stripe.

'What's on your mind, James?' he said.

James sat on the edge of the bed and looked around the room. It was exactly as he remembered it. His father had never changed the furniture, despite the fact most of it had belonged to Kathleen's grandparents. Similar to the study, the almost black mahogany made this room the darkest in the house. Each piece was oppressively large, from the wardrobe Frazer stood at now, to the four-poster bed, to the chest of drawers under the windowsill, to the bedside tables and the purely ornamental writing desk. It always made James think of 1950s noir, the black and white movies of Hitchcock in particular.

James hated the room. No wonder his mother had moved back into her own, smaller room after she and Frazer had stopped sharing the marital bed.

'Will you give this place a bit of a spruce when Ana moves in?' James asked, not wanting to launch into his request immediately.

Frazer raised an eyebrow.

'What makes you think she'll move in here?' he said. Then, before James could respond, he added, 'And, anyhow, you cannot improve on quality. That's what this furniture is. This wardrobe, eh?'

Frazer ran his fingers along the decorative grooves on the front of the door.

'This was built and carved by hand by a local carpenter in the 1920s. Isn't it amazing, aye, what you can do with your hands? This is real work, son.'

James glanced out the window, at the shadows starting to form in the garden as the birch trees at the front cast their long silhouettes. A car passed on the road outside, headlights already on.

It was just what Frazer did.

*Real work.*

James had stopped letting the implicit digs bother him when he realised just how little his father had ever achieved with his own life. Managing somebody else's money was hardly a rod with which to beat others.

'You've been hovering all day,' Frazer said, eyeing James.

'I haven't been *hovering*. I just wanted to speak with you.'

'Is this a conversation we should have in my study?'

James clenched his jaw. Always, with the study. You on one side, Frazer on the other, a headmaster facing an errant child.

His anger must have showed because his father smiled.

'Ach, keep your panties on,' Frazer said. 'I'm winding you up. Go on, spill it out.'

James swallowed. Get it over with.

'I've a show rolling into production soon,' he said. 'It's going to be big. I've an Irish broadcaster on board and a French company have signed up. I'm thinking, we get it on terrestrial first, then pitch it wider. Make the big bucks. It's about . . .'

'Ah, you know I don't watch television, Jimmy.'

James dug his nails into his palms so hard they nearly bled. His father hadn't called him that in years. A pet name, Frazer used to say. Yet, there was a tone that said the derivative was not uttered with affection.

'No,' James said. 'But you understand finance.'

Frazer didn't reply.

James took a deep breath.

'The French company – they're really enthusiastic, but they can't put in as much money as we need to get the show up and running.'

'So,' Frazer said, cocking his head. 'You will have to increase your end. Not ideal, but if it's to be as successful as you say it will, it's a small gamble for a large payoff.'

'Yes,' James said, enthusiastically. 'That's exactly it. It's just, I'm not, eh, it's not possible at this time for me to raise more finance.'

Frazer turned, his face a picture of surprise.

'But you're doing well, lad,' he said. 'I read your interview with *The Times* recently. Profile of a successful producer. Money is hardly an issue, is it?'

James could feel his insides spasming, he was cringing so hard.

'No, of course not.' He'd prepared this earlier. He knew how to appeal to his father and it wasn't as a charity case.

'It's the aesthetics,' he said. 'If I'm fronting the majority of the cash, it looks like other partners aren't as interested, that the project is not a priority for them. Broadcasters get finicky about things like that. But if there are outside investors . . .'

'But I'm not *outside*,' Frazer said. 'That is what you're getting at, isn't it? You know my position on money, James. Your grandparents left you all handsomely provided for. How you all used it was up to you. But there is no more in the pot. Not from me.'

James felt anger course through him. This wasn't going how it had in his head.

'I was hoping to appeal to your business acumen,' he said, the words sounding right but knowing he was fighting a losing battle. 'You've managed the family portfolio for years; you know a good investment when you see it.'

'Yes,' Frazer said. 'I do.'

He looked back to the mirror and began to knot the tie.

James glared at the back of his father's head, unable to keep the resentment from revealing itself.

'The portfolio is for the whole family. Mam would have wanted—'

Frazer cut him off.

'You had enough of a leg-up in the world. If I kept bailing you out, you'd never learn responsibility. You're thirty-five, James. A grown man. You live and die on your own choices.'

James stood so fast, the blood rushed to his head. He'd spent most of his younger years feeling inadequate. When he'd walked away from his hit show, it was to go on to bigger and better things. Success had silenced the voice in his head, his father's voice, the one that said *you're only playing at being a big boy, they can all see through you.*

He'd got to the top, hadn't he? On his own merit. He'd done what he had to, to get there.

But, without another show, the doubts had crept back in. The fear.

And he was fucking sick of it.

'Responsibility?' James said. 'How hard did you have to work for what you have? What exactly did you do before you landed on your feet with our mother? A few years of being a bank clerk up in Dublin didn't get you this lifestyle.'

'I would stop and think, James, before you go any further,' Frazer said, not taking his eyes off the mirror or the tie he was straightening. 'The point of the family portfolio is that you all inherit after I'm gone. Be careful about saying or doing anything that would jeopardise that.'

He turned and looked at James.

'And let's be honest, your inability to maintain your own finances has caused enough heartache already, don't you think?'

'What's that supposed to mean?' James said, panicking.

'I think you know,' Frazer said, and this time, he met James' eye.

James blinked, rapidly, as his father stared at him.

No. No, he couldn't.

'We all have our crosses to bear, son,' Frazer said.

James felt dizzy. He closed his eyes as the room began to spin.

He lived every minute in fear of losing the money he'd already invested in this project.

It would end him, if his other debts came back to haunt him.

Frazer selected a blazer from the wardrobe and walked towards James, who was struggling to make his tongue or his legs work.

'Do me a favour and check this tie knot, will you? I can't get it right.'

James stood up, his knees like jelly. He started to fix the tie, his head not even in the room. He realised then how close his hands were to his father's neck.

His father's old, wrinkled neck.

James felt a surge of something rush through him.

If his father ever told anybody . . .

As quickly as the rage came over him, it was gone.

A moment of madness.

James straightened the tie at the back, refastening the gold pin. A sudden pain – the sharp end had stuck into his skin.

A bright red bubble of blood sat on the tip of his finger.

'Ach, come on,' Frazer said, not even noticing his son was in pain. 'Let me buy you a pint. Put your investment problems behind you for a night. I'm sure you will work it all out when you get back to Dublin, eh? You're a top producer, Jimmy. You'll get the *aesthetics* right. It's all about the spinning, isn't it?'

Frazer headed for the door, still smiling.

James stayed where he was for a moment, still unable to speak or move.

But then he followed his father, his head hanging, filled with the familiar shame.

# ADAM

The day had passed easily enough.

The visit to their mother's grave had been unpleasant, obviously, but at least Adam had managed to keep up his pretence.

It was, to his siblings' minds, the first time Adam had been at the cemetery since Kathleen's death.

But that wasn't the truth. He'd been there already, once. As soon as he found out. He'd needed to see it, to kneel at its foot and to beg her forgiveness for a sin he hadn't meant to commit.

He'd never wanted to hurt Kathleen. He'd done everything he could to prevent it. But it hadn't been enough.

Now, as he got ready to go to the Strand Bar, Adam knew he would have to keep his wits about him.

Stick to the bits that are true, he told himself.

He met Ellen on the landing. She was leaning against the bannister, looking down at the hall below. She didn't look happy.

'Don't do it; you're loved,' Adam quipped.

'Sorry? What?'

Ellen stared at him.

'Throw yourself over. I was joking.'

'Oh. I'm not sure *you* should be making suicide jokes.'

Adam inclined his head in submission. She had a point.

Ellen had seemed distracted all day. Maybe all week. For the life of him, Adam couldn't figure out what was going on in her head. But then, he never could.

Adam joined her and looked down. Frazer was draping a scarf around Ana's neck, arranging her hair gently on the silk.

'You look nice,' Adam said, turning back to Ellen.

She looked the same as always, to be fair. Her hair plaited, her face pale, wearing her uniform twinset cardigan and vest, a pale pink this evening. Quality, but far too old for her.

'I haven't looked nice in fucking years,' Ellen hissed, with such sharpness that Adam almost took a step back. Before he could reply, she spoke again.

'Is she what she seems?'

Ellen was peering down at Ana again.

Adam sighed.

'You should just talk to him,' he said. 'Ask if he's okay with you staying at home. It won't be Ana's choice.'

'*If* he's okay with me staying at home?' Ellen turned and faced Adam. 'It *is* my home. Do you know how much I've put into this place over the years? You know what he's like. He's good at watching money grow. He's good at splashing it when he wants to show off. He's not so good at using it for the *trivial* things. I've put most of my wages into this house.'

'I bet you've kept the receipts and all,' Adam said.

'What if I have?' she said. 'None of you helped. If he died and the house went six ways, nobody would repay me. It probably wouldn't be standing without me. There was subsidence, in the garden last year. It could have affected the foundations. I paid . . .'

'He's told you he'll leave you the house, hasn't he?' Adam said.

'There's still the portfolio,' Ellen said, defensively. 'It's not like any of you would lose out.'

'But do you think he'll keep his promise now he's getting married?' Adam said.

Ellen pursed her lips, her cheeks flushing red.

'Clio said she'd walk down; I'm waiting for her,' was all she said, when she eventually spoke again.

'I'll go with you. Let's get her.'

Adam held his arm out, pointing at the steps to Clio's landing, allowing Ellen to walk ahead.

Ellen knocked and opened their sister's door, then walked straight in, Adam on her heel.

'What?' Clio snapped.

As Adam rounded the door, he could see Clio in the corner of the room, kneeling.

Ellen was watching her, quizzically, and Clio's face was flushed.

'What if I'd been getting dressed!' Clio continued. She stood up, tucking her tee shirt into her skinny jeans, where it had come loose.

'Were you praying?' Adam asked, bemused.

He didn't think he was imagining it, though – the carpet in the corner of the room seemed to be uneven, like it had just been pulled up and then hastily thrown back down, and there'd been no time to flatten it. Ellen's thin lips and curious eyes intimated she'd spotted it too and was thinking the same thing.

'I'll be down in a minute,' Clio said.

Ellen's eyes flicked to the carpet again. Clio glanced at it quickly, then at Adam. Her eyes were beseeching, a look he remembered from when they were kids and their father had happened upon a fourteen-year-old Clio beside a small pile of cigarette butts out in the garden. Adam, twenty at the time, had assumed full responsibility.

If helping her like that would put him in her good books, he was more than eager to do it.

'Come on, Ellen,' he said. 'Let's go down and see if Frazer and Step-Mommy Dearest are walking, too. We can interrogate her.'

Ellen left the room reluctantly. Adam shut the door firmly behind her, but not before noticing Clio drop to her knees again in the corner of the room.

What was she up to?

# KATE

The Strand Bar was heaving, full of people that Kate was surprised to find she remembered.

She'd thought that would have made her feel uncomfortable. All of these people knew old Kate. *King Kong Kate.*

But nobody spoke to her in a way that said their recollections of her were in any way negative. Instead, she was being hugged and kissed and admired. Several people had told her she looked fantastic and quite a few seemed to know how successful she was up in Dublin.

She supposed everybody had changed over the years and her dramatic metamorphosis was viewed as an example of somebody who'd gone in the right direction.

Kate made her way to the bar, feeling calmer than she had since the previous night's catastrophe.

She had wound herself up so much about her past. It had never seemed to fit with her life in Dublin. Yes, she came from money, but it was only money as far as where she grew up was concerned. It wasn't money like Cheng's or the circles he moved in. In her head, everything about her early life had struck her as parochial and unsophisticated and now she was wondering if perhaps she had underestimated the weight it carried.

The people of Spanish Cove and Albertstown were good folk.

And, when she really thought about it, she should probably feel more of the pride her father was always espousing. Cheng's family might be wealthy, but the Grants didn't come from the same renowned stock as Kate.

Why on earth did she feel so ashamed?

She needed more front, that was it. She had to stop seeing the negatives and concentrate on the positives.

Cheng hadn't answered any of her calls today. When she did eventually speak to him, Kate vowed to remember the way she felt right now about her family and her background. It might be a starting point for Cheng forgiving her. It might be the start of Kate forgiving herself.

Buoyed by a sudden sense of serenity, Kate found a gap at the counter and smiled widely, catching the attention of the server.

The woman, who seemed familiar though Kate couldn't put a name to her, approached.

'Do you sell champagne by the glass?' Kate asked.

The bar woman shook her head, but pointed to the fridge behind her.

'I can do prosecco by the glass or champagne by the bottle.'

Kate glanced over her shoulder at the crowd gathered in the corner of the bar. Several villagers surrounded the family and Frazer was buying drinks for anybody who came up to congratulate him on his engagement.

'Quite a celebration you have going on there, Kate,' the woman said.

Kate frowned, still scanning her memory for a name.

'Eva,' the bar woman said. 'I was more in Adam's . . . your brother's gang.'

She flushed bright red when she said it.

'Ah,' Kate said, her memory returning. 'The owner's daughter.'

Eva smiled. She was still pretty, Kate noticed, prettier perhaps than Kate remembered her, when Eva worked in the bar as a teenager, slightly more awkward and a little shy.

Had she and Adam been an item?

She wore a wedding band now, anyway. Adam had missed his chance with her. Like he had with all of them.

'I hear you're in the business yourself,' Eva said. A customer behind Kate harrumphed loudly but Eva seemed content to ignore him. 'Sorry – prosecco, Kate?'

'No,' Kate said. 'A bottle of Moët. Like you say, it's a celebration.'

Eva smiled and reached for one of the cooler buckets, before taking the champagne from the fridge.

Kate looked around her while she waited. When she'd started drinking in the Strand, it had been what you'd describe as an archetypal rural Irish pub. Dark wood furnishings, ruby red upholstery, Beamish beer mats, a menu consisting of roast of the day and fish for the vegetarians. Leaving the outside world and venturing in meant having to adjust to an almost complete lack of light, a condition barely troubled by the low-hanging, dust-covered, light-shaded bulbs.

The place had been completely overhauled in a nautical theme. The dark panels had been replaced with distressed, reclaimed planks, painted in a light blue. Ships' wheels were mounted on the walls; here and there an open-mouthed stuffed trout peered out from inside a glass box.

The tables were still oak but the chairs had been reupholstered in a blue to match the walls.

The menu now sang of the sea and each dish was accompanied with the previously strange and wonderful. Puréed celeriac. Beds of samphire. Sautéed sorrel.

It was adorable.

'Yes, my husband and I run a hotel,' she said, speaking louder over the rising bar chatter, when Eva came back to the counter.

'Not just any hotel,' Eva said, the admiration obvious.

Kate smiled.

'You want me to pop this for you?' Eva asked. 'Or will I have it brought to your table?'

'Pop it,' Kate said. She'd felt queasy earlier, but it had all but vanished and she was on form for a glass. And something to eat. 'Do you serve food, by the way?'

'Jesus!' the customer behind her cried. 'I just want a pint of Guinness!'

'It's on for you, Frank,' Eva called back, without even looking at him. She nodded at one of the other servers, who promptly placed a pint glass under the Guinness tap.

Kate watched as Eva popped the cork, then placed a sparkling clean flute on the counter. Eva began to pour, then looked up to say something to Kate. The words died on her lips as her eyes widened in shock.

Kate sensed rather than saw the door to the bar open and the crowd part. She turned, along with everybody else, to see what the fuss was.

Adam walked in. He'd stopped outside for a cigarette so he was behind the rest of his family. Kate gave him a pitying glance. The locals had heard he was back but this was clearly his first time down in the village proper and they couldn't hide their shock at seeing him in the flesh. She felt momentarily sorry for him.

Then she realised Adam was looking at her.

No, not at her.

He was looking at Eva.

Kate turned around. Eva was still pouring the champagne, her hand frozen mid-air; the liquid was now spilling over the rim of the glass and dribbling onto the counter.

'Hey!' Kate said.

Eva snapped back to attention. She looked down at the mess, appalled.

At the same time, conversations resumed, the crowd closed in again and Kate knew Adam was moving towards their family. She could hear the words of greeting to him and the whispers once he'd passed through each group.

'I'm so sorry,' Eva said. 'I'll get you a fresh bottle.'

'Don't worry about it.' The woman looked like she was about to cry. 'It's just a drop.'

Christ. Perhaps Adam and this woman had been really serious. Kate had had no idea.

Eva mopped up the puddle with napkins, still muttering about a replacement bottle.

'I'm sorry,' Eva said.

'It's nothing,' Kate responded, dismissively. 'Don't worry about it. No use crying over spilled champagne.'

She laughed, lightly, still enjoying her good mood.

'No,' Eva said. 'I'm *sorry*.'

Kate looked down. The other woman had taken hold of her forearm. She squeezed it gently.

Kate looked at Eva, puzzled. The other woman was gazing at her intensely; she seemed to be willing Kate to understand something.

Kate shook her head, confused. Then Eva let go. She turned to one of the other servers and said something, then walked to the other end of the bar. Kate watched her lift the countertop, then slip out the door that led to the back and the owner's quarters.

# ELLEN

Wine wasn't enough, tonight.

'What can I get you?' the barman asked, harried, tired. The woman serving with him had upped and disappeared and now it was him and some barely legal teenager working the bar.

'Whiskey,' she said.

'What?'

'Whiskey.'

'I can't hear you, love, you have to speak higher than a whisper.'

'For Christ's sake, I said whiskey,' Ellen barked.

She didn't turn around; she knew they'd all heard her.

So what.

'Jameson's, Johnnie Walker, Midleton . . . ?'

'Just . . . !'

The barman stepped back, a mask of customer service descending on his face, shutting down any more remarks his end.

He selected a glass but instead of filling it from the optic, he placed it on the counter. He reached for a bottle from underneath the bar and unscrewed the cap.

Ellen watched as he poured it into the glass, him watching her back, waiting for the nod.

She let him fill it well past its second measure, almost to its third, before nodding curtly.

'Thank you,' she said. 'I'm sorry.'

He nodded.

Ellen took a large gulp before she turned around and faced the rest of her family, who were all pretending there was nothing to see. Except her father, who was staring at her with narrowed eyes, as his fiancée sat unknowing beside him, engaged in meaningless small talk with Adam.

Ellen grabbed the barman's hand when he passed her her change.

'The woman with us,' she said. 'Do you know her?'

The barman didn't even ask who she meant.

'Ana, sure,' he said. 'Has a bakery in Wexford town. She's been in here a couple of times with your father.'

'Bakery?' Ellen blinked rapidly. What type of store had that news article mentioned? Jesus, why hadn't she remembered to read it?

Because she couldn't stop thinking about thirteen years ago. That was why.

Her head was a mess.

'Ellen!'

Frazer's voice carried over from the table.

She thanked the barman and returned to her seat.

Ryan was talking to Ana now, but the whole table was listening, as he told her about his writing attempts and how long he'd been living in Italy.

'Is it like travel-blogging?' Adam asked him.

'In a manner. It's personal accounts, what it's like for an expat, recovering from addictions, healing yourself through new experiences, blah de fucking blah. I'm trying to make it humorous but knowing me, it will read like *The Road* meets *War and Peace*.'

'You wish,' James retorted.

'You're very funny, Ryan,' Clio said. 'Even intentionally, sometimes.'

Ryan smirked. Ellen could see he was embarrassed at having to talk about himself when they could all hear that it meant a lot to him.

'It sounds like an addiction diary,' Frazer said. 'I'm not being smart, son, but do you really think you can earn money out of that? Aren't those diaries supposed to be tools to help you cope in the real world, eh?'

Nobody responded at first.

'Frazer,' Ana said. 'If it helps your son, it is a good thing, no?'

Ellen looked at her, surprised. The others, too, were taken aback. Her father smiled at his fiancée.

'Of course it is,' he said, patting her hand where she'd placed it on his arm. 'Ignore me. Sometimes I open my mouth and hear my own father. He was a tough old boot. Whatever's right for you, eh, Ryan?'

Ana beamed at him.

Ellen could practically feel her brothers and sisters starting to warm to the woman.

She raised an eyebrow and took another sip, willing the alcohol to work quicker.

'Whiskey, Ellen,' her father spoke again. 'You're not drowning your sorrows, I hope?'

'Why would I be drowning my sorrows?' she said.

'No reason,' Frazer answered, innocently. 'I'm only asking out of concern. It's a while since you drank properly, from what I recall.'

'Yes, well, we're all having an interesting weekend,' Kate said, and Ellen felt a surge of affection towards her.

'I'm just enjoying not being the epicentre of local gossip, for once,' Ryan said. 'Fair play, Adam.'

'Who cares what people talk about?' Clio scoffed. 'It's what they don't talk about that's always bothered me. You'll get used to it, Ana, small village life. Where an affair is the talk of the town but nobody wants to talk about the man who's beating the crap out of his wife or the daughter who slit her wrists. The shit that goes on here would make a capital city blush.'

'There isn't that much going on,' James said, scornfully.

'Bollocks,' Clio said. 'Teenagers growing up round here have fuck all to do. You know that. That's why they get up to no good. It's why we did, anyway. Half the women in here were pregnant in their teens.'

'Aye, well, I'll not let it be said there isn't always a place in my home for someone who's got into trouble,' Frazer said.

Ana smiled approvingly and Frazer beamed in return, ignoring the incredulous faces of his children.

'*Your* home,' Ellen interrupted, staring straight at her father. She couldn't help it. She didn't know if it was the whiskey or just the sheer stress of the last few days, but more likely it was what Clio had said and her father's response.

Today, of all days.

'Excuse me?' Frazer said.

'You said, "your" home,' Ellen repeated. 'You said, there's always a place in *my* home.'

'Yes?'

'Surely it's *our* home.'

Frazer narrowed his eyes. Ellen could feel everybody around the table will her to stop but she just couldn't.

'Well, clearly, it's the Lattimer family home,' he said. 'But it is *my* house.'

'You said . . .'

Ellen had barely got the words out of her mouth before her father raised his hand to quieten her.

'Not this again, Ellen,' he said, impatience oozing through his smile. 'Aye, you're thirty-nine now, lass. Nobody's going to blame you for wanting to fly the nest.'

Frazer laughed.

'You have this in Poland, Ana?' he said. 'Some of my kids I never see. Some of them love me so much, they won't leave.'

'Our children stay at home sometimes, Frazer,' Ana said, nervously. 'They mind their parents. It is a good thing.'

'*If* their parents need minding,' James said.

Ellen put down the empty glass.

'You know what today is,' she said, looking her father directly in the eye.

Frazer made a puzzled face, jutting his lower lip out like he had no clue.

'Sunday?' He smiled.

'You know,' Ellen said. 'Thirteen years.'

Her father's face filled with confusion, then, slowly, recognition. And then he looked ashamed.

Kate clasped a hand over her mouth. The boys stared down at the table, embarrassed, shamefaced.

'What day is it?' Clio asked. Nobody answered Clio and she glared at them all.

Blood rushed to Ellen's face. Her hair, plaited and hanging down her front as it always did, suddenly felt heavy and hot against her chest and neck. Her cardigan was choking her.

'I need air,' she said.

Then she stood up and walked out of the bar, knowing that now, for sure, everybody was looking at her.

# AFTER

'Do you want to tell me why you stormed out of the Strand Bar yesterday evening, Ellen?' the detective asked.

'Who told you . . . did you see that?'

Ellen shook her head. She'd lay a bet he'd been there. Everybody would be talking about Crazy Ellen, running out of the pub like the madwoman she was.

It was too much. It was all too much.

She didn't hear the detective's long, frustrated sigh. She didn't see the way he was looking at her – concern, mixed with suspicion.

Ellen placed her hands on either side of her head.

She was losing it again.

She'd already lost it.

'You see, it's obvious this weekend was stirring up a lot of feelings that you and your siblings would prefer to have kept buried,' he said. 'All I'm asking is, do you think it's plausible, with all these emotions running high, that somebody snapped tonight? Maybe not even intentionally? Alcohol had been consumed, you're in the middle of nowhere, Frazer upset all of you . . .'

'Yes!'

Ellen cried the word.

'Yes, what?'

'Yes, I wanted to bloody kill him. Yes, yes, yes.'

She stood up, her whole body shaking. The detective's eyes widened.

'I've wanted to kill him ever since . . .' she said, 'ever since he did what he did to me.'

Then she slumped back down on the chair and started to sob, with all the pent-up sadness and anger she'd felt for so long.

It felt like a relief and something breaking at the same time.

# CLIO

Clio leaned over the sink in the bar's bathroom and splashed her face with cold water.

After Ellen's abrupt departure, her father had seemed contrite, apologetic.

Clio didn't know if it was genuine or an act for Ana.

He'd ordered more wine for the table and Kate had arranged snacks, but nobody would tell Clio what had just happened and her stomach had seized up.

She looked at herself in the mirror. Her face gaunt, pale, black rings under her eyes. This place was draining her. Even more than New York had in the last couple of years. If that was possible.

'Can't live with them, can't fucking kill them,' she told her reflection.

Of all people, Rob Downes was in the corridor outside. He looked at her, curiously.

'I didn't know you were here,' she said.

'It's my local when I'm home with the folks,' he said.

'Oh, right. Yeah.'

'Saw you come in,' he said. 'Thought you were taking a while.

I wondered if I was supposed to follow you. Become a member of the Mile High Club or whatever the hell the pub equivalent is. The sticky yard? The drunk kilometre?'

He smiled and winked.

She shook her head, an eyebrow raised.

'Well, I didn't see *you,* and the fella I was expecting to follow me didn't get the message, so I suppose I'll just head back.'

'You absolutely sure about that?'

He came closer and she smelled his aftershave again. She was almost tempted.

'You complete me,' he said, in a mock American accent.

'What are you going to do, fucking eat me?' Clio snorted.

Rob laughed.

'It gets lonely 'round here, after dark,' he said.

'There's always Netflix,' she said.

And now he was bringing his face close to hers.

'Nice try.' Clio smiled and slipped past him, not as easy as it sounded in the narrow corridor.

'I'll never stop trying,' he called out as she opened the door.

'I'm sure there's a law that forbids that.'

'I am the law.'

Clio let the door swing shut behind her.

When they arrived home, instead of going straight to her room, Clio followed Ryan into his, Teddy at her heel.

'Clio, I'm tired,' he said.

She sat on his bed, throwing her legs up and resting her back against the headboard. The dog tried and failed to climb up beside her. She ended up pulling him on, awkwardly, grabbing his paws and under his belly. She was starting to worry he had arthritis. Wasn't that a big thing with dogs?

'I'm tired of not knowing what's going on,' Clio said. 'Fix that for me, will you? I thought you and I didn't have secrets from each other any more. I know the rest of them are . . . what's the word I'm looking for? Fuckers. But, us, Ryan?'

'We all have secrets, Clio. I bet you have things you don't want to tell me about New York.'

Clio felt her jaw clench.

'See,' Ryan said, nodding slowly. 'By the way, if that fleabag moults all over my bed, you can change the sheets.'

'He doesn't have fleas. Do you, boy? And I bet he's not the first dog you've lain with.'

'How very feminist of you.'

'You pronounced misanthropic wrong.'

Ryan kicked off his shoes and sat on the rug, legs crossed like he was about to meditate.

Clio looked down at his feet. Ryan had never worn socks in all her memory of him. Which meant, bereft of shoes, you were really aware of the little scars that lined the inside of his toes. Track marks. She'd have thought he'd try to hide them, but no. Ryan didn't bother.

'What did Dad do to Ellen?' she said.

'You really don't remember any of this?'

Clio shook her head.

'I suppose that makes sense,' Ryan said.

He started to count on his fingers.

'What are you doing? Will you just tell me?' Clio was exasperated now.

'I'm trying to remember when it happened. Thirteen years ago. I was about fifteen at the time so you must have been twelve, yeah?'

'I'm three years younger than you, Ryan, it's not rocket science.'

'I'm surprised you don't remember it at all, if you were twelve. Do you remember when Ellen wasn't living here?'

Clio scrunched up her face and reached back into her memories.

She'd been pissed off that year because she'd discovered her best friend at the time would be going to a different secondary school, one in Wexford town, while Clio was going nearby, to New Ross. It had seemed like the end of the world.

She'd some recollections of Christmas and Hallowe'en, because her mam always threw big parties.

Her strongest memory, though, was the time she'd gone paddling by the shore and her first period had started. Her mother had tried not to laugh when Clio told her of her fear she'd be attacked by a shark when the pains started and she saw blood on the insides of her legs.

She couldn't remember Ellen not being there, but, then, she barely interacted with Ellen when she was there. The age gap was too large.

'Was she away working or something?' Clio said.

'Yeah, that's what they said. That she'd gotten a job and moved away. She'd moved out, that was true. No job.'

Clio cocked her head, interested.

'Ellen had got her inheritance a few years before,' Ryan continued. 'And she was *wild*.'

'Ellen, wild? Twinset Ellen? Are you pulling my leg?'

'No.' Ryan smiled. 'Demon for the sneaky drink, she was. I'm surprised she didn't come up in my counselling sessions. Bad role model. Fierce pretty, too, and not afraid to show it.'

'I think Ellen's been body-snatched,' Clio said.

'You and her could have been twins,' Ryan continued. 'She'd a tongue on her that could slice you in half. I adored her. It was all fucking stamped out of her, though.'

He paused.

'Clio, are you sure you want to know this? We don't talk about this shit. We all have enough reasons of our own to hate him.'

Clio gritted her teeth.

'Tell me,' she said.

# AFTER

'Where did Ellen go?' Ryan asked, sitting down again at the small table. 'She never came back into the room.'

'One of the medics is seeing to her,' the detective told him. 'She got quite distressed. But she'd started telling me about what your father did, all those years ago.'

'Yeah, well,' Ryan said.

He looked across at the detective, then realised something.

'You don't know what happened, do you?' Ryan asked.

'Remind me.'

Ryan sat back.

'You don't,' he said. 'Ha.'

'What?'

'Nothing,' Ryan said. 'It's just, you're around my age, yeah? Ten years younger than Ellen or something, right? She'd be amazed if she realised that in actual fact, not everybody knows her past. None of us talk about it, you know. It was a promise we made her.'

'In the circumstances . . .'

Ryan hesitated. If he told the detective, the man would think it incriminated Ellen.

But there was little point in trying to keep it secret. And anyway, Ellen had nothing to do with Frazer's death. Ryan knew that. His sister wouldn't harm a fly.

'When Ellen was about twenty-five or so, she met some bloke,' Ryan said. 'He was from Wexford town. Ellen ran away with him. He bowled her over. Nobody knew what she saw in him. He was a total fuckwit. Been with half the county and, if you asked me, he had a head that looked like he shot out of the womb and landed face first on the hospital tiles. But, love is blind, and all that.'

'Why did she run away?' the detective asked. 'She was a grown woman. It wasn't the fifties; who cared who she was with?'

'He was married.'

'Ah. The gossips must have had a party.'

'They went to London,' Ryan said. 'You know what it's like around here. Talk of the town, she was. Frazer was, well . . . you know. Apoplectic.'

'Was he that moral?' the detective asked.

'It wasn't her morals he was worried about. It was her money. This bloke didn't cart her off for love. He took her on an extended holiday to burn through fifty grand. Everybody knew it. Everybody bar Ellen. Then the arsehole returned home, without her. So our dad went over to get her.'

'Was she too ashamed to come back?'

'Christ, no,' Ryan said, scornful. 'She didn't want to come back. Come back to be told *I told you so*? Dad arrived and found her in this bedsit, but she refused to go anywhere with him. She planted herself on her bed, took out a bottle of whiskey – so he told my mother, anyway – and proceeded to get pissed in front of him. So, being Dad, he locked her in.'

'He locked her in her own home?' the detective repeated, appalled and intrigued in equal measure.

'He told her he was drying her out. He did the same with me once, years later, except I probably needed it. Ellen was just having a good time. She didn't have a problem, per se, bar being a bit heart-broken and definitely unruly. But he left her there anyway, went back to his hotel, came back the following morning and sat on the steps outside the bedsit, telling her he'd bring her home when she was ready to behave herself.'

'So, she went with him in the end,' the detective said.

Ryan tugged at his lower lip, frowning.

'He left her there the whole day,' he said. 'Even when Ellen started to cry and told him she didn't feel well. Long after that.'

Ryan took a deep breath.

'Even when she started screaming in pain.'

The detective sat perfectly still, all ears.

'Ellen didn't know she was pregnant. But she knew there was something wrong. Eventually, Dad called the ambulance – and it wasn't even his choice, really. One of the other bedsit renters – and this wasn't the type of place where people asked questions – she came upstairs and read him the riot act. Frazer was embarrassed into it. Anyway, when the medics came, Ellen was nearly dead. She'd had an ectopic pregnancy. And it had burst.'

Detective Downes' eyes widened.

'It ended up, there was so much damage and bleeding they had to perform a hysterectomy,' Ryan said. 'Ellen was traumatised. She ended up in a . . . well, she needed help. She was there for months. When she came home to Spanish Cove, she stayed home.'

Ryan shrugged, sadly. Then he shook his head.

'That does not mean she attacked Frazer tonight,' he said. 'Ellen has lived in that house for the last twelve years and never had so much as a cross word with Frazer.'

'Anybody can snap,' the detective said.

Ryan sat forward.

'Frazer has done worse,' he said. 'If you're looking for suspects, Detective, you can land on any of us. But both Ellen and I know what our dad did to us. It's the ones pretending there was nothing wrong with their relationship with him – they're the ones I'd say were most likely to beat the shit out of him.'

# KATE

She wouldn't have heard them if she hadn't sneaked down to the kitchen to stuff herself with food from the fridge.

She couldn't sleep. The happiness she'd felt earlier had been fleeting. She'd too much on her mind.

Worry, about Cheng.

Guilt, that she'd forgotten a date that meant so much to Ellen.

Panic, that she was losing control over everything.

She wasn't even hungry.

She'd eaten plenty at the pub. She didn't know the psychology behind it, just that there was something about triangular-cut sandwiches that meant you were entitled to eat more than four, or what would constitute a normal-sized sandwich.

She'd had at least ten triangular sandwiches.

And seeing as Kate avowedly avoided all bread products generally, she'd already crossed the Rubicon for the evening.

She was helping herself to cheese and cured meats from the double-door Smeg when her ears picked up the soft murmur of voices in the garden.

Kate walked over to the window just to look out and make sure it wasn't an intruder, though that would be rare enough in this part of the world.

She saw her father and Ana on the swing chair. Frazer was frowning; Ana, too, looked worried and uncomfortable.

Kate leaned closer to the open window and picked up Ana's voice more clearly.

'We have made the promise to each other, Frazer. No secrets.'

'We also promised we wouldn't be involved in each other's business or families, Ana. Ach, the children are grown now. They stopped being my responsibility a long time ago and they were quick to let me know it. They can't just change their minds and start looking for Daddy to sort out everything.'

'I do not want the bad mark on our future before it has even begun. I have enough to worry about. It is not too late to change your mind.'

'I've told you. I trust you. Implicitly.'

Kate frowned. What did her father trust Ana with?

'It is not about trust. It is about putting your family first.'

Ana's voice was harsh and she was glaring at Frazer. Kate raised an eyebrow.

The empire was safe from Darth Vader. Princess Leia had this.

'You are my family, Ana.'

Frazer placed his hand on Ana's knee, trying to placate her. It didn't work. Ana crossed her arms, still aggrieved.

At that moment, Kate felt her phone buzz in the pocket of her dressing gown. She'd been carrying it around, hoping Cheng would ring or text. She'd tried him a couple of times since coming back from the pub and on each occasion, it had gone to voicemail.

She pulled it out and answered it, moving swiftly away from the window and leaving the kitchen.

'You're still up,' Cheng said. 'I was afraid I'd wake you.'

'I'm so glad you rang,' she answered and she was. She could feel her whole body flood with gratitude. She could cope with anything as long as she had Cheng on her side. Anything.

'I didn't want to go to sleep without talking to you,' he said.

'Me neither,' she said. 'Oh, Cheng, I'm so sorry. You know I love you more than anything. I can't bear the thought of you being angry with me. It's all a big mess. But, you know, it's actually going okay down here. We're sorting out some things. I promise, in the future, it will be different. No more lies. You will be as much a part of my family as I am of yours. If you want to be.'

'Kate.' Sharper now. He was still annoyed with her. Kate squeezed her eyes shut and racked her brains. What more could she do? What could she say?

'I was putting my things away in the wardrobe,' he said. 'And I know how tidy you are so I wanted to sort out the stuff you'd taken out but decided not to pack.'

She was at the top of the stairs now. She opened the door to her room, still listening, puzzled.

'I found them, Kate,' he said.

'Found what?'

'I . . . maybe I was looking. Yes, if I am honest, maybe I was trying to see if there was anything else you were keeping from me.'

Kate felt the blood in her veins run cold and a strange, fluttering sensation take hold in her stomach.

'You're taking diet pills, Kate? I actually had to look up what they were. For a moment, I thought they were contraceptives and, even at that, I was freaking out. But diet pills? Why? I don't understand. You work out, all the time. You watch what you eat. You're so . . . driven.'

'I'm not taking them,' she said, impulsively. 'They're old. I had some weight problems when I was younger. Hormones. But now I . . .'

There was a deathly silence on the other end of the phone. Kate was holding her mobile so hard, her hand started to sweat.

'There's a receipt in the box, Kate. You bought them before you left for Spanish Cove. And I'm guessing forgot to pack them.'

Fuck. And fuck.

'And I found your prescription. Valium?'

Kate sat down on her bed. She leaned forward, feeling like she might be sick.

'You'd no right to go through my things,' she said.

'You're keeping all these secrets . . .'

Something snapped in Kate.

She knew it wasn't in context.

She wasn't angry at Cheng. She was angry at herself. She was angry at her father. At Adam. At . . . all of them.

But Cheng was the one on the phone. He was the one judging. And she'd had enough.

It was the problem with being Frazer Lattimer's daughter. You walked an odd line where you were simultaneously better than everybody else while also feeling like you were never good enough.

She wouldn't let her own husband make her feel like that.

'Oh, for God's sake,' she said. 'Don't we all have bloody secrets, Cheng? I'm stressed! I'm stressed and when I get like this, I eat. And when I eat, I can't stop eating. That's how I'm built. And this life you and I have, where we're perfect and the hotel is perfect and everything is so bloody perfect, there's no room for me to be the size of a small bloody planet. So I take the pills and then I get mood swings and feel depressed and I take the other pills and . . . I can't be King Kong again! It's my business, not yours; can you just back off and stop going through my things!'

There was silence. Then a sharp intake of breath from Cheng.

'Fuck, Kate, I'm not proud I went through your things but that was just a drawer in your wardrobe. What's in the attic? Do you have more I don't know about? A lover? Valium, Kate. Didn't you say your mother practically . . .'

Kate laughed loudly, and it sounded like sheer desperation.

Cheng fell silent, evidently astonished.

'Oh, Cheng,' she said. 'Go to hell.'

She hung up. Then she flung the phone on the floor.

And reached into her pocket and took out the block of cheese she'd spirited in there.

She was munching on it when she heard footsteps outside her door on the landing.

She crossed the room and opened the door, but it was only James, heading towards his own room.

Kate was about to go back into her own when she paused.

'James,' she said, sharply.

Her brother stopped and turned.

'Did you tell Dad that I'd lied to Cheng?'

She could see, then, why James had gone into the production side of his business and not acting.

His face flushed bright red even as he uttered the lie.

'No,' he said. 'Of course not.'

Kate nodded, but she kept staring at him. James muttered something that sounded like goodnight, and went into his own room.

Kate returned to her bed, and picked up the cheese again.

Her father had known. He'd known.

Her marriage was falling apart and she was losing her bloody mind and it was all Frazer's fault.

She could kill him.

# AFTER

One a.m.

Over three hours since the detective had started questioning them all.

Over four hours since Danny had tried to breathe life back into Frazer's body.

It hadn't worked. Frazer was dead before he went into that water. Danny knew it, from the moment he'd seen the blood on the deck.

He'd still tried, though.

Danny watched Rob Downes writing frantically in his little pad as something occurred to him. Then he looked up at Danny and back down again.

'How long was Frazer seeing Ana?' he asked.

'A few months,' Danny said.

'But none of his children knew?'

'No.'

'Not even Ellen?'

'No.'

'You seem sure?'

'I am sure. Frazer told me. He wanted to keep it to himself.'

'So Frazer confided in you alone?'

Danny swallowed the lump in his throat.

'We were friends longer than I can remember. But, he had his moments, Frazer. I'm not going to lie – he wasn't always the best father. Though he tried, you had to give him that. And what do I know? I've no children. I don't know how hard it is.'

'Right.' The detective nodded.

Danny watched the other man think carefully about his next question.

'Adam and Ryan say Ana was below deck with them between 8 p.m. and 8.30 p.m.'

Danny shrugged.

'I didn't see her,' he said.

'Hmm. Do you know what happened to her previous husband?'

'Died,' Danny answered.

'Yes. But do you know how?'

Danny shook his head.

'He was attacked,' Rob said. 'Sustained injuries to the brain. He died from a head trauma.'

Danny frowned.

'Do you think Ana had something to do with this?' Danny asked.

'Do you?'

Danny swallowed again.

Maybe, just maybe, Danny would agree to tell the detective what he'd seen.

He didn't want to.

But it didn't look like he'd have much choice.

# RYAN

The bank holiday Monday had started wet. When Ryan came out of the shower that morning, he sat on his bed listening to the rain lashing against the window and the larger drops falling as they collected in the gutter that ran under the eaves.

Perhaps they wouldn't be able to have the party that evening.

But as the hours drifted on, the dark clouds cleared, and by early afternoon the sun put in an appearance, its rays making the puddles on the side of the road shimmer and the remaining drops on the grass blades glisten.

By the time the three brothers drove down to the yacht, boxes of bottles and glasses in the boot of James' car, they were all in tee shirts.

Ryan could only remember one other time they'd all been together in a car like this – many years previous, when James had started working in Dublin.

James had suggested a boys' blowout in a top nightclub in the capital. He rarely gave his family the time of day, except when he wanted to show them how well he was doing. But Adam and Ryan didn't second-guess his motivation on this occasion.

James knew actual celebrities and how to get into those places, even if Ryan was underage at the time.

Adam had been a little more reluctant. He was always quiet, Adam, much more of a thinker than a talker. And he had his head down in college; he was determined to do well in his second-year exams.

But he agreed to go along for Ryan's sake, who was positively fizzing at the thought of mixing with the great and the good. Nobody knew it, but he was already dabbling at that stage and he spent most of that night in the club toilets with a blonde and several lines of cocaine.

Ryan had realised early on that any inhibitions he had around women faded when he was high and, surprise, surprise, he was at his most entertaining when he was off his face.

It had been one of the last good nights. By the middle of that year, Ryan was using regularly.

Just over twelve months later, he'd have his first overdose. But that was all to come. And by then, Adam would already be gone.

Ryan felt no ill will towards Adam.

He did hate himself.

But, more than anybody, he despised Frazer.

It had cost thousands in therapy to be able to say that. Therapy, ironically, that his father had paid for.

The counselling had been professional enough to make Ryan understand that he too bore responsibility. They'd all grown up under Frazer's roof and only Ryan had become a drug addict.

Ryan had a propensity for addiction. He found it easier to live in the imaginary space he created for himself, and the longer he was there, the more crippled his emotions became. So he went further. It was a cycle.

But it began with Frazer.

You could make excuses for the man. Say that he had a tough childhood himself – and he had. Frazer's father had been, by all accounts, a cold, unpleasant sort. Embittered. An Irish man, he'd joined the British army and fought on multiple occasions, bravely. But when he returned to Ireland he'd been snubbed by his wider family and neighbours, who still bore the scars of the British colonial administration in Ireland. And when he then moved to Glasgow, he was snubbed for being Irish. Neither fish nor fowl.

So Frazer had grown up in a home filled with anger. But as an adult, things had worked out handsomely for him: he'd met Kathleen, the only daughter of one of the wealthiest and most-renowned families in South Wexford. A woman who was as soft and gentle as he was hard and unyielding.

Ryan knew Frazer loved their mother. But she didn't have the effect on him she might have had on another man. She tamed him, but she didn't control him.

It was still Frazer who ruled the roost, even if it was Kathleen's ancestral home they lived in and Kathleen's money they lived off.

Of all the children – and Ryan could never figure this out – Frazer disliked his youngest son most. Perhaps Frazer saw something of himself in Ryan, or he reminded him too much of somebody. Whatever it was, Ryan bore the brunt of his father's bad tempers and aggression.

Clio, though the youngest, had once made the most insightful analysis, and it had stayed with Ryan.

*You won't let him win and you won't go down,* she'd said. *Words slide off your back, so he uses his fists. But when he hits you, you stay standing. And you weigh nothing, so that's pure fucking hatred keeping you up.*

'Will you go back up to Dublin tomorrow?' Adam asked James.
Ryan brought himself back to the conversation in the car, his
mental meanderings put aside for now.

James was tense, Ryan could see it in his shoulders.

'Yeah, sure,' James said. 'I've enjoyed the few days off, despite
the . . . eh, circumstances. But it's all go up there, you know. Gotta
keep hustling. What about you in Paris? You kept on your toes?'

'More or less. I've got a large development underway at the
moment. A social housing project on the outskirts. The authorities
are trying to move away from the ghetto feel, get it right for the
working class and the new migrants. This time.'

'Speaking of migrants,' James said. He eyed Ryan in the rearview
mirror, then glanced at Adam, casually, like he hadn't been leading
up to this. 'It's killing me, the curiosity. Whose passport did you
use to get to Paris? Do you have a completely different identity
over there? Or did you pay somebody for a new one? I mean, that
would cost a few bob, wouldn't it?'

'I have my own passport.'

James frowned.

'I applied for a new one with the embassy,' Adam said. 'I just
said the last one was lost.'

'With what documents?'

Ryan could see Adam's jaw clench. He didn't like being asked
about his life in such detail.

'I had my birth certificate.'

'Did you?' James looked up at the mirror again, met Ryan's eyes.
Ryan, too, was interested to hear where Adam was going with this
one.

'You didn't take it from the house,' James said. 'Dad looked.'

Adam turned and looked out the window again.

'I ordered one online. You can do that, now.'

'Hmm.'

James looked back at the road, clearly not satisfied.

'If you don't mind me saying, James,' Adam said, 'you seem a bit more concerned about my movements to and from Ireland than why the hell I left in the first place. Don't you want to have that conversation?'

Adam shifted himself around for the last part of the sentence, so now his body was angled towards the driver's seat and he was looking directly at his older brother. Ryan could see James squirming, red blotches racing up the back of his neck.

Adam glanced in the back at Ryan and spoke to him next.

'What about you, Ryan? What do you want to ask me? How I dealt with the French healthcare system? How I got a social security number? Any specific details I can fill you in on?'

'To be honest, bro, I spent a good part of the last ten years drying out so I can't exactly pretend to be too concerned about your welfare when you were, what, sipping red wine in Parisian cafés and shagging gorgeous French birds.'

'It wasn't women I was sleeping with, anyway,' Adam said.

'Ah.' Ryan smiled. 'I see. Whatever floats your boat. What about you, James? Surely in your line of business, everybody is swinging every which way?'

'It's a myth that the TV industry is filled with people screwing all around them,' James said, haughtily.

'What is it filled with?' Ryan asked.

'Ruthless fuckers.'

'Ouch!' Ryan laughed.

James seemed to relax a little. Ryan could see Adam study him for a minute or so, then shift himself back in his seat.

'It is going very well, though,' James said, smiling. 'I've a new show going into production. I hope. Don't want to jinx it. We've got a few channels lined up. Including a French one, as it happens.'

Ryan could see him eye Adam sideways.

'Yeah,' James continued. 'We're looking for the final investors. We're ninety-nine percent there, but you're a businessman, Adam, you know what it's like. Once we get it over the line, that's it. I'll make millions on this one.'

James turned his head and glanced at Adam again.

In the back, Ryan had a much better study of their brother's face.

Adam pursed his lips and stared out the window.

Ryan observed it all. The play and the silent rebuttal.

# CLIO

Clio had planned to take Teddy for a walk on the beach but they'd only managed to get as far as the end of the road before he'd given up.

'Come on now, fatso. You haven't been beyond the garden since I got here. You're just going to grind to a halt if you keep this up.'

Teddy draped a paw over his nose.

Clio looked at the collie, lying on the ground with absolutely no intention of moving, and sighed.

'You're shitting me, right?' she said. 'You don't expect me to carry you home?'

He barked.

Of course he expected her to carry him. She'd been stupid enough to take him down here.

Clio looked back up the hill. The house was just a few hundred metres away but Teddy was heavy and the incline was steep.

'Fuck it anyway,' Clio said. She crouched down and picked up the dog.

He was lighter than she remembered but the distance added weight and by the time she reached the house she was fit to collapse.

She put Teddy down on the front step and shook out the knots in her arms before she could even raise them again to open the door.

When she did, Teddy strolled in ahead of her.

'You little . . .'

She followed him in.

She needed a shower, and her workout had only been about four hundred metres in length.

The sound of raised voices drew her towards her father's study. She'd been avoiding him, after what Ryan had told her last night, but her curiosity got the better of her.

'There is not enough there, Frazer; I will tell my girls to make more. But I need a cheque to cover the suppliers tomorrow.'

Clio arrived just as Ana's voice reached a crescendo.

She peered in through the open door. Her father had the phone to his ear, his hand over the mouthpiece, trying to look as though he was taking Ana seriously even while the smile broke out on his face. He caught Clio's eye.

'Ana, there are only nine of us on board and you've catered for the five thousand. But order more food if you like. I just need to finish these few calls and I'll be able to help. Do you know how hard it is to get people on a bank holiday?'

Ana threw her hands out, exasperated.

Ana, Clio realised in that moment, saw the coming evening as her audition for the role of family matriarch.

Clio wasn't sure if it was because the situation reminded her so much of other times, other events, when it had been her own mother remonstrating with her father, trying to get his help or attention for some such party they were planning . . . but she felt herself drawn into the room, wanting to offer some assistance to the frustrated woman facing Frazer.

'Is there anything I can do, Ana?' she said.

Ana turned and looked at her, surprised and grateful.

'No, no,' she said. 'It is so good of you to offer. I just want to make sure I have enough for everybody to eat. Your brothers have gone down to set up and everybody is being so helpful, but . . .'

'I'm the big ogre who's no help at all, eh?' Frazer sighed and laughed simultaneously.

'Let me give you a hand,' Clio said.

'If you are sure,' Ana said. She stepped forward and grabbed her notepad from Frazer's desk. At the same time, there was a loud yelp.

She jumped back, just as Clio noticed Teddy had followed her in and walked over to the desk. Ana had accidentally trodden on his paw.

The dog whimpered. Both Ana and Clio dropped to their knees to comfort him but Teddy pulled back his paw and growled.

Ana drew back quickly.

'Did that dog bite you?' Frazer said, standing up, his voice angry and alarmed.

'No, of course not,' Ana said. 'It is the dog who is injured. I am sorry, doggy. Bad Ana.'

'He's okay,' Clio said. 'You're all right, aren't you, boy?'

Frazer had come around the desk. He took Ana's hand, examined it.

'You sure you're okay?' he asked.

'Do not be silly.' She laughed.

'I'm allowed to worry about you.' He kissed her hand. 'All right, you have my full attention now. Order whatever you like and tell me what you want me to write on the cheque and I'll sort it, okay.'

Clio watched, amazed at how tender her father was with his fiancée. Everything and everybody else in the room was forgotten. And she saw how Ana enjoyed the attention.

Clio remembered what Ryan had said to her last night, after he'd told her about Ellen. Clio had asked how their mother had reacted to Frazer, after what had happened. And Ryan had reminded Clio that Kathleen had loved all her family unconditionally. Her husband, as well as her children. Plus, he added, Frazer knew when to use his charm.

Was Ana the same as Kathleen? Would she let Frazer get away with everything?

Looking at the two of them together, now, Clio had an awful feeling Ana would.

Which meant Ana was a problem.

# ELLEN

Sometimes, the internet was not enough to keep Ellen in touch with the world.

Today, the connection was painfully slow and Ellen had to quit out of the online banking page several times before she eventually managed to get it to load fully. She shouldn't have wasted the strong connection earlier to read about Ana's bakery, but it had been useful.

Stepmother was facing bankruptcy.

Ellen had already guessed it, even before she had landed by fluke on the article about the bakery going into receivership.

But did Frazer know? That was the question.

When her personal banking page came online, and Ellen's balance came up on screen, she almost wished she'd given up earlier.

Ten grand. That was all she had in the world. Enough to pay a deposit and a few months' rent, but certainly not enough to buy anywhere. And where would she rent? A place in Wexford town on her own? She was thirty-nine and she certainly wasn't fit to share with anybody.

No. Not Wexford town. She couldn't go there, anyway. He still lived there. With his wife. The one he'd gone back to. His wife and their three kids.

She'd found him on Facebook years ago and had been silently stalking him ever since.

How different everything could have been.

When she returned from London and, after a few months in the hospital, came home to Spanish Cove, she'd gone to find him. She wanted to tell him about the pregnancy and the miscarriage, all the bad things that had happened to her.

But somebody had got there first.

He called her a mad bitch and slammed the door in her face. He threatened her. Told her if she ever appeared on his doorstep again, he'd *smash her face in*. That she'd only been good for money and he wanted nothing more to do with her.

She was a slut, he said.

This man, who'd danced with her in the snow in the grounds of Somerset House, their hair speckled with crystal, icy flakes; who'd taken her to look in Christmas windows on Oxford Street and hinted at buying her a ring; who'd brought her champagne in bed in the Ritz and made love with her for hours on end.

She'd known he was married. She wasn't a homewrecker – he'd sworn it was over and she'd believed him. She'd fallen so hard.

She'd walked home in the rain; her mother had picked her up somewhere outside Albertstown and brought her back to Spanish Cove. Ellen sobbed at her own stupidity but her mother had cried the whole way, too, apologising over and over for letting her down.

It wasn't her mother's fault.

The others didn't know it but Kathleen had been on the verge of throwing Frazer out for what he'd done, until Ellen had begged her not to. She couldn't bear to be responsible for any more shame on their family. She'd brought enough, as her father had pointed out. And Frazer had been nothing but contrite since Ellen had returned to Spanish Cove.

Ellen looked away from the laptop screen and stared at herself in the mirror. Her hair hung almost down to her waist. She never coloured it or used heat stylers. It was silky and smooth, like all the Lattimer women's hair, but with no effort.

She lifted her brush and started to comb it in long, sweeping arcs.

Ten grand. She earned eighteen annually from the online tutorials, and she didn't have a whole lot of overheads. She insisted on handing over a nominal weekly amount to her father for rent and board. She wouldn't have it said that she was living in the house for free.

But she didn't spend money on going out, or on frivolities.

All of her money had been spent on the house over the years. Most of her savings had gone into keeping the thing standing. She had every receipt for everything she'd bought. The light fittings and curtains, the cushions in the sitting room, the new pots in the kitchen.

These things just appeared and her father expected them to. But he never asked how they were paid for. He never commented on their necessity or how they made the house look nicer.

She didn't mind. It was her house and she was going to stay living there. He owed that to her. It had never been said explicitly. But it was there, tacitly.

And once her siblings had all received their money from the portfolio, once Ryan and Clio were sorted with their trust funds, nobody would mind, would they? James and Kate were independently wealthy and by the sound of things, Adam hadn't returned for money.

Ellen would happily write off her own share of any inheritance money if it meant she could stay at home.

What could she do to stop her father from marrying Ana?

She heard car doors slamming outside. The boys were back from setting up the yacht.

When she heard the knock on her door, she logged out of her bank page and shut the laptop.

'Come in.'

James ducked his head in and smiled.

'The yacht looks good,' he said. 'You, eh, getting done up?'

Ellen was in her normal clothes and had just finished fixing a bobbin on the end of her plait. She looked up at James, but said nothing. He was sweating, just a tiny bit, but she could see it on the skin over his upper lip.

What had him so stressed?

'I was just wondering if I could have a bit of a word,' he said. 'You understand accounts, don't you?'

Ellen nodded. Where was he going with this? She hoped it wasn't business advice. She gave online tutorials for exams; it was simple and formulaic. She was loath to start helping out family members. It would expose how little she actually knew about the world of accountancy.

'Has he . . . has Frazer let you see the portfolio at all?' James asked. 'Do you know where it's at? Financially, I mean.'

'I wouldn't understand it if he did,' Ellen said. 'Investments have nothing to do with accountancy. Just because they're numbers, it's not all the same thing.'

'Right. I see.'

He still wasn't finished. Ellen stood up, hoping she could move him along. They hadn't been alone together since he'd arrived down but now, at close quarters, she realised that something about James made her uncomfortable. He was full of bonhomie but it seemed false, like he was putting too much effort in. And he'd practically driven his wife and daughter out of the house, despite – on the odd time he did visit home – raving about how fabulous they were.

'I guess I'm curious to know how he's doing,' James said. 'I'm fine, obviously. And Kate. But the rest of you – well, I wouldn't like to see this Ana one sneak in under the radar and make off with what's ours, you know. Yours, even.'

Ellen bristled. It was like he was reading her mind. But she didn't feel like she could be open about it with James. In fact, she felt defensive.

'It's a bit clichéd, isn't it?' she said, haughtily. 'Wicked step-mother makes off with the family jewels?'

'Clichés become clichés because they keep happening,' James said.

'Well, either way,' Ellen said, 'I haven't seen the portfolio. You know Dad. I'd have to ask and once I did, he wouldn't let me. Because I wanted to.'

James nodded. He was distracted. His phone was ringing again.

'Your work seems to really want to get hold of you,' she said.

'Work and everyone else.' He frowned. 'I'll let you, um, finish.'

He placed his hand on the door to leave, but hesitated again. 'Just one last thing. He hasn't been to see his solicitor at all, has he?'

Ellen frowned, confused.

'I don't know,' she said.

James nodded again, his lips pursed thoughtfully.

Ellen sighed. She couldn't help it. He looked like he had the weight of the world on his shoulders and he was her brother, after all. Anyway, what right had she to feel superior to him when it came to worrying about the family fortune?

'Are you . . . okay?' Ellen asked.

James paused.

'I'm a bit . . . distracted,' he said. 'I'm up to my eyes with work, and Sandra . . .'

He trailed off.

'Sandra what?' Ellen said.

She could see James weighing up whether to be truthful and then he just opened his mouth and started to talk. He was dying to tell somebody.

'She wants a baby. Out of nowhere. I guess I'm panicking a bit. I love Bella but I'm not sure there's space right now. In my head, I mean.'

Ellen flinched. Only James could think it was appropriate to have this conversation with her.

She cocked her head and examined her brother. He'd always been handsome. The best-looking of all the Lattimer men in a stereotypical way. The most charismatic. He had the best stories, the funniest gossip. But he was also the most shallow. The most in need of validation. And definitely not as bright.

And allergic to the truth.

'Sandra has traded on her looks her whole life, James,' Ellen said. 'She's forty and people spend more time looking at Bella than her, now. She's trying to stay on top of her appearance, obviously. But it's more animalistic than that. Sandra's fertility is waning and that's what men see, isn't it? She knows that. Not consciously, but somewhere inside her. You can fix it, in the short term, but you've got a longer-term problem on your hands. The absolute worst thing Sandra could have done was marry five years younger. She needs to be a princess. Not a queen.'

James stood there, agog.

Ellen shrugged.

'I . . . eh, well,' he said. 'Sounds like you missed your vocation, Ellen.'

She smiled, sadly. She'd missed bloody everything. And he was still as thick as two short planks.

'Um, see you later.'

James practically ran from the room.

Ellen shrugged again, for her own benefit. Then she turned and looked in the mirror.

What had James said that had bothered her?

Ellen stood there, clutching the brush so hard, her palm was starting to hurt.

She had it.

Why did James want to know if Dad had been to his solicitor?

She opened her computer again, but that was when she heard the yell, followed by sobs.

Ellen stood up so fast her chair fell backwards.

That was Clio's voice. And she was in distress.

# AFTER

'Did you take what the paramedic gave you, Ellen?'

Ellen looked up quickly, then down again. The detective was peering at her with that dreadful, pitying look she knew so well. She hadn't noticed it in him earlier but he'd obviously remembered.

Who she was.

What she was.

*Slut. Idiot. Crazy.*

Her father's names for her were delivered far apart and infrequently, but they'd been well chosen. It was like he knew what her ex had called her. The exact phrases that would cause her the most pain, especially delivered by somebody who was supposed to care for her.

Always whispered, always out of earshot of everybody, always said as if they were harmless and she was the one in the wrong to be so offended by them.

*If you wear that, people will think you're a slut, Ellen.*

'I'm fine,' she said.

'All right.' A pause. Ellen felt like her body was swaying, like they were still on the yacht and not in this cramped room with its minimal furniture.

'So, you didn't see Kate or Clio at any point during the half-hour period we've discussed?'

'I didn't . . .' Ellen hesitated, tried to make her mouth work. 'I didn't see anybody.'

'But you knew Adam, Ryan and Ana were in the cabin outside the toilet.'

'Mm.'

'But you don't know where James was either?'

A shake of her head. She thought she was shaking it. Or it was shaking her. She felt funny.

'Do you know, Ellen, whether James asked your father for money over the weekend?'

Ellen frowned.

'Don't know,' she said. 'He came to my room, right before, and started asking questions about money. He was being all weird. But he was correct to be worried. Ana's going out of business, you know. Little gold digger.'

'Sorry, right before what?'

'And he didn't give a shit when it all kicked off. James, I mean. He didn't come down.'

'Ellen, what kicked off? What did James call to your room *right before*?'

'Oh. Right before Dad did what he did.'

The detective looked very confused.

'Hang on,' he said. 'This was earlier today? Your dad did something? What? To whom?'

'Something very bad,' Ellen whispered. 'To Clio.'

# RYAN

He wasn't long back when it happened.

Ryan and James had left Adam down in the boatyard and when they'd come back up to Spanish Cove, Ryan had stood in the garden smoking, preparing himself for the night ahead.

He hadn't noticed his father emerging from the house, or realised that he was carrying something.

But he did hear the garage door go up.

He'd sauntered over, curious.

He didn't know what he was looking at at first. All he could see was Frazer's back and Teddy's hind, as he lay on the floor.

The dog's legs were thrashing, weakly, and the muscles in Frazer's arms were straining as he leaned over him.

'What's wrong with him?' Ryan said. Then, because he knew she'd been like a mother to that dog when she was a kid, he called for his sister.

'Clio! Clio!'

Before he realised what Frazer was doing.

'Is he having a fit?' Ryan came closer. And then he saw.

Frazer had his hand over the dog's mouth and nose. Teddy's eyes were wide, the pupils dilating, the white starting to burst with broken blood vessels.

'What the fuck?'

Ryan snapped out of his shock very quickly and tried to pull Frazer away.

With one arm, Frazer shoved Ryan violently backwards. Out of practice and not expecting violence, Ryan fell on his backside, hitting the concrete floor of the garage with a thump.

It was painful, but it didn't stop Ryan. He got up, tried again.

'Get off him!' he yelled.

But he couldn't drag his father away from the dog.

It must have only taken a couple of minutes. It felt like a lifetime.

The dog stopped struggling. The red and white fur ceased to shake and his legs became floppy.

Frazer sat back.

'You're so fucking brave, aren't you?' Ryan snarled, rage replacing shock.

And then Clio arrived.

She took one look and clasped her hand to her mouth in a sob.

'What happened?' she said.

'He's gone,' Frazer answered. He was barely out of breath. 'It's okay, lass.'

Great big tears spilled out of Clio's eyes as her father put his arms around her.

'He killed him,' Ryan said.

He watched Clio tense and her father drop his arms, defensively.

'He was sick, Clio,' her father said, slowly, like he was speaking to somebody with mental difficulties. 'It would have been a cruelty to let him go on. He was in pain and he was tired. I had to put him out of his misery. He was getting cranky. Look at how he reacted to Ana in the study. If that had been a child—'

'Don't!' Clio cried. 'He didn't even touch her. She hurt him.'

Ryan crossed the garage and took Clio's hand. He had to get her away from Frazer before she killed him, there and then.

He started to lead her from the garage but, when his father turned to pull a tarpaulin over Teddy, Clio let go of Ryan's hand and flew at Frazer.

'Why would you do that?' she sobbed. 'Why!'

'It's me who's been minding him all these years, Clio,' her father said, his voice pained. 'I'm upset, too.'

'Leave it,' Ryan said. 'Clio, come on.'

Ellen appeared. She looked at Clio, then at the floor, then at Ryan and finally at her father.

'Jesus, Dad,' she said, taking Clio's other arm. 'You're so predictable.'

Together, they left the garage, leaving their father alone with the dead dog and a look of remorse that carried no weight with any of them.

# AFTER

The second time the detective summoned him, James could sense a shift in the atmosphere.

The investigator had a cold look in his eyes. Something had changed. Somebody had said something.

'You didn't see what your father did to Clio's dog?' the detective asked, throwing James.

'It's half one in the morning. You've had my brothers and sisters in and out of here all night. And now you want to talk about the fucking dog? No. I didn't see what happened. And it was Dad's dog. Clio hadn't been home in four years.'

'Mm-hmm. So you weren't angry at Frazer?'

'It was just a dog.'

The detective sucked in his cheeks.

'I know she was upset by it,' James said, quickly. 'I feel sorry for her, of course. But sometimes it has to be done. The dog was old. Dad put it out of its misery. I suppose they're all painting him as some cartoon villain, but it was the garage or the vet, and at least he's buried in the garden now, not slung in an incinerator. Shouldn't we be talking about Ana's dead husband? What did you tell Danny happened to him again?'

'It was a random attack,' the detective said. 'A hate crime. Mr Wójcik was attacked by two youths who started yelling racist slurs at him, telling him to go home to Poland. It is a little strange, that's all I was saying. That her first husband would die from head trauma and her husband-to-be . . .'

'Yeah, exactly,' James said. 'You should be talking to Ana. She was obviously after his money.'

'Were you?' the detective asked, swerving sideways again. 'Did you ask your father to help you out financially this weekend, James?'

'No,' James said.

'But you were asking about the family finances.'

'I was,' James said. 'Because my dad had decided to remarry and I wanted to know where things stood for my family. I'm the eldest, it's my responsibility.' He laughed, lightly. 'You know what I do, surely? What I earn for a single series puts my inheritance in the ha'penny place.'

The detective hesitated, his pen hovering over the page.

'I Googled your IMDb earlier,' he said.

James swallowed.

'You only did that one show, wasn't it?'

'Several series of it, yes. But, in the industry, you do a lot that doesn't end up on your IMDb. Script consultation, that sort of thing.'

'Oh,' the detective said. 'I see. I would have thought you'd put everything on. Bulk up your CV, that sort of thing. That's what everybody else seems to do.'

James said nothing. The detective watched him for a moment, then moved on.

JO SPAIN

'When you all split up on the yacht, did you go to speak to your father?'

'No,' James answered.

'No?'

James shook his head.

'Where did you go? You weren't on the rear deck. You weren't downstairs. You weren't on the same side of the yacht as Kate.'

'I was up talking to Danny.'

'For a couple of minutes, I believe. Did you pass your father?'

'I don't know.'

'What do you mean? If you walked up the starboard side of the yacht, you must have seen him.'

'Yeah. I saw him for a second.'

'You talk to him?'

'No.'

James started to sweat.

'Why did you start the fight with Adam when you returned to the rear deck?'

'Because Adam started all this by coming back,' James snapped. 'Everything was fine until last week.'

'You sound really angry, James.'

James opened his mouth and closed it.

'Do you have anything you need to tell me, James?'

James turned his head slightly, and looked out the window.

He had a lot to confess to.

He'd done a lot of bad things.

And the guilt was overwhelming him.

238

# JAMES

He'd answered Lena, when she called the second time that weekend.

His CFO, the bank, his solicitor, his line producer, the French, Sandra – they could all wait.

But Lena. Oh, God, he needed her badly.

'You're back,' he said, relief flooding his voice.

She'd been in Denmark, auditioning for a part in a British/Danish co-production. A small part, but one that would stand to her and make her quite a lot of money.

And he'd got her the casting call.

'Yes.' She laughed. 'I am back. Or *jeg er tilbage,* as they say in Copenhagen.'

'Well?' he asked.

'I tried to call you, the other day,' she said, a hint of disappointment in her voice. 'You cut me off.'

He'd been in the car with his siblings, of course he had.

'I had a big meeting, sweetheart. I'm sorry. It's been non-stop. And I have that family thing I told you about. It's all stress.'

'Poor baby,' she purred down the phone. He felt his insides tingle. She'd take care of him when he got back up to Dublin. Lena was his fountain of youth. When he was with her, he felt like the man he wanted to be. He could see how she saw him – famous, successful, handsome. Not a kid playing at being a grown-up.

She never asked awkward questions. She never whined. She knew when to talk, she knew the industry and she knew when he just wanted to fuck or be quiet.

She was completely perfect.

'It went brilliantly,' she said. 'I got a callback!'

'I knew you would,' he said, smiling broadly. He'd already thought about what would happen if she got the role. The seed of an idea had planted itself; if Lena got this and got paid, and she knew he'd be giving her the lead in his production, then perhaps he could get her to let him take care of her earnings. Her current agent was a two-bit nobody.

'I can't wait to see you tomorrow and celebrate,' he said.

Already he was imagining her in bed; her gorgeous body writhing in sweat beneath him, her lips reaching up for his, her dark hair wrapped around his fingers.

'Oh, baby, I really wish I could see you tomorrow,' she said.

His erection shrank almost instantly.

'Why can't you?' he asked.

'It's just – a group of us, we said we'd do a creative workshop? Darius Lefoy is going to be there and I so badly want to meet him. There's this producer, he said that he reckoned I'd be a good opposite for Darius in this new show he's going to do.'

James took a deep breath.

'What producer?' he said, trying to keep his voice even.

'Did I not say? Lenny Michaels?'

She was keeping her voice light, too. Deliberately.

He'd feared this, of course he had. She was so eager to get herself out there. Willing to please. Willing to do what she had to.

And beneath it, an utter cutthroat. Like them all.

But it was important that he kept it together. She needed him more than he needed her. That's what she had to believe. And he still held the ace card of an actual lead role. Not a vague promise of one if she slept with him. Because she already had, and he'd stayed loyal.

'You probably mentioned it,' he said, dismissively, as though it wasn't important. 'It sounds like a great idea. Listen, babe, I have to run. I have this yacht party to get to and remember I told you the Netflix crowd were chasing me for a call? I think that's coming this evening.'

There was silence for a moment. He heard a rustle on the other end of the line.

And his heart beat, unnaturally loud.

'Are Netflix really interested, babe?' she said. Her voice had a patronising tone he hadn't heard before.

It was like being sucker-punched.

'Yeah, of course,' he said, his stomach wobbling with the lie. 'Why would you ask that?'

'Oh. No reason. It's just something Lenny said. Um, yeah, I'd better run, too. Darius is phoning later to arrange my lift for the morning.'

'I didn't know you two knew each other so well,' James said.

'It's just the circles we move in,' Lena answered.

*What circles?* James wanted to say. *You were a fucking extra on a soap when I met you.*

Instead, this false laugh emerged from somewhere inside him.

'Sure,' he said. 'Well, listen, you be careful, my little star. You're on the rise and everybody is going to want to hang out with you. Especially the likes of Lenny Michaels. I'll put a call in to my Danish contacts and see where things are at, okay? You're much bigger than Ireland, remember that.'

'That would be amazing!' she gushed. 'You're so right. Maybe tomorrow I could—'

James cut her off with an abrupt goodbye before he hung up.

What had he been thinking?

It was time he sorted out this shit.

Sandra would have to sell the apartment. She could have her baby; he'd let that be the quid pro quo. He still had his inheritance to come and a great show to make. And he had his darling Bella. His family, the one he'd made, that was all that mattered.

It would be okay.

The fight back started now.

He found the Danish producer's number on his phone, along with a leading casting director he was friendly with, and before he could stop himself, he banged out the text, attached a photo from the last party he and Lena had been at together and pressed send.

Nobody wanted an actress on set who was already hooked on cocaine at twenty-two.

It was all much more professional these days.

# ADAM

Adam had stayed down at the yacht when James and Ryan returned to the house. He liked being around Danny and the man needed help getting the vessel ready. He wasn't as young, or fit, as he'd once been.

The two older men, Danny and Frazer, were opposites in many ways. But Danny had more layers than most gave him credit for. He read – everything. He listened to current affairs. He enjoyed solitude but he also liked to reflect on the state of the nation. And, of course, he was deeply fond of Kathleen and, ergo, of Frazer, when she brought him back to Spanish Cove. His friends' children were the nieces and nephews he'd never have.

Whereas, Frazer . . .

It was just like his father to have planned a party for himself this weekend. Anybody could have seen it coming.

Danny had put him to work washing down the side of the yacht. It was already sparkling – Adam evidently looked like he needed to do something with his hands.

'You're quiet,' Danny said, looking over the side of the boat. Danny, who hadn't uttered more than the word 'coffee' in the last hour.

Adam examined his handiwork. The white surrounds of the black lettering that spelled out *The Countess* were gleaming.

'You worried about tonight?' Danny asked.

'Why worry about something that can't be changed?' Adam said.

'Doesn't stop most, Mr Philosopher.'

Danny stared out to sea. Adam resumed washing down the yacht.

'They got you under the spotlight up there?' Danny asked. 'Keep asking you questions? People love to talk. It's why I like the sea so much. The quiet.'

Adam considered before answering.

'It's a bit weird,' he said, thoughtfully. 'There's me and getting to grips with why I went missing for ten years. But then there's the new girlfriend and the possibility of the upset she'll cause. Dad has definitely given me a pass. Did you know he was planning to marry her, Danny?'

Danny paused.

'I might have had an inkling when he asked me for a loan of this a few weeks ago. You weren't even back then and he was planning a party for something. He was spending more time with Ana. I should have guessed.'

Danny patted the side of the yacht.

'Do you like her?' Adam asked.

'She's a good woman,' Danny said.

'Right.'

They worked in silence again for a few minutes, Danny busy on deck, Adam admiring his progress

Then Danny's head appeared again.

'Why did you do it, lad? Why didn't you come to me and talk about what was going on?'

'I don't know, Danny,' Adam said. It was the honest answer. He'd been twenty-one and the only solution to all his problems seemed to be to walk. He hadn't given himself enough time to talk himself out of leaving or into confiding in someone. Danny might have been an obvious choice but Adam thought at the time he was better off handling it on his own. That it was best for everybody that way.

'I wish you had,' Danny said.

Adam paused.

So did he.

He looked at the name on the side of the yacht. Then he lifted his hand, traced the letters with his fingers.

*The Countess.*

'You say Dad asked for a loan of this,' Adam said. 'I thought you'd just leased it for him. Is it yours?'

Danny nodded.

'Fuck, Danny, it's huge. Must have cost a bomb.'

'I take tourists out,' Danny said. 'Bought it with my savings but it's almost paying for itself. What else would I spend my money on? No wife, no kids. I've only ever loved the sea.'

Adam stood, dropped the washcloth in the bucket of soapy water and started to walk away. He lifted his hand to wave goodbye to Danny but didn't look back.

Kate was at the top of the pier talking to a strange man. Adam couldn't put a name on him but he'd a gut feeling he was a local. He wore an ill-fitting suit, grey, strained at the arms and across his chest. Young, but his face, while good-looking, had the older, weather-beaten appearance of a farmer.

'Adam,' Kate called. 'I came down for the chemist. You want a ride back up to the house? This is – um – Rob?'

The man with Kate held his hand out. Adam shook it, still none the wiser.

'Used to pal around with your sister,' Rob said. 'Clio? More, after you left. You wouldn't have known me, though I probably gatecrashed a couple of parties you were at. My older brothers would have been there.'

'Oh,' Adam said. 'Right. Yeah, sorry, I'm bad with faces.'

'Rob is a detective now,' Kate said.

It was a struggle, but Adam kept his expression blank. Rob was still shaking his hand, but he released it and Adam let it fall by his side, taking a step back simultaneously.

'I was just telling Clio yesterday, I think when they did that big search for you all those years ago, it set off something in my head,' Rob said. 'I never stopped wondering what had happened to you.'

Adam didn't know what to say. He stared at the ground, shrugged, embarrassed.

'Yeah,' he mumbled. 'Sorry.'

'Jesus, no need, pal. It happens, you know. I have the professional perspective now. Vast majority of missing cases, people just have a breakdown, walk out, whatever. It's good to have you back.'

Adam glanced up. Rob was staring at him and, while Adam knew the other man knew nothing, that he was just naturally interested, he still felt the urge to get away from him.

And was that . . . fuck.

Adam could see Eva from the pub in the distance.

Oh, Christ. Not now.

It was her. Eva stopped. Then she raised her hand.

She was waving at him. Uncertainly, nervously.

He'd been able to avoid her in the pub last night. He hadn't expected her to still be working there. But, thankfully, she'd disappeared almost immediately after he arrived.

He didn't want to talk to her. Not in front of Kate.

'Did you say you were heading up to the house, Kate?' Adam said.

'I . . . yeah. It was nice to see you again, Rob.'

Kate clicked the lock on the car. It was Ellen's, Adam realised. Not surprising, that. James wouldn't let anybody near the Audi and Frazer's car, with its old manual steering, was a bugger to drive.

Adam got into the passenger seat and, as they drove, watched in the side mirror as Rob, and then Eva, grew small and smaller. He raised his hand to his mouth, started to worry at his nails. He was a ball of tension.

'I've no recollection of that Rob whatsoever,' he said.

'He was around a bit more after you left,' Kate said. 'Bit of a rep as a ladies' man. I think he was Clio's boyfriend for a while.'

'Him? A ladies' man?'

'He still has the twinkle.'

*He has the hard stare is what he has,* Adam thought, but didn't say.

'What are you doing down here, anyway?' he asked Kate. 'What did you need in the chemist's?'

'Nothing. Painkillers. I just had to get out. Get some fresh air. They have about fifty different restaurants and pubs between here and Duncannon and not one gym.'

'Why would you need a gym when you can swim or run outdoors?'

'It's just what I do,' she said. 'I thought if I *did* something I always do, I would feel like I always do.'

'Which is?' he asked.

'In control.'

'You don't feel like you're in control?'

'Adam, I don't even feel like I'm in my own body right now. I feel tired all the time, out of sorts, and like I'm about to cry every bloody second.'

Adam looked straight ahead. The road rose ahead of them, empty, theirs the only vehicle, the sun shining on nothing but emptiness and isolation. To the left, the sea shimmered blue; to the right, moss and uneven stone pocked the cliff face.

'I'm sorry, Kate,' he said.

'For what?'

'For messing shit up for you with your husband.'

'I think I might have done a little of that myself,' she said.

Adam swallowed. It was about as honest as he'd ever heard Kate.

'I didn't know you were depressed,' Kate said. 'Back then, I mean. We all had our things, Adam.'

'This is exactly why I couldn't talk to anybody, Kate. Everybody had their own shit. You especially.'

'What does that mean?' she said. 'Me *especially*?'

'Come on, Kate.'

'Come on, what? I'm always worrying about other people.'

Adam was getting irritated now. He didn't want to have this conversation. He was still trying to figure out how he'd handle Eva when he eventually did have to talk to her.

But if Kate was going to force him . . .

'You worry what they think of you,' he said. 'It's not the same thing. And once you started to lose that weight . . . the rest of us could have dropped dead for all you cared.'

'That's not true.' Her face turned bright pink.

'It is true. You became vain and stuck-up and . . . and so full of yourself.' He snorted. 'You'd think you'd really worked to lose that puppy fat. But you didn't, did you?'

'I did work,' she spat.

'You didn't.'

The car fell deathly silent.

'You spent most of your inheritance on liposuction and a tummy tuck and fuck knows what else,' Adam said.

Kate banged her hand on the horn. Adam jumped.

And felt like an arsehole. He shouldn't have said that. She didn't deserve it. He was just in a bad mood.

They never spoke it aloud. That Kate had bought her new skinny self. They let her have her revised narrative. With the dad they had, she deserved it.

Had there ever been a time when Frazer wasn't mocking her eating habits? Or her weight?

Had there ever been a time when he wasn't pushing food on her?

And whenever Kathleen gently expressed concern that maybe Kate had a weight issue, Frazer would say, ah no, she's grand.

The man, to put it politely, was a fucking psychopath.

'Oh, so what,' she said, in that artificially light tone she had. 'It was my money. Compared to what you spent it on – running away.'

'Sorry,' Adam said.

'You're always sorry.'

'I am, though.'

'Grand. Whatever.'

Adam winced.

'Dad drove you to it. We all know. I'm not surprised you wouldn't let Cheng near him. Or the rest of us.'

Kate said nothing. She was seething; he could feel it off of her. They drove in silence back to the house.

# AFTER

Rob took the call, quickly, quietly.

His boss was en route. He wanted a brief summary – was it really worth his while coming down this late? Was Rob positive they couldn't mark this one up as an accident?

Rob gave him what he had. What he thought he had.

'Ah, shit,' his boss said. 'Well, it's been four hours now. You have to let them go home before they start looking for my number. I can't cope with complaints tonight. I'm bloody exhausted.'

'I'd have been quicker compiling these statements if you'd given me somebody.'

'Three serious incidents on one night, Downes, for crying out loud.'

'It doesn't matter,' Rob said. 'It's worked out better this way. They're starting to talk. I'm breaking them down.'

'Is it an issue, you knowing the daughter?' Quinn asked him. 'Clio, is it?'

'I know everybody down here, boss.'

'Hmm. Right enough. And you're sure about your theory? Frazer was the intended victim?'

'Yeah,' Rob said. 'I toyed with it being the brother who came back, but it doesn't add up. He looks nothing like the father. And as far as Adam being a suspect, I had one of the lads back in the station do a quick check on him. Adam Lattimer has no record in France – no run-ins with the law whatsoever – so I'd be surprised if he decided to come home after ten years just to murder his father.'

'Which one of them did, then?'

'I'm narrowing it down. I just need a little while longer, sir.'

A sigh. Quinn was sceptical and hopeful at once. When Detective Downes had been dispatched to Albertstown, they'd assumed it was an accidental drowning he was dealing with.

Sad, but quickly closed.

If this tragedy turned out to be manslaughter, or worse, then the best outcome for Quinn's department was a fast turnaround.

'I just think, if I let them go home at this point, and they're asked to come into the station over the next few days, the spell will be broken,' Rob said. 'They'll clam up and they'll have their solicitors by that stage. And they're all potential flight risks, in my opinion.'

'Right, right,' Quinn said. 'Okay, well, look, they're still clearing this road crash on the motorway. I'm going to make sure that's taken care of and then I'll be down. You have an hour.'

It was all Rob needed. He was about to hang up when Quinn spoke again.

'Downes, go hard on the captain. He might be like family, but he's not.'

And that was exactly Rob's plan.

# CLIO

Her face was still puffy but make-up would cover the worst of it.

Her father was right. Teddy was just a dog. A pet she hadn't even seen in four years.

It was shock. She'd get over it.

She wanted to go down to the garage. See him one last time.

But she couldn't.

The dog was dead.

Move on.

She read the letter instead, over and over and over, trying to keep her mind focused on why she'd come home in the first place.

*Teddy. On her lap. Sleeping at her feet. His familiar smell. His loyalty. In her arms. His laboured breathing as she nearly collapsed, carrying him up that hill. His only crime, loving her more than Frazer.*

He was just a fucking dog. What was wrong with her?

Her eyes skimmed the words on the page. This time, she almost got to the very end before the tears started to blur her vision.

When she finished, she folded it in half again and placed it in the envelope. She let herself feel sad and then she let the anger take over. That's what was important.

She heard footsteps outside on the landing. Doors opening and closing.

It was time.

Ana welcomed them onto the yacht.

Clio took a glass of champagne from her but then she saw Danny and used him as an excuse to get away. She gave him a quick hug and passed him a bag for the party.

Ana didn't know about the dog. Clio still wasn't sure if it would bother Ana, if she did.

Ellen put her arm around Clio and hugged her. Clio smiled thinly, gratefully, then hugged her back. One positive had come of this weekend: she felt a thaw in Ellen. And now Clio understood why her sister had become so cold in the first place.

Maybe, one day, she would tell Ellen about what had happened in New York.

The yacht started to slow. Frazer had asked Danny to bring them out far enough to feel like they were offshore but to a point where they would still be able to see the lights of the village.

Clio reckoned it was because he wanted people to see the yacht, to know they were on it for a private party and that they could afford the best of everything.

She sat back on the benches, propped her feet up on a small stool in front of her and sipped her drink.

The evening was balmy but the sky had started to cloud, the dusky, late sun behind them casting red light through grey plumes.

Perhaps it would rain again. Clio could see below deck from here

– the set of stairs that led to a large cabin. The yacht was large enough that, if the weather turned, they could take the party downstairs. Frazer was down there now, going through the box of fireworks with Danny. They'd decided to set them off early. Just in case.

Frazer wouldn't like his party to be a damp squib.

Clio snorted to herself at her own joke.

Somebody had put music on. Electric Light Orchestra's 'Mr Blue Sky', incongruously cheery and festive.

Adam took a glass from the table and sat down beside Clio.

'You okay?' he asked. 'Ryan told me.'

She glanced around the rear deck they'd all settled on. Ana was hovering by the catering table. Nobody to talk to, nobody looking to be taken care of.

'Go keep our new mammy company,' she said. 'I'm not in the mood.'

'Some people say losing a dog is like losing a child.'

'He wasn't a child.'

'Didn't you used to dress him in old baby clothes so he wouldn't get cold?'

Clio snorted, but she felt like she might cry.

'Don't pretend you care about anything in my life,' she said.

She got up and walked away, taking the steps two at a time below deck.

Danny and her father were laughing at something they'd found in the box of fireworks.

'Ach, lass,' Frazer said. His voice was apologetic, tentative. 'Look at these.'

Her father held up a pair of false teeth with ridiculously enlarged vampire fang incisors.

Clio put her hand to her chest.

'Where did you get them?' she asked.

'The fireworks were in the . . . storage,' Frazer said. She knew he'd been about to say garage but stopped himself. 'They must have fallen out of one of the old Hallowe'en boxes. God.' He shook his head gently. 'Do you remember her in these?'

Clio nodded, slowly. Her father looked different when he was like this, when he was being nostalgic. Kinder, somehow.

She summoned the memory, the last big Hallowe'en party they'd had when they were all together. Their mother carving out pumpkin after pumpkin, fake cobwebs in the hall and sheets draped over coat stands. Dressed as a vampire, wearing the fangs, all day.

She loved an occasion, did Kathleen.

'I vant to suck your vlood,' Frazer said, and laughed again. Then he shook his head and picked up the box of fireworks. He looked sad.

Clio swallowed. It was difficult to remember her father was human sometimes.

But when she did, it always caught her by surprise.

'All right, Danny, let's get these to the upper deck and set them off into the night sky. Mark my engagement with a bang!'

'Right enough,' Danny said.

Frazer lifted the box. Clio stood aside to let Danny go ahead of her.

'You okay?' Frazer said, as he too passed.

She nodded, begrudgingly.

'I'm sorry for earlier,' he said. 'It was necessary, but not necessary that you saw it. I didn't think you'd still be as close to the poor dog. Not with you having been away so long. I couldn't bear to see him in pain any more. But I should have taken him to the vet's. I appreciate how it must have looked.'

'It's fine,' Clio said.

'What age was he, anyway? He must have been about one hundred in dog years. Ach, a right good life, he had.'

'Sure.'

Frazer studied her, then nodded.

'You were always my favourite, pet,' he said. 'I'd never do anything to hurt you.'

Then he walked up the stairs.

Her eyes bored into his back as she followed him up.

Her breathing grew rapid, the sense of panic hitting her like a giant wave.

If she was his favourite, she could only imagine how it felt to be one of his other children.

# AFTER

'All right, Danny, help me out here,' Detective Downes said. 'The party was in full flight, from what I gather, but Frazer cut it short. Then you'd some engine trouble, am I right?'

'I couldn't get her to start,' Danny said, shrugging, like the intricacies of engines were as unpredictable as the ways of women. 'Like I told you. It choked, a few times. I had to take a look. The drive belt had slipped. Only noticed it when I saw the belt dust on the engine pulley. Got it sorted okay. But it caused a bit of a jerk. Not enough to do real damage. Certainly not enough to tip anybody overboard.'

Danny sat back with his hands on his chest, fingers laced. He hadn't a clue about boats, this pup.

'But the whole time you were up front, you could see Kate Lattimer on the port side of the yacht?' he said.

'Aye. She was holding her phone up in the air, looking for a signal, like. Thought the phone might slip, I did. She looked drunk.'

'I've looked at her phone. She was trying to get through to her husband. Her call log matches the timeline. So, if you could see her, you could see Frazer, too.'

'Yep,' Danny said.

'And did you see somebody with him, Danny? Did you see him arguing with anybody?'

Danny tapped his fingers against each other.

'I've known these kids since they were babies,' he said. 'I'm godfather to two of them.'

'Oh,' the detective said. 'I didn't know. Who?'

Danny looked down at his fingers.

'James and Clio,' he said. 'The oldest boy and the youngest girl.'

'Right. James said he was talking to you when the family dispersed. Is that true?'

'He was with me for a minute or two,' Danny said.

'And then where did he go?'

Danny stared at the detective.

And then he looked away.

# JAMES

James couldn't even think about drinking. His brothers and sisters seemed to relax as the evening wore on – eating the food Ana had organised from her little shop, knocking back champagne, acting like they didn't have a care in the world. Somebody had compiled a ridiculous playlist that was blaring out of the speakers at the front of the yacht and they were currently enduring Hall and Oates' 'You Make My Dreams'.

James had switched his phone off. He'd resumed ignoring all calls after Lena had got hold of him, including several from Sandra.

And just as well he had. His financial controller had rung the house and Sandra had answered, resulting in two panicked voicemails from her.

His wife wasn't the brightest, but, Jesus, she could solve the JFK conspiracy if she put her mind to it. She'd be a dog with a bone now until he confessed and told her just how up shit creek they were.

He had one last chance, by his reckoning.

He'd broached it wrong with his father. Frazer preferred the younger generation, he always had. It was clear he'd a soft spot for Bella, even though she wasn't blood. She probably reminded him of Clio at that age. Smart and pretty and rebellious. She even had red hair like Frazer had once had, albeit Bella's was dyed.

His father was the one man whose eyes James couldn't pull the wool over. He had to speak to him again and, this time, he'd have to do something he hadn't done in a long time.

The one thing his industry had taught him not to do.

He'd have to be honest. Instead of appealing to his father as an investor, he needed to tell him how broke James' family was. How Sandra and Bella, especially Bella, were going to suffer. They could end up homeless, for God's sake. It was that bad.

James would do his best to be on good form tonight, which meant keeping his wits about him and not drinking or arguing with anybody, just keeping an even keel.

Then, in the morning, he'd sit down with Frazer and explain it all. And hope for the best.

Frazer and Danny were standing on the upper deck, the fireworks display ready to go, a protective cordon set up around it. His father turned and waved at them all to tell them it was about to start. He caught James' eye and smiled and James smiled back so hard, he thought his face would break.

He oohed and aahed with the rest of them as the vibrant multi-coloured sparks exploded into the sky, trailing little gems of fire and a whiff of smoke and sulphur.

'It is beautiful,' Ana called, her face awash with happiness, bathed in an artificial orange glow.

And James smiled at her too because, after all, he didn't know how involved she was going to be with the purse strings.

The fireworks didn't go on for long. Frazer and Danny had many skills but pyrotechnics was not among them. After one almost got away from them, they both came down from the upper deck. Danny went up front but Frazer crossed to Ana and placed his arm around her waist, beaming.

'Let those be the only fireworks of our marriage.' Frazer laughed.

'A marriage without sparks sounds as dull as fuck to me,' Ryan drawled. 'Apologies for my language, Ana dearest.'

He raised his glass of sparkling water. Ana lifted her champagne, her smile grateful and pleased at once.

'No, son, no toasts yet.' Frazer turned and smiled at them all. James felt his antennae go up. There was something in Frazer's eyes that instantly put him, and he knew the rest of them, on edge.

'I have another announcement to make.'

'For fuck's sake,' Clio muttered, loud enough for James, standing beside her, to hear.

Frazer turned to face his fiancée.

'Forgive me if I get a wee bit sentimental, lass. But I want to tell you that when we met, the first thing that drew me to you was your courage. Like me, you didn't have an easy start in life. Like me, you made your way. And like me, you weren't afraid to travel to do so. I came to Ireland when it was difficult to get work. You came over with barely a word of English.'

Frazer spun on his heel and eyed all his children again. James winced. Something big was coming. Something bad.

'Ach, I knew when I asked this woman to marry me that I wanted to offer her the world, and it is the world to which I will bring her. After our wedding, we are going travelling!'

Frazer smiled at Ana again. She smiled back, but it looked to James like she was uncertain, concerned even.

'Frazer, perhaps now is not the time,' she started to say.

'Travelling where?' Clio asked.

'Everywhere. We're both in good health, we're not too old, we could live for decades. Aye, I want to see everything. And I want to see it with this woman by my side.'

'But . . .' Ellen said. 'How long are you going for?'

'For as long as it takes.' Frazer beamed.

'Frazer,' Ana spoke quietly, urgently.

'There's nothing here for us,' he continued, ignoring her. 'You've all grown up. We've no grandchildren. Your mother . . .' Frazer looked at Adam. James could see his brother visibly bristle.

'She always had this thing about me keeping the house,' Frazer continued, 'like it was a beacon for Adam to find in the dark. If it was still there, you might come home. And you did. So, now, I'm free from my promise. I want to thank you especially, lad, for releasing me. You'll never know how grateful I am for your return, now, of all the times you could have chosen. I'm selling the house to fund myself and Ana's adventure.'

Adam's face turned pure white.

There was a gasp. James didn't know if it had come from him, Adam, Ellen or somebody else entirely.

'You can't!' It was definitely Ellen who spoke this time.

The look on her face was primal, frenzied even.

'It's already arranged,' Frazer said, holding his hands out. 'I got through to the estate agent today. When Frazer Lattimer puts in a call, it's answered. Even if it is a bank holiday.'

Frazer puffed out his chest, thrilled with himself.

'Hold on.' James stepped forward. He had a cold feeling in his stomach. But his brain was very much in working gear. 'Why would you sell the house? Why not just access the investment portfolio?'

'The investments haven't been performing so well lately,' Frazer said, then shrugged as if it had nothing to do with him.

James ignored his own shock for a moment to register Ana's. His soon-to-be stepmother looked utterly appalled.

'I knew it,' James said, and he meant on both counts. His father had fucked up and Ana was a gold digger. He returned his stare to his father. Frazer met his gaze but he couldn't hold it. He looked away. A first for Frazer.

'Woah,' Ryan said. 'What do you mean, they haven't been performing? Surely it's up to you to make them perform? I mean, isn't that what you've done for all these years? That was your purpose, right? It's not like you'd anything else to do.'

In an instant, Frazer took a step towards his youngest son, his arm raised.

Ryan took a step towards their father, too, skinnier, smaller, still ready to take him on.

'Frazer!' It was the loudest James had heard Ana. She pulled at her fiancé's arm, yanking him backwards.

'I do not want this.'

'Of course you bloody want this,' Ellen said, her voice like ice. 'You gave him the idea. How's your little bakery going, eh? Did you expect him to bail you out or do you just want to get away from it all?'

'This is not my doing!' Ana's face filled with indignation. 'I don't want the travel. I have travelled enough.'

She glared at their father.

'And you said no secrets.'

Frazer looked taken aback.

At his side, James clenched and unclenched his fists. His heart was racing, his mouth dry.

Frazer ignored his children. He turned to Ana and placed both his hands on her arms.

'This is for us, my love. I will not have my life dictated by adult children who should be standing on their own two feet. Ach, I told Kathleen, I did, I said that money from her parents would spoil them. It would ruin them, leave them with a sense of entitlement. And I was right, wasn't I?'

Frazer looked at each of them in turn.

'You, James, you blew it pretending to be a big shot in the TV world, thinking you could fake it until you made it. And, by Jesus, you're still trying to make it. Kate and Ellen, hell, neither of you have the brains you were born with. And you, Adam, what did you do with your cash? We're not talking about that, are we? You all disappointed me. You let me down. Me and your mam. And you all ran off the first chance you got. You only stayed, Ellen, so you could get your hands on your siblings' inheritance.'

James was so angry, the veins on his temple were starting to throb. He looked around at the rest of them.

They were all focused on their father, absolute hatred in their eyes.

Frazer looked marginally remorseful to have brought upset to the evening, but that was always his way. Launch the bomb, then stand back and survey the damage with contrition. His father reached out for Ana again but she turned her body sideways, away from him. She seemed genuinely upset, James gave her that.

'It's getting a bit nippy,' Frazer said. 'I think we'll head back to shore. Somebody tell Danny.'

He took a cigar from his pocket as he walked away from them.

# AFTER

Adam was shivering, badly. His shirt had dried but his jeans still clung to his legs, damp and heavy. The blankets and foil wraps the harbour master had found for them were doing little at this stage.

They'd be sent home soon, Detective Downes had said.

But would all of them be allowed to leave, Adam wondered?

He glanced around at each of his siblings.

If the detective scratched hard enough, he'd surely find a motive for each of them to have killed Frazer.

With, thankfully, the exception of Adam, who hadn't even seen the man for ten years.

The door to the small office opened. Adam saw Danny walk past behind the detective, heading outside.

Danny glanced in at them. He looked . . . guilty.

Adam searched for what had happened in the detective's face. Had Danny said something that incriminated one of them?

'Could I see you one more time, Adam?' Rob said.

Adam nodded and stood.

'This is getting ridiculous,' Kate snapped, impatiently. 'We've been here over four hours now.'

'Almost there,' Rob answered.

Adam saw him glance at Clio, concerned, before he followed the detective through the door.

When they arrived in the small office being used as an interview room, the detective sighed.

'I'm not lying about my boss being delayed,' he said, as though he'd read Adam's mind. 'There was a pile-up on the N11 this evening and a small boating accident up along the coast. We're stretched. It's rare enough we encounter a night like this.'

'Look, has he been taken to hospital at least?' Adam asked.

Rob pursed his lips.

'You know, you're the first one to ask where your father is,' he answered. 'Frazer has been taken to the morgue in the hospital, yes.'

Adam stared down at the floor. He took a deep breath.

'There'll be a post-mortem,' the detective said. 'But that will all happen in the next couple of days. I believe you were first into the water? You didn't tell me that.'

'I'm the best swimmer.' Adam shrugged.

'Not James? He's the oldest.'

'I . . . he dived in. After.'

'Did you think you could save Frazer?'

'I don't know. We didn't understand at that stage. That he had a head injury. I just thought, if I get him out of the water . . . Danny gave him mouth-to-mouth but he was already gone. Ellen told us to stop. She could see it, even if we couldn't.'

'Right.' A pause. 'Okay, one last time. Tell me exactly what happened.'

Adam tried not to let his frustration show. He bit his lip hard, then spoke.

'We were on the rear deck and suddenly Danny ran up. He'd come to check on us after he got the boat going again. He saw blood and . . . then Dad, in the water.'

'Danny said, by his reckoning, you'd all had a pop at Frazer tonight.'

'Well, I suppose you could perceive it like that. Danny is my dad's best friend, so . . .'

'Hmm. So, you were with Ryan, Ana and Ellen when you all separated?'

'Yes. And I could see Clio, the whole time, standing at the rail on the rear deck. Kate was . . . I don't know where Kate was.'

'Danny saw her. She was on the port side.'

'Oh. Right.'

Rob paused a moment.

'What about James?' he asked. 'Where was he?'

'I don't know,' Adam said, blankly.

'Did James have any issues with your father?'

Adam laughed thinly.

'We all have issues. If you're asking if they fought this weekend, well, I imagine they did. I'm fairly certain James is broke and I'd bet his whole debt that he tried to tap Frazer for money. He was trying his luck with me earlier today, that's for sure. But, seriously . . .'

'And James was the last to join you when you all returned to the rear deck. Then he attacked you.'

'Yeah, but . . . look, I was winding him up. There's no point saying otherwise. And I think Ana was the last to arrive? Though, she came up from downstairs. I mean, I think she did. She was behind us.'

'James punched you twice, until you were forced to defend yourself.'

Adam took a deep breath again.

'I guess,' he said.

'And all because you *wound him up*? Seems like a strong reaction.'

'Dad had us all fuming. He was selling the house and had just told us the investment portfolio was empty. I'm well-off, it doesn't affect me, but even I was annoyed at that little stunt. Kate, she'd hardly need the money, either. But the others. It must have come as a shock. It was a mean thing to do. Nasty.'

'Did you have *any* reason to be at odds with your father, Adam?'

Adam hesitated.

'He is – sorry, he was – an arsehole. Enough to want to kill him? No. If anything, I'm the one who risked being done in this weekend. You know the score. I vanished. Broke my mother's heart. Killed her, truth be told. No matter how I try to defend myself, it's my fault she's dead.'

Adam stared down at the floor again.

'I came back to say sorry,' he said, softly. 'And now I've said it, I'm going back to France to start living my life again. They might not be able to forgive me, but I can start to forgive myself. I was just a kid, you know? I don't know what made me walk away, but I know I had no choice.'

'I understand,' Detective Downes said.

Adam looked up, surprised.

The detective nodded, his face full of compassion.

Then, he stood and opened the door, indicating the interview was at an end.

'My cousin did the same,' he said, before Adam left.

'Ran away?' Adam asked.

'In a manner. He hanged himself.' The detective placed his large hand on Adam's shoulder. 'I get it, pal. You've been away a long time. Lot of deaths down this way. Lot of sadness. It's just the way of it.'

Adam nodded grimly.

It could have so easily been him.

# CLIO

Clio found herself alone on the rear deck.

They all needed space and the yacht was large enough for them to disperse to various corners.

At one point, she thought she heard raised voices. But she couldn't properly discern anything over the music.

The Police were blaring from the sound system. Kate had reverted to all her favourites when she'd compiled the soundtrack for this evening.

Clio looked over her right shoulder to where her sister was standing, on the left side of the yacht, on her own. Kate had her phone in her hand.

Clio could feel a chugging beneath her feet as Danny tried to start the engine to bring the boat back to shore. It didn't sound healthy.

Slowly, the family began to reappear. Back to where the alcohol was.

Adam, Ellen, Kate, Ryan.

They were quiet for a while. Still taking it all in.

Then they began to bicker among themselves.

'Why are you upset, Ellen?' Kate snapped. 'You're not going to be bloody homeless. You must have a fortune saved. You've been living there rent-free for what, twenty years?'

'Leave her alone,' Clio said.

'Well, I'm hightailing it back to Italy tomorrow and I have to say, I'll be glad to see the back of this shit storm,' Ryan said.

'Maybe it's time you all grew up,' Kate snapped. 'Stopped running away from bloody everything.' She glared at Adam, Ryan and Clio.

'Fuck off, Kate,' they said in unison.

'What's grown up, Kate?' Ellen said, finding her voice. 'Spending almost every day starving yourself and being unhappy as sin? God, don't even argue with me. It's like you've been eating for two since you came down. Fat Kate is dying to get out of that skinny bitch you've squeezed her into. You're bingeing. Just like old times.'

Kate opened her mouth to reply but then she looked down at the glass of champagne in one hand, the Mowbray pork pie in the other. Clio could tell she wasn't even aware she'd picked the pie up.

James came back around the side of the deck with a face like thunder.

'What's the matter, James?' Adam said. 'Somebody else you've tapped for money told you to go and jump?'

Clio winced on James' behalf. There was a nasty tone to Adam's voice that screamed trouble.

James picked up a glass of champagne and downed it.

'I mean, if you just ask me out straight, maybe I can help?' Adam said. 'I'm bloody loaded, mate. If you'd lay off all that *it's an investment* crap for once, and admit you're a failure who needs to be bailed out.'

'I'm a failure?' James said, coldly. 'Say that again.'

Adam stared at his brother.

'You're a failure.'

There was a moment of stillness.

Then James punched Adam in the face.

Clio gasped.

Adam leaned over, blood spurting from his nose. When he stood up, James punched him again.

They were his best shots.

Adam recovered quicker this time and started to lay into his older brother.

'Oh, my God!' Kate exclaimed, clutching Clio's arm. Then she started laughing, manically. Clio watched, startled, as her sister clapped her palm to her head.

'I get it,' Kate said. 'I get it now. Eating for two.'

'Why are you laughing like a fucking lunatic?' Clio said. 'Look at them!' She looked back at their brothers. They were wrestling like two angry drunks. And Ryan was now trying to intervene.

'The timing!' Kate laughed. 'The timing is just perfect.'

Her expression contorted into one of sheer desperation. She placed her hand on her stomach and closed her eyes. Then she looked at the champagne glass in her hand, her eyes widening in alarm.

'Shit!' she said, and flung it like her hand was on fire.

Ana, who Clio hadn't even noticed standing there, ducked, but the glass nearly hit Clio. Her mouth fell open as the glass shattered and the champagne inside it shot through the air like a golden rainbow.

Kate took another glass and threw it. She'd cracked.

'Bastard!' James managed to get the word out despite the fact blood from his split lip had dribbled into his mouth and made his voice sound particularly funny.

'This is a disaster,' Kate cried, the carefully cultivated South Dublin accent vanquished, the flat vowels of her native county elongated and natural.

'For fuck's sake, lads!' Ryan protested.

Clio said nothing. She was in shock, witnessing the complete collapse of her family.

'Stop!' Ellen's voice was quietly desperate but it carried across the mayhem and, to Clio's surprise, it resonated.

The boys dropped their hands, exhausted, done.

Kate lowered her arm.

Clio knocked back the remaining champagne in her glass.

'And what do you have to say about all this, Brunhilda?' James spat. He nodded in the direction of Ana.

Her face said it all.

What had her engagement party become?

What sort of family was this?

What was she marrying into?

Clio snorted alcohol out her nose, causing a burning sensation in the backs of her eyes. Adam, hands on his knees, looked up and smirked. Ryan started to laugh.

The valve was opened, the stress released. Adam and James' blood-letting had proved cathartic and, in any case, the siblings were always going to be united in the face of their father's announcement.

The yacht jerked suddenly. Danny had got the engine going.

They all stumbled but quickly regained their footing.

'Where is he, anyway?' Kate said. 'He started all this. Where the hell is Dad?'

The music was so loud, nobody heard her at first.

'Where is Dad?' Kate shouted.

Clio stopped laughing and watched as they all shrugged and shook their heads. They had no idea where their father was. They no longer cared.

Until Danny came running down the side deck, yelling and hollering.

'Man overboard! Man overboard!'

Clio was the first to join Danny by the rails and the first of Frazer Lattimer's children to see him floating, face down, in the water.

He was already dead.

# AFTER

Clio hadn't expected to feel so upset.

When her mother had died, the shock had quickly been replaced with tears. She'd cried for what felt like months, until all the sadness turned to something else.

Anger. Hatred.

If you'd asked her, she would have openly admitted that she loved her mother more than her father and that she would most likely not mourn his demise. He was her family, but she had avoided her dad for years and could hardly play the loving daughter now.

And, yet, as the hours passed, the tears came.

I'm grieving for the father I should have had, she told herself. Not the man he was.

Rob was even more gentle when he spoke to her for the final time, perhaps noticing how blotchy her face was, aware she'd been crying. Probably much softer than he should have been. You could forgive him that. He knew her. Properly knew her. She'd been vulnerable with him, at her softest. She'd toughened up since, but he remembered her differently.

'I'm worried,' he said, pushing the freshly brewed coffee towards her and nodding at it, willing her to take a sip. She couldn't. Her throat was swollen tight; she barely felt like swallowing, let alone drinking.

'You have it wrong, Rob,' Clio said, weakly. 'We've been through enough. Tonight was . . . well, it was just us. You can't read anything into a few arguments, not with my lot.'

'Clio, you've said yourself, James attacked Adam physically when he returned to the deck. None of you can attest to where he was on that boat when you all separated . . .'

'Rob, I was standing up on deck on my own. Nobody was with me. Does that mean I killed my dad?'

'Adam saw you, Clio.'

'This is crazy,' she protested.

'It will be easy to establish if your brother has money problems. Let's say your father refused him a loan. Then tonight he announces there won't even be an inheritance. Couldn't James have just snapped? The way he snapped with Adam? Maybe he didn't even mean for your father to drown. He just hit him. Then he panicked when your father passed out.'

Clio kept shaking her head, incredulous.

'We all fell out with my dad at some point in our lives,' Clio said. 'And we all had words with him this weekend over various things. I had a go at him yesterday for how he treated my mam all those years ago. But even if you're right and James hit him, how are you going to prove it, Rob? If James is denying it?'

'I can't let you go home with a murderer, Clio,' Rob said. 'Why the hell do you think I'm keeping you all here?'

Rob sat back and studied her. Clio felt her face colouring.

'Do you think your father deserved to die, Clio?' he asked.

'Don't be stupid. I . . .'

'Please. Be honest with me. I'm not asking for an admission of guilt. Just, tell me what you think.'

'Yes.'

Clio inhaled sharply. She'd blurted the word before she could stop herself.

'I just mean . . . our mam shouldn't have gone first. It was the wrong way round. He wasn't a good man.'

'That's okay. It's okay to feel that.' Rob hesitated. 'And for all your problems with your siblings, you love them, right?'

'Yes.' She nodded emphatically. 'They're annoying as fuck, but they're my blood. I'm . . . angry at Adam. For what he did. But, I remember what it was like, when we were younger. When we were closer. Mam did her best but our house could be a . . . a difficult place to live.'

'Okay,' Rob said. 'We're getting somewhere. Thing is, Clio, in my job, you see a lot. I did a murder up in Wexford town a couple of years ago. I was only starting; my mentor was this jaded fuck who couldn't wait to get off the job. We had a man, dead at the foot of a flight of apartment stairs. Post-mortem said he was pissed, so it could have been a fall. But forensics said he went backwards and scuff marks on the steps and bannisters up top indicated it might have been a shove. We had witnesses, though, who said it was a fall. His wife, and a neighbour.'

Clio shrugged, unsure where this was going.

'We'd a file on the man. Domestic violence. He'd been in custody once or twice and the wife had been in Wexford General more times than you can count. My boss reckoned she pushed him. He figured the neighbour, who'd been listening to the wife having the shit kicked out of her for years, said she saw him fall to give the wife cover. We closed the file. Accidental death. Now, I probably shouldn't be telling you that, but you and I have history and there is a point.'

'Rob, I . . .'

'Just listen. You believed your father wasn't a good man. That doesn't necessarily mean you'd want him killed. But you also love your siblings. And if you happened to see one of them do something to your dad, it would be very natural to choose to keep quiet. Out of concern, or fear or . . . love.'

Clio's hands started to tremble.

'Clio, I already have a witness who saw James arguing with your father.'

Her mouth fell open.

'Danny was up front. He could see everything. And you were at the back. If you'd turned your head even once and looked up the right side of the yacht, you'd have seen the same thing.'

Rob was staring at her, imploring her to confess.

Clio wilted. She looked away before he could see anything on her face.

'Danny was your dad's best friend,' Rob continued. 'He's not a member of your family. He's fond of your family but, to be honest, he doesn't seem to care for James too much . . . And he's not going to keep your secrets. Not when I'm threatening him with obstruction.'

She swallowed.

'He saw Frazer and James quarrelling, Clio. He went downstairs for a couple of minutes and when he came up, they were both gone. But nobody saw your father anywhere else on that boat. The last time he was seen, he was arguing with James on the side of the deck where blood was spilled.'

'Why would he . . .' Words failed her. She looked back at Rob. 'Do you believe Danny?'

'I've no reason not to.'

He fell silent. Waited.

'I can't condemn my own brother,' Clio said, exhaling it in one big breath. Then, 'What does James say?'

'He told me to my face that he didn't say a word to your father after the party split up. He's already been caught out in a lie.'

Clio shrugged, but her face was starting to give it away.

'If you saw something and you don't tell me, I can't protect you, Clio. Your father might not have been a pleasant man but if James killed him, it wasn't self-defence. James wasn't a victim. He's not getting away with it.'

Clio lifted her hands to her face. She covered her eyes.

'I hated my dad, Rob,' she said, letting out a great big sob. 'So, why do I feel like this?'

She couldn't see him, but suddenly he had his arms wrapped around her.

'Because you're human,' he said. 'But Clio, we don't get to decide who lives and dies. No matter how we feel about them.'

She nodded.

'I saw them fighting,' she whispered. 'I turned around and they were arguing. I couldn't hear anything over the music. James pushed Dad. I looked away. I didn't want any more drama and I didn't care if James hurt him. I figured Dad would push back, anyway. Then everybody came back to where I was, including James. I didn't see my dad again.'

Rob tensed. Then he let her go.

He smiled at her, then nodded.

He had what he needed.

Clio began to shake properly when he'd left.

Her father was dead and her brother had killed him.

How was any family supposed to deal with that?

When she returned to the others, Kate was still in a state.

James was gone. Rob had asked him to step out again.

'What?' Kate asked Clio. 'What did he ask you? Did he ask you about James as well? Adam says he keeps asking about James. Did you see something?'

Clio hung her head. Kate gasped.

'This can't be right,' she moaned. 'James wouldn't hurt Dad, would he? Oh God, I think I'm going to be sick.'

She stood up abruptly, and in the small space, everything Kate must have eaten and drunk that day spewed forth. The others moved their legs and shoes out of the way as Kate cried and apologised, in between heaving.

'It's okay,' Clio said, rubbing her back. Ellen, too, stood and pulled their sister's hair off her face.

'You have a bug or something,' Ellen said. 'You're never this sick.'

'It's not a bug,' Kate sobbed. 'I can't believe the timing of this . . . oh, God, not now.' She shook her head. 'He couldn't have. I know Dad was a . . . he was a . . . but James?'

Kate stood up straight and wiped away a dribble of bile from her chin with the back of her hand.

All the secrets would come out now, Clio realised.

Kate had no idea just what her father had been capable of.

The letter was safe at home.

Maybe one day, she'd show it to Kate. She wouldn't grieve for their father, then.

Clio wasn't angry at James.

No matter what Rob said, her father had deserved to die.

That's when they heard him shouting.

'I didn't do anything!' James yelled. 'It's not me. For fuck's sake! I'm innocent!'

# PART II

## TEN YEARS EARLIER
### 2008

# MAY

# RYAN

It was bad. Skin-tingling, sweat-inducing, heart-racing bad.

Ryan looked around the dark, dirty room, utterly familiar to him now, and millions of miles away from what he'd grown up with. In the window, curtains, so full of holes they looked like they'd been attacked by dogs, failed abysmally in their attempt to keep out daylight. As the sun flooded through the rips, tiny dust particles danced in its glow and created illuminated stripes over the furniture and the addicts hiding in corners.

They were only yards from Wexford town centre, with its brand-name stores and restaurants, busy-bee workers and smiling, shopping families. But the occupants of this house could have been miles away. A different planet, another universe.

Up until recently, Ryan had been able to go whole days without taking anything. But lately, his in-betweeners, as he called them, had become briefer.

He was fucking up, he knew he was. He'd dropped out of school the year previous, to the absolute dismay of his mother. His father had just looked at him with that smug little expression that said his youngest son was meeting all his low expectations of him. But

Ryan had needed money. He needed to work. There was no point pissing around with final exams when Ryan knew he was good for nothing, going nowhere.

'But your writing,' his mother had beseeched. 'You write so beautifully, Ryan. You don't even need to study, that's what your English teacher said. You could sail into a degree course.'

Ryan had laughed. He'd been high as a kite at the time but back then the drugs were manageable, he could still function. His mother thought he wasn't taking her seriously, that he wasn't taking life seriously. She was wrong. Ryan wanted to live life to its fullest, to experience every single minute. To block out the pain and only feel the good. That wasn't going to happen in school, and certainly not in Spanish Cove, where his father watched him like a hawk, always ready to pounce, always ready to attack.

But, there were practicalities. He'd missed so many shifts at the ferry dock that he'd got his final warning. He'd tried to keep his drug use to weekends, but slowly it had become Friday to Sunday, meaning he missed Mondays in work. Then, as he was generally off on Monday, he started to miss Tuesdays. And on and on it went.

Last week, he'd gone on a four-day bender and he knew if he dared to show his face on the dock, they'd just laugh and tell him to take a run and a jump. A Lattimer he may be, but they owed him nothing.

He needed money. Badly. He was three years off his trust coming through and he'd already blown a hole in it.

Ryan was in trouble.

Worse than all of that, he didn't know who to turn to. He was breaking his mother's heart. She'd dragged him home too many times. And if he went to her, she'd get his father involved.

Daddy dearest.

*I'm right, you're wrong, I'm big, you're small.*

*You're nothing.*

*You'll be nothing.*

*It's my job to toughen you up. Look at you. You look like a little girl.*
*Grow up.*

Ryan couldn't actually remember a time when he wasn't being told to grow up.

Thing was, he'd never felt that young, or babied, to begin with. His mother only made so much effort with him to counterbalance the effect of Frazer and it still didn't drown out his father.

Ellen and Kate would barely look at him now. James stopped caring a long time ago.

Only Adam and Clio gave a damn and he didn't want to make their lives any harder.

Ryan lifted the crack pipe to his mouth and inhaled deeply. The fumes hit the back of his nose and throat, making his eyes water.

He fell back on something soft, opened his eyes and stared up at the ceiling, enjoying the warmth, and the numbness that he needed more and more.

Ryan was going to die. Either because he killed himself or because his dealer found him and killed him. Whichever way it happened, it was coming.

And he couldn't say he wanted to fight it any more.

# CLIO

'Did you see her brother up in town during the week?'

'Oh, my God, no, but my sister did. She said he'd pissed himself? He was hanging around outside McDonald's. She said he was begging. Wouldn't you just die, though! And them flouncing around Albertstown like royalty from the big house. Money can't buy class, that's what my mother says.'

The sniggering followed Clio all the way down the corridor of St Agnes' convent secondary school. They knew she could hear them. They didn't care. She was meant to.

She stopped at her locker, opened it with all the rage that could be directed at an inanimate object, jiggling the key angrily, throwing in the books she didn't need for homework and slamming it shut. She'd have to listen to those bitches, or bitches like them, on the bus the whole way home now. The journey would take forever – it didn't even go directly to Spanish Cove. The New Ross to Albertstown bus covered several senior schools on the way and twice as many villages.

Fuck Ryan anyway.

Clio was well able for her peers. She could easily claw their little eyes out if they so much as looked at her sideways. But she wasn't going to do anything to upset her mother. She couldn't bring any more trouble home.

Clio stomped out the main door and down the stone steps towards the road.

It was raining; she didn't care. Her long brown hair hung loose on her shoulders over the drab grey sweater that ran into an equally unappealing knee-length skirt. The middle of May and she was getting soaked. Only in Ireland.

She reached the pavement and was about to turn left for the stop where the school bus was already waiting when a car horn beeped repeatedly.

It was her mother's tiny Punto and Kathleen herself was hanging out the driver's window, waving frantically at Clio.

Clio jogged towards the car, her bag banging on her back. She jumped into the passenger seat and quickly pulled the door closed behind her.

'Is everything okay?' she asked, concerned. Teddy bounded around the back seat, trying to get at Clio to lick her face. She patted him, distractedly.

'I thought you wouldn't see me and you'd hop on the bus,' her mother answered. She brushed at the drops of rain that had landed on the sleeve of her blouse when she'd leaned out the window.

Clio frowned.

'But is everything all right? Why are you picking me up?'

'It's raining and I thought you might like a lift, for a change.'

Kathleen reached into the glove compartment on Clio's side and pulled out a brown paper bag.

'Chester cake fresh from the bakery,' she said, handing it to Clio.

The pastry was still warm; Clio could feel it through the paper. She grinned, threw her bag beside Teddy, who started nosing through it, and settled into her seat. Her mother probably guessed she was having a hard time and could do with a break from the school bus.

There was only one wiper working on the windscreen, luckily on the driver's side. Clio's view was a wall of water, so she observed her mother as she sat forward in her seat, squinting, like she always did when she drove. Her dark hair was pulled back in a soft ponytail, and the lines on her forehead were furrowed with concentration. More than that: worry.

'Has he come back yet?' Clio asked.

They hadn't seen Ryan in days.

Nobody in the house was talking about it, which meant everybody was thinking about it.

Her mother sighed.

'No,' she said. 'But I've heard some whispers.'

'Me too,' Clio said. She brought the cake up to the edge of the brown bag and took a bite, the icing sugar dusting her lips. She could feel the dog's breath on her neck. He wasn't having any of her treat. The last time she'd given him sugar, he'd got worms. The two weren't related, she knew that, but the mental scars of seeing the spaghetti-like strings emerging from his backside and onto her duvet had stayed with her.

'I thought you might have,' Kathleen said. She reached over and touched Clio's cheek.

'It's not something I want you worrying about, love,' she said.

'He's my brother.'

'But not your responsibility.'

Clio shrugged.

Kathleen's tone was light, relaxed, loving. The same as always.

Yet, Clio couldn't ignore the fact her mother's lips were so badly chapped they were almost bleeding and that this was the third day in a row she'd worn that blouse, even though she was fastidious about laundry and this one was stained at the cuff from last night's dinner.

By the time they reached Albertstown, it was starting to clear up a little.

'Thank God for that,' her mother said, rolling down her window to let some fresh air in. 'We'd have had to build an ark if that stayed down for the day.'

Even the simple reference to the weather brought Clio's thoughts back to Ryan. Was he indoors? Was he dry? Or was he passed out somewhere, soaked and cold and ill?

Her mother slowed the car as they approached the harbour. Clio didn't know why until she saw Danny coming up from the boatyard, his dark green raincoat open and flapping in the wind.

He took his hood down when he saw Kathleen and waved. When the car rolled to a halt, Danny ducked his head in.

'Hello there, young lady,' he said to Clio. 'Looking forward to the weekend?'

'Why, what's happening at the weekend?'

'I just meant being off school,' he said, confused.

Clio smiled. Danny was painfully bad with small talk. But he tried, for her benefit, especially.

'Oh,' she said. 'I've a lot of homework. It's my Junior Certificate next month.'

'Used to be the Inter Cert, in my day.'

'You didn't get anywhere near your Inter Cert, Danny McHugh.'

Kathleen laughed. 'You started bunking off and going fishing before you hit double digits.'

'You can have no secrets!'

Danny grinned. Then his face grew serious.

'Any word?' he asked Kathleen.

Her mother glanced sideways at her. Clio turned away, pretended to be interested in something outside her window.

'Only one of those wipers working for you?' Danny asked.

'Oh. Yes.' Kathleen took her cue. She rolled up the window on her side, then opened the door.

'Just give me a moment, love,' she said to Clio.

Clio bit into the remains of the pastry.

Her mother got out of the car and joined Danny.

You'd swear the car was a sound vacuum, Clio thought to herself. Though even if it was, she'd have been able to lip-read the pair of them, standing in front of the Punto, allegedly discussing the dodgy windscreen wiper, all the while dissecting Ryan's latest adventure.

*Frazer won't let him back in the house,* her mother said.

*He doesn't like being reminded he's failed,* Danny answered.

*But he's our son,* Kathleen responded.

*He's also a drug addict, Kathleen.*

Then she turned away and Danny did too and Clio had to content herself with their backs.

She lowered her window a couple of centimetres. She could hear them better now.

'Heaven knows, I should have stood up to Frazer more when it came to Ryan,' Kathleen said. 'After Ellen, I thought he'd learned his lesson about going too hard. Is this my fault, Danny?'

Clio frowned. After Ellen, did her mam say? What about Ellen?

Ellen did nothing and went nowhere. She was as good a daughter as you could get, if you were okay with having your twenty-nine-year-old still living at home.

'You're a great mother,' Danny said. 'I don't know what it is about the lad. Maybe he reminds Frazer of himself.'

'Oh, he does that,' Kathleen said. 'He was carved from the hip bone of him. If Ryan learned to back down, it wouldn't be so bad. I've taken his side so many times but how can I, now, when he's pushed us so far? I know what Frazer is like, but none of the others have gone off the rails.'

Danny reached out and squeezed Kathleen's hand.

'It's tearing our family apart,' Kathleen said. 'But they're as bad as each other, Danny. You know, I always wanted the children to have two parents who were together. Now I don't know if . . .'

Then her mother turned and looked at her and Clio cast her eyes sideways quickly so she wouldn't be caught spying. She leaned back and started to stroke Teddy's ears, barely noticing that all he wanted was to lick her sugary fingertips.

'You make sure you're taking care of yourself, pet,' Danny said to Kathleen. 'Don't forget, you matter, too.'

By the time her mam returned to the car, Clio had rolled the window back up and was pretending to be bored.

'Home,' her mam said brightly.

'That wiper's still broken,' Clio responded.

'It needs a part,' Kathleen answered.

Clio sighed.

Sure, she was only fifteen.

But did they really need to baby her so much?

# PRESENT

Rob's boss sat across the desk from the detective, surveying the file Rob had prepared.

Every other minute, he nodded; occasionally he grunted.

But, in general, his demeanour was uneasy and there was a lot of head shaking going on.

DCI Quinn had taken the top job in Wexford two years previously and the success of his department in delivering fail-safe books of evidence to the Director of Public Prosecutions had become legendary.

'Unfortunately, this family is well known to some of our colleagues,' he said, after surveying all the statements at the front of the book. 'Never a good sign. The youngest son was into drugs, did you know that?'

'I did. Didn't know he'd got involved with us.'

'Sadly, yes. And there was a missing persons?'

'Yep. The file is closed on that one, now. He came back while I was down in Albertstown.'

Quinn looked up.

'Christ, Downes. We'll keep you on. Any idea where Shergar is?'

Rob smiled, ruefully.

'The poor parents,' Quinn continued. 'Mother has a heart attack young and the father is murdered at the hands of the son. Even if he was a bastard, by all accounts. All that wealth? What a waste.'

Quinn grimaced and glanced back down.

'If you can just bulk out the evidence here. It's all a bit speculative in the absence of a confession or proper forensics. For now, I wouldn't feel confident sending this over. You'll have to do a bit more work, Downes. You have it right, though. It was that son of a bitch. Every other person on the yacht is alibied to the hilt. It's only been a week. You have time.'

Rob took a deep breath.

It all pointed to James Lattimer.

But there was something niggling at Rob.

They had witness statements, and even a rudimentary glance into James' background had shown a man suffocating amid debt, career failure and, quite possibly, extramarital affairs.

Rob couldn't put his finger on it.

But it was there.

There was some part of this story he still didn't know.

# MAY

# JAMES

The restaurant was new and popular and overpriced; exactly the sort of place that Sandra liked and precisely where James wanted to be seen on a night out.

And they were celebrating. He'd been working on a cheap-as-chips soap drama for the last few years as a line producer, but now he'd landed his first executive producer role.

It had been a gamble that paid off. A friend, with absolutely no confidence, had nervously entrusted him with a treatment and a pilot episode. The friend had been hoping for some feedback. James read it and instinctively knew it was something a national network would buy. And he'd been right.

Once he'd secured the commission, he was able to convince his friend that James was the only man who could get the programme made. That, in fact, the broadcaster had demanded James.

The friend, bowled over with gratitude, agreed. James didn't convey to him the station's real response; that it was the best treatment and pilot script they'd seen in years and they were prepared to spend big money on it. They'd put no conditions on, they just wanted it made.

James returned to the channel with the writer's express wish that James produce it.

James didn't feel guilty. He'd spotted an opportunity and taken it. If it hadn't been for him, the thing would never have been seen by the broadcaster in the first place.

At twenty-five, he was about to get the biggest break of his career. It was unprecedented, for somebody so young. And James was in his element.

The problem was in the details. He wasn't a production company. He was one man. But he had to look like he was the head of a new and thriving organisation. He needed money for lunches and dinners and expenses, an office premises that wasn't his back bedroom, a website and an assistant.

Just like when he'd got the job on the soap, he would have to fake it to make it. Executive producer fees were large, and James knew if this show did well, the network would commission another season and another, and who knew where it would go from there?

It was important, not just for him, but for his new family. Sandra was five years older and hadn't seen him as anything more than a bit of fun to begin with. She had her life, her daughter, and she needed a man who could provide for them both.

But James wanted her. He wanted her badly. She reminded him of himself: driven. Bella's father, an agent who'd promised Sandra a modelling career, had left when he found out she was pregnant. A single mother, Sandra had still managed to carve out some success on the magazine pages, but now, at thirty, she was looking to the future and determined to make a good life for herself and Bella.

James loved that little girl. He'd never in a million years thought he'd be the paternal sort but the way Bella looked at him made him feel warm inside. She hero-worshipped James, the super cool TV guy who wore Ray-Bans and Levi's and hung around with the stars and might one day be her actual dad.

He wanted to be adored like that. By Sandra and by his ready-made family.

So James had to do something epic to convince her that his inheritance wasn't a one-off, that he was capable of earning the money to keep Sandra in the style she wanted to become accustomed to.

They both deserved it.

He walked through the restaurant, smiling at people he didn't know, so the people who did know him would think he was well-networked. He arrived at the table just in time to hear Sandra ordering a pricey Saint-Émilion Grand Cru.

'Jesus, Sandra.' He laughed, nervously. 'The champagne when we arrived was the celebration, I thought.'

'This is my treat to you, darling.' She smiled. She cupped his hand in hers, the diamond engagement ring sparkling on her wedding finger. 'You prefer a good red to bubbles, I know that. An executive producer! I knew you'd make it.'

He grinned back. She was right. He was on top of the world and he couldn't let something as mundane as cash flow ruin it. Besides, James had never struggled to find money. He was a Lattimer – he'd arrived in Dublin slap-bang in the Celtic Tiger with fifty large ones in his pocket and a deposit good to go on a city centre apartment. Things were starting to fall apart in the country now and yet, he was still on the up. Fortune favoured him.

'Red,' he said.

'What? Oh, the wine?' Sandra was confused.

'No.' James smiled. 'I think that's what I'll call it. Red Productions. My new company.'

'Oh, perfect, darling!'

James nodded.

If he could just access another fifty grand, he'd be fine.

# ADAM

The summer was going to be a welcome break from college.

He had to get through his exams next week, but then he'd have a whole three months off. And he was going to enjoy it. The past month had been nothing but stress. He was struggling, he knew he was, but he reckoned he had it in him to pull some good grades out. He hoped. Some last-minute cramming should do it.

Eva caught up with him as he came out of the pub's off-licence, laden down with two trays of lager cans.

'Alco in training?' She laughed, twirling the end of her blond ponytail in that cutesy, falsely unconscious way she'd carefully cultivated.

His face must have betrayed him, because suddenly she was full of contrition.

'Oh, shit, sorry, Adam. I wasn't thinking. Any sign of Ryan?'

Adam shrugged. His brother was just one of the reasons he'd taken a break from studying this weekend and come down to Spanish Cove. The other was his friend's twenty-first. It was coming up in a couple of weeks and Adam had promised to help plan a party for it, including starting to stock up on booze. He'd done little to help up to now. And even when he arrived the previous evening, Adam had been immediately put to work on a futile search and rescue exercise in Wexford town. Ryan had been spotted there, off his face. He'd gone back into hiding as soon as Adam started trawling the streets.

'No sign,' he told Eva.

She helped him carry the trays over to the car he'd borrowed from his mate, then held the boot open while he dumped them in.

'What has you back from the big city, anyway? Just Ryan?'

They were inches apart and Adam could see almost every freckle on her face. Her eyes were a dull grey, darkened by the clouds overhead. A spot of rain fell on her cheek and he had to resist the urge to dry it, because if he touched her, she'd think it meant something.

Eva had been following him around for years and he knew she had the hots for him.

She was a good-looking girl; friendly, fun, smart. He was fond of her.

But he couldn't hurt her. He didn't want to hurt his parents, either, but that didn't mean he would pretend to be something he wasn't. It was selfish and would cause too much fall-out.

Women didn't do it for him. Never had.

'Micky turns twenty-one in a couple of weeks,' Adam said. 'There's a gang of us planning his party. Can't leave it to his mammy. She'd have us round for tea and fairy cakes.'

Eva laughed.

'Anyway, I'd best head on,' Adam said.

'Grand, so. Hey, Adam . . . can anybody come to Micky's party?'

'We need *anybody* to come. Little bollocks has no mates, bar us old gang from school. It will be a piss-poor show if we can't get half the village to turn up. We might as well just send the strippergram into his work.'

'Isn't he a porter in the old folks' home?'

'You can see the problem.'

Eva laughed.

'Can I come, then?'

Adam had walked into the trap. He knew Eva would see this as a personal invite from him. And then she'd expect to be in his company, when he really just wanted to spend the night with his mates.

Especially Lee, Micky's cousin, who, if Adam wasn't wrong, had sent him the right signals when he'd come up to Dublin with Micky a few weekends ago. Adam had never known Lee was gay but then, he doubted anybody knew Adam was, either. Albertstown was good at that.

So pretty and perfect and sin-free on the surface.

'Um, yeah, come along if you like,' he said, then looked away quickly.

Adam was about to get in the driver's seat when Eva called out to him again.

Jesus wept, what now?

'Isn't that James?' Eva said, pointing at the Honda convertible that had just pulled into the pub's car park.

It was James and he had the top down, even though it was still drizzling and would have been pelting down on the motorway.

*What is he like?* Adam thought, just as Eva opened her mouth and said:

'He's such a movie star, isn't he?'

She was blushing. Maybe Eva wasn't after him at all, Adam mused. Maybe he was just a route to his older brother.

But then she turned and smiled at him and he saw the quiet desperation in her eyes, the insistent imploring that only unrequited love can bestow.

He felt like the biggest shit in the world. And to make it worse, it wasn't like the village was crawling with single young men.

'I'd best go say hello,' he said.

He slammed the driver's door and walked with Eva towards the pub, parting ways as she returned to work while he approached James.

'Bro!' James said, and pulled Adam into a hug. 'Roof got stuck. The state of me driving down that motorway! The da said you were down here – fancy a pint?'

'Eh.' Adam looked back over at Micky's car. 'I'm driving.'

'Ah, one won't kill you, though. You're too sensible. Come on, I'm only down for the night.'

'They tell you about Ryan, then?'

James' features scrunched up in surprise.

'Ryan? No. I came down to see you.'

Adam was confused.

'Come on,' James said. 'Let your big brother buy you a drink. If you insist, I'll make it an OJ. I want to talk to you about something important. Hey, you can tell me all about this college course as well. You're nearly finished now, huh? You must come round to ours more. It's crazy I have to come down to Spanish Cove to catch you when we're both living in the capital!'

James was already walking towards the pub. Adam pulled his Nokia from his pocket and sent Micky a quick text.

*Sorry. Catching up with brother. See you later.*

Micky texted back immediately.

*Ryan?*

Everybody was thinking of Ryan. Except James, it seemed.

# PRESENT

Eva Casey had seemed more puzzled than alarmed when Rob had asked her to meet him down at Danny's yacht, *The Countess*, two weeks after Frazer Lattimer's death.

Although she was a few years older than Rob, he still knew Eva quite well. She'd worked in the Strand Bar her whole life, obviously, but she was also a proper villager. She'd got married and had kids in exactly the same place she'd grown up. To the best of his knowledge, she only left Wexford to shop in Dublin the odd time. Even her holidays seemed to be Ireland-based.

He heard her on the deck before he saw her.

'Down here, Eva,' he called up from below deck.

She appeared in the door frame, the sunlight casting her figure in shadow.

Still a fine thing.

Rob stroked his chin and smiled.

Those days were behind him, now. They'd got him into far too much trouble, his son excluded.

'Well, Detective, I'm surprised they haven't set up a haunted special on this boat yet,' Eva said. 'You know we local businesses are always looking for tourist opportunities.'

Rob smiled, grimly.

'You'd have to get it past Danny McHugh first,' he said. 'Can you imagine Danny leading a weird and grisly ghost tour?'

'He could be the main attraction.'

Eva came down the steps. She stopped at the end and looked around her.

'It's mad, though, isn't it?' she said. 'To think a man died on this boat.'

'He didn't,' Rob said. 'He died in the water.'

'You know what I mean. Wasn't there blood on deck?'

Rob nodded. All Frazer's, forensics had confirmed.

He would have died, even if he hadn't gone in the water. That's what pathology had added. Whatever he was hit with was so hard it had caused massive internal bleeding. There was a bigger build-up of blood inside Frazer Lattimer's skull than the spray on the yacht could ever have indicated. A subdural haematoma.

They still hadn't found the weapon that had been used; no doubt that had ended up in the sea.

Forensics were working hard now on his clothing. The water had washed away most of the evidence but they'd picked up a few trace elements that might prove helpful. Two weeks had passed since the murder and they still had James Lattimer in custody. The police had made a successful case to the judge that, with his international contacts, James was a flight risk. Turned out, he couldn't make bail, anyway. But he couldn't be held in detention forever – they needed to give the DPP a complete file so he could push for a trial date.

The cabin they stood in was a large space. Comfortable. The

yacht's interior was lined with cream leather couches. Glass lamps adorned the walls, so while it was dim, it was never too dark.

'You and Adam Lattimer, you had a bit of a thing going, back in the day,' Rob said.

'Where did you hear that?' Eva asked. Rob could see the tension in her face, the defensiveness of her body language.

'Just around.'

Eva hesitated.

'No,' she said. 'We didn't. It's just a rumour. Silly girl talk.'

'You sound . . .' Rob reached for the word. 'I don't know. Were you disappointed by that?'

Eva shrugged.

'It was what it was. I suppose I was lucky I wasn't with him. It would have been a bit shit when he disappeared for ten years, huh?'

'Yeah, I guess so.'

Rob said nothing. He waited for her to fill the space.

'Why are you asking?' she said.

'Just curious.'

'Hmm. And is that why you're here, on the yacht? I mean, you know who did it, don't you? Everybody is talking about it. James Lattimer killed his own father.'

'It's looking likely,' Rob said. 'But it takes a jury to convict and we need a strong case against him.'

'Well, what do you want me for, then?' Eva asked, looking concerned.

'You've nothing to worry about,' he said. 'Really. I just wanted to know if you'd any insights into Adam Lattimer from back in the day.'

'I'm sorry, I don't. That's the truth.'

Rob nodded. Fuck it, anyway.

He'd sent himself on this wild goose chase, maybe it was time he put an end to it.

He was about to offer to walk her back to the bar when he was struck by a sudden thought.

'Do me a favour,' he said, his whole body tensing as the notion filled his head.

Eva raised her eyebrows quizzically.

'The loo is over there, just down that corridor,' Rob said. 'Can you go in, close the door, and make some crying sounds?'

Eva looked left from the foot of the stairs, down the small passage beside her.

'Down here?' she said.

'That's it.'

'Eh. Okay.'

Rob sat back down on one of the leather couches and waited.

He heard the door click to the toilet.

Then he sat and listened.

After a minute, the door opened again.

'Can I come out?' Eva yelled.

'Yep,' he called back.

Eva reappeared.

'Were you whimpering in there or wailing?' Rob asked.

'Wailing,' she said. 'Think, Gwyneth Paltrow accepting her Oscar. Why, could you not hear me?'

Rob shook his head.

'No,' he said. 'I couldn't hear anything.'

# MAY

# ELLEN

Frazer had made Ellen drive around Wexford town with him for the fifth time that week.

She was sick of it. Sick of searching for Ryan. Sick of being in that town, with all the risks it carried. She wouldn't get out of the car but still, every time they stopped at a light she was sure she'd see her ex. Or worse, that her father would see him. The man who'd knocked up his daughter, spent all her money, then legged it back to his wife while Ellen ended up in the nuthouse.

The humiliation.

Why couldn't they just let Ryan be? If he wanted to waste his life, why not just let him? It was his choice. Ellen of all people knew that what other people thought was best for you wasn't always the case.

The only reason she'd consented to this carry-on was for her mother's sake. Her poor mam, who just wanted everybody to get along. Who went out of her way to try to ensure all their happiness. Who kept asking Ellen to give up on the safety of her online courses and go out into the world and try living again.

Ellen argued that that hadn't really worked out for her the first time.

Her mam was insistent, though. And Ellen was starting to dream, just a little.

If she went to Dublin, she wouldn't be alone. James was up there and doing really well, by all accounts. Adam was in college there and would probably stay and get a job in the capital. Kate was determined to move up, now she had the . . . well, Kate would describe it as 'the look'.

You'd think it was Paris or London Kate was referring to when she talked about the capital. The sexiest thing about Dublin was its airport.

Still, if Ellen went to Dublin, she wouldn't have the *fear*. Her ex was not the sort to stray and stay far from his home town, as she'd learned bitterly.

'Your head is in the clouds, lass.'

'What?' Ellen jumped when Frazer spoke to her. They were on the road home after another fruitless trip.

'I was just saying these roads need resurfacing. After a few days of rain, those potholes are lethal. But you're dreaming away there.'

'Sorry, Dad. I was just . . . distracted.'

'Well, maybe put those thoughts to the back of your head for the weekend and make sure to help your mother out a bit. She needs you at a time like this. It's no time to be acting the idiot. What must people think of this family!'

Ellen flinched. Then she turned and stared at her father.

Why was he even out looking for Ryan? He'd no interest in finding him.

And why did he keep insisting Ellen come with him?

A cold feeling crept into her stomach.

Was he bringing her into town on purpose?

Was he enjoying her discomfort?

He'd begged for her forgiveness when she'd eventually come home after London. But she'd always suspected he thought she'd got what she deserved. She'd heard him muttering under his breath, any time he got frustrated with her.

She knew what he thought of her.

Ellen swallowed.

She needed to start seriously thinking about Dublin. Her father mightn't agree, but it was what her mother wanted.

She was twenty-nine, already too old to be living at home.

If she didn't get her skates on, she could end up being stuck there.

If she didn't get out of that house, she could end up murdering her father.

# JUNE

# CLIO

'Adam, my exams are over, I'm fifteen and, for the love of fuck, will you not just bring me!'

Clio was growing frustrated now, unable to think of any more convincing arguments, and ready to cry, curse, bribe, or do whatever the hell was needed to get Adam to sneak her out of the house and into Micky J's twenty-first.

It had been a horrible couple of weeks. Her mother had eventually found Ryan in a squat in Wexford town and almost convinced him to come home. But when he saw that their father was waiting in the car outside, he had refused to go. That hadn't been helped by Frazer getting out of the car and physically dragging Ryan out onto the street, where he was only prevented from beating his youngest son half to death by Kathleen and a passer-by.

Her mam had barely spoken to Frazer since and the atmosphere in the house was tense.

It wasn't just the fight she'd had with her husband. Clio sensed there was more going on with her mother.

Kathleen, who never gave up on any of them, had finally accepted she'd reached a stalemate with her youngest son. She couldn't force

Ryan to come home. She couldn't make her husband deal with the situation any better. And she couldn't put the lives of the rest of her children on hold any longer.

Clio couldn't bear any of it. She was mad at Ryan, furious with her father and disappointed with her mam. On top of that, she knew she'd fluffed most of her Junior Certificate exams because of the stress. Even languages, which she loved.

Adam sighed. She knew he was distressed, too. He'd finished his own exams and confided in his younger sister that he reckoned he'd screwed up a couple of them. Worrying about Ryan had proved too much of a distraction, even for his cramming skills.

'If I bring you –' he said, and Clio leapt at him, wrapped her arms around him and covered the side of his face with kisses.

He laughed and put her back down on firm earth, wiping the side of his face with a pretend disgusted look.

They were in the garden, standing on the bottom slope looking out over the sea, the place Adam liked to go to smoke. It was just out of the view of the house, out of sight of their parents, even though he was nearly twenty-two and didn't even live there any more.

'*If* I bring you,' he continued, 'you will not get slaughtered on my watch. If I catch you drinking, I will crucify you. And no sex, drugs or whatever else you get up to at fifteen these days. Let Ryan be your cautionary tale.'

Clio rolled her eyes dramatically.

'Spanish Cove,' she said. 'Where fun goes to die. I cannot wait to move out of here.'

'Wait your turn, pipsqueak. Your older sisters aren't even married off yet, as Austen would say. Here's one of them now. Jesus, Rocky Balboa look out.'

JO SPAIN

They watched Kate running up the road towards the house. Her morning workout was almost at its end, but tackling the climb up the hill was the toughest part.

'She's starting to look anorexic,' Adam said, shaking his head. 'You'd think the operations were enough. Fuck's sake.'

'She looks great,' Clio responded, defensively. Kate was all right, always passing down clothes and make-up she wasn't using any more, and nowadays they were clothes Clio actually wanted to wear, not the tents that Kate had worn up to this year.

'Kate!' Adam called out.

Their sister slowed to a halt and walked the last few yards towards them, then bent over and clutched her knees, breathing deeply.

'That bloody hill,' she panted.

'You should do your 10k downhill, then ring one of us to collect you.' Adam laughed.

'What would be the point of that?' Kate said, genuinely puzzled. 'Jesus, Adam, do not blow that in my face. Ryan won that bet you had to piss Dad off with smoking; you can quit now.'

'Ryan's not here,' Adam said. 'It falls to me to wind Dad up now.'

But he turned sideways to puff on the cigarette.

'You want to come to Micky's party later?' he asked.

Kate frowned.

'You're kidding? Your mates are little sleazeballs, Adam. The last time I saw Micky he tried to feel me up.'

'I would have thought you'd enjoy the attention. That's what all this . . .' he drew a circle in the air around her with his hand, '. . . is about, surely?'

'All *this*, is for me. Anyway, I can't. I'm starting in the hotel on Monday morning and I want to spend this weekend beautifying myself.'

'You're going to be a receptionist, sis, and Dad is still having fucking kittens you're going to be working like a pleb,' Adam said.

Kate snorted.

'I'm front of house and Dad more than anybody should be grateful I'm willing to work my way up from the bottom. Anyway, the sooner the better I am out of this house and away from you fuckers.'

She glanced at Clio and raised an eyebrow.

'Why do you look so pleased with yourself?' she asked. 'Is Adam bringing you?'

'If you tell Mam, I will spit in your tea every day for a month,' Clio said.

Kate tutted.

'Carrot, not the stick, Clio,' she said. 'What you should have said is, if I don't tell Mam, you will bring me tea for a month.'

Clio felt a bubble of panic. Kate wouldn't really rat her out, would she?

'Relax,' Kate said. 'It's not me you want to watch out for. Do not breathe a word to Ellen or she will rain all over that parade. You know she's the party police.'

Clio nodded obediently. Not a fucking hope she'd confide anything in Ms Proper Knickers.

Her mother, though, had an inner eye. And, even distracted, Kathleen managed to guess that Clio was planning something.

Kathleen was carrying a huge basket of laundry when Clio went back up to the house. Normally Clio would offer to help, but she was desperate to get into her room, to go through her wardrobe and see what she could wear on this illicit night out. She had a feeling Rob Downes would be there. She was only fifteen and he was nearly eighteen, but she had the absolute hots for him. Lads her own age were arseholes.

'You've a smile on your wee face that says you're up to something and you're very happy about it,' her mam said, breathing heavily as she put the laundry load down.

'No, I'm not,' Clio said, turning bright red.

'Now I'm convinced there's wrongdoing afoot,' her mam said. 'And I suppose that's the smell of Frazer's cigars I'm picking up right now, nothing to do with cigarettes at all.'

'I don't smoke,' Clio said.

'Because you tried Adam's and you don't like it any more?' Kathleen said, an eyebrow raised.

Clio hovered, one foot in her room already, praying her mam would let her go.

Kathleen picked up the laundry, then paused. She reached in and pulled out a black dress, one of Kate's new ones.

'I don't know who this belongs to,' Kathleen said. 'Stuff just goes into the laundry these days and gets lost.'

She held it out to Clio.

Clio took it, surprised and delighted.

She met her mother's eye.

Kathleen smiled, then went on her way.

'No drugs, no sex, no more than one glass of whatever you're having and get home safe afterwards,' she called back over her shoulder.

Clio laughed, happily. Summer was here. She was going to a party.

The shadow of Ryan hung over them all but it had lifted a little. For now.

# RYAN

He was in trouble.

Ryan hadn't taken anything in weeks but he still couldn't go home. He couldn't go near his family because he'd be putting them in danger. And it was all down to his own stupidity.

When he'd first met Aaron Dempsey, Aaron had seemed like the funniest, trendiest bloke Ryan had ever encountered. He was from a nice area on the south side of Dublin, a middle-class family and, while they probably weren't *Lattimer* people, Aaron and Ryan had clicked.

Because Ryan didn't really feel like a Lattimer himself.

Aaron was up for a laugh. He was a few years older than Ryan but he didn't treat him like a kid. He brought him to clubs, made sure he always had drugs, sorted out the women at the end of the night.

Aaron had his back.

Until Ryan started getting messy. That's how Aaron described it. Ryan was messy. Like a toddler who couldn't get through a meal without making a shit of himself.

Ryan couldn't understand it. They were taking the same drugs at the same parties, but it seemed to hit Ryan harder.

Then, Aaron started to cool off a little. He wasn't around as much, he didn't crack as many jokes when he was and there weren't as many invites.

Eventually, Aaron started to turn on Ryan.

There were no more freebies or mate's rates.

Debts were being called in.

Ryan had been a fucking idiot. He'd thought that, because Aaron spoke nicely and had been raised properly, he was trustworthy.

But Ryan didn't know Aaron.

He didn't know the gang Aaron was involved in or how dodgy they were. He didn't question why Aaron was living in Wexford and not Dublin.

It never dawned on Ryan that Aaron might have *had* to leave Dublin.

That his friend might be the sort who targeted people who could afford it and reeled them in.

That his friend could work for top Dublin gangsters. Bad people, who'd put Aaron to work in Wexford in order to clear his own debts.

Fucking crazy people.

Ryan was in a hole.

He'd run up a bill of twenty grand. He couldn't even figure out how. He couldn't put his finger on any single amount that was overly large, though he knew he'd snorted a shitload of crap up his nose and pumped a gallon into his veins.

But how did you do that? Twenty grand, puff, gone.

It didn't even seem like real money.

In three years' time he'd inherit his trust fund plus interest, probably close to sixty thousand. But that was in three years.

He didn't have that time. They'd told him they'd kill him.

They'd threatened his family.

When it was just him, he'd been able to accept it.

But now it was the people he loved.

Ryan was starting to panic. And in the middle of his problems, the police arrived.

They'd found him sleeping in an alley and brought him in to sober up.

The next morning, the detective, an older, seemingly friendly man, had sat down with Ryan and told him his options.

To Ryan's horror and amazement, they knew all about Aaron Dempsey and they knew all about Ryan. They knew who Aaron was connected to; they knew how he operated.

The cops couldn't target the ones higher up the chain. But they could nail the likes of Aaron.

And Aaron would lead them to somebody else.

It was in Ryan's interest to talk to them, the detective said.

Ryan listened, but he didn't really hear it.

He knew he only had one option.

He wasn't a tout. That would be sinking to the ultimate low in his father's eyes. You took responsibility for your own actions, Frazer always said.

Ryan had to pay his debts.

# PRESENT

'What are you doing here this late?'

Rob looked up when he heard his boss, Quinn. He rubbed his eyes, tried to get some moisture back into them. They were dry and itchy. He'd been reading for hours.

'I'm working,' Rob said. 'What are you still doing here, sir? Isn't it the charity ball tonight?'

'Eh, I'm working late, too,' Quinn said, air-dropping inverted commas on the *working*.

Quinn was most likely trying to avoid the annual police fund-raiser, this year being held in aid of a local homeless shelter. Rob felt nothing but sympathy for his boss. He, too, had no problem donating to a worthy cause. But Rob wanted to do it without having to smile like a fucking gobshite and nod along to inane anecdotes from the top brass. You didn't see them from one end of the year to the next but when it came to a social event, there they were, all suited, booted, present and correct.

Rob, though, wasn't just killing time to avoid the ball. Nor was he hiding in the office because his ex, once again, had reneged on the agreement for him to have his son. Two years of fighting for regular access was wearing, but Rob was fucked if he was giving up. She could cite the couple of times he'd let her down – because he'd been busy on the job – but that hadn't happened in months. Now, she was just being a total bitch.

No, Rob wasn't just keeping himself busy.

Rob was reading every piece of information he could lay his hands on that had anything to do with Ryan Lattimer, Aaron Dempsey and a well-known drugs gang with Dublin links.

'Just doing a bit of research,' Rob said.

Quinn peered over Rob's shoulder.

'Drugs?' he asked, puzzled.

'It's like you said.' Rob nodded. 'We'd opened a file on Ryan Lattimer and a certain Aaron Dempsey ten years ago. Officer in charge was Kevin Horan.'

'Dead.'

'Dead,' Rob agreed. 'The copper's curse. Heart attack a month before retirement. Anyhow. Good cop. He got an arrest for Dempsey at the time. Ryan wasn't dealing, just buying.'

'Begging your pardon,' Quinn said. 'Why are you still scratching at that closed scab, Rob?'

Rob sat back.

'I think Ryan or Adam Lattimer, or possibly both, might not have been entirely truthful with me about what happened on the yacht. Little inconsistencies keep cropping up. Like the fact they both claimed Ellen was in the toilet. Ana is saying she can't remember anything after the shock of seeing Frazer in the water. She, allegedly, can't even remember being downstairs herself, let alone where Ellen was. But the lads have stuck to their story. The thing is – I don't think they did know where Ellen was.'

Quinn shrugged.

'If Ellen Lattimer came up on deck and went and fought with her father, Clio Lattimer, for one, would have seen her, so she'd have to be lying too.'

Rob nodded.

That's what he was worried about.

'Make sure you don't run out of time with this,' Quinn said. 'The brother is the obvious one; you know that. Don't start peering in shadows for bogeymen. When it looks, smells and barks like a dog, it's a damned dog. Build the case you have, Downes.'

'I am, sir,' Rob said. 'Just dotting the i's.'

And swatting little flies, Rob thought to himself.

# JUNE

# ADAM

They'd pulled off a humdinger of a twenty-first for Micky.

It hadn't been without its challenges.

The football club they'd booked had fallen through with days to go.

Adam, knowing he was screwing up his exams anyway and in need of a distraction, decided to be the best friend he could be and had piled in to sort it out. He clenched his jaw and rang Eva, who, absolutely thrilled to be needed and reading much more into it than was there, had managed to talk her dad into giving them the function room upstairs in the Strand. He offered it at half price and Micky's mother, once she'd come to terms with the party having a lot more alcohol at it than she'd have liked, had stumped up the funds for the venue. Her son was coming of age. There'd be plenty of battles ahead and his choice of bride was the hill his mother had decided to die on.

Adam had feared the bar would be more difficult to get Clio into, but, made up as she was, nobody recognised her as little Clio Lattimer from up in Spanish Cove. Even he was surprised at how old she looked; she almost could have been one of Adam's mates from college.

By eleven, the party was in full swing.

That was when Ryan came in.

Adam spotted him immediately. It was like there was an invisible string attaching him to his brother; it lay idle on the ground when they were apart but tugged when he was close.

Ryan looked okay – well, not okay – his face was gaunt, haunted, and he didn't look like he'd eaten in weeks. But he appeared to be sober.

He stood at the edge of the party, looking around him, lost and desperate.

And, Adam realised, scared shitless.

Adam went straight over and put his hands on his brother's shoulders.

'What is it?' he asked, because he knew something was up and there was no time for bullshit small talk.

'I'm in trouble,' Ryan said.

Adam pointed to the door and led Ryan back downstairs and out to the car park. They walked down to the harbour and sat on the edge of the pier, legs dangling above the water, the night air warm on their faces and bare arms.

And that was where Ryan told Adam all that had befallen him; how he'd walked, stupidly and innocently, into the trap and how he was stuck there, like a dying fly in a web spun with superglue.

'Why didn't you just tell me?' Adam asked, when Ryan had spilled the whole sorry tale. 'Why didn't you ask for help ages ago? You know I have money.'

'It's your money,' Ryan said, and shrugged, like it was obvious. 'And I took the drugs. It was my choice.'

'That doesn't matter a damn,' Adam said. 'You're my brother.'

Ryan smiled thinly.

'What about this detective, Horan?' Adam said. 'You can't just let these Dublin fuckers get away with it. It was you this time, Ryan, but they obviously do it to people over and over. I'm not saying you're not a total idiot for getting addicted in the first place, but they clearly know what they're doing. They know how to lure people in.'

'They'd kill me,' Ryan said. 'And they've threatened the rest of the family, too. I told you. That's what's worrying me the most. I know what they're capable of. These aren't rational people, bro.'

'They can't get away with it,' Adam insisted, shaking his head.

'They can and they will,' Ryan said. 'It's what they do.'

Adam frowned. No. He wasn't accepting that.

'I can sort you with the money,' he said and Ryan exhaled a breath so fraught with emotion, Adam could tell he'd been holding it in for weeks.

'Adam, I can't . . . I don't know how to thank you.'

'I know how you can thank me. You're going into rehab.'

'I've been clean for a week. I haven't gone near anything. I don't need . . .'

'You're not pulling a George Bush Junior on me. You're going to proper rehab. It's the only condition I'll set.'

Ryan hunched his shoulders and looked down at his feet and the deep, dark water below.

Adam knew Ryan would fight it, but Adam would make sure that was what happened. And a lot more would happen too, once Adam had his way.

'Listen, you stink, man,' he said. 'Go up to the house. Have a bath. Then go give Mam a hug and say sorry. Tell her it's going to be different from now on.'

Ryan tensed.

'She won't want to see me.'

'She will,' Adam said.

'Dad won't.'

'Fuck him. It's your home. Let him try to refuse you entry with Mam there.'

'She saw what he was willing to do to me up at the squat, Adam. She saw what he was capable of.'

'She saw a father angry with his drug-addicted son, Ryan. Give her a break.'

Ryan sighed.

'You come with me,' he said.

'I can't. I have to make a phone call. I need to sort this money.'

Ryan examined Adam for a moment. He must have heard something in his brother's voice. But he didn't pursue it. Adam knew he was too exhausted to do so. It had taken all Ryan's energy just to come back and admit he was at the bottom. Now he'd handed over the burden, he needed somebody else to pick it up.

He stood, hovered over Adam for a moment, then walked away, shoulders slumped.

Adam watched him go. He hated seeing the defeat in his brother's gait, the shake in his hands.

Ryan had always been the more sensitive one. Or had it been that he'd been the one more picked on by Frazer? What came first, the chicken or the egg?

But Ryan also had that weird ability to hide what he was feeling, even while he felt it the most – to pretend that life was water off a duck's back for him.

They were close in age but hadn't fought the way most brothers did. Adam was the nurturing sort; he knew it himself, knew it was unusual. He'd always looked out for his siblings. Especially the ones who needed it. And Ryan needed looking after.

Adam took out his phone and dialled James. He let it ring but there was no answer.

He stood and walked back to the pub and took the stairs back up to the party.

He got through to his older brother just after midnight.

'Adam!' James exclaimed, full of the joys. He had drink on him and, by now, so did Adam. He'd gone straight to the bar after leaving Ryan and checking on Clio, and ordered a double measure of whiskey.

'How's it going, bro?' Adam said. He had to shout over the noise and strain then to hear what James was saying.

'. . . at a party, sounds like you're at one now,' James said.

'What?'

'Go somewhere quiet!'

Adam slipped out of the main function room and onto the stair-well. He had to stand aside for somebody to pass him – it was Lee. He smiled uncertainly at Adam and Adam realised Lee had followed him out, but hadn't understood he was on the phone.

Adam smiled ruefully. They'd kissed, once, over the last couple of weeks. He knew they were building up to more. Maybe even tonight.

'I'm at Micky's twenty-first,' Adam told James.

'Ah, course, course. You were helping him out, weren't you? You're a decent pal, bro. Has it been a good night?'

'Epic.'

'Brilliant. We're just home from a party ourselves. It's a big week next week. We start looking at casting. How are you, anyway, is everything okay? You were worried about exams, weren't you?'

'Yeah,' Adam said. 'That doesn't matter, though. It's . . . Ryan's back.'

'Oh. Right. Well, that's good, isn't it? Hopefully he'll get some help. Listen, Adam, is there something you need? It's late and Bella's still awake. I promised her a story. Fuck. Used to be piss-ups and hangovers. Now it's My Little Pony and early starts. I'm getting old before my time.'

'James, it's, um, it's about the money I loaned you.'

There was silence on the other end of the line.

'I . . . eh.' Adam was struggling. 'Do you need it all?'

'What do you mean, do I need it all? Do you think I would have asked for it all if I didn't need it?' James laughed nervously. 'And it isn't a loan, Adam. It's an investment. We've been through this.'

'It's just, I might need it to bail out Ryan.'

Adam couldn't see James but he knew the expression that was on his face. Disbelief, annoyance, anger. Of all of them, James had the least time for Ryan. James' mentality was firmly on the side of the survival of the fittest.

When he'd asked for fifty grand, James had promised Adam that he would have it back twice over by the end of the year. Adam had inherited fifty-eight thousand in total and as his father had paid for his degree, and Adam was working part-time, he had been content to let the money sit in his account. It was a temptation, but he wanted to keep it for after college. For travelling or a deposit on an apartment or something.

When James had contacted him, he'd allowed himself to be talked into giving James the loan. Let it help him with his career. They all knew James was going to be huge. He'd already been a producer on a soap and now he was making his own show. James was going places.

And when James would pay Adam back, even if he hadn't made a profit, Adam would have the money sitting there for when he needed it.

But he needed the money now. Or twelve thousand of it, anyway.

'Adam, the money is gone,' James said.

Adam didn't think he'd heard him right.

'Gone?' he repeated.

'Yes. Gone.'

'But . . . it's only been a couple of weeks.'

'It's not gone, gone.' James sighed. 'It's gone into the company, like I said. It's not in my hands, it's in the accountants'. It's paying for equipment and offices and a salary . . . Adam, I explained all this to you when I asked you to make the investment.'

'But Ryan's in trouble,' Adam said, and already he knew he was fighting a losing battle.

James said nothing.

'Shit,' Adam said into the silence. Then, 'Have you any personal funds, James? I mean, do any of you? I still have eight grand. If we can pitch together, we can . . . he needs twenty.'

'Jesus Christ!' James practically roared. 'Adam, can you hear yourself? Give Ryan twenty k? Twenty fucking k? So he can shoot it into his veins? Do you know what drugs cost, Adam? He'll go through that in a matter of weeks and he'll be back for more.'

'It's to pay off a debt—'

'No.' James cut him off. 'No. Listen to me, Adam. I love Ryan. He's my brother. But even if I had the money, I wouldn't give it to him. He's made his choice. And I love you, Adam, so I can't let you do this. It's not our job to bail him out. He can bail himself out or . . .'

James didn't finish.

Adam felt anger surge through him. It was *his* money. There might be logic in what James was saying, but . . .

'So, we can't bail Ryan out but I can bail you out, is that it?' Adam said. 'Doesn't seem fair.'

'Now, hold on,' James said. 'It's not comparable. I've asked you to come in on a successful—'

'I want my money back.'

Adam had the phone gripped so hard in his hand, his palm cramped.

'I can't give you the money back. Are you listening to me? There is no money.'

'I want it back,' Adam snapped. 'Give it back or I'll . . .'

'What? What will you do? Tell Mammy and Daddy? For crying out loud, Adam, we're in our twenties. Go tell Dad you made an investment with me and changed your mind. Tell him what you want your money back for. See what he says. This is the real world, Adam.'

Adam closed his eyes, frustration washing over him.

'They're going to kill him,' he said, his last attempt. 'James, they've threatened to kill Ryan. They've told him what they'll do to the girls. One of the men involved, he . . . he's just out of prison for throwing acid in his girlfriend's face. He had a kid with her. You think they can do that to one of their own and they wouldn't hurt one of our sisters? And they've said they'll do all that and then they'll find Ryan and gut him. He only has us, bro. Dad would see him dead before he gave him a cent, you know that. And it will break Mam's heart if she finds out.'

There was silence again.

He had him. Adam knew it. They were family, they were brothers. James could be single-minded but he wasn't a sociopath.

'Sorry,' James said. 'Can't help you.'

Adam was left listening to the dial tone.

He was still standing there, in shock, when Lee returned.

Lee took one look and brought Adam upstairs and into one of the back rooms.

And in his shock and distress, Adam let Lee comfort him, their first proper time, not the most romantic but a moment when Adam needed to be held and loved the most.

It was bittersweet.

Then the night took a turn for the worse.

They'd just finished and had their arms locked around each other, smiling, a little shy at the intensity they'd both felt, when Eva walked in.

Her face.

Adam, even though he'd tried not to string her along, even though he'd never expressed an interest, knew he'd broken her heart.

'You . . . you fucking pervert,' she said.

Adam, guilty and panicking, pushed Lee away. He tried to button his flies, his fingers clumsy, his hands sweaty with fear. And all the while, he ignored the hurt look on Lee's face.

'Eva,' Adam said, beseechingly. 'Please. I'm sorry, but please. Don't tell anybody. It's nothing.'

She'd choked on a sob, then her face had filled with stunned hatred.

'The fucking nerve of you!' she shouted.

Then she stormed out.

'Fuck!' Adam cried.

'It's nothing?' Lee said, quietly. '*This* is nothing?'

Adam spun on his heel.

'I'm sorry,' he said. 'I didn't mean that. It's just . . . shit, Lee. We're screwed.'

'What's the worst that can happen?' Lee said, bitterly. 'People will find out we like each other? Are you that embarrassed about me?'

'It's not you,' Adam said. 'My father will kill me. Are your parents going to be happy? You said they didn't know, either.'

'They don't know, but they suspect. I was thinking of telling them, anyway.'

Adam shook his head, miserably. His parents didn't suspect. Nobody did. And if Frazer got so much as a whiff . . . Adam's life would be over.

He must have looked pretty desperate, because Lee's anger seemed to fade.

'Your father won't kill you,' he said, gently. 'I can . . . I can come with you. If you want me to. We can tell him together. It might be hard at first but . . .'

'You don't know him,' Adam said. 'You have no idea.'

Frazer had picked on Ryan all his life and his constant refrain had been how *soft* the boy was, how people must think he was *queer*.

Frazer hated Ryan. Calling him gay was the worst insult Frazer could conjure.

In that moment, Adam just wanted to disappear.

# CLIO

Something was up with her brothers. She didn't know what, but there were plans afoot.

It had only been a few days since Micky's twenty-first.

That night, Ryan had come back and Adam had stayed down in Spanish Cove.

Since then, at every opportunity, the two of them had been in conclave, conspiring.

Something was going on and Clio was being left out of it and it drove her nuts.

Worse, whatever it was, it wasn't going well. Clio sensed from the permanent desperation on Adam's face, and the look of defeat on Ryan's, that Adam was trying to convince Ryan of something and failing badly.

She'd happened upon them, in the kitchen, two nights previous. She'd been sneaking in from being out late with Rob, hoping her clothes smelled of brine and not cigarette smoke and that her lipstick wasn't too mussed from their first kiss.

She knew Rob had a reputation but she also suspected a lot of it was generated by the overactive imaginations of bored teenagers and the willingness of Rob himself to be seen far and wide as a stud. He was nothing but sweet with her and, she suspected, possibly inept. If he was some great lover man, she'd yet to see it in action.

He refused to have sex with her, for a start.

*'It's statutory rape,'* he said.

*'I won't report you.'* She'd laughed.

Surely, if he was as much of a rabbit as he let on, he wouldn't be able to wait? She was *nearly* sixteen. He actually sounded like a prude, talking about the law all the time.

But he still kept her out well past her bedtime.

The naughtiest Lattimer of all, she thought, as she let herself in the back door as quietly as possible, trying not to giggle.

She was in the boot room, removing her shoes, when she heard them.

'I have a plan,' Adam said. 'You just have to trust me.'

'It's not going to work,' Ryan replied.

'I'll make him listen.'

'What's not going to work?' Clio asked, opening the door to the kitchen.

But they'd clammed up, read her the riot act for being out late and then shooed her off to bed like she was some kid.

Clio didn't know what was going on with them.

She just knew something bad was coming and everybody else was oblivious to it.

If only she'd told somebody.

That would be her nightmare for years to come.

That she should have told somebody.

# PRESENT

Rob could see Clio, sitting on the wall, watching the Passage East ferry pull away.

He stopped the car and got out, but didn't approach her straight away.

He rested on the bonnet for a moment, admiring her, the way she sat, the hunch of her back that said she was ready for any foe and would pull your fucking head off and shit down your neck before she'd let you get the better of her.

'Clio,' he called, on approach.

'Detective Dickwad,' she called back. Her affectionate term for him, since he arrested her brother. Still, she let him talk to her. She wanted progress updates. Clio was waiting for Rob's whole theory to fall apart so James could be released and Rob could be fired or sued or whatever he deserved. She'd told Rob that, in so many words.

'How are you doing?' he asked, plonking himself on the wall beside her.

'Find out what my dad was hit with yet?' she answered.

He sighed.

'Straight to business, hmm?' he said.

'Just wondering if you're still capable of doing any part of your job,' she said.

'You know I can't tell you all the details,' he said. 'You wouldn't want them anyway.'

'I'm pretty fucking un-shockable,' she said.

'Okay. He was hit with something hard. The water washed away any detritus, so we can't identify any residue to tell us what it was. But we can tell from the indentations it wasn't entirely smooth. It had an uneven surface.'

'He was hit with something hard?' she repeated. 'Well, I, for one, feel safe in my bed at night, knowing you're in charge.'

Rob said nothing. They watched the ferry move further away from the dock, its backwash sending ripples through the water.

Then, movement in his eyeline.

Danny McHugh was walking up the road towards them. He was concentrating on the ground, his head low. He looked like he'd been carrying a terrible weight ever since James had been arrested. Yet, Rob had practically had to drag his evidence out of him.

He was their godfather, Rob remembered. James and Clio's. He hadn't given up James lightly.

'Detective,' Danny growled, when he was upon them. 'Clio.' Much softer for her.

'Danny,' Rob said. 'Nice morning.'

Danny nodded.

'Just heading up to yours, Clio,' Danny said.

'Why?' Clio said, coldly. 'What could you possibly want with my family, Mr McHugh?'

Even Rob flinched at her tone.

'I'm checking in on Ellen,' Danny said, in obvious discomfort.

Rob stood up. He was uncomfortable standing between the two of them. Though part of him thought he should stay to act as referee.

Clio herself had admitted to seeing James arguing with Frazer. But Rob knew she mightn't have if Danny hadn't already blabbed.

She blamed Danny in order to feel better about herself.

'I'll be off, so,' Rob said. 'I was just passing.'

Clio said nothing. Danny nodded, just the once.

Rob started to walk back to the car, but then he paused.

'Eh, Danny, I was just wondering about something,' Rob said.

'Yeah?'

'The yacht's engine that night. You said the drive belt had come loose.'

'Yep.'

'How long were you below deck when you went to check what was wrong?'

'Just a couple of minutes,' Danny said. 'Like I told you.'

'You said in your statement that before you went down, you saw James with Frazer, but when you came back up, the deck on that side was clear.'

'Yep.'

Rob cocked his head.

'I guess I'm just surprised,' he said.

Danny stared back, confused.

'An experienced sailor like yourself,' Rob said. 'Drive belts slipping are common enough, but somebody like you would surely have checked all that before you left port?'

'I did,' Danny said. 'There must have been a lot of draw on the alternator. That's—'

'I know,' Rob said. 'Too much load. I've looked it up.'

Danny nodded, still watching the detective.

'Was anybody else down near the engine, do you know?' Rob asked.

Danny looked genuinely shocked.

'No,' he said. 'I'd have noticed.'

'Would you?' Rob said.

Clio glared at Rob.

'Hang on,' she said. 'What are you getting at? Are you back-tracking now? Do you think James didn't hurt Dad?'

'I'm just wondering if James thought that far ahead, that he'd even planned delaying your return to shore. Plus, the engine could have been deliberately sabotaged to make sure Danny had to go below, out of the way. But James would have needed access and, as you say, Danny, he wasn't near the yacht's engine. Nor anybody else . . .'

Rob turned and walked away.

# JUNE

# ADAM

'It's not a question of choice,' Adam said. 'You have to do this. For Ryan.'

He stared at his father, willing him to feel what he felt, to see what he saw. But the face that met him on the other side of the desk was impassive.

They were in Frazer's 'study', as he called it. The room he liked to shut himself in so he could properly manage their mother's family money. Who knew what he got up to in there all day long? Ryan had always reckoned their father had a stash of porn magazines in his desk drawer.

Frazer sighed, impatiently.

'I'm warning you, Adam, this is my choice and you will not breathe a word about any of it to your mam,' Frazer said. 'I won't have her upset because of that selfish shit for a minute more. The nerve of him. To come back here and bring this trouble to our door. To drag you into it—'

'He's not dragging me into anything!' Adam said. 'He's my brother. He's *your* son. We have to help him. I have eight grand. You just need to give me twelve. I can leave college and work and

I'll pay you back within a year, or when James gives me my money back, whatever comes first. I'm already good with computers, I can get a job in a bank, do what you did.'

'You'll leave college over my dead body,' Frazer boomed. 'The amount of money I've put into that already and you almost in your final year?'

'For fuck's sake!' Adam felt like screaming with frustration. 'Meet me halfway, will you? Why won't you help?'

Frazer's face turned bright red. He clenched his fists, but then he opened them, placed them flat on the table and took a deep breath.

'I am helping,' Frazer said, after a moment, and a lot more calmly. 'I'm helping Ryan help himself. He was mollycoddled by your mother for years and look where it got him. I did my best to toughen him up and still it didn't work. And if we help him now, we will be trapped in that cycle. When does it stop, Adam, tell me that? It doesn't, that's the truth. And now you're looking to ruin your own life as well. Two sons, dragged down by the actions of one. I'll not have it.'

'He's not a drug addict because you failed to toughen him up,' Adam said, shaking his head, incredulous. He couldn't believe his father's lack of awareness. 'Dad. Give him this chance. It will mean the world. It's all he needs to see. I swear it.'

Frazer stood up.

'I'm done here, Adam. And so are you. I want Ryan out of this house. And if you can't accept that, the same goes for you. Your mam and I have given you everything. This is not how we expect to be repaid. It's destroyed her and it's destroying me.'

Adam hung his head. Then he stood, crushed. He didn't know where to go from here.

He couldn't land this on Kathleen. Adam loved his mother but the very fact Frazer was here, and not Ryan, showed what side she'd taken and, in his heart, he couldn't blame her for it. Ryan was a fucking idiot.

But he was still family and it wasn't his fault he was the way he was.

It was their father's.

Frazer came around the desk to face him. He placed a hand on Adam's shoulder.

'You're a good son, lad,' he said. 'Ach, the best. A diamond between two godawful idiots. Your sisters are what they are. Clio, there's hope for. She has spirit, that lass, we all know that. But you, Adam. You're the man of the house after me. That's a tough place to be but I know you're capable. You'll understand why I am how I am. One day.'

Adam nodded, dutifully.

He was already starting to formulate his next move.

It all came together quickly.

It had to.

Eva hadn't told anybody his secret yet, as far as Adam knew. She was avoiding him; she seemed to have disappeared off the face of the planet, but he still lived with the fear. He'd know, if she told everybody. He'd know from the looks and the whispers. And then he'd know because his father would beat the crap out of him and look at Adam the way he looked at Ryan.

Disappointment bordering on contempt.

And there was Ryan to worry about.

He'd run into some fuckwit junkie mate who'd tried to give him a bag of grass and Adam knew worse would follow soon. Ryan was panicking and in that state of mind, he was vulnerable.

If Adam didn't sort this out, Ryan was going to kill himself.

The money had been the hardest part. He'd forged his father's signature plenty of times in the past, but on minor things like school notes. Writing a bank draft for the fifteen grand Adam was planning to steal left his hands a bit shaky.

He'd decided to go over and above what he needed from his father, just to make a point. That, and he'd need a few quid to help him when he left.

Once he had the cash, he would have to act fast. His father wouldn't be long noticing it had been taken from the account.

He'd made Ryan contact Aaron Dempsey and arrange the meet. Then Adam had accompanied his brother. They'd handed over the twenty grand at a house party, in bundles of notes in a black bin bag. It was amazing how small twenty grand could look. And then Adam had got Ryan out of there fast, before Aaron could pull a buddy-buddy routine on his brother and convince him the past was the past, it had all got out of hand, and sure, here's a foil wrap, no hard feelings.

On the way out of the house, Adam had pulled Dempsey aside.

'You might have taken my brother for a fool, but I knew what you were the second I saw you,' he said.

'Oh, yeah?' Dempsey smirked. 'What's that, then?'

'The scum of the earth,' Adam said.

Dempsey laughed in his face.

'Your brother will be back,' he said. 'Got a little inheritance coming in a few years, hasn't he? Everybody knows about your family. He'll be through that in a week, guarantee it.'

'Watch yourself,' Adam replied. 'Just watch yourself.'

Dempsey laughed again. Adam shuddered. The dealer reckoned he was untouchable. And you only had to look at the people at the house party to realise it was probably true. The sons and daughters of respectable Wexford people, all vulnerable prey for somebody like Dempsey, with his nice, well-spoken, middle-class image. It was terrifying.

Once Ryan was safely deposited at home, Adam went to the police station in Wexford town. He left an anonymous package for Detective Kevin Horan, including photographs of Dempsey distributing drugs to minors at the house party – one of them a judge's daughter – along with Dempsey's phone number and the address of his current rental property.

Ryan was okay with the plan up to a point.

The point where Adam disappeared.

'You can't,' he'd argued. 'Dad will do his nut and Mam will go mad with worry.'

'It's crucial,' Adam said. 'Once the cops pick up Dempsey, all it takes is one bit of bad luck and he'll connect being ratted out with us. You need to go into rehab and there isn't a place for you yet. We can't risk that gang getting their hands on you before there is. If I run, I look guilty. His people have to spend some time looking for me before they come for you. Because you'll need to be sober to steer clear of them, Ryan.'

'This is fucking stupid,' Ryan argued. 'At least tell Mam! And I need you here, Adam. Dad wants me out. It's only you and Mam keeping me here.'

'I can't tell Mam,' Adam said. 'She'll never agree to it. And she'll go mental when she finds out I did all this without telling her.

'Ryan,' Adam sighed, 'You have to let me do this. You have to trust me. My life won't be worth living anyway, when Dad finds out I've taken that money. No offence, but he already hates you. For me to do something like this, it's way worse, do you understand? And I've . . . I've other reasons for wanting to leave. I don't want to talk about them but, to be honest, this couldn't have come at a better time. I have to get away for a while.'

'But what will the rest of them think? They'll think you've had an accident or something. Or worse!'

'I've thought of that,' Adam said. 'I know it's not great, but it's just for a few weeks, Ryan. I'll let Mam know I'm okay as soon as I can. And you have to be there for her, right? She'll just think the pressure of college has got to me, something like that. I won't be the first to choke and do a runner before my final year. I've failed my exams, for fuck's sake, it'll be obvious I'm stressed. She'll be worried for a few weeks, tops, and then I'll be in touch. It's not going to kill her. I won't even take my passport, all right? She'll know I'm not far. I'll borrow yours and you report it missing in a while – get a new one. I can pass for you.'

'Adam, if she starts thinking you've . . . I don't know, harmed yourself or something . . .'

'Mam?' Adam scoffed. 'She knows me better.'

Ryan looked at Adam, pleading, but he was already giving in. He didn't have a better plan and so far, everything Adam had done had worked out.

'But if you go and we don't know where the fuck you are, how will we find you? If nobody knows who you are, what if something actually does happen to you?'

345

Adam shrugged. None of that would come to pass. It would be fine.

It was a mad plan.

A terrible plan, you might say.

But Adam couldn't see any other way. And he knew it would all work out.

But there was something he didn't plan for.

Something he should have planned for.

# PRESENT

Kate Lattimer held her hand over her stomach the whole time she was sitting with Rob. He didn't know how many weeks pregnant she was, but it couldn't be a lot. She was as flat as a pancake. In a matter of days, though, she'd slipped into full maternal mode.

'I apologise for keeping you at the harbour master's office so long that night,' Rob said. 'I obviously wasn't aware of your, er, condition.'

Kate pursed her lips but looked slightly mollified.

She'd already told him she wasn't going to make a complaint about that, though the very fact she mentioned the word *complaint* made Rob nervous. From what he'd gathered, her husband was incredibly wealthy and big into litigation when necessary.

'What did you want to see me for?' Kate said. 'I have a doctor's appointment shortly, before I head to my solicitor's office.'

'Ah. Yes. Well, it's that, really. We've already had communication from your solicitor, Kate.'

'It's Mrs Grant.'

'Oh.' Rob sat back, took a deep breath. It was like that, so.

'Well,' he said, gathering himself. 'I wanted to explain to you,

Mrs Grant, that your brother already has a solicitor – he was appointed to James by the State because James obviously has no means to retain his own representation. Your solicitor can, of course, consult with your brother, if that's what you choose, but he doesn't practise criminal law, from what I understand?'

'Please don't talk to me as though I'm stupid, Detective. My solicitor has only contacted you to inform you that he will be assisting us in finding the *correct* representation for James. My brother is innocent. I'm not having my son or daughter growing up with their uncle in prison. How will that look?'

'Here's the thing, though.' Rob sighed. 'Nine people got on that yacht. Eight got off. It wasn't an accident. Which one of your siblings are you happy to see banged up for your father's murder? Or do you think whoever killed him should get off?'

Kate winced.

'Perhaps you're trying to deflect the blame onto Ana or Danny? Do you want to change your statement about that night? Are you absolutely sure you could see Danny at the front of the boat?'

There it was. Rob's one niggling suspicion that Danny McHugh might have pulled the wool over his eyes, that Kate had been so happy to have him alibi her that she'd alibied him back.

'Of course Danny was bloody there,' Kate said, and Rob's fire was instantly put out. He knew, just from the look of her, from the sound of her, that Kate was telling the truth. She might lie to herself about plenty of things, but not the stuff that mattered. She wasn't going to give Danny an alibi if it meant throwing James, her actual family, to the wolves.

'And you and I both know Ana wouldn't have the strength to

attack my father, even if she wanted to,' Kate continued. 'Hit him, maybe. But lift him over a rail? Hardly.'

'So . . .' Rob held out his hands.

He watched as she clutched her stomach even tighter, staring down at the thin sweater, probably imagining the new life growing inside her.

'I'm so sorry all this tragedy has been inflicted on your family,' Rob said. 'I can't imagine how you're dealing with it all. I know your own relationship with your father wasn't the best—'

'Excuse me, I had a perfectly normal relationship with my dad,' Kate said, her face colouring. 'I loved him to bits. I want justice for him. That's not what this is about. He's never going to meet his first grandchild and that saddens me, terribly. But what matters now is moving forward. James has a child, too, even if it's not by birth. We're family. We need to pull together. How would it look, otherwise?'

Rob had stopped listening. On the desk, his phone had buzzed with an email. And he could see from the subject line and the first few words of the correspondence that it was from the forensics team and it was significant.

# AUGUST

# RYAN

Adam's plan had seemed like the only option.

But it was flawed. Ryan had known from the start but it became abundantly clear in the time that followed.

Six weeks after Adam disappeared, the gang that ran Ryan's dealer picked Ryan up on the coast road and bundled him into their car. He hadn't even seen them coming and wouldn't have realised who they were if he had.

He'd been distracted, thinking about Adam. Six weeks without contact and Ryan couldn't hold it together any longer. He'd assumed Adam would be in touch by now. So, he had to talk. He had to get back into the house and tell his mother what had happened.

As expected, without the obstruction of Adam and with Kathleen going up the walls, his father had thrown Ryan out. He'd still had the sense to do it behind Kathleen's back. Ryan didn't fight it because he, too, thought that it was for the best. It meant he wouldn't be tempted to blab.

And, given Kathleen took at face value Ryan's word that he'd decided to stay at a mate's, it was obvious where her focus was at the moment.

But Ryan knew from Clio that the family was growing more distressed by the week about Adam's disappearance. Even James seemed worried, though Ryan suspected he was panicking that somebody would discover he hadn't given Adam his money back when he was asked for it. He certainly hadn't told anybody he'd borrowed it, even when Kathleen discovered that Adam's bank account was more or less empty.

When the gang members threw Ryan into the back seat of their vehicle, he'd yelled blue murder. Some well-aimed punches had put paid to his protests and, once he was battered, bloodied and quiet, they'd driven a few miles before pulling to a halt.

Their accents were thick north-side Dublin, rough as fuck, and their faces completed the look. Hard, unforgiving, dangerous.

'You're lucky you paid your debt,' the big one in the passenger seat said. He hadn't taken part in the beating. He was the boss, a little cooler than the other two, not one to get his hands dirty. 'If you hadn't, you'd already be dead.'

Ryan whimpered. He was afraid to lift his head, so his view of everybody was from the angle of the leather seat, looking up.

'Your brother, though, he wasn't so lucky,' the man said.

Ryan froze.

'Tried to do a runner, didn't he? Your Adam. After squealing on our Aaron. Did he think we wouldn't find out? We've got people inside the cop shop, pal. He didn't get very far, though. Your brother. And you can't squeal with a slashed throat.'

'What?' Ryan spat through a mouthful of blood.

'Yes, sir,' the man said. 'Won't be talking to anybody now. Sorry, pal, I can't even tell you where we buried him. I can't remember. I sure as fuck wouldn't be able to find him again.'

The roaring in Ryan's head drowned out the vicious laughter of his three captors.

'You just spread the word now, like a good boy,' the man said. 'I'm sure you'll be back down with your old druggie pals in no time. Let them know what happens when somebody rats on my people.'

Ryan felt the damp start to spread down his jeans. It wasn't the beating that had caused him to urinate. Ryan had taken worse from his father. He'd wet himself purely out of shock.

The man looked down and shook his head.

'Not on my fucking interior,' he said.

The car door opened, and Ryan was pulled out.

The three men stood over him. The two monkeys, snickering. The boss, looking out to sea.

'It's a beautiful part of the world all the same,' he said. 'Used to holiday near here, when we were kids. Before they started doing cheap flights to Alicante. Anyway, we'd best be heading.'

He turned on his heel. Expensive leather shoes, that's what Ryan saw, as they walked away.

Then they spun back to face him.

'Your poor mother's heart must be broken. I saw the piece in the paper begging for any information on Adam. Tell you what, if one of my sons was responsible for the death of the other, I don't know how I'd feel about that. If I were that son, I'd probably top myself.'

Ryan watched in silence as the car doors slammed and the engine revved, the spinning wheels sending dust flying in his direction.

# PRESENT

James Lattimer was a shell of himself.

Rob sat in front of him, studying the other man, remembering all those times he'd seen pictures of him in the papers and glossy magazines, at film openings and on chat shows. Of all Clio's siblings, James was the one Rob was most familiar with. Not because he'd met him much in person, but because of his fame.

He was a far cry from the celebrity circuit now. He looked exactly like everybody else in the remand centre. Skinny, suffering from a combination of stress, carb-laden food and a lack of natural light and decent exercise.

'I didn't murder my father,' he said. 'Yes, we argued. I've admitted that. I should have told you from the start. I needed money. And I'd just found out that he'd blown the family portfolio and was selling the house to fund his fucking . . . is it even a mid-life crisis when you're in your sixties? Of course, we argued. But I didn't kill him. I walked away from him and he was fine. This is madness, pure madness.'

'We've statements to say you were the last person with your father and we know he didn't accidentally fall into the sea, James,'

Rob said. 'You don't fall over a railing that high. And he didn't jump. He was unconscious before he went in. Did you hit him? Did you push him, maybe?'

'I never laid a finger on him. When I went back to my brothers and sisters on the rear deck he was alive and breathing. He was puffing away on that stupid cigar, I swear. I need to see my wife. I need to see my daughter. They haven't come in. Can somebody organise for them to come in?'

'I'll see what I can do,' Rob said. 'We can't force your family to visit you.'

'This can't be happening. I'm innocent!'

'Just tell me the truth, James.'

'I am!'

'You never laid a finger on Frazer?'

'No. I swear it. I didn't touch him.'

Rob sighed. He leaned into his laptop bag and took out a file. He opened it and placed it on the table, pushing it towards James.

The language had been simplified for the layman. The Director of Public Prosecutions, who'd just been sent the whole case file, had received the official, technical explanation.

James scanned the words. Then he looked up at Rob, confused, terrified.

'Then how do you explain that?' Rob said.

James hung his head.

# OCTOBER

## CLIO

As the months had worn on and there was no sign of Adam, everything had deteriorated.

At the start, her mother had been convinced that Adam had just run off to get his head straight. Within days, a letter had come from his landlord returning the deposit on his flat and expressing regret at losing a good tenant.

Then his exam results had come in. They'd been addressed to Spanish Cove. He'd failed several modules and would have to resit them in September.

September came and went and still no sign.

He's panicked, Kathleen told them all. She was angry at herself for missing the signs. It was because she'd been so caught up in Ryan's problems, she said. Ryan, who'd moved out and started taking drugs again and then, in August, overdosed. He'd barely survived and was now in a clinic refusing to talk to any of them. The doctors were straight with the family – if Ryan didn't want to be helped, nobody could save him, and they didn't know if the overdose was intentional or not.

Through it all, Kathleen had carried them. She held steadfast in her view that Adam was okay, in spite of what others around them were starting to say; what her own family were saying.

Some days were harder than others. Kathleen was only human. Clio never said anything, but she'd noticed her mother taking the odd pill, late in the evening, which Clio guessed was to help Kathleen sleep.

And, sometimes, Kathleen popped one in the afternoon.

Clio's dad wouldn't even speak about Adam. He reluctantly helped with the search parties but his overriding emotion seemed to be anger.

Kate and Ellen were convinced their brother had committed suicide. They didn't say it aloud, but it was in what they didn't say. The way they refused to talk about finding him, or a future that contained him.

James suggested Adam had done a runner, too, but as time wore on he also fell into the suicide camp. He was thoughtless enough to suggest it out loud and Clio had wanted to kill him.

Clio picked at a thread on the side of her pillow.

She didn't want to upset her mother by letting her know how distressed she was.

Her mother was their rock. She always had been. When there were arguments in the family, when one of them clashed with Frazer or when they fought with each other, Kathleen was like the diplomatic corps. Sensible enough to know when to take sides and when to stand back and support both. But the stress of the last year was taking a strain.

Arguing with Frazer was taking its toll.

She knew, the minute she took the first stair, that they were at it again. This time, from the sounds of it, in Frazer's room.

Clio wasn't sure how her parents had ended up sleeping separately. She'd asked her mam once, and Kathleen had laughed and said Frazer snored like a train. Another time, she'd claimed she'd got into the habit of taking Clio into a different room at night so as to not wake Frazer when Clio was being fed.

Clio didn't believe either version entirely, though she reckoned it might have been an amalgamation of both.

Ryan used to say Kathleen had moved into a separate room for contraception's sake.

*'You broke her, Clio. You never slept for more than two hours at a go when you were a baby.'*

To which she'd told him to fuck right off.

Clio walked silently along the landing until she was just outside Frazer's room. She needed money. She wanted to go out and she wasn't going to let their fighting interrupt her plans.

But her hand hovered on the door, just short of pushing it open.

She wanted to hear what they were saying, first.

'I just can't understand why you're not doing more to find Adam!' Kathleen said. 'It's like you're not bothered. But Adam isn't Ryan. You love Adam!'

'I love Ryan,' Frazer replied defensively.

Outside the door, Clio raised an eyebrow. Yeah, right.

'I don't mean . . . you know what I mean, Frazer.'

Her father sighed.

'Aye, I know. You think I gave up on Ryan and now I'm giving up on Adam. Do you think so little of me, Kath? I haven't given up on Ryan. I'm paying for his rehab, aren't I? I'll just not bloody indulge him with his other nonsense. He's a junkie, pet. Tough love, that's what he needs.'

Clio could almost hear her mother flinch.

'Well, they say nothing happens without cause,' Kathleen muttered.

'I am not responsible for that lad going awry,' Frazer snapped.

'I'm not saying you are, Frazer, but you were always fierce hard on him. Anyway, look.' Kathleen's tone changed; it was more pleading now, less accusatory. 'Adam is what's important now. I know he's out there, Frazer. We just need help to find him.'

'It's a waste of bloody money. The lad will either come back, or he won't. If he doesn't want to be found, do you think it's fair to go looking?'

'I need to know!' Kathleen sobbed the sentence.

There was silence for a moment or two. Clio's stomach contracted.

'Aye,' her father said, eventually. 'I know, lass. I know. I hate to see you so upset, I really do. It kills me. These pills you're taking – are they helping? Do you want me to get you more?'

'I don't want any more pills, Frazer, I want my son back. My sons – I want them both back. They're my babies.'

'Maybe if you got a higher dose . . .'

'Just agree with me on this, Frazer! Get a private detective. Please. If we find Adam, we don't need to make him come back. I'll be happy to know he's alive and safe.'

Clio held her breath.

'Okay,' Frazer said. 'We'll do it. If it makes you feel better, we'll do it.'

Clio heard her mother sob again, but it was more an exhalation of relief.

She lifted her hand and knocked on the door, before opening it.

Kathleen turned her face away. She was standing, facing Frazer as he sat on the bed.

Frazer's face softened when he saw her.

'What can we do for you, love?' he said. 'Your mother and I were just talking.'

'Yeah, I know,' Clio said. 'Eh, can I have a loan?'

Frazer smiled.

'Ach, like the loan I gave you last week? Are we totting these up, lass? Do I get to charge interest?'

'Usury is a sin,' Clio replied.

'Now, with smarts like that, you could easily get a summer job!' Frazer laughed. At the same time, Kathleen turned and smiled.

'How can we deny you?' she said.

Clio smiled, thinly.

'My wallet's downstairs.' Frazer sighed, for effect. 'I'll go see if I can shake a few pennies from it. You can make me a cuppa before you go wherever you're flitting off to with my money.'

'Pinky promise,' Clio said.

She let her father pass her, but stayed in the room with her mother.

'Mam, is there . . . is there anything you're not telling me?' she asked.

'What do you mean?' Kathleen asked, puzzled.

'Did Adam – did he do something?'

'Like what?'

'I don't know,' Clio said. 'He just, he didn't seem himself those last few days, when he was here. Was he in trouble or something? Did he say anything to you or Dad?'

Her mother crossed the room and put her hands on Clio's shoulders.

'He didn't tell me anything was wrong,' she said, her voice thoughtful, considered. 'But that doesn't mean there wasn't. I've gone over and over it. Adam knew I was worried about Ryan, so I've absolutely no doubt he was protecting me. But I would have known if something was badly wrong. Oh, love, I know what people think. I know what they're saying. Nothing bad has happened to Adam, though. I'd feel it in here. He'd never hurt himself. Not in a million years. And if there'd been an accident, we'd know by now. He just needs some time. I'll still bloody kill him when we find him, mind. But, until somebody tells me otherwise, that's what I'm going to keep thinking.'

Clio nodded. She wanted to tell her mam that she thought something had been going on but she couldn't find the words. Not when her mam was worried enough.

And so Clio let herself hope. She let herself imagine this man her dad planned to hire would find her brother. Or at least be able to tell them what had happened.

She couldn't know that by the following spring, he would return with the worst news.

That Adam was probably dead.

She couldn't know that her father would convey that to her mother.

And that he would badger her to accept it, at exactly the same time as Ryan took a turn for the worse.

And that her mother's heart, fit to burst with love for them all, would finally burst with sadness.

Months later, it would only be Clio and Ellen and their father left in Spanish Cove. No Adam, no Ryan. James enjoying his life in Dublin. Kate scarpering up there as fast as she could. Her mother cold in the ground.

From eight to three.

From loud to silent.

From loved to . . . nothing.

# PRESENT

Rob knew Clio was sitting downstairs in the station.

He'd multiple missed calls from her, along with texts and emails.

Now she'd arrived in his work place and was waiting for him. There was no escape.

He clicked out of the email he'd just received from the DPP confirming the trial date.

Then he took a deep breath and rang down.

'Send her up,' he said.

She arrived in a flurry of dark hair and even darker mood, slamming the door shut.

'You're fucking ignoring me,' she said.

'Shh.'

Rob placed his finger on his lips. Then she looked to the side of the office.

Johnny was asleep in his buggy. The tot could fight his nap for hours, but once he was down, he was out. The slamming door hadn't woken him, but Rob didn't want to test the theory of just how much noise Johnny could snore through.

It was the first time his ex had let him have their child in weeks

— even if it was only because her mother had let her down and she had a pressing hair appointment. Rob wanted to show he could do a good job and her turning up to a screaming toddler and an angry woman in his office wouldn't cut it. Especially if she wasn't happy with her highlights.

Rob thought he saw Clio soften, just a little. Johnny could do that to a woman, with his cherubic face and angelic golden curls.

But then Clio was glaring at Rob again and he knew she wasn't placated. If he was hoping to get at her via her maternal instincts, he might be waiting a while.

'What's going on?' she hissed. 'You dropped that little bomb about the engine the other day and then went off the radar. What do you know? Was all this planned?'

'Why are you so agitated?' Rob hissed back.

'I'm still in the house with Ryan, Adam and Ellen,' she said. 'Kate is up and down and she's on a crusade to get James released. If it wasn't him, if it was one of them that did something, I need to know, Rob.'

Rob sighed.

He shouldn't be having these conversations with her.

But he and Clio went way back.

How could he not talk to her, he told himself.

'James attacked your father,' he said.

Clio's face turned blank, right before it fell.

'I'm sorry,' she said. 'I'm glad, but I'm not glad. I don't know what to think any more. Should I be happy it was James? No, obviously not. I'd rather it was a big mistake and it was an accident. But I can't help it. I'm relieved it isn't one of the others. I've never been close to James.'

Rob nodded. He understood.

'How do you know?' Clio asked. 'For sure, I mean. What's changed? He's still saying he didn't do it, isn't he?'

'Yes,' Rob said. 'But, he can't deny forensics.'

'What forensics?'

'James admitted to arguing with your father that night,' Rob said. 'But he claims it was just verbal. He denies your statement that he pushed Frazer. He says he told your father he should change his mind about selling the house and apologise to you all. He said there were some raised voices but nothing physical and then he walked away. Right onto the rear deck where he started punching Adam, with what sounds like the slightest of prompts.'

Clio nodded, clearly anxious, waiting for more.

'The majority of the forensic evidence on your father's clothing suffered the same fate as his injury — it was washed pretty clean. But, we picked up trace blood on his clothing. Most of it was his, except for some on his tie.'

'On his tie?' Clio repeated.

'Take it where you get it,' Rob said. 'The blood belonged to James.'

'So how does he explain it?' Clio asked, shocked.

'He can't.'

'What's your theory?'

'My theory? I don't play that game, Clio.'

She eyed him, unblinking.

Rob sighed.

'Your father might have lashed out at James. According to all your final statements, Frazer almost hit Ryan during the family argument. So, perhaps he snapped when James confronted him.

He hit him, and some of James' blood landed on his tie. Then, when your father was walking away, James picked up something and swung it at him. James panicked, realised what he'd done and threw your father overboard. The DPP's office is going for something more straightforward. That James injured himself when he attacked your father and some of his blood ended up on Frazer when he lifted him over the side rail.'

Clio seemed to shrink.

'I'm sorry, Clio,' he said. 'It's circumstantial for the most part, but the lie is damning. There's really no doubt that your father was attacked and lifted over that rail. On top of everything else in the file, including your statement . . .'

Clio covered her eyes. When she removed her hand, she stood up.

Rob couldn't think of anything to say to stop her leaving. He just knew he really hoped that this wasn't the last time they'd see each other.

'Clio, can we . . .'

'Let's grab a drink some time,' she said.

'I'd love that.'

She nodded.

'He really is a beautiful kid, Rob. You should be proud. Didn't you do good?'

Then, with a glance back at Johnny, she left, closing the door softly behind her.

# PART III

2014–2018

# NOVEMBER 2014

# CLIO

She'd jumped at the chance of the trip.

She'd turned twenty-one the previous April and had barely cele-brated the occasion. Instead, she'd concentrated on saving in order to go travelling and now her real celebration would be two months in Paris with her friends.

It had taken a good chunk of her savings. She'd been working as a care assistant in Wexford General for the past two years, as a candy-striper, for want of a better name, pretending she might go into medicine proper one day. Anything to keep her father at bay, with his pushing and pushing that she go to college and get a decent career. She'd convinced him that care assistant was a step on the ladder. Even if the pay was shit.

He point-blank refused to fund her popping off to Paris on a little sojourn, though. Ryan had finally got himself clean and fled to Europe. Kate had practically eloped with some bloke in Dublin. She wasn't talking to Frazer at the moment because, on the very first occasion of meeting him, Frazer had asked Kate's fiancé Cheng if he was actually Chinese, or if his parents had come over on the boat from Vietnam and now ran a chain of Chinese takeaways so they had to pretend. They were all now being punished for Frazer's rudeness. Kate was determined none of them would meet Cheng.

They never saw James, either. He seemed to have disappeared once his run of TV success came to an abrupt end. Three series of a hit show and then the station cut it. James was trying to spin shite about wanting a new challenge and being the one who walked away.

And Frazer wasn't holding out any hopes for Ellen.

Clio was his baby. His last great hope for proper success for the Lattimer clan.

He hadn't begrudged her the trip. Two months of culture and civilisation was a good thing. He admired those who wanted to travel. He just wasn't going to pay for it.

Not only that, but the bastard told her he'd put a stay on her trust. He needed to be sure, he told her. To access the trust, she had to show she could be trusted.

The rest of her siblings had gone off the rails, spent their money like it was water.

Or disappeared with it.

If Clio could make it to twenty-two without losing the run of herself, then they'd talk.

Clio couldn't decide if that conversation would go along the lines of *thank you very much* or *go fuck yourself.*

Clio loved Paris. The only thing she missed about home so far was the sea and Teddy. She enjoyed the wine, the food, the people.

But she didn't think France was where she'd want to settle. Clio wanted somewhere a bit edgier, a bit less classical. She'd been musing about London.

Still, as experiences went, Paris was a good one.

That morning, she walked along the banks of the Seine, rebuffing the attempts of the early-riser portrait artists to paint her – for free, they claimed, but she'd been stung like that before.

She enjoyed the musky smell of the river, the freshness of the trees overhead, the bustle of morning traffic, angry beeps at the *putains de crétins* who dared to switch lanes without indicating.

The smell was changing now, to fresh croissants and thick black espresso. *Petit déjeuner.*

Clio felt her stomach rumble. Her travel companions thought she was nuts. No matter how late they partied, Clio was up early every day, needing to walk, to see the water. They'd emerge around lunchtime and stumble to the nearest café for hair-of-the-dog carafes of red wine and toasted baguette sandwiches.

Clio liked morning. She liked breakfast. And she needed some now.

She walked to the café on the corner near their cheap hotel and ordered her usual. Pain au chocolat, freshly squeezed orange juice and café au lait.

It was the most expensive meal of her day, the consistent indulgence she allowed herself.

Clio sat in the window, looking out at the passers-by on their way to work, the authentic Parisians, not the tourists who emerged after ten, hoping they'd be early enough to skip queues at the Louvre and have the Champs-Élysées as their own private avenue.

The people outside were the ones who staffed the offices and the shops and the foyer ticket boxes. And Clio loved to watch them. The French had coined the term *chic* – she'd grown up with that innate knowledge, but being in Paris let her fully understand it. The men strolled with the confidence and arrogance of people who owned half the world. Or once had, at least. The women managed to simultaneously look like they'd risen at 4 a.m. for their beauty routine and just rolled out of bed looking like that. Sleek make-up and high heels, elegant coats that swung around slim, toned legs.

Clio was admiring the self-assured sashay of a young woman around her age when she saw him.

Adam.

He walked past, hands stuffed in the pockets of a dark overcoat, shoulders hunched forward, the familiar evening shadow on his chin and cheeks, the dark, serious eyes.

Adam.

Clio gasped. And, almost like she was floating, she slipped off the high stool and exited the café, forgetting her scarf, not buttoning up her coat, just falling out onto the street, the cold air hitting her full on and still not waking her from her dream.

She chased him – not running, but walking as fast as possible, almost stepping out in front of a car emerging from an underground car park on Rue de la Cité, before a fellow pedestrian grabbed her arm.

She muttered *merci*, then continued on. She still had him in her sights.

She was under no illusion. It wasn't him, really. This had happened to her before. Not just with Adam, but with their mother, too.

When she caught up with this stranger, she'd get ahead of him and look at him and be filled with the same crushing disappointment she always felt when she realised the people she loved were still gone, after all.

At the corner she was just behind him and as he turned, she saw his face.

And realised she'd been wrong about being wrong.

This was him. Six years older, but still him.

'Adam!' she blurted, shocked, amazed and appalled, all at once.

He kept walking. Faster.

She clasped her hand to her mouth. She'd never considered, she'd never even imagined . . . she'd been prepared to be disappointed but she hadn't been ready for the absolute flood of emotions that hit her when she realised her brother was alive and well and walking around Paris.

A crowd of American students started to move en masse in the direction of the Panthéon.

Adam walked with them.

Clio lost sight of the top of his head as the young tourists swarmed around her, but she kept moving too, along the Rue Soufflot, towards Place du Panthéon. She spotted him then, at the front of the group, walking up the steps of the great building, all of them going inside.

She followed, her shallow breaths and racing heart drowned out by the hubbub of the American students, all chatting and laughing loudly.

'Madame! Miss!'

Clio stopped, distracted from her chase.

'Ticket!'

Clio threw ten euros at the cashier and grabbed the card, flashed it quickly at the security guard at the next desk.

Then she was inside, and it was quiet, except for footfall, the odd cough, a zip being opened. The smallest sounds echoed in the large space, up to the high ceiling and around the marble columns.

The building was divided into four, a cross-like structure fanning

out from the magnificent dome at its centre. Clio walked quickly
up the middle. She thought she'd seen Adam moving towards the
far end.

What was he doing?

Was he avoiding her?

By the time she'd got to the great monument at the rear, she'd
lost sight of him again.

'*Pardon,*' she said to an elderly woman beside her. 'Is there an
exit down here? *Sortie?*'

'*No.*' The woman shook her head. 'No exit. *Crypte.* Crypt.'

Clio shuddered. Of course she'd end up hunting for her presumed dead brother in a crypt, of all places.

There, a set of stairs.

The American tourists were scattered around the building behind
her. It was still early; there weren't many others here, just the odd
visitor like the woman she'd just spoken to.

She couldn't not follow. She had to see for certain that it was him.

She took the set of stairs.

Below, she found herself in a long, dimly-lit, musty-smelling
corridor.

It was completely silent and seemingly empty, though she
couldn't see if anybody lurked behind the arches to either side.

Clio started to walk, conscious of her breathing and the sound
her boots made.

To her left, a shadow caught her eye.

A statue in front of the tomb that housed the man himself.
Voltaire, his long nose and charismatic profile given life by the lights
cast on the structure. Clio had jumped, and this was just stone.

If it wasn't Adam down here, but a strange man, was she safe?

Who would hear her, among these ghosts and graves? Clio hadn't seen a security guard beyond the front desk.

Faced with a fork in the tunnel, she chose left.

The great writers were interred here. Hugo. Dumas. Her hands trailed over the inscriptions carved into the walls outside their tombs.

With each passing moment, she was growing more uncertain, more convinced she'd imagined things and yet, still scared that she was right.

A laugh behind her, some way away. Clio flinched. It was just another tourist, she told herself.

'What am I doing?' she whispered, just to hear something, to reassure herself.

She slowed her breathing; inhaled deeply through her nostrils.

The air down here was damp. Full of dead things.

And then, out of the corner of her eye, something moved.

She turned.

Adam. Standing there in one of the arches, Émile Zola's tomb behind him.

Clio groaned.

She started to back away. One foot after the other.

He reached out to her.

'Clio,' he said, his face as shocked as hers must have been.

'You . . .' she said. 'What are you doing here?'

Adam laughed. She knew it was involuntary, she knew it was a nervous reaction, but it still enraged her. It made her want to slap his face.

'I thought I heard you call my name. I thought I was imagining it. I hear you all, all the time. I see you all. I was convinced I was going mad.'

'You ran away from me.'

'I . . . I didn't. I was coming here. I'm studying the building's foundations.'

Clio shook her head. No, this was all wrong. She was the one who was going mad. She stared at him, mute.

'Oh, my God, I'm so glad to see you,' he said. 'How is everybody? How's Ryan? And Mam?'

This couldn't be happening. It was a nightmare. Clio hadn't got up this morning, she was still in bed and this was a bad dream.

Yet, there was the sound of more tourists entering the crypt and her stomach was full of pastry and coffee and . . . it was just Adam who shouldn't be here. Everything else existed; everything else was where it was supposed to be.

'Are you serious?' she said. 'How is Mam?'

Adam's face filled with fear.

'I know everybody hates me,' he said. 'I knew, when I didn't hear back. I just . . . it's been six years, Clio. It wasn't *that* much money I took. And God, I didn't choose to be gay. I'm sorry, I'm so sorry I had to do it the way I did. I realised as time went on that running away was so fucking stupid, but I was so young. It seemed like the best option. And, you're here, now. It's . . . mental.'

'No. No no no. This can't be happening.'

'Clio, it's happening.'

'Mam is dead.'

Adam's face did nothing for a moment. Then it registered. His eyes widened. His mouth fell open. It was he who took a step back this time.

'What?' he whispered.

'She's dead!' Clio came towards him. 'Mam is dead. She's been dead five years.'

Adam emitted a sound, something between horror and dismay.

He collapsed onto the concrete, the slap against his knees sounding hard and painful. He brought his hands to his eyes.

'Don't you dare cry,' Clio exclaimed. 'You have no right. You vanished. You disappeared and she fell apart. And then Dad told her . . . ugh! It doesn't matter. It's your fault. You killed her. I can't – I can't even look at you.'

'I . . . I didn't. I just took money. I told her. It was to help . . .'

Adam started to hyperventilate.

Clio put her hand to her stomach. She was going to vomit.

At that moment, a small group entered the tunnel where she stood, freezing when they saw the small drama being played out in front of them.

Clio started to walk. Then run. She couldn't breathe. She could barely see through her tears. Her legs felt like lead, but still, she ran.

She could hear him after her – at least she thought it was him – running, trying to catch her, but she was too fast.

Outside, the street was more crowded. The tourists were all out and about now, filling the steps, smiling for selfies with the Eiffel Tower in the distant background, then turning to get the same facial shots but with the giant columns behind them.

She stuck her hand out, summoned a cab. Then she was in it, gasping for air, sobbing and muttering a jumble of barely coherent French and English that told the driver to just go, anywhere.

Back in the hotel, she packed her bag, adrenaline coursing through her, as she spoke to a customer service agent from Aer

Lingus, who patiently explained that they could change her flight from next week to today but that it would cost almost double what she'd already paid for the ticket.

'Whatever!' she'd shouted at the phone. She'd put it on loud-speaker and left it on the bed so she could sit on her suitcase to close it.

What had Adam been on about? He was gay? That was hardly why he'd disappeared, was it? Because he was fucking gay? And what had he said about money? What was that about?

'Okay, um, miss, I can do that for you now,' the airline rep said. 'Is there anything else you would like me to help you with?'

The zip on the suitcase stopped resisting and pulled itself closed. She stared at the wall of her shared hotel room, the faded, peeling wallpaper, and realised in that moment that she couldn't go home.

She'd seen Adam. But who could she tell? Their mother had died waiting for Adam. Ryan had taken Adam's disappearance par-ticularly hard. He'd overdosed. Frazer wouldn't talk about his son. Ellen never talked about anything. Kate had moved on. She wanted nothing to do with their family. And James didn't care.

Adam had abandoned all of them.

Clio, most of all.

She wasn't going to be the one who broke it to them that he'd done it intentionally. She couldn't even imagine how they'd react.

It was better to forget it had ever happened. If Adam wanted to go home, let him. Let him do the explaining. She wasn't going to be the messenger that got shot and she didn't want to be there for the fall-out.

Clio started to plan.

She'd been seeing some guy from Wexford town on and off over the summer and he'd been talking about going to the States. He had a J-1 visa, which meant he could work there for the year. He'd encouraged Clio to abandon her Paris plan and do the same, but she wasn't a student and she couldn't be arsed applying for a green card.

But what if she just went? What if she took the rest of her savings and flew to New York?

She knew she couldn't live up to Frazer's expectations of her. On the scale of things, she'd barely let him down yet and he still looked at her in that way that said she was a disappointment, that he'd expected more. What would he be like when he realised just how flawed she really was?

'Yes,' she told the helpful Aer Lingus customer representative. 'How much is a flight to New York from Dublin?'

# RYAN

Rome was everything Ryan imagined it would be. Art, culture, architecture. Stunning women, little bastard pickpockets.

It was good for the soul, but it wasn't good for the head. Too much temptation in a city like this. Too much on offer.

It was far enough away from Ireland and everything he'd left there. But not far enough from the drugs. And while that wasn't what he was looking for, it was what he knew he'd end up finding.

He had an idea, though. His latest girlfriend came from a little town beside Lake Garda called Limone. She'd invited him to spend the weekend with her and sail on the lake, maybe enjoy some walks in the hillsides.

It was cold, deserted this time of year, but it was also at its best. No tourists clogging the narrow road that ran around the lake, no street hawkers touting tacky wares, no hiked-up menu prices. Just the locals and inexpensive, excellent vino and the best food.

He was an artist, wasn't he? Ryan should spend some time with her, let her be his muse.

He had been walking along the Tiber every day, but he missed a real expanse of water. Something that reminded him of home.

The good bits.

And he needed a break from his search for Adam.

Two years clean, two years searching. He wasn't giving up, but he needed a rest.

Minding himself – it was important to do that.

Adam drove into Rome the day before Ryan planned to leave.

Ryan had never got his head around how Adam had been able to find him in just a few months, when Ryan had spent twenty-four months searching for his brother.

Ryan had covered half of Europe on the meagre money he'd managed to scrape together. Frazer had refused to hand over Ryan's trust fund, but Ellen had helped him out once or twice and Ryan worked wherever and whenever he could.

He had so much to atone for.

So much shame to absolve.

Adam, apparently, had the money and the reach that Ryan didn't. He strolled into the lobby of the cheap *ostello* Ryan was staying in, charmed the receptionist into giving him a spare key to the single room Ryan had acquired and let himself in.

Ryan was sitting on the narrow bed at the time, rubbing cream into the scars that still itched on his feet. The door opened and there was Adam, larger than life, standing in its frame.

'What the fuck happened?' Those were Adam's first words.

Ryan couldn't even say his brother's name. Adam was like an apparition. Ryan could have been tripping, for how real it all felt.

'Mam died?' Adam said. 'Mam died!'

No small talk. It was as if almost seven years hadn't passed, like they'd just picked up a conversation they'd been having the other day.

Then Adam broke down in tears and Ryan could see this wasn't new to him – that he'd been crying for weeks, months even.

'Why did nobody tell me? Why . . . ?'

Adam slumped on the bed beside Ryan.

'We didn't know where you were,' Ryan said, still shocked.

'But I told you I'd contact you!' Adam said.

Ryan shook his head, utterly confused.

'Adam, go back. How the fuck – how did you find me? I've been looking for you. And how do you know about Mam? Where have you been?'

There were so many questions, Ryan barely knew where to start.

'Where have I been?' Adam said. 'Where have *you* been? I waited, fuck, I waited, Ryan. I thought something had gone wrong. Any one of a number of things. I thought you all decided it was safer for me to stay away, because of your dealers. I thought Dad had lost his shit over the money and you were all banned from talking to me. I was convinced Eva had opened her big mouth and I was dead to him, to all of you. But I'd nobody to talk to! I'd nobody to check in with. I tried ringing you, after a few months had passed, but your phone was dead. I was too terrified to contact the others.'

Ryan was still shaking his head, trying to process what he was seeing and hearing.

'I was starting to come to terms with being on my own,' Adam said. 'Then Clio turned up in Paris last November. I thought she'd come to get me. But then she told me about Mam and she was *furious*. Doesn't she know? Ryan? Doesn't Clio know what we did? Why we did it?'

Ryan wanted to die. He stared at the floor.

Adam was alive.

It was as he imagined. The whole tragic mess.

This was why people took drugs. This . . . fucking reality. The pain of it. It was unbearable.

'Nobody knows,' he whispered.

'What?'

Adam clasped his hand to his mouth, looked like he might throw up.

'Nobody knows. When Mam died, I was in rehab. And I was . . . I was too ashamed to tell them when I came out.' Ryan started to weep. 'Aaron's boss, weeks after you went, told me that they'd found you. That they'd dealt with you. He said you were dead, Adam. It had been six weeks and he seemed to know everything. You hadn't been in contact and I thought they were telling the truth.'

'He said I was dead?'

Ryan nodded grimly.

'He said it and I believed him. Why wouldn't I? I knew they were more dangerous than you believed. You would never have ratted on them, if you'd fully understood what they were capable of. So, I thought you were dead and it was all my fault. It all went downhill from there. Dad had already kicked me out of the house by then and I was in a state. After that, I overdosed. Deliberately, accidentally, I can't tell you what was going on in my head. I sobered up for a while, but I still couldn't tell anybody what had happened. I thought – they'll never forgive me. He planted that, in my head. Aaron's boss. Then Mam died. And I . . . I overdosed again.'

Adam rubbed his head, incredulous, devastated.

'Adam, I'm so sorry,' Ryan said. 'I thought it was better they thought you'd just walked out than knowing you were dead – and that I was responsible. I was a cowardly little shit, I know that.'

Adam placed his two hands on the back of his neck and breathed deeply.

'Please, forgive me,' Ryan said.

Adam shook his head.

'It's not you who needs to be forgiven. I did this.'

'No,' Ryan said.

'I did,' Adam said. 'I shouldn't have left you to deal with it all on your own. I knew you weren't strong enough. But I had to get away. Before Eva told everybody I was gay. I don't understand why you're here now, though. What are you doing in Italy?'

'Looking for you,' Ryan said.

Adam frowned, looking utterly confused.

'I got clean, a couple of years ago,' Ryan explained. 'And by then I'd started to wonder. They said they'd killed you but there was no body. That wasn't that gang's style. A few years later they battered Aaron Dempsey to death and left him on a street in Wexford town. He'd got out of jail and had been skimming from his dealing profits. Reckoned he was owed, I guess.

'I realised that they'd have let your body be found. You'd have been a warning, too. With my head straight, it started to make sense. They were fucking with me. They wanted me back on the drugs; they wanted me spreading tales about what they'd done to you so I'd learn a lesson and others would, too.'

Ryan stopped. He was babbling. But it was all true. Not as articulate as he'd like, but this was how he'd come to the conclusion that his brother wasn't dead, after all.

'We . . . we have to find Clio. We have to tell her.' Adam started to pace around the small room. 'This is a disaster. She hates me. They must all hate me. I need to tell them.'

Ryan shook his head.

'We can't tell Clio,' he said.

'We're telling her,' Adam cried.

'No, I mean, we *can't*. She went to the States with some bloke. She's living there illegally. She's sent a couple of cards but she won't tell us where she is. She's changed her number. She doesn't want to know us.'

Adam turned and hit the wall with his fist. It was cheap plaster; it caved. Ryan imagined it must have hurt, badly, but Adam made no sound. Instead, he rested against the wall, his back sliding down it. He collapsed into a sitting position, brought his knees up to his chest.

'But I contacted you,' Adam cried. 'Like I said I would.'

'No,' Ryan said, shaking his head. 'No, you didn't.'

Adam looked up at him, appalled.

'I did. Of course, I did.'

Ryan shook his head.

'I waited for you to get in touch,' he said. 'You never did.'

'That's wrong,' Adam said. 'Ryan, that's not what happened.'

# MAY 2015

# RYAN

It had taken Ryan a few weeks to summon the courage to return to Spanish Cove after Adam found him in Italy.

Once there, he wanted to make sure he could search the house when it was empty, which was proving more difficult than he'd imagined.

With Frazer, it wasn't so hard. His father left the house most days, in the car more often than not, and at least once a day he walked Teddy.

Ellen, though. It would take a rocket launcher to get her moving.

She'd pop to the shops in the village every so often, but mainly in the morning when Frazer was at home.

So, in the end, Ryan had to seize the moment while she was still there.

He searched his father's bedroom first. Silently. He'd had experience of being stealthy. He'd often taken money or pieces of his mother's jewellery in the past when things were bad.

But it wasn't there.

So then he tried the study.

Everywhere he thought it could be.

The desk. Under the floorboards.

Ryan was starting to panic.

Was Adam telling the truth?

Of course he was. How could Ryan even think that?

What if his father had destroyed it?

Wouldn't that have been the most sensible thing to do?

But Ryan didn't think so.

His father liked to have his secrets. And this one proved that Ryan was involved in Adam's disappearance, that Ryan had lied to all of them. It proved other things, too, but his father would ignore those little details.

He would have kept it, Ryan was positive.

And then he found it. On the bookshelf in the study, in among old tomes, covered in dust.

Ryan almost made it out of the house unseen.

Just as he was opening the front door, he heard Ellen coming down the steps behind him.

'What are you doing here?' she said. No hello. No small talk.

Ryan turned.

'Why are you here?' he asked.

She frowned.

'It's my home,' she said.

'Course,' he said. 'Miss Havisham.'

She coloured, but didn't come back with anything smart. Ryan felt like kicking himself. Frazer had done this to them. Made them smart-arsed and cruel. Ellen didn't deserve that. She'd been nothing but good to Ryan.

'Sorry,' he said.

She shook her head, dismissively.

'I just came back for something,' he said. 'I'm going again.'

'Where?'

'Home. I mean, my home.'

'Oh.' She hesitated. 'Are you . . . are you okay? Do you need anything?'

'I don't need money,' he said, the humiliation burning through him because Adam was funding him now and he'd no right to be proud. Or to take his brother's cash, again.

'No, I didn't mean . . .'

Ellen shrugged.

Ryan put his hand back on the door, but then he paused.

'Ellen, has Clio been in touch recently?'

'No. There was a card on my birthday. Best wishes and a big kiss she wanted me to give the dog.'

'No address?'

Ellen shook her head.

'Post stamp?'

'Still New York,' she answered him.

'Needle in a haystack,' he said.

'Are you going to look for her?' Ellen asked, puzzled.

'I . . . no. I just wonder about her,' he said. 'I want to know she's okay.'

'She's living off the radar, Ryan. You know that. And the last time she . . .'

Ellen trailed off.

'What?' Ryan said.

'The last time she rang, Dad was . . . He gave her one of his lectures. How she'd let him down and . . . you can imagine.'

'Yeah,' Ryan said. 'I can. Wouldn't exactly encourage you to come home, would it?'

'You know what he's like. When he wants her to come back, he'll turn on the charm. Or the blackmail. He still hasn't given her her money. Or you yours, obviously.'

Ryan shook his head. He didn't even want to talk about it.

'If she contacts you, will you let me know?' he said.

Ellen nodded.

'And you,' he said, before leaving. 'How are you doing?'

Ellen looked surprised to be asked.

'I'm okay,' she said.

Ryan nodded.

'He'll get his,' he said. 'Dad, I mean. One day.'

Brother and sister looked at each other.

'You should know something,' Ellen said.

Ryan held his breath.

'If I ever get the chance, I'll kill him, Ryan.'

Ryan nodded.

If he ever got the chance, he'd help her.

# PRESENT

The dial tone was a single, long drone. It rang three times before Rob's contact picked it up.

'Detective McGrath, fifth precinct.'

'McGrath.' Rob smiled. 'Can't believe you're at your desk, ya fat fuck. Well, actually, I can. It's not like you'd be out on the beat.'

'Fuckin' Irish, you got ten pounds on me, pal, at least.'

The American chuckled, a deep gravelly laugh that Rob remembered fondly from McGrath's trips home to his extended Wexford family.

'I suppose you got my email, Irish?' McGrath said. 'Or is this a polite how ya fuckin' doing call 'cause you've shit all to do in that bucolic backwater?'

'Yeah, I got your mail,' Rob said. 'Thanks for that. Told me fuck all.'

'You're welcome.'

They both laughed.

'Not much more I could find,' McGrath explained. 'Your gal was undocumented.'

'So was your granny,' Rob said.

'Again, fuck you very much.'

Rob smiled.

'So that's the official info,' Rob said. 'What did you find unofficially that you couldn't put in the mail?'

Silence down the line. Then:

'You're a smart so and so, aren't you? You know I can't be sure of this, now.'

'Tell me anyway,' Rob said. 'When did we ever let the facts get in the way of a good suspicion?'

'Well, I showed that picture you sent over to some colleagues and one of them recognised her.'

'From?'

'He ain't saying. She never got done for anything but if he recognised her . . . well . . . he wouldn't be the nicest fella. Or the cleanest, if you catch my drift. Happy to turn an eye for certain things.'

'Got ya.' Rob felt his stomach turn.

'Yeah. Looks like little Clio had it rough enough here. What you after her for, anyway?'

'Her father was murdered,' Rob said.

'Shit. She do it?'

'No,' Rob said, but even he heard the hesitation in his voice. 'Her brother's going on trial for it. I'm just doing some digging. For myself.'

He knew it was James. He knew it.

So why couldn't he silence his doubts?

The feeling that, of all of them, Clio was the one everybody would protect?

Clio or Ellen.

How could you not want to protect her? Protect both of them?

He barely heard the rest of McGrath's banter, but he hung up with a laugh and a promise to arrange a trip to the Big Apple, including a crawl of all those pubs staffed by the undocumented Irish.

Whatever about Ellen, Rob knew that Clio's life had been filled with trauma.

And, clearly, it hadn't ended when she'd left Spanish Cove.

Somebody like that could easily snap. In self-defence or in rage.

What mattered now was making sure she didn't suffer any more.

Because Rob couldn't help it.

He was a silly fool, a country boy playing at being a great detective.

A cop who had the good sense to know when to look the other way.

To know when justice had been served.

But more than any of that . . .

He was still in love with Clio Lattimer.

# CLIO

It was her lowest point.

Okay, she'd reasoned, she wasn't exactly an innocent when it came to men. She'd flirt if it meant they'd buy her dinner or a few drinks. Take her to a club or a show or give her a job.

She knew her power and she wasn't afraid to use it.

Dinner and tickets were all very well. But rent was her biggest outgoing.

And while her place was cheaper than most places in New York, it was still money and it needed to be paid. She couldn't risk moving somewhere else without documents, even if she wanted to.

When the guy had first come on to her in the bar, Clio thought he was just some sleazy older businessman who wanted to buy her a few drinks, maybe slip his tongue down her throat or cop a feel.

But he wasn't the sort to offer a free-ish lunch. When she returned from the ladies and smiled encouragingly at him, he leaned over and whispered in her ear.

'One hundred dollars if you'll suck my dick.'

She recoiled.

Clio had no issues with sex. She'd screw anyone, if she was in the mood. But on her terms, in her way.

She wasn't a prostitute.

Is that what this guy thought?

'Bastard,' she said, and climbed back off the bar stool.

He followed her out, grabbed her arm on the pavement and feigned surprise at the tears in her eyes.

'Hey,' he said. 'I thought that's what was on offer. I didn't realise. It's this city, you know? I didn't mean to insult you. A buddy told me that's what was available in that bar. He's an ass. But it's still on me. I was crass and offensive. I should have known a good Irish girl like you wasn't that sort. I guess, I thought, people get desperate. Who am I to judge?'

She was so tired, and so hurt, that she didn't have the strength to tell him to shove it. She wanted to accept his apology and move on. Slowly, because she was wearing heels and didn't have the cab fare for ten blocks.

'Let me buy you a drink,' he said. 'Please. Let me apologise.'

So, she accepted his snake oil.

When she woke up in her apartment the next morning, he'd left two hundred dollars on the floor by the bed.

He'd got off on it, she realised. She'd let him have sex with her because he'd bought her dinner and drinks and been nice, but he had to pay her. He was probably married. Paying for it meant he wasn't cheating. She was a whore, he was a client. It was a business transaction. He'd have headed out the next night boasting about how he popped a young Irish girl's cherry.

That, incredibly, wasn't the worst bit.

Rock bottom was actively going out to find the next man to pay for it.

It had been going on for months. She never put a name on it, what she was doing. She just knew it was helping to make ends meet.

If you'd asked her what was required to sell yourself for sex, she'd have scratched her head to come up with an answer. You didn't need training, that was for sure. Whatever you thought you should say or do was probably not it.

There were no words, no certain look, no real actions you had to take. You didn't stick *apprentice prostitute* on your résumé and wait for job offers.

It was probably the sheer desperation in your eyes that did it; that, and the ability of a man who wanted it to sniff you out. Like the first guy.

Sometimes, they acted shocked when Clio said she needed money. It wasn't payment, she said, she'd just be really grateful if they could help her out. Other times, they gave her money before she even asked.

She'd done it, what, about twenty times now? She'd even drunkenly had sex with a cop a couple of times, too numbed to it to worry about the risk.

A hundred dollars on the pillow. Cheaper than dinner and drinks and much more effective.

Sex, part-time job, vodka, sleep, walk, eat, job, sex, vodka, party, vodka, sex.

It was pretty much in that vein that Clio approached Christmas 2016.

Her present to herself would be to sort out her shit.

2017 would not include sex with strangers for money.

Happy holidays.

She needed a plan. A life plan.

She nearly died when Adam and Ryan turned up.

She wasn't sure how they'd found her.

Clio lived off the grid and New York was a big place with a lot of people.

But then, what were the chances that she'd have bumped into Adam in Paris?

Ryan told her later that Adam had found him the same way. He was wealthy, Adam, had resources. He'd worked hard, used his brains – he had brains, it transpired. Just not when they were needed.

It had still taken her brothers long enough. Ryan hadn't been in hiding when Adam caught up with him. Clio was actively making herself untraceable. Not just from the authorities. She lived in fear that one day her father would turn up and try to drag her home. She wouldn't put it past him. For the past few years she'd mainly sent cards to Spanish Cove, afraid to even phone again in case she wound up on the end of another of her father's monologues about what a disappointment all his children were to him.

They were waiting for her, in the barely-certified-by-the-city diner two doors up from her apartment. She'd called in to get her usual Philly sub when she heard her name. Her full name.

Clíodhna.

Nobody called her that in New York. Nobody really called her that at home either, but certainly not here, where it required a double backflip, aligned planets and the ability to speak in tongues to pronounce anything in Gaelic. You'd think the Irish didn't own half the city.

'What the actual?' she said, glowering at the pair of them.

'We need to talk to you and don't even think about scarpering, darling,' Ryan drawled.

And then they'd herded her in the direction of her apartment.

'So, you found out, Ryan,' she said, slamming the door when all three of them were inside. 'Do the others know you're alive, Adam?' She glared at her brother. 'They sure as fuck didn't hear it from me. They'd have thought I was delusional. No way was I letting them know about you.'

It wasn't strictly true. Clio *had* tried to tell somebody.

She'd rung Kate, not long after she moved to New York. She'd had a few drinks and the secret had become, in a word, unbearable.

She'd started by telling Kate how she'd thought she'd seen Adam in France.

*'I was just eating breakfast and he walked past and I could have sworn it was him—'*

*'Oh, Clio, for God's sake, you were like this the whole time after Mam died. Do you remember?'*

*'But, Kate, this time—'*

*'Yes, I know, and it will always be like that.'*

*A noise in the background, somebody calling Kate. Clio heard her answer in that false accent she used these days, a bastardised version of south-side Dublin with a central London twang.*

*'Kate? Kate, I need you to listen to me. This is important. Adam . . .'*

*'Clio,' she said, returning to the phone. 'Are you drinking heavily? I only ask because it runs in our family, let's be honest. You sound like you've had a few. You and Ryan . . .'*

397

'*Are you fucking serious?*'

And that's when Clio knew Kate was no use to her any more. Her sister had changed. She was . . . aloof. Cold. Uncaring.

So, Adam's French existence had remained a secret.

'You need to listen to Adam, Clio,' Ryan said. 'Nobody else knows where he is. Not yet. We've been living on the continent, both of us. And we've been over and back here trying to find you. You need to hear what I have to say, too. And you need my apologies. This is my fault. Not his.'

They had her then. She was curious. She wanted to know what they were on about.

So, she listened as they told her what had happened in 2008, how Ryan had messed up and Adam had come to his rescue. They told her about Adam's daft plan to dig Ryan out of a hole, including how James had more or less thrown his family under a bus. And then they told her how Frazer had refused to bail Ryan out.

She wanted to kill the pair of them.

'You absolute fucking morons,' she raged, apoplectic. 'Adam, you, especially.'

Clio was fit to be tied. She was furious.

But more, she was exhausted. Completely and utterly exhausted. New York had worn her down. The last few years had finally caught up.

Clio sat on the edge of her bed, and cried.

It was late, but the city still hummed outside, the horns still beeped.

'I don't get why you didn't tell the rest of us. That's what's unforgivable. Ryan – I'm sorry, Ryan, but it's true, you were a fucking basket case. Adam, Mam would have helped.'

Adam stared down at the cheap carpet on Clio's floor.

'I thought it was for the best,' he said. 'I needed to get out of Spanish Cove. And I didn't know how Mam would react to me taking that money. She seemed to be of a mind with Dad about Ryan.'

'She wasn't,' Clio said.

'You're not always right,' Adam said. 'You've sanctified Mam but she stood by Frazer, you know. Even when he hurt us.'

'I'm not listening to this! You have no idea what Mam went through.'

'Did she stop Dad from throwing Ryan out after I disappeared?' Adam asked.

'She didn't realise until after, and anyway, she was worried about you and Ryan was . . . Ryan was taking drugs again.'

Ryan looked down at the floor.

'I wasn't, Clio. Not when he threw me out. Not properly, anyway. He did that because he knew what I'd done. He knew I was in trouble with a gang and he didn't want it brought to his door.'

Clio opened her mouth, but closed it again.

'It doesn't matter,' Adam said. 'None of this is Mam's fault. I didn't tell her because I had a plan.'

'Oh, Jesus wept. The plan! How did that work out for you?'

'I . . .' Adam hesitated. He looked at Ryan. Ryan nodded.

Adam reached into his pocket and pulled out an envelope.

'Read this,' he said and handed it to Clio.

'What?' she said, taking it sceptically, disdainfully. 'You've written your feelings down?'

'Don't knock it,' Ryan said lightly, though it was anything but.

Clio sighed and opened the letter. She began to scan the words, but after a few seconds the page became a blur. Her eyes stung as they filled with tears. What was this?

She picked up the envelope and looked at it.

It was addressed to Kathleen Lattimer, Spanish Cove, Wexford, Ireland.

The watermark on the stamp was barely legible but still there. 15 August 2008.

Clio looked up at her two brothers.

'Read it,' Ryan repeated.

Clio looked down at the page.

'Dear Mam,' she began.

*Dear Mam,*

*Please, please, please, don't be angry or upset. And most of all, please don't want to kill me.*

*I am safe, I am well, I am okay. Ryan will fill you in on all the details. I asked him to wait until I contacted you and I presume he's got a place in rehab now, like we planned.*

*I just need you to know, for now, that I left of my own volition. I didn't run away because I was depressed or had issues or anything like that.*

*Mam, I had to take some of your money and I'm sorry but I know you won't mind. Ryan needed it. He was in really bad trouble and I swore I'd help him. I asked Dad, but he didn't want to give it to me. So I went around him. That's the truth. He refused to help us. He had his reasons, but they're for him to explain.*

*Please don't be angry at me for not asking you. You'd already dealt with a lot and both Ryan and I agreed we wouldn't put you through any more until this was all sorted.*

*It's best that I stay away from you all for a little longer, just in case. I have some funds, I can work and I'll wait for things to blow over. I'm attaching a postbox number. Please, contact me when you get this. I don't have a phone yet. I know I'm being paranoid, but I'm trying to make sure Ryan's dealers can't trace me.*

*I'm sorry for the last few weeks. I didn't want to cause you or the girls any pain. It's a bit mad, but Mam, it's for the best. And Ryan has promised to straighten himself out. It was the condition I made.*

*Stay safe and talk soon.*

*All my love,*

*Adam.*

*P.S. I don't know if you've heard any rumours about me down in the village. If you have, I know you'll understand. I can't help who I am.*

Clio dropped the letter to the floor.

'I don't understand,' she said, feeling numb but knowing it was only the precursor to something more awful. 'You sent this after six weeks. The post stamp says it was delivered to Wexford. So where did it go?'

'It came to our house,' Ryan said.

'No.' Clio shook her head, dismayed.

'It did.' Adam nodded.

'They hired an investigator and everything,' Clio wailed. 'He told Dad he'd traced you to London and everything pointed to you being dead. Dad convinced Mam to believe it; he *convinced* her. There was no letter. I heard him – he was getting her prescription tablets, he was . . .'

Clio stopped, panic rising in her chest.

'I found this,' Ryan said, 'in Dad's bookcase. He'd hidden it. He took it before Mam saw it and he hid it. Then he told Mam that Adam was dead. Clio, there *was* no private investigator. There was no trace of Adam in London. Dad wouldn't spend the money. He made the whole thing up. Adam hacked his bank accounts – years back. No money was spent on anything untoward in 2008 or 2009. No huge PI fees. Of course there weren't. Dad knew Adam had done a runner. And he knew why. He hid this letter because he was ashamed. He hid it, because it told Mam that Dad was a liar and a prick.'

'I need a drink,' Clio said, reacting, her whole body on fire, every nerve ending jingling. And Adam had gone back out, found an all-night liquor store and returned with vodka.

'I needed you to know,' Adam said. 'I needed you to know I would never have left you like that. Both of us,' he looked at Ryan, 'have had our demons over the years. But we never meant to hurt any of you. You or Kate or Ellen or . . . Mam. Dad and James, to hell with them. They're—'

'Evil,' Clio said. 'They're fucking evil. I saw Dad promise Mam he'd get an investigator. He made a whole story up about you being dead – he . . . lied! He lied to her face, to all of us. And then, when she was dead, he told the rest of us that the investigator had made a mistake. He must have known he'd be found out if you came back, so he lied again. And James was the first one to suggest you were dead, Adam. He never even mentioned the money he took from you. Neither he nor Dad did, even when Mam was wondering why your account was empty. Ryan, at that point, why didn't you . . . ?'

Anger at her brother overtook Clio again. She launched herself at Ryan, smacking and scratching. She wanted to kill him. Ryan took it – it was Adam who called a halt, pulling her off before she could do any more damage.

'I'm sorry,' Ryan said, tears coming fast. 'I was such a screw-up. I thought Adam was dead and I didn't think any of you would forgive me. For Adam or for Mam. I'm sorry. I'm so sorry.'

Clio collapsed on the floor against the bed. None of it made sense and yet it all did. They'd always been the closest, the three of them. And she knew Ryan had only ever meant to destroy himself. Not anybody else.

'Why?' she choked. 'Why didn't you tell Ellen or Kate about Adam? They're still in Ireland, you knew where they were.'

'Kate is busy with her own life,' Ryan said. 'And Ellen is . . .'

'What?'

'She's delicate,' Adam said, and the two brothers looked at each other. 'We need to mind her. If she found out about this, it could . . . it could break her.'

'She's fucking useless, is that what you're saying?'

Clio shook her head. She couldn't understand any of it. It would take a lifetime to come to terms with it all.

'So,' Ryan said. 'What now? Do we tell the others? Pick up where we all left off?'

'No,' Adam said. His voice was so cold, Clio looked up sharply. Adam's face was almost unrecognisable, it was so filled with hatred. His pupils seemed darker and his lips thinner.

'Well, what?' Ryan said.

'We get revenge.'

Adam said it like it was the most obvious, basic response.

He met Clio's gaze and held her eye contact.

Her stomach filled with butterflies; a tingling sensation crept over her whole body.

All that heartache. All those wasted years.

Kathleen, dead.

Clio was the one who'd found her mother. Her eyes open, cold as ice, blue in the face, her features constricted in pain. Her mouth, so often fixed in a smile, contorted into something snarling and ugly.

She'd fallen half out of the bed; her nightdress had ridden up around her waist, leaving her little dignity, and Clio hadn't been able to lift her back up on her own, to cover her mother up. The book she'd been reading was still open on the bedside table. John Grisham. Her reading glasses were resting on it. A glass of water, the dregs of tea in a cup, a little lipstick on the rim.

The vial of prescription tablets sitting on the bedside table, nothing left inside.

It was only ever hinted at. Clio couldn't believe that her mother would intentionally overdose. That she'd leave them, after all they'd been through. Her heart had just failed, Clio told herself. And the coroner had agreed.

But her father . . . he'd made little remarks. Like he had no role, like it was all Kathleen's fault.

*She was fond of the sleeping pills*, Clio had heard Frazer whisper to the paramedics.

Kathleen had wet herself and it was that little detail, the stench of urine, the stain on the sheets, that almost ruined Clio.

A woman so full of life, a woman who'd given them all life, gone.

In the years that followed, Clio tried to live up to her father's expectations, pretending the house wasn't shrouded in grief, that nothing was wrong and their family hadn't been torn asunder. There was never any mention of Ryan or Adam or anything amiss.

Frazer had decided that they shouldn't all dwell on Kathleen's death, that they should move on.

And then her father had refused to give Clio her trust money.

The things she'd had to do to survive in New York.

How she'd had to live.

All of it flashed before her eyes, like a film reel rolling.

'Revenge?' Ryan echoed, confused.

'All of this,' Adam said, 'do you think it should go unpunished? He destroyed us. They both did. Dad and James.'

Adam was still staring at her, waiting.

And Clio felt it. The first inkling of an agreement.

'We need to plan this and we need to get it perfect,' Adam said.

'Plan what?' Ryan said. 'What will we do to them?'

Slowly, Clio started to nod.

'Whatever we have to,' Adam said, still focused on his sister.

She nodded, slowly, then quicker.

Ryan looked from one to the other of them.

Clio wasn't worried about him.

Ryan would do whatever Adam asked. He owed them that.

'And I know who's going to help us,' Adam said.

# PRESENT

'Has Rob guessed anything?' Ryan asked.

Clio and Adam were sitting on the porch swing. Ryan sat cross-legged on the ground in front of them.

The will reading was the following day. Kate was down and she and Ellen were inside the house, cooking dinner.

Clio looked over at the kitchen window. Her sisters were smiling, but in that sad way they all had now. Like it was beyond them to be happy after what had happened.

Not that any of them missed Frazer one little bit, really.

Clio, Adam and Ryan had broken the vow of silence they'd made to have this one conversation. Because, after tomorrow, they would go their separate ways again. And nobody would discover what they'd done.

'Rob doesn't know anything,' she answered Ryan. 'He was asking a lot of questions for a while there. Got me worried. But, in his words, the forensics sealed it.'

'How the fuck did James' blood end up on Dad's tie?' Adam asked. 'Danny saw James arguing with Frazer but he didn't see Frazer hit James. That's what he says, anyway.'

'Danny would never lie to us,' Clio said. 'Anyway, *I* saw James push Dad. And who cares if James left evidence on him?'

'I care,' Ryan said. 'The plan was to punish James for a while. Not get him a life sentence. That cop friend of yours will hammer that blood home to get a conviction, Clio.'

'What's a life sentence, these days?' Adam said. 'Can it be any more than ten years, with good behaviour and all that shite?'

'Fuck, you don't need to keep reminding me it was ten years, Adam,' Ryan snapped. 'It's just . . .'

'What?' Clio asked, when he trailed off.

'I feel guiltier than you,' he said. 'This all started with me.'

'Is that what you still think?' Clio said.

Ryan nodded.

'Because that's bullshit,' she said. 'This all started with Dad beating the shit out of you, Ryan. And fucking with Kate's head when it came to her weight. And belittling James so he became an even bigger cunt than he already was. And destroying Ellen's life. And making Adam live abroad for ten years thinking none of us gave a shit about him. And breaking my heart. That's where it started. You know it and we know it.'

Ryan stared down at the grass under his legs.

'You need to start believing it,' Clio said. 'He fucked us all over. You can't crack now.'

Her brother nodded.

'I don't feel any guilt,' Adam said. 'We've protected everybody. Ryan and I have vouched for Ellen and Ana. Both Danny and Clio could see Kate. And I could see Clio almost the whole time. *Almost.* Let James try to clear himself.'

Ryan shrugged.

Adam looked over at Clio.

'Where *did* you go for those few minutes?' he asked.

'I was just wandering around,' Clio said, her eyes fixed on him. 'Why? Have you been wondering if I did it?'

'I wouldn't blame you if you had,' Adam said.

Clio nodded, grimly.

'I just wish I'd killed him years ago,' she said. 'But I didn't. James did. It's the least he could do.'

It was the line she'd rehearsed, over and over in her head.

Adam nodded.

'Yes,' he said, encouragingly. 'He did. James killed our father.'

DECEMBER 2017

# RYAN

A whole year had passed.

The plan had been slow in coming together.

Partly because they were all in different countries. Partly for . . . other reasons.

It had been Adam's idea to get revenge. But Ryan, the one who was able to move in and out of Spanish Cove easiest, had put most of the plan in motion. All Clio had done at her end was get back in touch with her family, to make it easy for her to go back when the time was ready.

And within six months, they'd have carried it out.

He listened to the transatlantic dial tone ring three times before she picked up.

'We're on?' she said, not even opening with hello. Adam had bought them all pay-as-you-go mobiles specifically for contacting each other. They'd kept it as limited as possible. It was imperative nobody knew that they'd been in contact for all this time.

'We're on,' he said. 'Mam's anniversary notice will be published in May. That's the first step. Adam will use it as an excuse to come home.'

'Good,' Clio said, and Ryan could almost hear her nerves jangling down the phone. He was far more nervous but he couldn't let it show. They already assumed he was the weak link.

'When we do it, we'll all be together and we can alibi each other,' he said.

'Don't say it like that,' Clio snapped.

'It's the truth, Clio. We're going to kill our father. One way or another. Have you thought it through? Are we strangling him in his bed? Battering him over the head? Stabbing him in turn?'

'Ryan,' Clio cut him off. 'Only one of us will kill him. We've discussed this. And we'll agree when it gets closer who, where and when. He'll plan something to make himself the centre of attention, you know he will. It will be a party or something. It's the one thing about narcissists. They're eternally predictable. And we'll make sure we have all the information in advance so we can finalise things.'

Ryan sighed. She was right, he knew she was.

'It's still going to be hard,' he said.

'It's not going to be you, don't worry,' Clio said, impatiently. 'You are up for this, aren't you, Ryan?'

Ryan nodded, holding the phone tight in his hand, his cheek resting on the mouthpiece.

'I'm not going to let you down,' he said. 'If it's what you and Adam want.'

'We have to pretend it's the first time we've spoken in years,' Clio said, ignoring him. 'It has to be the most convincing performance of our lives. And I have to absolutely despise Adam. He needs to be pitiful and I need to hate him.'

'We're ready. I've heard Adam do his piece to camera. I was almost ringing a suicide hotline for him.'

Clio laughed thinly.

'And we can't talk about anything when we're there. Not even when we think we're alone. We've no idea who could be listening. Do you understand, Ryan?'

'Clio, stop lecturing me.'

'I'm not. I'm just nervous.'

'I know.' Ryan sighed. It would be difficult, not discussing it when they were all together. Playing at being strangers for a whole weekend. But it was essential.

'And . . . everything else is in place?' she asked. 'Is he ready?'

'We all know what we're doing,' Ryan said.

'Okay.'

A pause.

'I guess I'll see you this summer,' she said.

'Yeah. Clio, you got rid of the letter, didn't you? We don't want Dad finding it. He'll know we know.'

'Sure,' she said.

He didn't believe her. He knew Adam had made up his mind, from the moment he'd met Clio in Paris. But Clio had needed to see that letter to understand what their father was capable of. She'd be reading and re-reading it, right up until they killed Frazer.

Ryan knew she would.

# PRESENT

# ADAM

The reading of the will passed peacefully enough.

Frazer Lattimer had never got around to altering his last wishes. He'd presumed the house would be sold before he died and he'd have spent that money, so any standing will would have been null and void anyway.

There was no provision for Ana. The will had been updated when Kathleen died and the recipients were the same as they had been in 2009. Ana had returned to her failing business and life in Wexford town, possibly feeling like she'd had a lucky escape. Frazer's children knew she definitely had.

So, the house was to be sold and divided among each of the Lattimer children equally. The portfolio was to be dealt with in the same manner – whatever was left of it. It wasn't as bad as Adam had feared. Frazer wasn't overly risky or greedy. He'd just made bad investments. He was out of his depth, unable to recognise his limitations. A simple bank clerk elevated to a manager of a huge sum of money and unable to admit he wasn't capable.

Adam reckoned his own business advisors could turn it around for the family.

The stay on the trust had been lifted for Ryan and Clio. Ryan was attempting to give all his money to Adam and Clio but they wouldn't allow it. Instead, they'd agreed to manage it for him, to help him buy his own place in Italy and make sure he didn't have too much cash available. He knew he was capable of slipping at any time. He was determined not to, but he had to be prepared.

The will made small bequests to various charities and friends – Danny, mainly, though he hadn't been invited to the reading.

When they gathered in the dining room afterwards, with tea and coffee and cake, they talked it through. Ellen, while distressed, was being as magnanimous as she could be. They'd been through enough. It was time to move on.

'I think it's fair,' she said. 'And James is going to need the money from the house for his legal fees. He can't afford to fight the charges without it. When I last spoke to him, he said Sandra had threatened to divorce him; she found out he'd remortgaged everything. But her apartment, at least, is safe. It can't all come down to you, Kate.'

Adam exchanged a glance with his other siblings.

'We're not selling the house, Ellen,' he said.

She frowned, confused.

'But . . .'

'We've agreed,' Kate said. 'I will help James, if he starts telling the truth. He won't or can't explain his blood on Dad. It pains me to say it, but that Rob Downes is right. Dad deserves justice.'

Kate placed a hand on her stomach, something she was doing a lot these days, Adam knew. She was beginning to show a tiny bit. It was probably more fat than baby, she kept telling them proudly. Apparently, Cheng insisted on treating her day and night and he wouldn't let her walk anywhere, let alone work out. He was fussing over her, hand and foot, and she was happy to let him.

Adam knew Kate would never be perfect. His sister had many flaws. But she seemed to be more content than she'd been in a long time, and her husband was happy to let the past stay in the past. The baby had quite possibly saved them from a lot of pain.

'But, James,' Ellen protested.

'I'll buy James' share out,' Adam said. He had no intention of giving James money, of course. Not unless he begged. James owed him fifty grand plus interest.

Ellen looked around them all, confused.

'You two need it,' she said, finally, looking at Clio and Ryan.

The two of them shook their heads.

'We have our trust funds,' Clio said.

Ellen sat down hard on one of the dining chairs.

'You'd do that, for me?' she asked, looking to each of them.

'I don't need money,' Adam said. 'Just somewhere to call into when I come home every now and again.'

Ellen gave them a bittersweet smile.

'Mam would have been happy for us to keep this place,' she said.

'Yes,' Adam said. 'She would have. And you're owed it, Ellen. He owed you. We're paying his debt.'

Adam crossed the room and put his arm around Ellen. She let him. Kate coughed uncomfortably, but out of the corner of his eye, he saw Ryan give her a gentle shove, until she smiled, embarrassed.

Adam also noticed Clio took that moment to slip away.

His phone beeped. He knew who it was. He'd got her first message early that morning. It had taken him a moment or two to figure it out. *Got your number from Kate. I'm so sorry. I want you to know I never told anybody. E.*

Eva.

He'd sent her a text back to say it wasn't her fault. She'd obviously been worrying about it for ten years. They'd agreed to meet for a coffee and a chat before he flew back to Paris.

Normal people doing normal things.

# RYAN

The call connected straight away.

Ryan had crept off to his bedroom shortly after they'd had their conversation in the dining room. He didn't want his siblings to overhear.

Ryan couldn't get beyond the guilt he felt. This all came back to him, after all.

'Hello?' the voice on the other end of the call said.

'Bella?' Ryan said. 'It's me. Your, eh, Uncle Ryan. How are you?'

Silence.

'Fine,' she said, eventually. 'Was it today?'

'What?'

'The will reading?'

'Oh,' Ryan said. 'Yeah.'

'He leave anything to me or Sandra?'

Ryan said nothing.

'Typical,' she said.

'I'm sorry, Bella. How are you both coping? How's your mother?'

'She's . . . she's talking to James again.'

'Oh?'

'Yeah.' Bella paused. 'He's got her convinced he's innocent. He seems to think this will end up on Netflix some day as a documentary. À la *Making a Murderer* or something.'

Ryan had to stop himself from laughing.

'She's all over it,' Bella said, happy to talk now, her excitement getting the better of her. 'She was going to divorce him but now she's organising a film crew to meet him while he awaits trial and . . . well, *money*. She fucking loves it. More than anything, I guess.'

'I see,' Ryan said. 'It sounds exciting.'

'Yeah. Um, I probably shouldn't be saying it to you. Frazer was your dad and all.'

'James is my brother,' Ryan said.

'I don't really get it.'

'What?'

'Family,' Bella said. 'I've always felt . . .'

'Alone?' Ryan suggested. Bella said nothing, but he knew that's what she meant.

'Me too,' he said.

'He was a good dad,' Bella said. 'But, he's not my real father. Thank fuck.'

He listened to her breathing for a moment.

'Are you going to go to New York?' he asked.

'I don't know. Everybody seems to be going to Toronto, really. It sounds a bit more fun. A challenge.'

'You know what's challenging?' Ryan said.

'Where?'

'Home.'

'Eh, yeah. Um, listen. I gotta go.'

'Something important?'

'Ariana Grande is dropping her new video on YouTube. I want to be the first to view it. I've never been the first.'

'Very important, then,' Ryan said. 'Speak soon?'

'Um. Okay.'

She hung up.

Sixteen, on the cusp of adulthood. With James and Sandra as role models.

God love her. Hopefully she'd be all right.

Ryan lay back on his bed and looked out at the sea.

James deserved it, he told himself again.

He deserved to be framed.

He had to keep telling himself that.

# CLIO

She found him up at Kathleen's grave.

Of course, that's where he was.

The light was starting to fade from the day, but it still caught the leaves on the trees, burnished golds and reds and yellows. It was early August but June and July had been hot and Kathleen always said a sweltering summer brought an early autumn. She'd been right.

'Danny,' Clio said.

He looked up from the soil he'd been raking.

Her mother lay separate from their father.

He'd been buried with his in-laws in the shade. None of the siblings wanted Frazer resting with Kathleen.

'Just thought I'd give up here a clean,' Danny said.

Clio watched him for a moment.

'We told Ellen anyway,' she said. 'She'll be staying in the house.'

'She happy 'bout that?'

'Delirious. She did want us to sell for about five minutes, so James would have money to fight his case.'

Danny clicked his tongue.

'We dealt with it,' Clio said.

'Any word?' Danny's raking slowed.

Clio shrugged.

'Rob is now convinced it's him, even if it might get thrown out in court. Or, if he's not convinced, he certainly isn't interested in asking any more questions.'

Danny nodded.

Clio was seeing a lot of Rob. They all knew.

It was dangerous, but Clio couldn't help it. She was growing so fond of him, and, she thought, him of her.

Danny stood, slowly – Clio extended her hand to help him. He winced in pain when he was upright. The cancer was affecting all his joints now.

She looked down at the beautiful job he'd done with her mother's grave.

'Did you love her, Danny?' Clio asked. 'I mean, really love her? In that way? *The Countess*. It's a Yeats play, isn't it? *The Countess Cathleen*.'

'Oh, aye,' Danny said. 'I really loved your mother. But not in that way, pet, no. I think you know that. She was like a sister to me. And at first, I thought Frazer was good for her. If he made her happy, I was happy. But, as time went on, I knew and she knew the man was deeply flawed. I should have done something, much earlier.'

'We couldn't have known how low he'd sink to maintain control,' Clio said. 'He was my dad, Danny. I loved him. Despite everything. Even I couldn't believe what he was capable of.'

'I know, pet.'

'He killed my mother,' Clio said, looking down at the grave.

Danny exhaled, sadly.

'He deserved to die,' he said. 'You see a sick dog, you put it out of its misery.'

Clio nodded.

Frazer would have agreed.

'But you remember your promise,' Danny said.

Clio sighed.

'Yes,' she said. 'I remember.'

'I take the blame, on my own,' Danny said. 'I fought with Frazer over how he was treating all of you. I picked up whatever I could lay my hands on, I don't even know what it was. A bottle or something. I hit him over the head. I panicked then, and threw him overboard. Then I ran down to you all and said I'd spotted him in the sea. It only took me a few seconds. None of you knew anything. None of you saw anything. You stick to the stories you told. I'll write it all down in the letter I leave.'

Clio felt the tears sting her eyes.

'That's what we agreed,' Danny said. 'I'm the oul' fella. You're the ones with your lives ahead of you. I'm the one who's dying.'

Clio nodded. Yep, that's what they'd agreed.

And somewhere on the ocean floor was the large rock that she'd taken from her mother's grave, the one she'd brought onto the yacht that night and handed to Danny, the one that had been used to concuss her father so he'd drown when he hit the water. It was the only part Adam would let her play.

'Did he suffer?' she asked, the guilt heavy in her stomach.

Danny shook his head, firmly.

'He was puffing away on his cigar,' he said. 'Oblivious. He didn't even see me.'

Clio nodded again.

So much careful planning.

As soon as Adam had contacted Danny and told him everything, he'd offered to help.

To get vengeance for Kathleen.

When Danny found out Frazer was seeing Ana and got a hint of Frazer's plans for a party, they knew that was the moment.

A death at sea, with no chance of any witnesses, bar family. Clio, Danny, Adam and Ryan able to keep the others in the dark and out of the way.

And James left exposed, somehow, some way.

It was perfect.

Frazer did everything they predicted.

Adam returned.

Frazer's money was paid back.

The lost son grovelled, claimed he'd had a breakdown.

The rest of them were ordered home.

Threats, not bribes.

They'd all be excluded from the will if they didn't comply. Even Clio.

Right to the end, such low opinions of his own children.

And the knowledge, later, that he wanted them all there just to tell them he was going to screw them over.

Danny held out his arm and Clio linked it.

The man who'd been more of a father to her than her own dad.

He had very little time left.

That's what had simultaneously slowed down and sped up the planning in the end. Danny's ill health and then his terminal diagnosis.

She still hoped he'd live. She, a devoted agnostic, had found herself praying for it every day, weeping at the thought of him being gone.

But she knew he would be, eventually.

And James would have been punished enough. If he was convicted, Danny's deathbed confession would exonerate him, particularly as the bulk of the evidence the cops had on James was speculative to begin with.

Hopefully, Rob wouldn't think Danny's confession was penned out of guilt and a desire to protect his godchild.

Clio rested her head on Danny's shoulder.

When Danny died, they'd bury him with their mother.

All that had gone in with her father was the letter that he'd hidden for so many years.

The letter that, had he given it to Kathleen when it arrived, would have given her something to live for. And would have brought Clio's family back together.

Clio had tucked it under Frazer's body as she'd kissed him goodbye.

# ACKNOWLEDGEMENTS

*Six Wicked Reasons* is about a dysfunctional family. I'm lucky to have a book family that functions very well. Thank you Stefanie Bierwerth and Nicola Barr for keeping me in good ideas, laughs and a positive frame of mind, even when I want to bin every word and start from scratch. And thank you wider team, Rachel, Milly, Sharona, Cassie, Hannah, Bethan, David, Jon, Breda, Ruth, Jim and Elaine – basically Quercus and Hachette Ireland, for taking the end product and launching it like a rocket ship into the reading world, every time.

Of course, each book takes a whole lot of effort and endurance from my real family, too. Thank you Martin and my lovely children, for all the tea, snacks, turning on the big light, shoulder rubs and general support when I disappear off to word-count world. I know this is a collective effort to get us to the mansion with the Mercedes in the garden and I appreciate your efforts. This time next year? Decade? We'll get there.

And thank you all my terrific friends. I know the fact you think it's an outrage I haven't won a Nobel prize for literature by now says everything about how much you love me, and isn't proof that you're all completely crazy. You're right. Give me all the prizes.

My final and most important thanks is to you, the reader. I'm just a scribbler with some stories. You read my books and made me an author. It's a dream come true.